THE GAME

A HIGH-STAKES CONSPIRACY OF POWER, POKER, AND PROFIT

BRANDON KELLER

Black Rose Writing | Texas

The author grants the final approval for this literary material.

First printing

This is a work of fiction. Names, characters, businesses, places, events, and incidents are either the products of the author's imagination or used in a fictitious manner. Any resemblance to actual persons, living or dead, or actual events is purely coincidental.

ISBN: 978-1-68513-625-3 (Paperback) 978-1-68513-626-0 (Hardcover)

Library of Congress Control Number: 2025934573
PUBLISHED BY BLACK ROSE WRITING
www.blackrosewriting.com

Printed in the United States of America
Suggested Retail Price (SRP) $23.95 (Paperback) 28.95 (Hardcover)

The Game is printed in Minion Pro

*As a planet-friendly publisher, Black Rose Writing does its best to eliminate unnecessary waste to reduce paper usage and energy costs, while never compromising the reading experience. As a result, the final word count vs. page count may not meet common expectations.

For my wife, Jill, and children, Erin and Aidan.
For my parents, Bonnie and Jack, and John and Cecilia.
For my siblings, Kristina and David.
I love you.

THE
GAME

CHAPTER 1

Tyler steps into the empty elevator and leans against the cool marble wall. Only thirty-five floors stand between him and the beginning of his weekend. He glances at his watch—10:15 p.m.—and wonders if any of the other two thousand Mid-Atlantic Financial Services employees are still here. The building's probably empty, other than late-night security.

The elevator hums to life, beginning its descent while Tyler yawns and rubs his eyes. Another sixty-hour week in the books.

He loosens his tie and checks his phone. Nothing more from Anna. A good sign, he hopes, after her earlier text saying Aunt Virginia and Marco were already drunk.

The elevator glides past the tenth floor. He leans back, spotting a small maintenance sign tucked against the corner of the wall. *Hope they fixed whatever it was*, he thinks absently, before pushing himself off the wall.

Seven. Six.

Without warning, the elevator jerks to a stop and plunges into darkness.

Stumbling forward, Tyler slams against the closed door. His phone flies from his hand, and he hears it smack on the granite floor. He drops to his knees and pats the cold floor until he finds it then stands and illuminates the elevator control panel with its light.

Telling himself everything's fine, he presses the button to open the doors, but nothing happens. His heart races, and he jabs the button again—once, twice, three times—still no response.

Starting to panic, he tries the alarm button. Nothing. Just as useless as the others. Sweat breaks out across his body, and he has to remind himself to breathe normally.

Gotta get out of here.

He wedges his fingers between the door panels, trying to force them apart, but they don't budge. He wipes his sweaty palms on his pants and calls 911 on his phone.

The elevator lurches again, this time slowly rising in the darkness.

No! Wrong direction.

"Nine one one, what's your emergency?" The operator's voice pierces the quiet, a lifeline to the outside world.

"I'm trapped in an elevator," Tyler says, his voice shaky.

The lights flicker back on, momentarily blinding him. The elevator picks up speed, shooting upward.

"Are you okay?" the operator asks.

Tyler blinks, his vision adjusting. He sees the floor display race from twenty to twenty-five to thirty.

"Sir?" the operator's voice blares.

"I—I'm fine. The elevator's moving now," he stammers, watching the display flash forty then blank out entirely.

The ascent slows, and the elevator grinds to a halt. Its doors slide open, revealing a long, empty hallway.

"Do you still need help?" The operator's voice startles him.

Tyler hesitates and steps into the sterile hallway. "No, sorry. False alarm," he says, though he's not quite convinced himself.

He hangs up and takes in his surroundings. The hallway is bare, with concrete floors and plain white walls. No decorative art, no polished hardwood—none of the sleek corporate decor he's used to seeing in the most important building in Baltimore. He looks up. A small plaque above the elevator reads "41."

Tyler frowns. The Mid-Atlantic building only has forty floors. A chill creeps up his spine. He shrugs off his blazer and shivers in his soaked shirt. He eyes the closing elevator doors. *No way I'm getting back into that thing.*

He turns around and studies the hallway. His gaze lands on a single door at the far end. *Stairs, maybe?*

He makes his way toward the door and cautiously pushes it open. No stairs in sight, but the walls here are a deep burgundy, and a luxurious Persian rug runner stretches across the ebony floor. It feels like a different world.

Voices echo from around the corner—men talking and laughing. The pungent scent of cigar smoke wafts through the air, stronger with each step.

Tyler rounds the corner to find six men seated in plush leather chairs around a table with green felt stretched beneath their fingers. One man shuffles a deck of cards, and another sips from a cognac glass.

Tyler catches movement out of the corner of his eye. Before he can turn to see what it is, a hard object slams into the side of his head. His vision blurs, and the world goes dark.

CHAPTER 2

A dull ache pulses in Tyler's skull, dragging him back to consciousness as a deep voice cuts through the haze.

"Let him up, Max. He looks harmless."

The assailant yanks Tyler to his feet, pats him down, then disappears into the shadows. Tyler sways on his feet, his vision swimming as he stumbles toward the bigger man, his fist raised, more out of instinct than strength.

Another voice, sharper and more direct, grabs his attention.

"What are you doing here?"

"How the hell should I know?" Tyler snaps, the words spilling out before he can stop them even as the familiar voice makes him catch his breath. His muscles lock up, heart hammering in his chest, and he turns slowly, dreading the confirmation of what he already knows. Regret floods through him as he looks right at Mike Hayward, CEO of Mid-Atlantic Financial Services. Hayward's eyes widen slightly, his mouth curling into a faint smile.

Tyler's leg trembles. He struggles to steady himself, feeling the weight of Hayward's stare.

"I work here. For you. Well, for your company."

Hayward glances at the two cards he's holding and frowns before returning his gaze to Tyler.

"What's your name?"

"Tyler Rush, sir. I'm an analyst in the Financial Services Division. I work for Rob Walker." His whole body is weak.

Hayward stands and walks toward him, exuding calm control. "Take a seat."

He places a firm hand on Tyler's shoulder, guiding him to the chair. The rich scent of Mike's cologne hits Tyler like a rush of adrenaline, snapping his focus back. Tyler sits, sinking into the plush leather as he tries to steady his breathing. He rests his elbows on the arms of the chair and glances around, his head swiveling—*is that Barry Knowles sitting next to me?*

Mike nods at a man across the table. "Paul, you're a doctor. How about you give him a quick once-over? He took quite a hit."

Tyler's cheeks burn. *Paul Thompson? Here?*

"He's fine," Paul mutters and looks away.

How the hell does Paul know Mike? And what's an actor like Barry Knowles doing here? Hollywood isn't exactly next door.

Tyler watches as Mike glances between his beet-red face and Paul's forced disinterest, trying to make the connection.

Paul may have been the first in his family to attend college, may have finished first in his class at Johns Hopkins Medical School, and may have become the first African American head of the Food and Drug Administration. But in Tyler's opinion, he's a first-class hypocrite.

Another man with bushy, salt-and-pepper hair leans forward, flashing a too-white smile. "You sure you're okay? Let me grab you a drink … a stiff one."

Tyler nods, grateful for something normal. "Water's fine, thanks."

The man tilts his head slightly, apparently amused. "Water? All right then." He stands and ambles toward the wet bar in the back. Tyler watches him, thinking he looks familiar but not able to come up with a name.

Mike leans in, his voice low.

"I'll ask again. What are you doing here?"

Tyler takes a deep breath and rubs the side of his head where it still throbs. His fingers brush over a patch of matted hair.

"The elevator malfunctioned. Brought me here by accident."

He breaks eye contact with Mike and examines the table. Gold coins glimmer on the green felt. Five stacks stand in front of Mike's chair, each about twenty coins high. The other men have varying amounts, some neatly stacked and others less tidy. A large pile sits in the middle of the table.

Looks like a high-stakes game of Texas hold 'em. What would it be like to play with these big shots?

Tyler glances back at Mike, who is still staring at him, eyebrows raised.

"There's only one passenger elevator that comes to this level," Mike says, "and it's out of service." His tone is flat, but Tyler catches the slightest hint of irritation.

"Apparently, someone didn't get that memo," Tyler says before he can stop himself. *That's twice,* he thinks. *Need to keep my mouth shut.*

Mike frowns and glances at the man returning with Tyler's water. "Preston, you used the service lift, didn't you?"

Tyler finally places him—Preston Sinclair, Chair of the Senate's Armed Services Committee. He's seen his face on CNN and Fox News.

What the hell's going on? A leading senator, the head of the FDA, a famous actor. All here with my CEO for a Friday night card game?

Preston hands Tyler the chilled bottle. "Yep. Donny brought me up on a maintenance elevator." He chuckles. "Not the nicest ride."

Mike returns his attention to Tyler and softens his tone. "I'm not sure how you got on that elevator, but it was a mistake. My apologies for the confusion. It won't happen again."

"No worries," Tyler says, trying to sound casual.

He sucks down the last of the water and crinkles the plastic bottle in his hand. He notices blood on his fingers. *How hard did that idiot hit me?*

Barry Knowles laughs beside Tyler. "What kind of elevators you got here in Baltimore, Mike? New York rejects?"

A bearded man joins in with a chuckle.

"Mike," the man says, "this kid has hustle, staying this late on a Friday night while you're already two drinks in."

Mike silences them with a raised hand. "Tell me, Tyler, what are you doing in the office this late?"

Tyler shifts uneasily in the chair before straightening up and clearing his throat. "Perfecting some programming code," he says, his voice a little steadier. His hands rest on his lap, fingers tapping against his thigh as he gathers his thoughts. "I noticed a depreciation entry we missed in last year's tax return. That got me thinking—there might be other missed opportunities. So I wrote code to find them. It's snaking through our financial system as we speak."

Mike frowns. "Writing code? You said you're a financial analyst."

"Yes, but I'm an AI junkie." Tyler pauses. "I've been experimenting with ways to apply machine-learning concepts to boost our performance."

The bearded man leans forward and peeks at the two cards that lie in front of him. He glances at his stack of gold coins then folds his arms and focuses on the far wall. His behavior screams *bluff* to Tyler.

Mike's eyes narrow. He's clearly interested. "And how does this code work?"

"Think of it like a virus, except it's friendly. It's working through our financial database, looking for entries with characteristics like those of the missed depreciation opportunity I found. As it identifies new candidates, the program automatically recalibrates itself to consider the new information before it continues its search. It keeps learning, gets smarter, in a sense."

Mike cocks his head. "You set up and implemented a deep learning algorithm by yourself? No business case, no project plan, no massive cross-departmental team?"

Tyler beams. "IT approved it as a pilot project. It's still early, but it appears to be working. The code runs on its own, allowing us to relax and enjoy other activities." He nods at the table and smiles. "But don't be fooled. It's called *artificial* intelligence for a reason. At its core, it's still just following instructions. There's no such thing as true computer intelligence."

Mike smiles. "That's what they say. Let me know how it turns out."

Tyler feels everyone staring at him—except Paul, who is looking down, and the man with the beard, who is laser-focused on the wall.

Did I get to first base, or did I just strike out?

Mike gestures toward a door in the rear of the room. "Well, this has been enlightening, Mr. Rush. But now, if you'll come this way, I'll escort you out."

Tyler stands, his legs stiff and unsteady, and follows Mike across the room. His heartbeat pounds in his ears, and he wipes his clammy palms on his pants. Mike stops by the door and locks eyes with him.

"I trust you'll keep what you saw this evening to yourself," Mike says. "Understood?"

"Yes, sir."

Tyler takes a step but then turns back to Mike.

"What is it?" Mike asks.

Tyler hesitates then blurts out, "The beard is bluffing."

Mike's eyes dart to the table. He shakes his head, bemused. "The service elevator will take you down. Donny's waiting for you on the ground floor."

Tyler thinks about the elevator, and his heart begins pounding again.

Mike strolls ahead. "Or I can direct you to the stairs."

"The elevator will be fine," Tyler lies.

The ride down is uneventful, and a minute later he's outside the building and enveloped in the comforting grip of a muggy Baltimore summer night. By the time he crosses Pratt Street, his shirt is sticking to his skin. He glances back at the Mid-Atlantic building.

Did that really happen?

As his mind calms and his pulse slows, he becomes more aware of the pulsating pain in his head. *Hang on*, he tells himself. *A few more minutes and I'll be in my apartment, soaking in a hot bath.*

He reaches the Inner Harbor and strolls along the water's edge. The boats are mostly settled for the night, tucked away safely in their berths. Only the water taxis are still awake, ferrying partiers back and forth between downtown and Fell's Point.

In the surface of the still water, he sees the facades of restaurants and bars that are still open, their shapes like constellations formed by the reflection of their lights. He takes a deep breath, and the remaining adrenaline washes away from his body, leaving him exhausted.

Tyler reaches his building, smirks at the elevator, and plods up twenty-one flights of stairs. He lumbers down the hall, aching to relax in the tub then fall into bed.

As he approaches his apartment, he notices a dark shape slumped against his door. His heart thumps.

Tyler's night is not over.

CHAPTER 3

Tyler stoops down in front of his apartment door.

"Anna," he whispers to the dark shape.

She's curled up, asleep. He taps her shoulder until she stirs. When she opens her eyes, he helps her stand and pulls her into a gentle hug, relaxing slightly as she leans into him. He pulls a key from his pocket and scans the dimly lit hallway. It's empty, and the air is stale, faintly smelling of disinfectant and old carpet. He unlocks the door, and they step into his apartment where the low hum of the refrigerator fills the silence.

He remembers her earlier text and asks, "Aunt Virginia and Marco kept drinking?"

She nods, her shoulders sagging. She seems to relax now that she's with him.

He takes the small duffel bag from her shoulder, and as she raises her right arm, he notices faint, reddish marks on her forearm—like fingerprints left by being grabbed too hard. He stares at them for a moment, his chest tightening. The sight of them pulls him back to his own childhood memories of Aunt Virginia's sharp words and Marco's heavy-handedness.

Tyler gently touches her arm. "Did someone grab you?"

Anna lowers her gaze and shrugs. "Auntie, but it's nothing serious. Marco actually told her to stop—shocking, right?" Her voice wavers, and a few tears slip down her cheeks despite her effort to stay composed.

Tyler sits beside her, wrapping his arms around her slender frame. "Do they know you're gone?"

"I'm not sure."

He pulls back and squeezes her hand. "We should get going."

Back in the hallway, they stand in front of the elevator doors. Tyler crosses his arms, his body stiff.

Too tired to deal with another elevator ride tonight.

Anna watches him closely. "I doubt they're coming after us."

He nods, but the thought of being trapped again sends a shiver through him. "Let's take the stairs anyway."

They descend in silence except for the sound of their footsteps echoing off the cold concrete walls. When they reach the lobby door, Tyler grabs the handle and hears the ding of the elevator from the other side. He and Anna exchange a glance, and he opens the door a crack.

Two police officers are boarding the elevator.

"Good call," Anna whispers.

Tyler exhales, relief flooding through him as he mouths a silent prayer. *Thank you.* Sometimes it's better to be lucky than good, he thinks.

Thirty minutes later, they're lying on twin beds in a dingy West Baltimore motel room. Tyler tosses and turns on the hard mattress. The air is thick with the stale odor of cigarettes, mixed with the sharp scent of cheap, overused cleaner. It's as if the walls are closing in on him as he tries to make sense of it all—*how has it come to this?*

He can't shake the anger gnawing at his gut. He turns, the coarse sheets rubbing against his skin, and stares at the ceiling. His thoughts drift back to the court hearing that led to the restraining order limiting his access to Anna. Virginia had spun the narrative so perfectly, convincing the judge that Tyler was a danger to Anna's well-being— that he had instigated her repeated attempts to run away, the last of which ended with her being mugged at gunpoint. A nauseating wave of exasperation crashes over him, and he sinks deeper into the worn mattress, wondering how everything spiraled so far out of control.

The only positives are that Anna is safe with him at the moment and that the motel takes cash without asking for an ID. He glances over at Anna. Her fragile form is a stark reminder of everything he's failed to fix. He clenches his fist beneath the covers.

"I'm so lucky you're my brother," she whispers, catching him off guard.

Her words slice through him, leaving an ache in his chest. She deserves to be safe, not stuck with Virginia and Marco.

His thoughts swarm, and the familiar regret returns. *If only I'd spoken up before the accident*, he thinks, *it never would have happened.* That thought always haunts him, and it's quickly followed by the painful reminder—*if only I hadn't told Paul the truth afterward.*

The thoughts eat away at him, sharper than any pain Virginia or Marco ever inflicted.

Anna sits up. "Don't take me back there tomorrow."

Tyler's heart sinks. Every time she asks, saying no gets harder. He wants nothing more than to say yes, to promise her safety and freedom. But he knows it's impossible right now. He hates not being able to give her what she wants, what she deserves.

"I'll drop you off early. They'll still be passed out," he finally says, his voice quieter than before.

She looks at him, her eyes pleading. "But I want to live with you."

"I'm close, sis. In nine months, I'll have enough to hire an attorney. I'll clear the restraining order and start the custody process."

"Nine months?" She flops back onto the mattress, groaning. "Let's just leave, Ty. We could disappear, go to Ocean City, like you always talk about us doing with Mom and Dad when I was little."

For a few seconds, Tyler lets himself imagine the two of them free, with no more court battles, no more threats. Just peace. Then reality crashes back just as quickly. Running isn't freedom. It's a trap.

"But Anna—"

"We'll be caught," she says, her voice flat, rehearsed. "And then you'll go to jail, and you won't be able to help me at all."

He swallows hard. "I've run it through my head over and over. We have to stick to the plan."

"Borrow the money from Greg," she suggests, her voice small, almost desperate.

His jaw tightens, but he says nothing. He's not about to rely on his buddy Greg—or anyone. Instead, he shifts the conversation away, trying to push the thought aside.

"It's time for bed," he says softly, knowing it won't make the ache in her eyes go away.

Outside, the low rumble of bass echoes from a passing car. Tyler gets up and peeks through the slats of the broken blinds, half-expecting Marco's old Cadillac to pull up. Instead, a blue Mustang rolls down the street.

Anna watches him from her bed. "I keep telling you to ask for help," she says, her voice weary, "to take charge. But you don't listen. You just worry. And beat yourself up."

He pulls the blinds back into place, trying to block out the neon glow of the liquor store across the street. Her words sting, hitting too close to the truth. He turns to her and says, "I saw Paul tonight. After work."

"Who?" she asks, frowning. "You mean Paul, the jerk?"

Tyler sits on his bed. "He pretended not to recognize me."

Anna sits up straighter, her eyes focusing as her face stiffens. "What a loser. If I ever see him, I'm going to punch him in the nose."

Tyler chuckles. She means it, too.

The room falls into silence again, and Tyler stretches his arms, his muscles taut with tension.

"Let's relax and get some sleep. Tomorrow will be better," he says, though he isn't sure he believes it.

He lies down and reaches for the lamp, but Anna beats him to it, switching it off and curling under her covers.

Tyler struggles to fall asleep. His mind is a whirlwind of memories—the accident that set everything in motion a decade ago, Aunt Virginia's twisted control, the life they should have had. He turns toward Anna's bed, watching her sleep.

Someday soon, I'll fix this, he promises.

CHAPTER 4

Mid-Atlantic CEO Mike Hayward flips from channel to channel on the television perched next to his monitor. CNBC, CNN, Fox News. So much information spewing out every minute of every day. A protest in London, an earthquake in Indonesia, a partisan battle in Congress. And those are just flecks of dust in the giant storm of data constantly being generated. Digitized nuggets of knowledge are everywhere—in the wires, in the walls, flowing through the air.

He reaches out his hand, flutters his fingers in the air, and wonders what important factoids are gushing unseen between his knuckles at this very moment. He grabs an imaginary handful, closes his fist, and can almost feel them slipping through his grasp on their quest from here to there. Frustrated, he knows they are just outside his ability to seize and put to work.

He takes a bite of the thick Italian hoagie resting on his desk and quickly grabs a napkin to wipe the olive oil running down his chin. Despite all the progress in financial technology, data science, and information aggregation over the past few decades, humans can still only harvest an infinitesimal amount of data from the vast, nutrient-rich field of information surrounding them. It's like having access to thousands of acres of ripened wheat but processing barely enough to make the bread for his sandwich.

That will change soon ... in a big way. If things go according to plan.

He strolls to one of the many windows framing the perimeter of his cavernous corner office and surveys the city—his city—from his fortieth-floor vantage point. He raises a hand to shield his eyes from the sun, now well into its daily westward descent. Beyond the office buildings, the hotels, and the sports stadiums lie street after street of row houses that some Baltimoreans take pride in. Mike is not one of them. At one time, maybe, they represented a fine abode for folks on the rise, working hard to better themselves and their families. Now, too many of them are a rundown, unkempt blight on his beloved town.

His cell phone dances across the desk behind him, and he reaches for it.

"Good evening, Preston," he says.

"I talked to Crowley. He sounded interested but ultimately declined."

Mike frowns. "Why?"

"Said he didn't want to bring any undesirable attention to the president as he begins his reelection campaign."

Doesn't want undesirable attention? Mike snorts. *He's a magnet for it.*

Mike hangs up abruptly. "How embarrassing," he mutters to himself.

He does not like to be embarrassed. Why had he listened to Preston's idea to invite the sitting vice president of the United States to join the game? *He's a Democrat, for crying out loud.* Mike hopes the Council of Elders was correct in its decision to elect Preston as its newest member. Sure, Preston is a seasoned senator, Mike thinks, but he's missed the mark on this one.

He takes another bite of his hoagie and paces back to the window.

What's Crowley's view like from his office at 1600 Pennsylvania Avenue? He's probably sitting there now, stroking donors and political allies, ignoring my gift. He'd respond differently if I were sitting at a Manhattan address.

The remnants of meat and bread in Mike's mouth turn sour. He's tired of taking a back seat to these high-profile leaders, the ones celebrated on the cover of *Forbes* and the front page of *The Wall Street Journal*. He's tired of always proving his name belongs among the industry's elite. He gazes across the panorama of West Baltimore before him. He's tired of his city being the forgotten stepsister, always out of view, hidden in the shadows of those beloved fraternal twins—New York City and DC.

Mike's face breaks into a wry smile. That will also change soon, he thinks.

In a very big way.

He gathers the waxed paper and grease-stained brown bag that remain from his dinner and tosses them in the trash. Fueled for a couple more hours of work, he reflects on how much he enjoys this time of day—no underlings stopping by for direction, a break from the constant barrage of emails, a respite from the steady stream of vendors clamoring for coveted face time with the most important man in Baltimore.

How many others are here, still working away? he wonders. Not many, he knows. When he returned after his quick four o'clock meeting next door, he'd nearly been trampled by the wave of people heading home for the day. *What happened to the work ethic that built this country over the last century? Now, it's all about remote work, family time, and work-life balance.*

What a joke.

Most people have forgotten that working for him is a privilege, not a right. Not all of them, though. Some still care, still sacrifice.

I bet Tyler Rush is still working away.

•   •   •   •   •

Tyler rubs his eyes, thinking he should leave soon. He glances at his watch. Ten past seven. As soon as he finishes validating the budget template, he'll head out. It's been a busy Thursday, with no time to dig into the expense spreadsheets until the building emptied a couple hours ago.

He hears footsteps behind him.

"Greetings, Mr. Rush."

Tyler jolts at the unexpected voice and turns his head to see Mike Hayward standing three feet away.

"I'm curious about the results of the code you wrote to look for tax depreciation opportunities," Mike says, his onion breath filling the air. "I thought you might still be here."

Tyler opens a file on the computer monitor in front of him. "It's been running since last Friday. So far, we've identified seventy-eight entries that will save $248,000."

Mike focuses on the monitor, his eyes scrolling down the list. "Remarkable." He places a hand on Tyler's shoulder. "This is the kind of innovative thinking we need here."

"I've been obsessed with AI since middle school. There's a genuine opportunity to apply sophisticated analytics and data science in the financial arena. I've spent the past year researching this." He looks up at Mike. "A lot's been done already, but it's mostly centered on high frequency trading and quick arbitrage opportunities. There's still plenty of blue ocean to discover."

"I'm impressed. And intrigued." Mike's eyes are bright. "Neither of those things happens too often."

Tyler straightens himself higher in his chair, pleased by the compliment.

Mike extends his hand for Tyler to shake. "You are making a difference, young man. More than you realize." He holds the handshake for a few seconds then smiles. "Tell you what. I'm going to add you to an investment task force, accelerate your learning."

Tyler grins. "Thank you, sir. I can't wait."

"I've also got an algorithm I want you to look at. It makes stock recommendations, but the results have been hit and miss. Poke around at it. Let me know what you think."

The unexpected goodwill coming his way is hard to fathom, and Tyler hesitates a moment, his stomach knotting as doubt creeps in. It's hard not to wonder if he's capable of handling what's being thrust at him. His fingers grip the armrest tightly, but he forces a smile.

"Bring it on," he says, hoping his voice doesn't crack.

"That's the spirit." Mike turns to leave. "I should mention … the algorithm is extremely confidential." He takes a step then looks back over his shoulder. "By the way, you were right. The beard was bluffing." He chuckles. "Instead of folding, I raised. He folded immediately."

Mike winks then strolls away.

CHAPTER 5

"Deepak. This is Mike."

"Good evening, sir. Greetings from Bangladesh. How are you this fine night … or day, I suppose, for you?"

Mike does not waste time on pleasantries. "How are things progressing?" he asks.

"We've conscripted over two million computers. We expect to increase that number by one million per month, possibly faster."

"That's good." Mike leans back in his office chair, the leather creaking beneath him, and kicks his polished shoes up onto the desk. "Any detection problems?"

"None, sir. The virus remains completely hidden. We're monitoring traffic on both mainstream and dark net sites. Not a hint that anyone has noticed our project."

Mike runs the numbers in his head. By year's end, his cyber army will be comprised of nearly ten million drafted computers with a collective appetite for processing data and information that is almost unlimited. Even then, it will be premature to activate them. They will need to be properly linked to function at full capacity.

The result? Magnificent—the equivalent of harnessing the computing strength of all seven billion human brains on Earth. More powerful, really, as his network will operate as an interconnected artificial mind he can unleash on the world to do his bidding. Each node will work in harmony, like a perfectly tuned symphony, creating beautiful music never heard before, with him—Mike Hayward—holding the conductor's baton.

There's just one missing ingredient.

"What about the code?"

Deepak sighs. "Not so good."

"I'm tired of hearing that," Mike says, teeth gritted. He shoves his feet against the edge of the desk, sending his chair sliding back with a dull screech. "I've paid too much for that answer, Deepak."

"Yes, Mr. Hayward. But you must understand—what you are asking for is incredibly complex. Some of the team believe it's impossible."

"Fire those people." Mike stands abruptly, and the chair spins behind him. "They're holding us back."

"They are still talented scientists. I did not mean—"

"Nonbelievers are a cancer. Get rid of them."

Despite his outburst, Mike knows how difficult the task is—that's why the code is so valuable. It's the missing ingredient he can sprinkle on his network of robotic mercenaries to let the magic begin. Fringe computer scientists refer to it as the "Einstein Code," mythical lines of code that would allow computers to make the leap from being mere cooks following instructions to Michelin-starred chefs generating the recipes themselves. They would possess genuine human intelligence and creativity, dwarfing ChatGPT and more recent advancements in artificial intelligence that are lauded in the news and at nerd conventions.

Mainstream scientists dismiss the Einstein Code as an impossible figment of dreamers' imaginations—but Mike knows it's achievable. Science fiction is about to turn into reality.

With me as the conductor, imagine the power I'll have. His vision blurs slightly as he pictures the future. *I'll be king of financial exchanges across the globe. Industry captains will come to me for guidance, seek my approval. News stations will follow every move I make. And that's only the beginning. The possibilities are endless.*

But I must be the first.

Something stirs deep within him. He stretches his arms way up, feeling the satisfying pop of his joints as he lifts onto his tiptoes, releasing tension.

"Sir?" Deepak's voice crackles over the phone. "One more thing. We lost Dr. Conti. He quit yesterday."

Mike curses under his breath. "What about Dr. Kimura?"

"She's still with us."

"Why did Conti leave?"

"He wouldn't say, but I'm afraid he's going to a rival group."

"New Horizon?"

"I don't think so. I found out he's moving to Romania. Râmnicu Vâlcea, Romania."

"Find out why," Mike says, and he ends the call.

New Horizon is one thing, Mike thinks. He can keep tabs on them. Râmnicu Vâlcea is a more disturbing development. He has several contacts in the quaint Romanian town that has evolved into a hacker's paradise. But he hasn't heard of an outfit there hiring neuroscientists.

Who are they? Are they after the same Holy Grail? How deep are their pockets?

The thought of a rival group poaching his scientists is unnerving. Mike's thoughts race—years of work and millions of dollars have gone into building this operation, and he can't afford to be second. With a swift motion, he presses another button on his phone.

"This is Drag," answers a rough voice.

"Proceed with Plan B," Mike orders then hangs up.

If his money and experts can't create the code from scratch, he'll steal the seed he knows exists. That will get things moving.

He sinks into the guest chair in front of his desk, suddenly feeling the strain of exhaustion settling into his bones. Nothing has gone right today, but he feels better knowing Plan B is in motion. And that Plan C is coming together. The Einstein Code can't elude him forever. He will get it soon … no matter what it takes.

An alarm sounds on his computer, pulling him from his thoughts. He sits up and logs into the network of security cameras. Surveillance would be the honest word, though Mike prefers to believe he is merely monitoring his employees. He scrolls through feeds until he finds the one he needs. The resolution is crystal clear, even the audio from the hidden microphones comes through perfectly.

He studies the faces in the meeting. Puppets, he thinks. They hang on Ed's every word after he introduces himself as vice president of investments and proceeds to lead them down the wrong path—just as Mike suspected he would. They probably wonder why they're here, not realizing it's a tryout, an important audition.

Mike's script requires that he select just the right person. Someone possessing confidence to act under pressure, someone blessed with a large dose of resourcefulness, and, most importantly, someone driven by a fuel of much higher octane than the low-level motivation powering a garden-variety overachiever.

His eyes narrow as Ed instructs this all-star team to spend their most important asset on a list of regurgitated investment options provided by other firms.

He grimaces. At one time, he had thought Ed had the potential to be special.

He studies the faces of the puppets, one by one.

Natasha is focused, her eyes scanning the report in front of her. She is a star in the making. She leans over toward Greg and mumbles something. Greg nods, his unruly blond curls bobbing in front of his smiling face. Mike knows those curls and goofy grin mask a razor-sharp mind.

His close friends chide him for the vast time he invests scrutinizing his puppets, but he is convinced it's the number one reason his company's revenues have grown sevenfold under his reign.

And he isn't being disrespectful thinking of them as puppets. He views everyone as a puppet, a part of the grand performance he's conducting.

Except his ex-wife. She was just a bitch.

Mike spots Tyler on the screen. Doubt etches the young man's face as he reads Ed's list.

Mike wills him to say something. *Come on, kid.*

"This is pointless," Tyler blurts out, loud enough to cut through the room. "We're chasing butterflies."

Yes! Mike couldn't have phrased it better himself. *Chasing butterflies. Exactly.*

Ed glares at Tyler, the weight of his gaze silencing the room.

Tyler lowers his eyes. "That didn't come out right."

No, Mike thinks, don't lose your guts now. *It did come out right.*

Ed frowns, drumming his fingers on the polished wood. "Oh? Please enlighten us. Why, exactly, is this pointless?"

Tyler fidgets with his tie, takes a deep breath, and looks Ed straight in the eye. "Your solution to improve returns is to bring us a list of prepackaged investment products peddled by other companies?" His voice hardens. "That will not increase our returns."

Mike leans closer to the screen. *There's the fire.*

"These sophisticated financial instruments have the potential to provide above-average returns," Ed says, settling back into his leather chair with a faint squeak. He taps a pen against his teeth, the sound sharp against the tense silence. Sunlight filters through the shades, casting long shadows across the room. "Tell me, Mr. Rush, what's wrong with looking at high-quality investment opportunities assembled by the world's leading investment banking firms? All carrying top-notch ratings from Standard & Poor's, I might add."

"If you're trying to find a gem," Tyler says with a firm voice, "I can tell you it won't be from a well-vetted product offering from Goldman Sachs that's been carefully crafted for the benefit of Goldman Sachs."

A vein pulses in Ed's forehead. His face flushes with anger as he stands, hands on his hips. "Your many years of investing experience taught you that, I suppose?" His voice is mocking. "If you have a point, Mr. Rush, will you kindly work your way in that direction?"

Tyler slides a neatly folded piece of paper across the gleaming surface of the conference table. "I researched our competitor, New Horizon, after seeing their name in the meeting invite. They are consistently achieving higher returns with lower volatility. We're playing it safe, while they're finding smarter ways to invest."

Mike nods his approval at the screen, a smile forming. *Now there is a special puppet.* He increases the speaker volume and licks his lips.

Ed snickers. "You should know—and Mr. Hayward should as well—they are not our peer. We provide a broad scope of financial services. They specialize in serving the top one percent. I don't know why the CEO insists on comparing us to them." He glances down at his fingernails. "And I surely don't know why he added you to this team."

Tyler grabs a bottle of water from the table and takes a deliberate sip, his eyes never leaving Ed's. "But we're both investing to achieve maximum returns for a set risk tolerance," Tyler says calmly, "and they are killing it."

Mike leans even closer, impressed. Tyler is holding his ground. *Good.*

"What's *your* brilliant solution?" Ed snaps.

"We need to investigate how they're doing it. There's no way they're following the crowd."

Ed dismisses him with a wave of his hand. "They're not just going to hand over their strategies, Mr. Rush. This committee will follow my approach while you go off chasing windmills."

Tyler's jaw tightens. He starts again, his voice measured. "Ed … Mr. Rogers. I'm not trying to be difficult. It's just that in the finance department, we often research competitor approaches to—"

"This is investments, not finance! If you don't have a specific, actionable recommendation, then I suggest you keep your mouth shut for the rest of the meeting."

Dead air fills the room. Everyone stares at Tyler.

Ed has backed the young analyst into a corner, Mike observes. How will he respond now? *Don't give up, Tyler. Keep fighting.*

"That's what I thought," Ed says after a moment of silence from Tyler. He turns his attention to the rest of the young professionals. "Now, team—"

"Buy Republic-Cola," Tyler says, his voice ringing out.

"Republic? The soda company? That's your big idea?" Ed bursts into laughter. "I better end the meeting so everyone can rush out to buy some."

Tyler doesn't flinch. He rises from his chair, his face calm, and walks out without a word, leaving Ed laughing behind him.

Ed might be laughing, but Mike isn't. His instincts tell him Tyler's onto something. He closes the video and reaches for his phone.

"Morgan Brown, at your service."

"Where's Republic trading?" Mike asks.

"One moment," his broker says. "Republic-Cola is currently $114 and change. Thinking about short-selling it? Expecting it to tank?"

Mike looks up, running quick calculations in his head. "Buy 100,000 shares."

Morgan clears his throat. "I must advise against it. Republic's got a D analyst rating, sir. It does have a high dividend. If that's what you're after, give me an hour to research a solid recommendation with a big yield."

"I wasn't asking for your opinion."

Mike listens to the clatter of Morgan's fingers punching a keyboard.

"I've got your account pulled up," Morgan says. "Purchasing 100,000 shares at market price. And … it's in."

Mike is just about to hang up when he hears Morgan's voice again. "Mr. Hayward, I've got to ask. Do you have a tip?"

Mike lifts the receiver back to his mouth. "Call it a hunch."

He stands and strolls toward the door. Is he being foolish, placing an eleven-million-dollar bet on the whim of an inexperienced analyst who tossed his recommendation out in the middle of a verbal jousting match?

He doesn't think so. He has learned a lot about Tyler in the past couple weeks, and he is certain the young man isn't bluffing with his stock recommendation. Years of studying body language at card tables have taught Mike to trust his instincts. *Tyler is speaking the truth.* And after all, Mike may soon be betting much more on the back of Tyler

Rush than measly soda bottles … because he has just made his final decision.

•   •   •   •   •

Tyler grabs a cup of coffee and stops by Greg's office on his way back to his cubicle.

"Got a few minutes?"

"Sure." Greg tilts his head back and dumps the last crumbs from a Fritos bag into his mouth, earning a pained look from Tyler.

"Don't blame me," Greg says. "I'm helpless against the power of Fritos, the pinnacle of human achievement in processed corn."

"You're messed up." Tyler chuckles and drops into a chair across from Greg's cluttered desk. He can never understand how Greg eats so much and stays so skinny. Greg's brown leather belt—complete with an oversized cowboy buckle—hangs loosely on his hips, more decorative than functional, as if it's just marking the space between his torso and legs.

Tyler's stomach growls, and he absentmindedly rubs his belly, spilling a few drops of stale coffee onto his shirt.

"I'm messed up?" Greg raises an eyebrow. "Look at you, bud. You can't drink a cup of coffee without making a mess." He tosses the empty bag into the trash with a flick of his wrist. "You can't even get through a meeting without ticking off a VP."

"Yeah, it wasn't my finest moment." Tyler groans, wiping at the coffee stain on his shirt.

"Hey, it's not entirely on you. Ed's been on edge. Something about the commodities market going haywire this morning. Corn futures, I think."

Tyler nods. "I've been on edge too. And he pisses me off."

"What's done is done." Greg shrugs. "But I gotta ask, what was with that Republic recommendation?"

Tyler thinks about the poker game he saw, and about Mike's cryptic instructions regarding the investment program. He remembers Mike's warning to keep everything under wraps. "I probably should've kept my mouth shut."

"Agreed. Ed killed the meeting after you walked out."

"I get it." Tyler rocks back in his chair, balancing on the two rear legs. "We're invading his territory."

Greg points a finger at him. "You're the smartest guy I know, but don't let your big ol' mouth get ahead of you."

Tyler stands and turns to look out the window. He catches a view of Camden Yards a few blocks away, thirty-seven stories down. "What time do the Os play tonight?"

"Seven." Greg pulls out his phone and swipes through a ticket app. "You want to go?"

"I can sneak out by then. You game?"

"Heck yeah." Greg looks up from his phone. "Didn't you used to play shortstop?"

"In high school, until I got too tall."

Greg grins. "Ramirez is out tonight. Hamstring injury. Maybe they'll let you play … in the game."

They both laugh, the tension from the day easing for just a moment.

CHAPTER 6

Three days later, Tyler powers off his laptop. He's ready to leave the office and meet a group of friends for Friday happy hour before attending Anna's eight o'clock basketball game. As he grabs his messenger bag and steps out of his cube, his desk phone rings. He looks back. The caller display reads *Exec—Admin.*

Could it be Ed? Is he an executive? There's been no word from him since their intense encounter at Hayward's investment meeting earlier in the week.

Tyler's thoughts swirl. *Ignore it? Or answer it?* One deep breath— he answers.

"Tyler Rush speaking."

"This is Lance Hudson, Mr. Hayward's administrative assistant. He'd like to see you in his office."

Tyler pauses before answering, "I'll be right up." He hesitates another moment then asks, "Where's his office?" He's never been on the fortieth floor where the C-suite executives roam.

"Walk through the glass doors when you exit the elevator. Tell the receptionist you're here to see me."

Guess I'm in trouble because of Ed. Damn.

After a short, uneventful ride up five stories, Tyler enters a different world. The open space behind the receptionist stretches out half the width of the building, free of the cubicle walls and general clutter that consume the offices he normally frequents. Floor-to-ceiling windows provide an unobstructed view of the city from this, the highest floor of the tallest structure in Baltimore.

Highest official floor, he reminds himself.

The air smells cleaner up here, as though the higher altitude filters out the stress that brews below.

Lance emerges from a door at the end of the room and nods. "Follow me," he says.

They march down a hallway past the darkened offices of the chief operating officer and the chief financial officer, along with the empty desks of the administrative assistants assigned to guard each of their doors. Tyler's shoes echo in the eerily quiet corridor. A large room stretches along the far wall, spanning the length of three limousines.

"Boardroom," Lance says, his tone clipped and businesslike. Without waiting for a response, he turns abruptly.

Tyler pivots to follow him and gets his first glimpse of Mike Hayward, visible through the glass wall of his luxurious office, typing on his keyboard. He looks insulated from his company in this personal kingdom that takes up the entire southwest corner of the fortieth floor.

Lance opens the glass door of Hayward's office, motions for Tyler to enter, then closes it behind him.

Tyler's attention is immediately drawn to the ornate desk. Carved into the front of its walnut facade are a roaring lion, a peacock with intricately designed tail feathers, and a hawk with its wings pulled back, diving toward an invisible prey.

"Nice, huh?" Mike asks, waving Tyler forward. "This piece was hand-constructed for Lord Philip Renwick in 1896. He later commissioned Spanish wood sculptor Juan Consuelos to add the carvings."

Tyler nods, as if the names are familiar to him.

Mike steps behind the desk and gestures toward the panoramic view wrapping around the corner of the building.

"What do you think?" he asks.

Tyler whistles. "Unbelievable."

Mike strolls toward the far end of the office. "I want to show you something."

Tyler follows Mike through a glass door that opens onto a wide terrace brimming with ferns and tropical greenery. Many mornings, Tyler has gazed up from the street below and noticed this balcony that juts out ten feet from the face of the building, but he never imagined it held a lush jungle oasis forty stories above the gritty streets of downtown Baltimore.

The faint scent of damp earth and tropical plants mingles with the undertone of cigar smoke. Water cascades down multiple rock falls, almost drowning out the murmur of the city five hundred feet below. Tyler's breath catches as the surreal atmosphere of Hayward's high-rise paradise intoxicates him.

He trails behind Mike along a winding path, maneuvering around a massive stone fountain, careful not to trample the manicured grass surrounding it. A cool breeze whispers through the terrace, causing the lush ferns to rustle softly. The air is crisp against his skin, a welcome contrast to the stuffy confines of his cube. As they near the edge of the terrace, a wave of vertigo washes over Tyler. He chases the feeling away.

"Have a look," Mike says, leaning casually against the railing, peering over the edge.

Tyler inches forward, his feet refusing to obey as his stomach knots. He leans back, the magnetic pull of the dizzying height tempting him to retreat further. With deliberate effort, he steps closer, the metal of the railing cool beneath his fingertips. His legs wobble as he dares a glance down at the tiny figures below—the people moving about their evening in the Harborplace market, completely unaware of the man staring down at them from so far above.

"What a view," Tyler whispers, gaping down and beginning to feel larger than life in this rarefied air. He clutches the rail so hard his knuckles whiten as the realization hits that only this thin barrier separates him from a five-hundred-foot drop. A fresh wave of dizziness surges through him.

Mike chuckles softly. "You need to get your sea legs. This height can be a little overwhelming at first."

Mike pulls back from the railing and sits in one of the cushioned patio chairs nearby, motioning for Tyler to join him.

Why am I here? Tyler wonders. *Maybe it's not because of Ed ... but surely the CEO has better things to do than shoot the breeze with me.*

"I've been thinking about the work you did on the tax savings initiative," Mike says. "I also spent some time reviewing your contributions to the Matterhorn acquisition and the Gen Re reinsurance deal."

He reaches for a cigar case on the table between them, offering one to Tyler, who shakes his head no. "I see potential in you," Mike continues, biting off the tip of a cigar and lighting it with a practiced flick. "Lots of potential, as a matter of fact."

Tyler flushes. "Thank you, sir."

"It's not just a compliment—it's a fact." A cloud of smoke drifts lazily from the cigar, framing Mike's wide smile.

Tyler thinks of the late nights he's poured into the investment program and the countless hours spent at the office. *He's right. I do have potential.*

"Speaking of potential ..." Mike waves his hand toward the harbor. "Did you know Baltimore almost became the capital of the United States?"

"No, I never learned that."

"It's not in the history books. Many things aren't." Mike gazes into the distance, far beyond the city's outskirts. "It was after the Civil War. Some influential folks tried to make it happen. They almost succeeded, but due to an unfortunate twist of fate—an unlucky flip of the cards, you might say—the DC advocates won the day."

"That would've been something," Tyler says.

"Yes, it really would have. This is a great town. It produced the two of us, right?"

Tyler laughs, and his stomach unclenches slightly. "I suppose so."

Mike smiles, his eyes fixed on the horizon. "People forget about Baltimore, think it's just a gas stop between the Washington powerbrokers and the New York elite." His eyes become glassy. "That'll change one day—and sooner than you think."

Tyler's not sure whether to be inspired or unnerved by the CEO's words.

"Enough about Baltimore," Mike says. "There's something else I want to discuss." He rises and returns to the railing, casting a glance back at Tyler. Tyler follows, sliding up next to the building's edge with more grace this time.

Mike turns to him. "I've got an unusual proposal for you."

Tyler tenses, feeling the gravity of the moment.

"I'm going to offer you a chance to enter our Executive Development Program. Understand, this is unprecedented—I've never offered this opportunity to someone so young." He places a hand on Tyler's shoulder. "But you're ready for it."

A surge of excitement streams through Tyler's veins followed by incredible disbelief.

Mike's expression turns serious. "This is a big step. Consider it carefully, and let me know when you decide. If you opt in, there is no turning back."

Tyler nods. "I'd love the opportunity to contribute more, to learn more." He smiles. *And to make more money so I can save Anna.*

"I'll have my VP of Human Resources, Julie Caruthers, send you the details. Read them thoroughly. We'll meet next week to further discuss it."

It's everything he can do to not accept on the spot, but Tyler holds back.

"Trust me," Mike adds, "this will be life-changing. But it won't be easy."

Tyler watches as a red-tailed hawk circles overhead, moving in slow, deliberate arcs against the summer sky, as if patiently waiting for the right moment to strike its prey.

Mike turns around and leans back against the railing. "Tell me, have you had a chance to tinker with the investing program?"

"I spent last weekend going through it."

"First impressions?"

"It's pulling in massive amounts of information from thousands of sources—news briefs, social media posts, traffic reports, weather predictions, court decisions—and trying to compile, categorize, and link the information to create stock recommendations."

Mike nods. "The key is that it will provide those recommendations before the financial markets have been able to connect the dots, allowing me to take an equity position before anyone else realizes what's about to happen." He puffs on his cigar. "At least, that's the goal."

"It sounds like insider trading," Tyler says. "Except that it would be completely legal."

Mike glances at him. "Have you unearthed any stock recommendations that might interest me?"

"It gave me a strong buy for Joker-Cola."

Mike's head snaps toward Tyler. "Joker?" His hand darts to his pocket, and his phone is halfway out before he finishes the word.

Tyler continues. "The program picked up on a comment from their CEO, buried deep in the transcript of last week's quarterly earnings conference call. He was responding to an analyst about fresh marketing strategies, and he mentioned an upcoming meeting with Football USA executives. No details, though."

"From that it recommended buying Joker?"

"There's more. It linked that information with a tweet from the league's commissioner about the value of old friendships in business—he and Joker's CEO have met several times over the years—and with multiple sources indicating Football USA team owners would meet late this week to approve a major endorsement contract."

"Sounds like a done deal," Mike says.

"Maybe. But it also pulled in a Facebook post from the owner of Glamour Salon that Lilly Stebbins would be in for a treatment this past Tuesday morning."

"The actress?"

"And wife of Mark Stebbins, Republic's new president." Tyler glances at Mike. "And the Glamour Salon is located in the lobby level of Football USA's Washington, DC, headquarters."

Mike nods slowly, the puzzle pieces appearing to fall into place. "So the investment program deduced that Joker and Republic were both meeting with Football USA to try to secure a major deal."

Tyler nods. "And since Joker has beaten Republic in the last seven branding duels, the program concluded with an eight-nine percent probability that Joker would become the official sponsor of Football USA by tomorrow."

A gust of dry summer air from downtown breezes up across the balcony.

"Then I should buy Joker in the after-hours market," Mike says.

"I wouldn't recommend that."

Mike pauses, his brow furrowing. "Why not? Is the model wrong?" He scratches at a spot on the metal surface of the railing.

"Not wrong exactly but incomplete. It missed a few crucial factors—the fact that Republic's new CEO is a closer with a stellar sales record, for one. Football USA also has a statistical bias toward partnering with local companies, and Republic's headquarters is just ten miles up the Potomac from their DC offices. Plus, the new CEO and the league's commissioner have a personal history—their fathers were fraternity brothers decades ago."

Mike leans back, appearing impressed by Tyler's rapid analysis. "You figured all this out last weekend?"

Tyler nods. "The program had access to the data points but didn't flag them as relevant. They were scattered and not connected. I manually added the missing pieces, feeding them into the algorithm. Once I did, the odds flipped—ninety-four percent in favor of Republic."

Mike stares at Tyler. "You manually adjusted the program?"

"Not a permanent fix. I just forced it to consider the additional variables."

Mike drops the stub of his cigar to the ground, steps on it to extinguish it, and kicks it off the edge of the balcony.

"I'd like you to automate that adjustment within the program."

Tyler blinks, taken aback by the enormity of the task. *Automate it? That would be like asking a machine to think like a human. Is that even possible?* The scope of what Mike is asking sinks in. He hesitates for a few seconds before responding.

"This won't be easy. Your request goes beyond the abilities of the deep learning model I built for the tax depreciation project. It would need to understand the questions to ask itself and see the links that seem unrelated. But I'm willing to give it a shot."

He sidles up next to Mike and peers over, watching the stub fall. The faint creak of the railing under his grip reminds him just how high they are.

•   •   •   •   •

Mike studies Tyler as he leans over the railing and looks straight down. Impressive how quickly the young man has mastered his nerves, he thinks. And the speed at which he's dissected the algorithm? Exceptional. The same algorithm for which progress has stalled halfway around the globe, despite millions in funding, dozens of top scientists, and every resource Mike can conjure to push the project to the finish line. The same algorithm with the potential to change the world.

One problem, though, Mike realizes. He checked today's stock prices earlier and found Republic down five percent for the week, while Joker was up four on strong rumors of a pending deal with Football USA. It seems the algorithm's original prediction was correct.

It seems Tyler is wrong.

"Your explanation about the adjustment is logical," Mike says, "but the market doesn't seem to agree." He reaches for his phone and pulls up a financial news feed, intending to show Tyler the price changes for each of the cola makers.

Tyler looks up and shrugs. "Good thing neither of us loaded up on Republic stock."

Mike snorts and gazes out over his city. *Have I rushed to judgment with Tyler? Been blinded by my desire for him to be the one?*

His phone vibrates with a new notification. "Football USA Strikes Deal with Cola Maker." He presses the link and holds the device in the air so Tyler can also view the screen.

A face emerges against a backdrop of a high-rise in the District of Columbia. "Rumors have swirled throughout the financial markets all week that an endorsement deal between Football USA and Joker-Cola is imminent."

Mike prepares to hide his disappointment. Losing a few bucks isn't a big deal. He'd just hoped Tyler would've been correct.

"To everyone's surprise, however, minutes ago, Football USA Commissioner David Blakely appeared at a press conference with Republic-Cola CEO Mark Stebbins."

Mike grunts then turns the volume up a notch.

"Republic is already up sixteen percent in after-hours trading. Joker stock is being punished by this surprising turn of events. According to my sources, no one saw this coming."

Mike stares at the screen, grinning. "Well, I'll be damned." *One person saw it coming all right, and that person has unknowingly made me over a million dollars in three days.*

Impressive—no question, my young protégé here deserves a starring role in the script that is still being written.

A helicopter passes overhead, slicing through the calm summer air. They both watch its slow flight across the city.

Yes, the time is right. Tyler is ready.

Mike breaks the silence. "What did you think about that poker game?"

Tyler hesitates. "I didn't tell anyone, sir."

"That's fine. Wasn't a trick question." Mike casts the bait. "Do you play?"

"I did in college. I even thought about going pro." Tyler grins. "Most of my friends and I shared that dream."

Mike chuckles. "I can understand. It's a fascinating game." The bait is still out there, bobbing along on the surface of their conversation. "Do you have any questions?" He looks at Tyler. "About the investing code? Or about the Executive Development Program?"

Tyler watches the chopper working its way westward.

"I do have one question." He pauses then plunges ahead. "If I join the program, can I play?" He glances at Mike then adds, "In the game?"

A bite! Mike hides his joy. "That's an interesting question."

Tyler shifts uncomfortably. "If I'm out of line—"

"No." Mike waves away his concern. "In fact, it would be a tremendous networking opportunity for you." He starts to reel in the line, slowly, carefully. "I'll give it some thought."

Far behind the helicopter, the bright sun is beginning its descent for the night. In its path, barely visible against the horizon, a wall of gray clouds slowly marches its way forward. Neither man pays any attention.

•   •   •   •   •

Tyler sits in a corner of the junior high bleachers, not exactly blending in with the sea of jeans and work boots in the crowd scattered around him. His dress slacks and starched white shirt stand out, he realizes, but at least he left his coat and tie in the car. He would have changed into casual clothes, but after meeting with Mike, it took a mad dash to arrive at the school before Anna's game started.

Tyler glances around the gym for the third time, reconfirming that Virginia and Marco are not in the audience. It would shock him if either of them ever showed up for a game, but he knows caution is necessary. His nest egg needs to go toward lawyers who can clear up this legal mess and help him get custody of Anna—not to defend him for violating a court order.

Tyler wipes sweat from his upper lip. The summer league games are brutal in a gym with no air conditioning. Several large fans above the court move the air around, but they provide little relief for the spectators.

Partway through the second half of the game, Tyler frets about his impulsive request to play poker with Mike and his rich and powerful friends. *So stupid.* He would like a chance to get his hands on their money, of course. *But come on.* Mike, to his credit, hadn't laughed in his face.

As soon as Tyler had blurted out his request, he remembered Paul. *Would he be there again? Talk about awkward.*

The shrill pitch of a whistle cuts through his thoughts. He realizes he's missed most of Anna's action on the court while ruminating on his meeting with Mike.

"Foul! Two shots."

Tyler watches Anna move to the free throw line, and he glances up at the scoreboard. Tied up, twenty-eight apiece. Two seconds remaining in the game. *Come on, Anna, you got this.* He knows she's not confident. Things never seem to work out in her favor.

Anna bounces the ball once. Then twice. She fumbles her catch after the second bounce. Then she shoots.

Tyler can tell the ball is off course. It bounces off the right side of the rim. Anna's head droops. He wants to cry and wonders what he should say after the game to make her feel better.

The referee hands Anna the ball for her second attempt. She bounces it once and stops. She takes a deep breath and stands still. Ten seconds pass. Then twenty. She looks around the gym, spots Tyler, and waves. They smile at each other.

She faces the basket, rises to her full height, and shoots. The ball swishes through the net. Game over.

Anna's teammates rush to her, give her high fives and hugs, then whisk her off the court.

Tyler strolls to the hallway outside the exit from the girls' locker room. Leaning against the wall, he nods at the waiting parents around him and enjoys the moment.

After five minutes, Anna emerges with two other girls, all giggling and replaying their favorite moments of the game. She sees Tyler and halts her conversation midsentence. She runs over to him and wraps him in a bear hug, quickly, before rejoining her friends. Tyler follows them out of the school.

As he nears his truck in the parking lot, Anna drops back in step beside him. He always drives her home after games, especially when it's dark. Well, almost home. Close enough to ensure she enters the apartment safely while he remains unseen by the other occupants.

"Anna? Is that you?" The voice is loud and slightly slurred. It's unmistakably Marco's. He emerges from a mongrel of a car covered with patches of primer and sporting mismatched tires.

Tyler can't believe it.

Marco stops when he recognizes Tyler. "Well, look who we have here. The college graduate in his fancy clothes, no doubt making all kinds of money. Does he ever remember his aunt and uncle anymore?"

Tyler cringes at Marco calling himself "uncle."

"No, never a cent for them—not even after all they did for him." A wave of cheap cologne, infused with notes of an even cheaper whiskey, washes over Tyler as Marco approaches. The older man's heavy breathing fills the space between them, labored and loud.

Tyler steps back to create a comfortable amount of space between them, but Marco immediately moves forward to fill the gap.

"We have to go, Anna," Marco says. His eyes stay locked on Tyler as he speaks. "We'll need to think about a punishment for disobeying our order to stay away from him. And *you* …" He jabs a finger into Tyler's chest. "I ought to call the cops and have you arrested for violating the restraining order—again."

Marco no longer physically intimidates Tyler. His thick arms and linebacker shoulders protrude from his soiled tank top, but these days, it's his belly Tyler notices first. The years of constant six packs of beer and cigarettes have added to a self-inflicted punishment and have slowly disintegrated his health into the sad version standing before Tyler. Marco's breath is ragged and tinged with alcohol.

"Call the cops," Tyler tells him. "You're drunk. I'll take my chances with an appearance before a judge if it means you getting a DUI."

"Get in the car," Marco says to Anna then glares at Tyler. "You. Stay away from her." He turns and takes a few uneven steps toward his vehicle, his feet dragging across the hot asphalt.

Anna moves to follow him then turns back. "It's fine, Tyler. I'll go with him."

"No!" Tyler's yell causes the heads of a few nearby parents in the parking lot to look their way. "Let me tell you something, Marco, and try to use the few sober brain cells you have left to understand this. Anna is not riding home with you. I'm going to drive her to your apartment. I'm going to drop her off. *Period*."

"Son of a bitch!" Marco turns back around and charges forward. He swings his fist at Tyler's chin, but Tyler sees it coming and ducks left. The miss causes Marco to lurch forward, and Tyler straightens up, shoving hard on the older man's back. Marco crumbles to the pavement, heat radiating up into the air as he struggles for breath.

Tyler stares at the crumpled form in front of him and immediately regrets what he's done. He should have kept his cool. Anna will be the one who pays for his selfishness, not him.

CHAPTER 7

The blaring alarm jolts Tyler awake. Groaning, he reaches for his phone to silence it before rolling out of bed. He's supposed to meet Greg in an hour for their Saturday morning run.

He ambles to the kitchen of his studio apartment and brews a pot of coffee. As the machine gurgles, his thoughts drift to Anna. *Did she get home okay? Was there fallout from last night?* He sends a text to check on her then takes a deep breath, trying to push the doubts aside. Filling his mug to the brim, he walks to the sliding glass door leading to the balcony overlooking the harbor.

Shielding his eyes from the bright morning sun, he surveys the scene below. The air is humid, almost sticky against his skin as he takes a sip. Below, the harbor is mostly still, save for the soft hum of boat engines preparing for the day. The faint smell of saltwater lingers in the breeze, mingling with the aroma of his coffee. His eyes settle on the marina a quarter mile away, where seagulls harass the anglers loading their boats, squawking and diving at the buckets filled with bait.

After finishing his coffee, Tyler heads back to the kitchen. He cracks a few eggs into a pan, adds a slice of toast to the side, and eats in silence, his thoughts turning to his conversation with Mike. The idea of a high-stakes poker game—one that draws in CEOs, actors, and senators—lingers in his mind.

Once he's done eating, he grabs his laptop and types, "Baltimore high-stakes poker Mike Hayward," hoping to uncover any mention of the mysterious game.

He scrolls through the first page of results and advances to the second. Halfway down, an entry catches his eye.

Was our History Decided by a Deck of Cards? | Truthrevealed.net

www.truthrevealed.net/civilwar/secrets/thegame/story?id=348 732

*Dec 29, 2008—We investigated rumors of a secret **poker** game. **Stakes** couldn't have been **high**er. Abraham Lincoln, Jefferson … Jonas **Hayward** … still today in **Baltimore.***

Not an exact match but interesting. Tyler clicks the link.

Unavailable Page >>Error 5724?<492394402129

Going back to the previous page, he rereads the entry—2008. It's so old, no wonder the link is broken. He navigates to the Truthrevealed.net website, but his phone alarm blares again. He glances at the screen then grunts and closes his laptop. *Time to meet Greg.*

Outside his building, Tyler waits on the patio and enjoys the sound of harbor water gently lapping against the moorings. In just a couple hours, a flood of tourists will overrun the now peaceful harbor.

He stretches on his toes to loosen his calf muscles. Beads of sweat are already dripping down his temples. *Could it possibly be more humid?* He looks to his left toward Pratt Street. *Could Greg ever be on time?* He glances down and kneels to tighten his laces. *Could that poker story really be about the game?*

Greg finally appears, jogging along the sprawling boardwalk next to the Inner Harbor. He owns a condo in a high-rise a few blocks away. As he approaches, Tyler falls in next to him and they run beside the water.

Greg skips over an empty bottle lying in his path. "'Sup, bro."

Tyler nods and wipes his forehead with the back of his hand as his sneakers hit the brick pavers, each step heavy. His calves ache, but he keeps pace with Greg, trying to shake off the lingering exhaustion from the week.

Greg grimaces. "Don't know about you, but I'm dragging. Barhopping with Jen and her friends at Fell's Point till two."

"Is that three dates with the same girl?"

Greg grins. "I know. It goes against my civic duty to remain available for the ladies."

Tyler punches his friend's arm. "Hey, do you know how to access a web page with a broken link?"

Greg nods and asks, "Why'd you bail on happy hour?"

The bit of the internet story said Hayward. Wasn't Mike, but still … Tyler thinks.

"Dude, you need a date," Greg says. "You can't just work and worry."

"Maybe next time."

"Jen was going to set you up, then you didn't show. Made me look lame."

Tyler runs a few steps in silence. His breathing syncs with the rhythmic pounding of their shoes striking the ground.

"I was in Mike Hayward's office."

"Say what?" Greg reaches over and flicks Tyler's ear.

Tyler slaps his hand away. "He wants me to join an Executive Development Program."

Greg scoffs. "Crazy talk."

They turn and pass in front of the National Aquarium.

"One year of experience," Greg says. "You're still a babe in the woods."

"I've helped on some big projects."

"I've danced the jig for eight years," Greg says. "Outstanding performance reviews. Never had a whiff of the accelerated deal."

Tyler shrugs.

Greg points a finger at him. "It's a big deal. Bob Silverstone was in it. Became CFO."

"There's more to it," Tyler says. Over the next several minutes, he tells his best friend about the game and the investment algorithm. "You better not tell anyone, even Jen. Or I'm toast."

Greg nods. "You might be able to play?"

Tyler shrugs.

"I'd stay away from it," Greg says.

"Probably good advice."

The boardwalk turns into Key Highway, and they pass the Ritz-Carlton Residences.

Greg points at a waterfront condo. "There's your old home."

Tyler bites his lip, remembering a time when he and Anna lived with their parents in this comfortable condo. Aunt Virginia was simply an ordinary annoying relative then, someone to be endured on holidays. Then his and Anna's lives were turned upside down, and they had to move to Aunt Virginia's apartment—only four miles north but a world away. Plywood slats replaced spotless glass panes, and dingy liquor stores replaced juice bars. Their new world was brushed over with background paint on a canvas constructed by men like Mike. But it's a world very real in Tyler's memory and a world that currently consumes sweet Anna.

He shakes his head and glances at Greg. "Help me find the internet story."

Greg kicks his knees high in the air for no apparent reason, normal behavior for him. "Gotta be a cached page."

"I need your help."

"Really? You're the programming genius."

"Yeah, but we both know who the world-class hacker is."

Thirty minutes later, the sweaty pair ambles into Tyler's apartment. Greg makes a beeline for the living area, and Tyler stops to grab two waters from the fridge.

"Don't sit on the—" he starts to yell but then hears the groan of springs as Greg collapses onto the couch. "Thanks a lot."

Greg looks up from Tyler's laptop on the coffee table in front of him. "Need your password, bud."

Greg's fingers dance along the keys, and five minutes later, he pushes the laptop toward Tyler.

"Was Our History Decided by a Deck of Cards?"

By Brett Sommerfield on Dec 29, 2008

Outrageous? Unbelievable? Shocking? Yes. Yes. Yes. And, likely true!

Two weeks ago, someone emailed me a photo of the following letter, purported to have been written in 1887 by Elijah James, a close friend and adviser of Jefferson Davis.

December 14, 1887

Dearest Samuel,

I fear this will be the last time I write to you. Each breath requires great effort, and the rattling is louder.

Before my passing, I need to share the events of early 1861. Seven states had joined our Southern cause, but nine remained uncommitted. After a month of no progress, Mr. Davis grew concerned that the momentum would be lost and proposed a game with Mr. Lincoln.

Still staring over at the screen, Greg reaches for a loose end of the sheet covering the couch and mops his brow.

Tyler pokes the side of his head with a finger. "Stop using my sheet as a sweat rag and scroll down." He reads on.

On the twentieth day of March, they met at The Willard Hotel in Washington and played five-card draw. Jonas Hayward and I served as official observers, watching as a thousand coins were traded back and forth between two great warriors, the gold shimmering in the lamplight.

The great battle raged for three days and nights. In the end, Mr. Lincoln won five states to Mr. Davis's four. Within three months, Virginia, Arkansas, North Carolina, and Tennessee had seceded, while the rest passed resolutions supporting the Union.

"Jonas *Hayward*," Tyler says. "That's why it got snagged in my search."

Greg nods and scrolls the rest of the way down. "Ask your new bestie about it when you're jibber-jabbering about CEO stuff together."

"Yeah, right. What else does it say?" Together, they continue reading.

> The gold coin I have enclosed with this letter is exceedingly important, of much greater value than its mere weight. It is embossed with a special mark, a chevron with thirteen stars. The person who possesses this coin is the custodian of the game. You see, my dearest son, a table, a deck of cards, and four chairs continue to be used to solve some of the most important conflicts that arise in these United States.
>
> Upon my death, you will be contacted with instructions on how to use this coin. If this responsibility is too much to bear, you may contact Jonas Hayward but no one else. I assure you, I am of sound mind as I pen these words. Now I bid ye farewell.
>
> Your father,
>
> Elijah James

Greg rolls off the couch. "Sounds like a pile of BS to me."

Tyler stares at the screen. "I saw gold coins at the game."

"Careful there, bucko. This is way out there."

"What's a chevron?" Tyler asks.

"It's like an upside-down letter v." Greg empties his pocket and examines the quarter and two dimes in his hand. "Dang. I'm not the custodian."

Tyler snorts and points at the screen. "There's more there, at the bottom."

> Quite a letter, but is it real? Newspaper records indicate both Lincoln and Davis were in Washington, DC, in March 1861. Archived financial records show a suite and six rooms booked at the Willard Hotel in the name of Jonas Hayward.
>
> More to come, as the truth must be revealed!

Tyler stands and paces toward the window. "Could it be true?"

"It's on the internet. It must be."

They both laugh.

"I'm going to contact this guy," Tyler says, "Brett Sommerfield. See if he has information about a high-profile game in Baltimore."

"Want me to see if Elijah and Jonas are real?"

Tyler nods.

Greg jumps to his feet. "Gotta run. Jen and I are going to Frederick this afternoon. Be back tomorrow night."

Tyler sighs as he watches his friend leave to spend time with his girlfriend. One day, he thinks, as he sits alone in his apartment.

CHAPTER 8

Tyler sips from a steaming mug of coffee and flips through the mountain of New Horizon financial exhibits piled on his desk. He scours 13Fs, 10-Qs, and annual statements, searching for clues. He knows most investors think it's impossible to time the market, predict the movement of individual stock prices, buy and sell at the most opportune times, but New Horizon appears to be doing the impossible.

Do they have an investment program? An algorithm that can do what Mike's code cannot?

He types an email to Ed to share this information, hoping it might bridge the crevice between them. Before he finishes, an instant message from his boss appears on his screen.

Rob Walker: *Please come to my office.*

Tyler winds his way through the thirty-fifth floor, crowded today because most of the hybrid folks come in on Mondays. He stops by the break room to refill his coffee before arriving at Rob's office. Noticing someone is already inside, he pauses at the threshold.

"Come in," Rob says, motioning him inside but avoiding direct eye contact. "This is Human Resources Manager John Mather. I asked him to join us."

John stands and offers a firm handshake, his smile tight.

Could this be about the Executive Development Program?

"Thanks for stopping by," Rob says, his voice higher pitched than normal and his face flushed. "Have a seat next to John. I'll shut the door."

Tyler frowns and sits. The quiet drone of the air conditioning is the only sound in Rob's tense office, and Tyler shifts uncomfortably in his chair.

I don't think that's why I'm here.

Rob finally settles into his seat, fiddling with a piece of paper. "There's an issue I need to discuss with you." He turns briefly to John then faces Tyler. "Ed complained that you acted inappropriately in the investment task force meeting. Says you tried to take control of the group."

Tyler's heart pounds. "That's not what happened."

John leans toward him. "Ed states you were disrespectful and disruptive," he says then glances at Rob. "Isn't that how it's written on the red counseling form?"

"You're writing me up?" Tyler asks. "Is this a joke?"

John shakes his head while Rob grimaces.

Tyler pinches the bridge of his nose and closes his eyes. "I've got an email ready to send Ed that explains what I was talking about in the meeting."

Rob claps his hands together. "Well, hopefully that'll put this to rest." He pushes the paper across the desk. "Just sign the form, and we'll move on."

"When Ed sees my email, I'm sure he'll realize this counseling form is a mistake, guys."

"I can appreciate why you're concerned," John says, "but it's not a big deal. Many of our best performers have been written up once or twice. It's difficult to climb a mountain without skinning your knees a few times." He laughs, but Tyler doesn't. "Sign the form. It signifies acknowledgment, not agreement."

Tyler pushes the paper back across the desk, unsigned. "If you check with Ed, he'll agree this isn't needed."

Rob raises his eyebrows at John.

John nods. "Send your email, and I'll check with him." He pauses, rubbing his temple. "It would be easiest to sign the form, though."

Tyler slides his chair back and stands. "I'll send the email."

He returns to his desk and finishes the note to Ed, summarizing his findings about New Horizon. He reads it three times before pressing the send button, making sure it sounds respectful.

Two hours later, Tyler meets Greg in the lobby for lunch. Exiting the building, they slam into a wall of early August heat and a blinding sun. Quickly donning sunglasses, they hurry two blocks over to Sally's Subs, enter the cool restaurant, and sit in their favorite booth near the front window.

In a matter of moments, Tyler fills Greg in on his eventful morning.

"You did the right thing," Greg says, still chewing his cheesesteak. "I've written up a few knuckleheads for poor performance. HR says it's no big deal, but those things stick around. Just don't start a war with them."

Tyler shakes his head. That's the truth. He snags a piece of chicken and pops it in his mouth. "Were you able to find anything about Elijah James or Jonas Hayward?"

"They were both real, living humans. But that's not the interesting part."

Tyler freezes, his sub halfway to his mouth. "Yeah?"

"Jonas is Mike's great, great … actually, I can't remember how many greats, grandfather."

Tyler sets his sandwich down. "You're serious?"

Greg nods, unfazed, as he squeezes more ketchup onto his cheesesteak. "Yep. Mike's family tree is all over the place—senators, governors." He points a French fry at Tyler. "Mike's just the first Hayward to go corporate."

Leaning forward, Tyler lowers his voice, eyes intent on Greg. "I did some digging. Brett Sommerfield, the guy who wrote the article, died two months after it was published."

Greg's eyes narrow. "How?"

Tyler clasps his hands in front of him. "Carbon monoxide. Faulty heating system, no detector."

Greg watches two brunettes stroll by the window then looks back at Tyler. "So no follow-up articles?"

"Right." Tyler's voice tightens as he recalls Sommerfield's story.

"Guess you'll have to ask your buddy Mike if his grandpa's grandpa saved the Union." Greg laughs hard, snorting soda out of his nose. "Ow. That burns." He looks over at Tyler. "Make sure *you* don't get burned … if you manage to weasel your way into the game."

CHAPTER 9

"Are you up for the challenge?" Mike asks. He's sprawled in a captain's chair, his legs resting on the table in front of him.

Tyler sits ramrod straight, too nervous to enjoy the view of the Ravens' football stadium through Mike's floor-to-ceiling window. It had been a dull Wednesday afternoon until *Exec—Admin* displayed on his phone a few minutes earlier.

"I read all the material," Tyler says. "Even talked to Mr. Silverstone earlier this week."

"Bob is a terrific example of this program working to perfection. Shaved a good ten years off his path to the office of the chief financial officer." Mike flares his nostrils. "But Bob didn't need to overanalyze the decision."

Tyler scrutinizes his CEO. He'd expected Mike to be impressed by his initiative in meeting with the CFO to perform due diligence on his own.

"Learn to trust your gut, young man. Don't overthink your destiny."

Tyler raises his hand. "I've given the wrong impression. I was *in* from the moment you asked."

Mike leans forward. "Understand, once you venture down this rabbit hole, there's no turning back. Word will get out."

Tyler's stomach churns. "I'm in."

Mike leans back and beams. "Your life will never be the same."

Bile fires up Tyler's throat, and he gulps it down and forces a smile. Needing a distraction, he points out the window. "The Ravens' first preseason game is this weekend."

The older man's eyes never leave Tyler. "How has your experience been on the investment team?"

Tyler freezes. *Relax. Deep breath.* "Ed and I got off on the wrong foot."

Mike sighs and shakes his head. "I'm disappointed to hear that."

Tyler's mind races. *Am I officially in the accelerated program? I haven't signed the paperwork yet.*

"You need to be able to handle pressure, master your nerves, and make the correct decision."

"I already fixed the misunderstanding. I shouldn't have mentioned it."

Mike nods. "Schedule a meeting with Julie in HR. She'll be your coach in the program. I will personally be your mentor." He stands and strolls to the terrace door. "Step outside with me."

The terrace is as green and vibrant as it was the week before, but still, something seems off to Tyler. A knot of unease tightens in his stomach as he follows Mike. *Must be this height giving me the creeps.*

An early evening wind blows from the east, whisking in salty, frothy air from the deeper waters of the Chesapeake Bay. The building sways ever so slightly with each gust. He feels dizzy as he follows Mike outside.

"You asked about joining the game," Mike says. "I don't think it'll work."

They are standing at the edge of the balcony, looking at the harbor and bracing themselves against the force of the unobstructed wind. Tyler holds the railing to steady himself, searching for the right words to change Mike's mind.

Mike focuses on something out on the water, maybe the large sailboat leaving its berth. "The game's been around for a while," he says, "and the diversity of the participants has expanded over the years, but never have we allowed someone in who's so young ... or unestablished." He looks at Tyler. "While you possess great potential, your actual achievements are limited."

Tyler's mood slumps. Another chance to save Anna has just slipped away.

"I suppose it wouldn't hurt to let you stop by once, though, as a visitor, to meet some folks before we start playing." A Baltimore oriole lands between them and perches on the railing, its song a melody rising above the whistling harmony of the wind. "Needless to say, I expect complete confidentiality. Without equivocation."

Tyler perks up. "Absolutely."

"Come to my office after work on Friday, about six." Mike's phone rings, sending the bird off in a flutter of orange-and-black feathers. Pulling the device from his pocket, he glances at the screen and silences it. Without a word, he walks back inside and Tyler follows, wondering whether Paul will be there on Friday night.

Should I ask? No. Mike would expect me to be able to handle the situation.

As Tyler nears the door to leave the office, Mike calls out, "Don't fret about Ed. He's a moron."

·   ·   ·   ·   ·

Mike watches Tyler depart and considers whether he is playing his cards correctly, engaging the young analyst without scaring him off. The type of puppet required for this role is someone who would not shy away from the events that lie ahead.

Will Tyler be up for the challenge?

Mike pours two fingers of Blue Label into a tumbler and paces back to the terrace, but he does not take a sip. Not yet.

He reaches for his phone to return the earlier missed call but hesitates, continuing to stroll to the building's edge, stretching out the anticipation. Leaning on the rail, he swirls the glass under his nose, momentarily intoxicated by the rich, smoky aroma and the thoughts of his own future.

Curious, he watches the folks trudging across Pratt Street forty floors below, consumed by the daily struggles of their mundane lives, seeking happiness from a trivial purchase from one of the harbor stores, hoping for the gift of a meaningless compliment from one of their superficial friends, all the while wasting the powerful computers God blessed them with. Such a shame. Each human cranium contains the perfect creation of a hundred billion neurons but sits mostly idle. What little is tapped into becomes cluttered with emotional garbage, irrational thoughts, and impulsive desires, leaving the entire apparatus bogged down.

Luckily, there are visionaries like me, Mike thinks, *to watch over them—to lead them and their city into a bright future.* Soon, they will cross the Baltimore streets with their heads held high, rejuvenated by being part of something bigger than themselves, something grand.

Mike takes his first small sip of Scotch and lets it sit in his mouth. The deep, mellow flavor lingers on his tongue as he looks out over the city.

He knows that with his network of conscripted computers and the Einstein Code in his hands, his power will skyrocket. The bounds of his empire will become limitless. He can feed his motley army of laptops, desktops, and server mainframes with an all-you-can-eat data buffet of news articles, social media posts, stock tickers, weather forecasts, and thousands of other sources. Once embedded with his special code, his minions will function as one, sifting through the impossibly vast barrage of digital output. They'll share information at light speed, make connections between seemingly unrelated factoids, and build intricate data webs that will reveal masterpieces of world events yet to unfold.

The idea of efficient financial markets will be shaken to its core. Mike will possess a real-life superpower, the ability to see into the future. And as a result, he will be respected more than anyone else in history.

Mike recalls the Indonesian earthquake he'd seen on the news. Important to those whose houses were destroyed, no doubt. Most of the rest of the world shrugged its shoulders … because no one was able to connect the dots. But what if that seismic event causes a reduction in the country's rice production? Just enough so that exports must be canceled to African nations that are short of food staples because of the fifty-year drought plaguing their continent.

What if Zimbabwe has a secret deal with Vietnam to supply the African country with enough of the important white grain to properly feed its population? Hungry refugees from surrounding nations— South Africa, Botswana, Mozambique—would descend upon Zimbabwe and tax an already fragile infrastructure.

Philip Dziike would surely exploit the resulting chaos to lead a coup and usurp power from his older brother, the current president of Zimbabwe. And Philip Dziike has expansion on his mind, an African Manifest Destiny of sorts.

This would be crucial information, the kind the world would care about. The first to predict it could invest early in Philip's ventures, later securing lucrative export agreements for coffee, diamonds, and natural gas—investments that would pay dividends for years to come.

This kind of valuable information could be leveraged by someone who could accurately see into the future, someone who controlled millions of computers equipped with the Einstein Code—someone like Mike.

He eases the smooth Scotch down his throat and looks out over his beloved city from his fortieth-story perch, admiring the tranquility of the Inner Harbor, the beautiful architecture of the fine hotels and office buildings, and the magnificent stadiums housing the Orioles and Ravens.

Suddenly, the wind shifts and engulfs him with the putrid smells of urine-soaked street corners at the intersections of forgotten roads lined with the disgraceful hovels that litter too much of the city. He shakes his head, discarding the embarrassing images from his mind and filling it again with his future vision. His knowledge will be coveted by presidents and parliamentarians, by dictators and democrats, by any leader who wants to remain relevant.

His own fiefdom right below him will change as well. Those urban shanties will be mowed down to make room for tech company headquarters, sparkling condos, and record-breaking, five-thousand-foot-tall engineering and skyscraping marvels.

Forget Dubai. Forget New York. His own Charm City will become the envy of the world, the Silicon Valley of the East, the Singapore of the West.

Mike looks down at the long line of pedestrians strolling up Charles Street toward the hub of the city. He watches them closely and in his mind replaces their nameless mugs with the grimacing faces of beleaguered politicians who will soon march in those same footsteps—after their forty-mile trek up from DC—to what will then have become the new political capital of the world. Manhattan stockbrokers will trip over each other, racing to be first on the scene to access the new Baltimore Stock Exchange. The spreading grin on his face cannot be contained.

Mike imagines himself watching it all unfold from a balcony terrace like the one on which he now stands, but a hundred twenty stories closer to the clouds, basking in the homage thrust on him while he rules all wisely, like God watching His children, always one step ahead. Ancestral pride fills his soul as he foresees his beautiful city finally becoming what the Haywards have long envisioned for it.

Mike sighs and slowly takes another sip. He's reached the culmination of his egotistical orgy and cannot grind any more pleasure from his musings. It is time to make the call.

He hears a voice answer immediately.

"This is Drag."

"You got the information?"

A pause. "We got a problem."

"Don't tell me that," Mike yells. "What the hell do you mean, a problem?"

"Stumpy dropped him. Four stories. Splat. One less professor for Harvard to brag about."

"You killed him?"

A new voice comes through the speakerphone. "Wait. Dat's bullshit! You were 'posed to have his legs. Besides, you know I only got t'ree fingers on my strong hand, Drag. You try holdin' a fat squirmer like him with only t'ree fingers."

Mike closes his eyes and shakes his head.

"Did you get any information from him?" he asks. "A copy of the code?"

"We did not." Drag's voice is subdued. "You want us to visit the girl?"

Mike winces. A troublesome question. That plan is further down the alphabet than C or D. Hopefully, it won't come to that.

"No." He ends the call and downs the rest of the whiskey in one big, frustrated gulp. Peering across the street at the harbor, he waits for the alcohol to flush through his body and calm his now agitated nerves along its path. He watches a sleek yacht leaving the harbor, its course surely plotted to conquer an unknown destination. He knows his own destination, but the path to get there is changing. Plan B is now dead. Plan C is in the works. Is it the right approach? Is there another way?

He scrolls through the contacts on his phone. Sergey Volkov. His team could hack in, get what he needs. Mike is certain they could penetrate the intense wall of security that less sophisticated operations have been unable to pierce. There is one glaring problem, though, and it isn't the ten-million-dollar fee. Sergey is a thinker. He'll wonder why Mike would pay such an exorbitant sum for what seems like simple corporate theft. He'll wonder why the information Mike is seeking is protected with security equal in sophistication to that protecting the secrets of the Pentagon.

He'll wonder, *What is this computer code I'm stealing?*

And if he figures it out, Mike would never see it. Sergey has never advertised himself as a man of his word, and if he put the code up for sale on the black market, there are others with the resources to bid its price into the stratosphere.

Like an unknown outfit in Râmnicu Vâlcea, for example.

No, Mike accepts his current path is the right one.

Tyler Rush is now Plan A.

CHAPTER 10

Late Friday morning, Tyler grinds out an opinion paper detailing the accounting treatment for a new investment being reviewed by Ed's team, but he keeps thinking about Mike's invitation to meet some of society's elite later that evening.

What should I say? How should I act?

He tries to imagine himself being suave and making clever remarks that will make everyone laugh. Then he remembers Paul.

But maybe Paul won't be there.

Focus, he thinks. He is analyzing a confusing investment derivative based on the daily volatility of spot oil prices. His task is to determine how to best reflect the invested asset on the financial statements. Ed's team will evaluate the quality of the investment itself and decide whether to make the purchase. Tyler remembers seeing it listed as an option in the previous investment meeting. Apparently, Ed completely ignored his advice and is pursuing it.

Although the scope of his assignment is crystal clear—determine the accounting treatment—he hasn't been able to resist peeking under the hood. He wants to know for himself if it's a sound move. It certainly looks good on the surface, but he's built an Excel model that unearths a fundamental flaw for an investor. If oil prices increase in a sustained manner for three to four weeks, the investment will sink.

He leans back, his chair creaking in resistance. What to do with his analysis? He can include his concerns in the opinion paper, but perhaps this is another opportunity to strengthen his working relationship with

Ed. If he quietly shows the VP what he has found, he can let the older man run with it, decline the investment, and get the credit when it later blows up in the marketplace.

They're meeting in—he glances at his watch—about twenty minutes. Ed scheduled the meeting, and Tyler assumes it's in response to the email he'd sent him earlier in the week, the one with the research he'd gathered about New Horizon.

Tyler pauses and pictures himself deflecting the compliments that will come his way about the quality of his analysis. It will be a bit uncomfortable, but he's ready to get past their previous confrontation. Better to sacrifice a bit of his own glory so he can build a bridge with Ed.

After he finishes his work, he takes the stairs two at a time and climbs up four floors. Arriving a few minutes early, he pokes his head into Ed's open door. The vice president of investments is at his conference table with several others, and he waves Tyler in.

As Tyler enters the office, it becomes apparent he can stop worrying about having to deflect compliments. Occupying the two chairs on one side of the table are his boss, Rob Walker, and Rob's boss, Vice President of Finance Carla Perez. On the other side sits John Mather from human resources.

The room becomes eerily quiet, the kind of abrupt silence that occurs when someone walks into a room and everyone stops talking in midsentence because the subject of their conversation is now within earshot. John is looking in Tyler's direction, his face a perfect poker mask. Rob, meanwhile, fixates on the far wall with his hands behind his head, as if oblivious to the fact that Tyler is fewer than five feet away.

Ed gestures toward two empty chairs. "Pick one."

Tyler frowns, glances at each face, then takes a seat. "Was my email helpful?"

Ed pauses before speaking. "I've been busy investigating an opportunity," he says. "A *real* opportunity."

"Please tell me you're not talking about that oil derivative from Sachs."

Ed's face reddens.

All the work I did, and he's chasing a junk investment.

"I guess it's better than wasting your time on something mundane like Republic-Cola," Tyler snaps.

Ed's eyes dart around the table. "Carla?"

She establishes eye contact with Tyler. "Our corporate handbook states that all performance issues must be in writing and acknowledged by the recipient." She glances at Rob, then at John, and finally back at Tyler. "You refused to sign."

Tyler looks around, bewildered. Everyone is staring at him. "What happened was a misunderstanding."

Ed half-stands. "It was *not* a misunderstanding. You refused to sign the form." He sits down. "John, Rob?"

They both stare back at him.

"Is Julie Caruthers available?" Tyler asks. "She can clear this up." His frustration is building. His intentions had been good. Why does Ed refuse to see that?

"You know Julie?" Carla asks but then shakes her head. "Doesn't matter. The bottom line is that I have a fellow executive who isn't happy. Plus the fact that you ignored company policy."

"I did not ignore it." Tyler's voice is throaty and he quivers in his chair. His heart hammers against his chest. He wants to scream out, *"This is not fair!"*

He takes a deep breath and lets it out slowly. Everyone is watching to see his next move. Another deep breath. He thinks of Anna as he exhales, and the tension releases.

"I'll sign the—"

"Too late," Ed snaps. "It's been four days. We already have your termination paperwork completed."

"But if he's willing to sign the form?" Carla glances around the room.

"He's insubordinate. And unprofessional. End of story." Ed directs his glare at John. "Give him the papers." His eyes sharpen, and he turns to focus on Tyler. "You can sign them and get your last paycheck. Or not sign … and not get paid. This time, it's your choice."

John collects the stack of paperwork from the table and straightens it.

"Keep it." Tyler is calm, the tempest of his frustration having blown through. "Before I sign anything or go anywhere, I want to talk to Julie."

•   •   •   •   •

An alarm flashes on Mike Hayward's screen: *Security needed in office 39004 (Ed Rogers) to assist with employee termination (Tyler Rush).*

Ed is insecure, not a big secret, Mike thinks. *Still, I hadn't expected him to be such an idiot.*

Mike stands abruptly, knocking his chair over, and strides out of his office.

•   •   •   •   •

What's the proper corporate etiquette when you're waiting to be escorted out?

Tyler amuses himself thinking about the answer, but his humor vanishes when he considers the impact of losing his job on his ability to free Anna from Aunt Virginia and Marco. How have things escalated to the point of him being fired? He's sure Julie would help him if she were here. Maybe she'll still be able to fix things.

The seconds tick by. Carla, John, and Rob are riveted to their phones. Ed's gaze is laser-beamed on the door just behind Tyler's shoulder. Finally, there's a knock and the door opens, but it isn't the security guard. Or Julie.

"Mr. Hayward." Ed jumps up from his chair.

Mike's eyes scan the room.

"We're handling a termination," Ed says. "Is there something I can do for you, sir?"

"A termination?"

"An analyst in the finance department. Insubordination issues."

"Why are you involved?" Mike asks and saunters over to Ed's desk. He picks up one of Ed's business cards. "You're in charge of investments."

"Sir," Carla says, "Ed contacted me about an employee issue, but I'm having second thoughts here."

Mike perches on the front of Ed's desk. "Give me the paperwork."

John shoots out of his chair and bounds over with it.

Mike riffles through the pages and nods. "A termination is definitely in order."

Everyone hears Ed exhale audibly.

Mike rips the papers in half and tosses them in the air. The pieces scatter and flutter to the ground.

"Ed, you're fired."

Ed sinks down into his chair.

"My mistake was not doing this years ago," Mike says.

"Mr. Hayward." Carla stands and appears confused. "We're still a year away from having someone ready for an executive role to replace him."

Mike eases himself from the front of Ed's desk and walks to the door. He turns to Carla.

"Tyler will take it."

"What? He's just an analyst."

"He *was* just an analyst. Now he's VP of investments." On his way out he adds, "Congratulations, Tyler, you have a window view now."

With that, he is gone, leaving a room full of awkward silence. Tyler slowly stands, picks up his report, and walks out, trying not to shake as he does so.

He takes the elevator to the ground floor, purchases an ice-cold bottled water and two hot dogs from a street vendor, and strolls along the Inner Harbor to soak up the noontime sun. He arrives at Federal Hill, at the far end of the harbor, and settles onto his favorite bench. He takes a bite of the first dog.

The downtown office buildings fill the horizon beyond the harbor, their sleek exteriors of concrete, stone, and metal masking the very human drama unfolding inside. Maybe someone in the Bank of America building just found out she got hired and can't wait to call her boyfriend with the news. Maybe someone else is getting fired.

Tyler wonders what that's like—getting fired. Did Ed call his wife right away? Or is he driving home in confusion and despair, worrying about the mortgage, car payments, and future college expenses? Tyler doesn't like him, sure, but there's no satisfaction in watching his life fall apart.

Tyler wonders if a building somewhere in his view holds someone getting an unexpected promotion. Not just a promotion but being exalted to a position they don't deserve, with little in the way of qualifications or confidence to handle it.

He could empathize with them, that's for sure.

He glances at his watch. *Time to get back to work.* Groaning, he rises and starts back across the harbor, wondering what else could happen today.

When he returns to the office, there's an odd vibe in the air. Several coworkers who usually greet him with a "hello" avoid eye contact as he passes through the lobby. On the elevator, a client services manager who has never paid Tyler much attention suddenly seems interested in where he lives and even invites him to a party.

Everything is off balance, as if his mind is processing events a few seconds after they happen. Arriving at his cubicle on the thirty-fifth floor, he finds two people from the information technology department packing up his computer.

"You're moving my stuff?"

"We're retrieving it." The young woman with brown bangs smiles at him. "You're getting one of the newer, more powerful laptops with greater security privileges."

Her head disappears beneath his desk, fumbling with the mess of wires that are connected to the power strip. He steps aside as the other tech—is his name Steve?—exits his cubicle carrying an armful of his old equipment. He passes Tyler without making eye contact.

The woman finally pokes her head out and extends her hand for him to shake.

"Liz." She smiles. "Your new device should be configured in the next half hour. I'll deliver it to your office up on the thirty-ninth floor. I already gave your iPad and iPhone to Michelle."

"iPad?" Of course, there will be perks with this new position. "You gave them to whom?"

"Your executive assistant, Michelle."

Tyler retreats a step, feeling dizzy. A surge of energy wells up inside him as the full realization hits. Vice president. Thirty-ninth floor corner office. Employees reporting to him. New equipment. Additional responsibilities. An executive assistant. He wants to cheer and cry at the same time.

Instead, he stumbles to Greg's office, shuts the door, collapses into the nearest guest chair, and makes his friend a therapist for the next hour.

CHAPTER 11

Jill Young takes a deep breath as she finally finishes working through the report she received from Francis earlier in the week. His latest musings include several key insights, thoughts that should help improve the algorithm. She nods her head, excited to adapt the theoretical observations of the professor to the practical investment algorithm she first unveiled three years earlier ... after five prior years of research and development.

In her role as chief financial officer of New Horizon, using her MBA training has become second nature, but what really gets her juices flowing is melding her passion for computer science with her natural ability to navigate the world of high finance.

She glances outside. It's a scorching afternoon, and she strolls to her window and peers down at the sunlit professionals fifty-eight floors below who are wilting in black and navy suits as they hurry back to their Wall Street offices after late lunches. She rarely takes time for lunch, not since getting promoted two years earlier. There aren't many twenty-nine-year-old CFOs in Southern Manhattan, and she wants to be sure she's earning her keep.

One observation in the report keeps replaying in her mind—something about a new type of inhibitory neuron. It might be the key to pushing the algorithm closer to replicating human thought and fixing the recent hiccup that caused such a commotion in the corn futures market. It feels like the final piece of the puzzle they've been chasing.

She and Francis have spent countless hours refining their algorithm, each step inching them closer to making machines think more like humans. The professor has been creeping along the edge of the brain research frontier, generating idea after idea for Jill to convert into code for their algorithm to process. Some of their ideas have become functional parts of the program, though most have not. Yet, despite the challenges, their algorithm continues to evolve, handling increasingly greater complexity.

After some thought, she thinks she can create the code to replicate the function of the neuron he's discovered, but she has several questions about how it might interact with the current structure of the neural network after she integrates it. Plus, it's a good excuse to have a conversation with her best friend. Her mentor. The only living person she trusts.

She moves back to her desk and dials the familiar number. She plops down in her chair, banging the side of her knee on the corner of her desk.

"So stupid," she mutters and massages her knee as she waits for Francis to pick up.

"Francis Stanard's phone."

It's a woman's voice. Odd.

"I'm calling for Dr. Stanard," Jill says, already sensing something is wrong.

A sob breaks through the silence on the other end. Jill sits upright, her body tense.

"He's dead."

Jill drops the receiver, her chest heaving. This can't be real, she thinks. Chills sweep through her.

"Hello? Hello?"

Jill barely registers the voice on the phone before the dial tone kicks in.

"Not again," she whispers.

She hasn't experienced this feeling—not this intense—since her mom died nine years earlier. She has worked hard to never feel this way again.

It must be a mistake.

She reaches for the keyboard on the desk in front of her and types rapidly. "Dr. Francis Stanard, Professor of Computer Science, Harvard."

The page fills with hits related to this prolific expert, but the first headline is the only one she sees. She clicks on the news story and frantically scans the words and sentences.

"Found on the sidewalk ... four-story abandoned warehouse ... Condor Street ... Boston ... toxicology reports negative. Possible suicide."

Jill sinks to the floor, her head resting against the desk, chest tight as grief takes hold. The tears come freely, and she doesn't attempt to wipe them away.

Makes no sense, she thinks. Such a good, sweet man with so much to live for. So dedicated to his profession.

And her only true friend.

Time blurs as she mourns in solitude—thirty minutes stretch into what feels like hours—before she finally gathers the strength to stand and leave the building. After wandering the streets of Lower Manhattan for an hour, she returns to the office late in the afternoon.

The pain gnaws at the edges of her thoughts as she tries to focus on the work in front of her. She briefly considers going home, but her condo is the last place she wants to be right now—empty, quiet, offering no relief from the ache rooted deep within her.

Saying a prayer for Francis, she flips through the stack of resumes on her desk, seeking distraction. The candidates are applying for a position two levels below her, but she takes pride in being involved in every hiring decision within her sphere of influence. It pays off down the road, she knows.

She picks up her phone and calls Stewart Beechum, her manager of investing.

"The resumes you sent me. Are these all of them?"

"I pre-filtered them. Took out the weak ones."

She believes him. The pile in front of her is chock-full of Ivy League degrees and loaded with amazing personal accomplishments. Some candidates have actual work experience, but many are fresh out of school. Judging from the names, there's a nice assortment of Asians and Caucasians, no doubt sprinkled with some Black candidates and quite a few Latinos. A lot are men, but even more are women.

Each person is so specially and uniquely qualified, they all look the same to her.

"Send me the rest. I'd like to give them a quick once-over."

Jill gives New Horizon credit for ensuring diversity in the traditional sense, and her team is well balanced with a nice mix of skin colors, social views, and political leanings, but she knows that diversity extends in other directions, too. What about an average student who has fought their way through a learning disability? Or a single mom determined to provide a good life for her infant? They think differently than the perfectly packaged paper candidates paraded in front of her. They provide another kind of diversity, another perspective that she wants to hear.

That kind of diversity extends to her personal life, too. Maybe that explains her single status. She wants someone who isn't so polished all the time. Someone who isn't so serious and intent on treating life like a competition, on doing whatever it takes to win.

Someone like Francis. She thinks of him again and cries until she can't anymore.

She will continue their work, she decides, but it will never be the same. Without Francis, it's just her now, carrying the weight of their shared dreams alone. But she will see it through—for both of them. Exceptional investment returns are just the beginning. He was excited about how much good the algorithm could accomplish once it was fully functioning. From the children in Burundi, waiting for charitable imports of food that never make it, to the mothers in Sudan, standing in front of empty pots, waiting for ingredients that never arrive, most of the suffering in the world is needless, preventable. What's lacking is the information infrastructure necessary to connect the food to the people, to connect the solutions to the problems. Information. Data.

And the ability to employ it in intelligent, diverse ways that no one has ever done before.

CHAPTER 12

After leaving his "therapy session" with Greg, Tyler walks into his new office for the first time and finds that his new executive assistant, Michelle, has neatly arranged his work files, supplies, and personal belongings.

"I turned your thermostat down to seventy," she says. "It gets warm in this part of the building late in the day."

She's a wonder, he thinks, as he calms in her presence. He had expected the demands of the new responsibilities to crush him on day one, but her attention to detail is making his transition smooth. A dependable assistant might be exactly what he needs to survive in his new VP role.

Settling into his chair, he adjusts the backrest and takes in his sleek surroundings. The sense of ease surprises him, though an undercurrent of doubt lingers. Is he truly ready for the pressure that comes with his new title—Vice President of Investments? Despite his past successes, this role is different, and the promotion happened so quickly.

He glances at the silver wall clock, tired and grateful the weekend is near. Then he focuses on a budget spreadsheet, later waving goodbye to Michelle when she leaves. It's five-fifteen—forty-five minutes until he's supposed to meet Mike and rub elbows with some VIPs. Maybe they'll even let him stay and watch.

Finally, it's six o'clock, and Tyler grabs his briefcase, turns off his light, and takes the stairs—only twenty-two of them now separating him from the C-Suite—to the fortieth floor. He strides straight to

Lance's desk, just outside Mike's office. Michelle advised Tyler that, as a vice president, he was no longer required to check in at the reception area. Lance's desk is empty. Apparently, he's already escaped for the weekend.

Mike waves him in, not looking up from his monitor.

"Welcome, my new vice president of investments." He glances up briefly then returns his attention to the screen. "What initiatives have you spearheaded thus far?"

Tyler's stomach flips, and Mike looks up again, breaking into a belly laugh. "Couldn't resist."

Tyler forces a chuckle as Mike checks his watch and says, "Let's head upstairs. It's been quite a day for you—one you won't soon forget."

Tyler nods, fully agreeing with that sentiment.

The stairs are hidden behind a nondescript door in the back corner of the office. Following Mike, Tyler realizes they're entering the poker room through a door right next to the one he had exited three weeks earlier. A lot has changed since then.

Mike leads him past the gaming tables and into an adjoining room. Sizzling steak and the aroma of cumin and chili powder instantly capture Tyler's interest. A fajita bar is set up against the back wall to his right. His stomach growls.

"Mikey! Hello, honey."

The smooth voice comes from one of the cocktail tables. It belongs to a tall, slender woman with long blonde hair that cascades down her back. She glides across the room toward them, one hand balancing a lime-green, icy drink—likely a frozen margarita—at shoulder height. As she reaches them, her free hand winds gently around Mike's waist, and she plants a kiss on his cheek. Her eyes flicker over Tyler, sweeping from head to toe before resting on Mike.

"Alyssa, say hello to the newest, and youngest, member of my executive team."

Tyler accepts her outstretched hand.

She smiles then glances over her shoulder. "I must get back to Vivian."

Tyler follows her gaze and spots a middle-aged woman, decorated with colorful, sparkling jewels and just the right amount of makeup, standing alone at one of the tables twenty feet away.

Mike nods and turns his attention back to Tyler. "Grab some food and join the guys."

He gestures to the other side of the room, past a half dozen cocktail tables, to an area with several chairs forming a half circle around a coffee table, a flat-screen television on the wall in front of them. Tyler recognizes Senator Preston Sinclair from his previous encounter at the game. He's chatting with two other men Tyler doesn't recognize. A fourth head leans forward, visible now as he retrieves a plate of food from the table.

Tyler grimaces. It's Paul Thompson. His stomach clenches, and his hunger vanishes. He takes a deep breath and approaches the men. "Eat the frog," his mom used to say when he was young. Always tackle the most challenging task first, and your life will be better. Right now, the frog is a balding Black man in a blue suit.

Preston glances up and waves Tyler over. The others are glued to ESPN's *SportsCenter* on the television. Tyler walks toward Paul, who now holds his plate in his lap, about to take a bite of his tortilla.

Paul looks up and frowns, his eyes widening as he abandons his upcoming assault on the fajita. Wrinkles erupt across his forehead. He abruptly stands, and the plate of food in his hand flutters, sending a strip of steak rolling off the edge and onto the floor. Dropping the fully loaded dish onto the table, he says, "Excuse me, gentlemen. I need to make a call."

Preston stands and greets Tyler with a handshake. "Nice to see you again. I heard you'd be stopping by." The senator's eyes then flash to Paul as he disappears to the adjacent room. "Guess Mike didn't give him a heads-up." He looks back at Tyler. "You know each other?"

"Our families were close, years ago."

"He's a good man, Paul is. Done a lot of good for a lot of people."

Tyler is tired of hearing it. He nods politely, relieved when Preston moves on to introduce the others. One man owns the largest privately held Port-A-Pot business in the US.

Noting Tyler's reaction, Preston chuckles. "Don't feel too bad for him. He doesn't have to deal with half as much crap as I do in Congress. From the other side of the aisle."

They all laugh comfortably. No awkward concern that someone in the group may have a different point of view. "That's his better half over there, talking to Mike's fiancée."

Another man steps forward and shakes Tyler's hand. "Why exactly are you here?"

"To network with you gentlemen before you play."

The sound of a helicopter catches their attention. Everyone swivels toward the wall behind the fajita station and listens to the distant roar of an approaching engine, its blades whipping the air. There are no windows on this floor, but the unmistakable sound of aircraft near tall buildings commands attention.

"That'll be the Whitfields," the Port-A-Pot owner remarks. "I'll let Mike know." He wipes his face with a napkin, stands, and ambles away.

The conversation turns to baseball, and Tyler is comfortable joining in. After several minutes, a loud male voice with a strong New York accent fills the room.

"Why're you guys in here stuffing yer pie holes when you should be in there gettin' ready to lose yer money?" The new arrival waddles into the room, a wide smile pasted on his friendly face, the tails of his oversize, custom-made dress shirt falling out of his pants. "I'm gonna get some grub, too, I guess."

"Hey, Tony," one of the men yells, "if you get any fatter, you'll need a bigger engine for that helicopter."

Tony turns to pull his wife beside him and slides his right arm around her. As he leads her to the buffet, he lifts his left hand casually and extends his middle finger toward the heckling men. They laugh even harder.

Mike strolls up. "I sent the service elevator down to get a couple hedge fund execs, then we'll be ready to play."

"Just one table tonight?" Preston asks.

Mike nods.

"Who the hell are you?" Tony is standing at a food table a few feet away and is staring at Tyler, momentarily distracted from his plate of overflowing meats, beans, and guacamole.

"This is Tyler Rush, my VP of investments. He's here to learn how to become gluttonous and obnoxious and, of course, filthy rich."

"All right, all right. Stop bustin' my balls. You ready to play some cards, young fella?"

Mike interrupts before Tyler can speak. "He's here to socialize. He'll be leaving before we start playing."

"Too bad," Tony says.

Tyler finds his voice. "Yeah, I was hoping I'd be flying home in your chopper tonight. Maybe next time."

His comment earns a hearty chortle from Tony. "I like this kid. He's a funny guy. You should ditch Mike and come work for me. I'll actually pay you some money. New York kinda money." He stops talking and shovels in a mouthful of guacamole.

Tyler loosens his tie and smiles.

"Anthony, honey." Tony's wife is an attractive, older woman sporting a multi-carat, sparkling diamond on her ring finger. "We're going to visit several shops and get a drink at the harbor. Let me know when you boys are wrapping up."

The ladies exit through the foyer just as the hedge fund execs arrive. They appear to be a couple—a tall, trim man named Evan and a gorgeous brunette. The remaining men enter the poker room to settle at the table near the wet bar. Ten chairs surround the oval table—one for the dealer and nine for the players. One chair remains unclaimed.

"Why don't you let the kid play?" Tony's voice booms through the room. "It looks like we got an open chair."

Paul sits across the table, arms crossed and glaring at Mike—who doesn't seem to notice.

"He isn't invited," Preston says. "It's time for him to leave."

Mike rises and pulls Tyler aside, guiding him toward the back bar. "It looks like we have an extra seat."

"I know how to handle myself." Tyler smiles quietly at Mike and hopes he can live up to his own hype. "And I *am* an executive now."

Mike scratches the tip of his chin. "I'll set you up with five thousand dollars in chips. Consider it a bonus for your new position."

Tyler's smile grows wider.

"We play Texas hold 'em," Mike says. "The stakes are no-limit."

Tyler nods and considers how many thousands of hands of hold 'em he played in college. Too many to count.

"It'll be a bit different here than you're used to," Mike says.

"Bigger stakes. I get it. I'll be careful."

"It's more than that, young man. You can bet *anything* you want at *any* time … not just the chips in front of you."

A bolt of anxiety shoots through Tyler. Mike is right. Being able to bet *any* amount at any time—even money he doesn't have—is a twist he has never encountered. This could get dangerous quickly.

It could also create opportunities, he realizes, and a surge of excitement dilutes his fear.

Mike places his palm on Tyler's shoulder and nudges him back toward the waiting faces.

"Don't wager more than the five grand, and you'll stay out of trouble," Mike whispers to him, and then he speaks loudly to the group. "I'm happy to announce Tyler is joining us. I've explained the rules. He's good to go."

Tyler counts one smile, which is on the face of Tony, and six frowns. He knows he must play it cool to show he belongs.

Lance Hudson, Mike's administrative assistant, materializes from the other room, pushing a cart filled with chips, cards, and a mahogany-brown leather ledger. Tyler now realizes why he hadn't been at his desk earlier—he was up here preparing for the game.

Lance distributes the chips in various stacks and denominations to each player. No cash changes hands, but he records the value of each player's initial investment.

Tyler inventories his chips and finds forty white ones worth $25 apiece, forty of the $50 reds, and twenty of the $100 blacks. Serious stakes for him. Apparently, not for the others. He notes that their huge piles dwarf his modest buy-in. As he arranges the chips, the weight of them in his hand provides a momentary grounding amidst the heavy stakes of the evening. The room buzzes with low chatter, but he feels the eyes of the seasoned players, including Paul, tracking his every move.

Tyler speaks softly to Tony beside him. "No gold coins?"

Tony shakes his head. "Only for special occasions."

Clay chips are fine with Tyler, and the familiar texture is comforting. He instinctively stacks and shuffles them with one hand, creating a slight clicking noise as the chips from the two stacks merge into one, a technique he perfected during hours spent passing time at card tables in casinos and at dormitory games with friends in college.

"Looks like you know what you're doing there, slick," Tony says as he watches his moves, "but do you really understand how this game works?"

Tyler nods once.

Lance finishes making his notes in the ledger, and he rolls his operation out of the way and over against the wall. He returns and sits in the dealer's chair.

One of the men eyes Tyler's meager pile of white, red, and black chips. "You look a little young to be here."

Tyler glances across the table at Mike, who stops arranging his large stack of black clay long enough to look up and catch Tyler's eye. He then resumes tinkering with his chips.

"Feel free to use your age and wisdom against me," Tyler says and laughs comfortably. He knows he needs to smooth over any conflicts, not wanting to give Mike any chance to change his mind.

Preston clears his throat and looks over at Tyler. "It would be prudent for me to provide a summary of the no-limit betting rules. The stakes can quickly spiral upward."

"I appreciate it, but it's unnecessary," Tyler says.

"Maybe the kid will get lucky," Tony says. "My first time in the game, I won eighty large in one hand." He points at Paul. "From you."

Paul seems lost in thought, his eyes unfocused as he runs his fingers over his closely trimmed, graying goatee.

Tony speaks more loudly. "Remember that hand, big guy? The one I played against you my first night."

Paul's head turns to meet Tony's stare. "What's that?" he says softly. "Oh, yes. Quite a night."

The hedge fund woman glances over at Tyler. "You sure you're not getting in over your head?"

Before Tyler can answer, Mike raises his hand in the air but keeps his eyes focused down at the table. "Enough. He's not a Supreme Court nominee. He is my guest. I invited him."

•   •   •   •   •

Tyler is up about five hundred dollars ... five hundred thirty, to be exact. His chips are arranged in neat stacks so he can tally them with a quick glance. This group plays with antes instead of blinds, but other than that, and their unusual no-limit betting rule, it's the same hold 'em he has played for years.

He's been playing cautiously, only staying in with powerful cards and folding quickly if his chances diminish after the flop. It isn't the most exciting—or profitable—way to play poker, but it permits him to carefully protect his stake while listening to the table conversation and scrutinizing the occasional betting wars that emerge between two, or sometimes several, players. It also allows him to closely watch, and mentally catalog, each person's idiosyncrasies in various game situations.

Hand follows hand, and Tyler is becoming more comfortable. It's not so different from the lower stakes games he played in college. He yawns as the tall hedge fund exec—Evan—opens the betting with a $100 black chip. Tyler looks at his hole cards and finds the seven of spades and three of hearts. Lousy. He folds.

Tony raises a hundred. Mike calls the bet, which now stands at two hundred after the raise. The hedge fund woman calls, and everyone else folds except Evan, who tosses another black chip into the pot to stay in as well. There's a thousand dollars in the pot, including the antes. It's enough to get everyone's attention.

Lance turns over the "flop," the first three community cards. Eight of clubs, eight of spades, and five of clubs.

Community Cards: 8♣, 8♠, 5♣

Evan checks. Tyler figures he doesn't want to risk additional money until he sees how the other players react to the flop.

"Three black chips," Tony says without hesitation and flips them into the pot. "Gotta get the chumps to fold."

Mike nudges Tony's ribs with his elbow and peers at a man across the table.

"I think it'll take more than that," he says and pushes a stack of ten black chips toward the center of the table. "I raise. Seven hundred more."

Tyler leans forward, resting his forearms on the table, finding the excitement just what he needs. His attention drifted as the game wore on, the long day catching up to him. Warmth fills the room—it's a few degrees hotter than when they'd started. The air feels denser now, thick with the scent of leather, alcohol, and freshly dealt cards. Rolling his shoulders, Tyler works out the kinks in his muscles.

The hedge fund woman places her cards face down on the felt and pushes them away, signaling her decision to fold.

Evan methodically counts out twenty red chips into two stacks of ten—a thousand dollars—and peeks at his hole cards again. He casually throws the chips into the pot, and each neat stack crumbles into a messy pile of clay discs.

"I'll keep you honest, Mike," he says. "I call."

Tony winks at Tyler and distorts his face into mock incredulity.

"Hello! Am I invisible here? My three-hundred-dollar bet didn't scare anyone even in the slightest?" He flicks his cards toward the middle of the table. They collide with a stray chip, bounce into the air, and land face up, revealing the four of clubs and the seven of diamonds, an awful hand. He'd clearly been bluffing and now is abandoning his charade.

"Two players in," Lance says and deals the fourth community card face up—the "turn" card. It's the ace of clubs.

Community Cards: 8♣, 8♠, 5♣, A♣

Tyler suspects Evan is holding two clubs and has just hit a flush. He's noticed that Evan tends to bet heavily after making a strong hand but plays cautiously with drawing hands until they come together. If Evan had a powerful hand before the ace of clubs appeared, he would have started the betting in the last round instead of checking and calling. If his hand lacked serious potential, he would have folded. So, two clubs as his hole cards make sense to Tyler.

Tyler also picked up a clue when Evan called the last bet with two stacks of $50 red chips when he had plenty of $100 black chips. Memorizing the mathematical odds was a necessary step to mastering the game, Tyler knew, but he had long ago discovered that understanding the psychology of the other players was the key to his unlocking enough profit from poker for him to quit his part-time college job. He'd learned that some people had an irrational attachment to the higher denomination chips, so when they used a pile of smaller chips to call a bet, it meant they weren't as confident about their hand.

Tyler had become expert at reading these "tells" that unknowingly provide information about a hand for anyone observant enough to read them.

"Action's on you," Lance says, nodding at Evan.

He tilts his head up. "Check."

Tyler is surprised. If Evan has a club flush, why doesn't he make a large bet? Mike is an aggressive player, so maybe by acting weak, he's trying to trap Mike into bluffing with a big bet. Then Evan can hammer him with a monster raise.

Mike also checks, apparently not taking the bait. The pot remains at two thousand three hundred dollars.

Lance turns over the "river," the fifth and final community card. It's the six of diamonds.

Community Cards: 8♣, 8♠, 5♣, A♣, 6♦

"Time to raise the stakes," Evan says, eagerly placing five $1,000 green chips on the table. "Five thousand."

Surely Mike will fold, Tyler thinks. It must be obvious to everyone that Evan has a flush.

But Mike doesn't fold. "I raise," he says softly, "twenty-five thousand more." He adds thirty green chips to the pot, and he stares straight ahead, his face blank.

What a bad time to bluff, Tyler thinks. Doesn't he know he's up against a flush? He studies Mike's face but is unable to ignore the growing mound of chips on the table. There's enough there to buy a new car, he realizes. Or to give a custody lawyer a hefty retainer. It's the largest pot of the night.

Wait, what is that? Tyler is suddenly alert. Mike's right eye squints, just for a millisecond, a subtle movement, but Tyler is sure of it. Mike's eye closed a tiny bit, and a hint of a wrinkle formed around the socket. His right cheek also lifted ever so slightly.

Most players wouldn't have noticed it, Tyler knows, not unless they had trained themselves as he had. He isn't sure what it means, but now he's more invested in the hand's outcome. *Is it possible Mike has a tell?*

Evan frowns and scratches his chin, studying Mike as if he's a hostile witness. "You know what I think?" His cross-examination begins. "I think you're trying to buy this pot. But not this time." He reaches beneath his chair, retrieves a black leather attaché case, and sets it on the edge of the table, extracting ten wrapped stacks of hundred-dollar bills.

"This is one hundred thousand dollars," he says proudly. "I call your twenty-five-thousand-dollar raise and raise you back another seventy-five thousand." He lays the bills neatly next to the mountain of chips in the center of the table.

"The action's back on Mike," Lance announces.

Mike leans back, his hands resting on his stomach and his fingers pressed together in a steeple. All chatter around the table has ceased. Tyler is seated next to Evan and can hear his breathing, which sounds like Greg after a few miles into a run. Tyler looks across the green felt at Mike and wonders what he's thinking. He'd pay to find out.

Tyler is certain Evan has the better hand, most likely the club flush. Mike checked on the previous card, which suggests he still needed help to make a strong hand, and the six of diamonds on the river isn't likely the card he was hoping for. Surely, he'll fold.

Mike slowly leans forward, picks up his gin martini, and takes a sip. The table feels charged, as if the air crackles with expectation. Tyler's pulse quickens, matching the dull thud of Evan's foot tapping on the floor. The scent of the martini—sharp gin with a hint of citrus—wafts toward him as Mike casually lifts the glass to his lips again.

"I raise," he announces.

Tyler is shocked.

"Your seventy-five thousand, and … let's see." Mike sets his drink down. "I'll raise a quarter of a million dollars."

Evan flinches severely.

The hedge fund woman gasps, and the Port-A-Pot owner rests a calming hand on her shoulder. Someone else shakes his head, muttering a curse, while Preston nods knowingly—clearly no stranger to Mike's audacity.

Tony giggles. "He's got you up shit creek without a paddle," he says, though it's not clear if he's talking to Evan or Mike.

Paul stares at Tyler, seemingly oblivious to the action.

Mike looks thoughtful.

Almost too excited to breathe, Tyler watches it all. If Evan has a club flush, then either Mike got extremely lucky on the last card, or he's on a stone-cold bluff, testing his opponent's resolve with his massive bet.

Seconds tick by. Then a full minute, and another.

Finally, Evan speaks. "I call," he says and flips over his hole cards, smiling nervously. Over seven hundred thousand dollars is committed to the pot. He shows the king of clubs and the ten of clubs, revealing the ace-high club flush Tyler suspected. It's the best possible flush.

Community Cards: 8♣, 8♠, 5♣, A♣, 6♦

Evan's Hole Cards: K♣, 10♣

Mike's Hole Cards: ?, ?

Mike presses his lips together. "Nice hand."

Evan slumps forward, relieved, and releases his breath in one big whoosh. The hedge fund woman reaches toward him, her arms extended, ready to embrace him.

Then Mike inserts the knife. "It is a nice hand but unfortunately … not quite nice enough." He casually tosses the ace of hearts and ace of diamonds onto the table, twisting his blade and gutting his opponent's hope.

Community Cards: 8♣, 8♠, 5♣, A♣, 6♦

Evan's Hole Cards: K♣, 10♣

Mike's Hole Cards: A♥, A♦

Mike has a full house. He made his hand on the turn but was patient enough to just check, waiting for Evan to make his move on the river. Masterfully played, Tyler thinks.

Completely fooled me.

Evan doesn't complain. "I have fifty thousand left with me. I'll wire the other two hundred on Monday." He stands and brushes his hands down the front of his slacks. "Gentlemen, thank you for the game. Mike, would you be kind enough to call the elevator for us?"

As the game breaks up, Tyler watches Mike greedily corralling his army of chips and bills. It's a truckload of money, but more importantly, Tyler has gained valuable information. Mike has an Achilles heel, a subtle eye twitch that indicates he has a monster hand, a tell that Tyler knows he can and will exploit for his own benefit.

For Anna's benefit, he corrects himself.

Mike pauses from raking in his winnings and glances at Paul. "You've barely said two words tonight."

Paul smiles—or maybe grimaces. Hard to say which, Tyler thinks.

Mike rises, walks to the bar, and reaches for a bottle. The rest of the players chat as they head toward the foyer, leaving Paul and Tyler alone at the table.

Paul stands and clears his throat. "It's been a long time."

Tyler doesn't respond.

Paul moves closer. "Frankly, it caught me off guard. Seeing you."

Tyler nods.

"Congratulations on your success," Paul says. He squeezes Tyler's shoulder then adds softly, "Be careful with this game. Mike always looks out for Mike."

With that, Paul strides away to join the others.

Tyler stays seated and ponders the first pleasant words spoken between the two of them in ten years, as well as the first kind touch he's received from Paul since his son, William, died in the van accident.

CHAPTER 13

On Saturday, Tyler wakes up refreshed after nearly ten hours of deep, almost unconscious sleep. He always spends the second Saturday in August with his family, so he doesn't have to pound the pavement with Greg today.

He drives three blocks up Charles Street and stops at a café to place a to-go order for a picnic for two, packed in an insulated cooler bag. When it's ready, he continues driving two miles farther north and parks close to the entrance of Green Mount Cemetery.

He steps out of the car, picnic in hand, and waits on the sidewalk for Anna. A light breeze ruffles the leaves in the tall trees that are abundant in this area, and he shivers. It's refreshingly cool today.

The concrete beneath his feet is stained a dull, reddish brown, and to his left, just past a multi-story apartment building, a side street stretches out, lined with lonely-looking row houses. He notices an old man with a white beard sitting on his porch steps, staring at nothing, and watches him for a while.

A voice rings out behind Tyler.

"Ty!" It's Anna, out of breath. "I got here as fast as I could."

He drops the cooler bag onto the sidewalk, wraps his arms around her, and lifts her off the ground, her warmth contrasting with the cool breeze.

Putting her down, he glances at his watch. "It's almost ten."

"I ran all the way here." She takes a few deep breaths. "Marco insisted on taking me to breakfast."

"Marco?"

"Don't worry." She points at the bag. "I told him I wasn't hungry. I just got a cup of coffee."

"You drink coffee?"

She rolls her eyes and bounces ahead through the cemetery entrance.

They meander along a bumpy, stone lane and through vast, green fields dotted with headstones, monuments, and statues of people once famous. Full, tall oaks and sugar maples provide shade, comfort, and clean air. It is so different from the dirty streets lined with dingy apartments where Anna is forced to live right now.

Tyler thinks about Marco. And Anna.

A small crowd gathers near several headstones ahead on the right.

"Tour group," Anna says, "tossing pennies on the graves of John Wilkes Booth and his friends."

Tyler appreciates the gesture, the face of Abraham Lincoln on the pennies an eternal reminder of the wrong they'd committed.

They wander along in silence. Anna reaches out and slaps the trunk of a stray maple tree that butts against the paved path. Tyler watches her closely. She seems okay, but it could be a facade, he thinks.

"I'll be able to start the custody process sooner than I expected," he says.

Anna throws her arms around him. "When?" she asks, her voice soft and hopeful.

Tyler smiles, a warmth filling his chest that he hasn't felt in a long time. "Very soon."

"Did you finally ask Greg for help?"

"I got an unexpected promotion. A big one."

Anna grins and skips ahead, up the hill to the chapel, which offers a beautiful view of the sprawling city in the distance. It's a quiet place, perfect for their time together. They'll picnic behind it then visit the graves of their parents and their brother—their usual routine.

CHAPTER 14

Tyler strolls into his office at seven thirty on Monday morning. Michelle rises from her desk and follows him inside. The floral scent of her perfume is nice, not too strong, he thinks.

"I've set up your schedule for today. It's synced on all your devices. Don't forget the eight o'clock with Julie Caruthers. She might have some exciting news," Michelle says with a smile. "Also, Ed had a standing staff meeting with his direct reports at nine every Monday. You want to keep that meeting?"

He nods and sets his bag on the small conference table.

"Michelle?"

"Yes?"

He smiles sheepishly. "Who are my direct reports?"

She laughs. "You have three … Cindy, Art, and Kat. I'll email you brief bios." She taps her pen to her lips. "I'll ask Julie's assistant to have their performance files ready for you when you meet her in"—she examines her watch—"just about thirty minutes."

Tyler nods, glancing at his desk as he mentally prepares for the day. He connects his laptop to the docking station that allows him to access the company's network and prepares to get to work. Michelle is still standing by the door, watching him.

"There's something else," she says.

He looks up.

"Please give me a chance before you make any long-term decisions."

He smiles. "You have nothing to worry about."

She relaxes. "I thought you might have your own person you'd bring in to replace me."

My own person? What an odd thought.

He spends the next half hour reviewing emails before walking to his meeting. Julie's office isn't far, a quarter of the way around the thirty-ninth floor. Her assistant hands him three manila folders as he walks past her desk. Each is labeled with the name of one of his new employees.

Julie greets him at the door to her office then closes it behind them. He sits in an uncomfortable chair facing her desk, and she goes around to her leather swivel chair.

"Congratulations on your promotion." Her voice is monotone, her expression neutral.

He leans forward in anticipation of what she'll have to say.

She peers at him over the frames of the thin reading glasses that rest on the lower bridge of her nose. "I have a form here that documents your new title—vice president of investments—effective last Friday, August 7th, and your new salary." She pauses and coughs into her fist. He leans closer. "Your new salary will be twelve thousand dollars."

Twelve thousand per month. Almost double his previous salary.

I'll indeed be able to rescue Anna sooner.

"To be clear," Julie says, "that's twelve thousand per pay period."

Sparks shoot down his spine as the significance of the news sinks in. Mid-Atlantic pays twice a month. *I'll be able to rescue Anna much sooner than I expected.*

"That's incredible!" He leans back. "I mean, wow!"

"We're all very happy for you." Still the monotone voice, with the hint of a frown forming at the edges of her downturned mouth.

He checks his enthusiasm and sits for a minute, digesting the news by himself.

"You'll also be entering the Executive Development Program." She pushes a folder across the desk. "You've reviewed the paperwork and are aware of the level of commitment involved?" Her chin is tucked into her neck, creating the sensation of looking down at him.

He nods, but he can't hold back the big smile plastered across his face.

"Being in the program will not reduce the expectations associated with fulfilling your new role." She frowns again, deeper this time.

He opens the folder and flips through the stapled packet. Each page is warm—fresh from the printer, no doubt—and the paper feels thick in his fingers, its weight matching the significance of the words to him.

It hadn't occurred to him that moving to the executive floor would also mean nicer paper.

He produces a fountain pen from the breast pocket of his shirt and signs his name on the last page. He pays particular attention to adding a slight wave to the horizontal top of the letter T in his first name and extending the curve of the R to form a border beneath the rest of the letters in his last name.

Just like he had practiced over the weekend.

Julie provides a schedule of biweekly coaching sessions he'll have with her, monthly mentoring meetings with Mike, and internal supervisory training sessions that will cover more topics than he can possibly absorb. His mind drifts as she delves deeper into the details of the schedule.

When Tyler's first official coaching session with Julie finally ends, he returns to his office and hands Michelle the schedule so she can enter it into his calendar. He's a couple minutes early for his nine o'clock meeting with his direct reports, but a man is already seated at the head of the conference table. Tyler recognizes him but doesn't know his name and can't recall ever speaking to him. The man's hair is cut military short, and his clean-shaven face is chiseled with lines of experience.

Tyler glances at the personnel files he's carrying, hoping for a clue— Cindy, Art, or Kat.

"Morning, Art," he says, dropping the files on the corner of his desk before rounding the table to greet his employee. Art offers his hand but doesn't stand. The calluses on his palm and the way his shirt bunches at the shoulders hint he's a regular at the gym.

Art smirks. "I always enjoy meeting members of *upper* management."

Tyler isn't sure how to respond. Does one of those classes Julie signed him up for cover how to deal with assholes?

Two females chatting in soft voices enter the door behind him.

"You must be Tyler," a stout woman says. She has long, flowing auburn hair and a generous smile. "I'm Kat McDonald, director of strategic investments."

Next to her is someone he knows. Cindy is a friend of Greg's, and the three of them have enjoyed lunch together several times.

"Hi, Cindy," he says.

After the introductions are complete between the four of them and everyone is seated at the table, Tyler begins his meeting.

"I want to start by acknowledging the awkwardness of the current situation." He looks at each of them, one by one. "But now is the time for us to move forward. I'm eager to work with you."

Art tilts his chin up and crosses his arms, accentuating the rippling muscles in his forearms.

"What do you know about investments?" he asks Tyler.

"That's what I have you three for." Tyler picks up his pen, ready to write. "Now, Art, what are you working on?"

"Reviewing our external adviser fees. I'll save us ten basis points by putting it out to bid."

Tyler jots a note on the yellow legal pad in front of him. "Stop working on that."

Art's jaw juts out as he looks across at Tyler. "Ten basis points applied to our portfolio of invested assets would create savings of four million dollars a year."

"Thanks for the explanation. Now stop working on it."

Art leans forward, his arms still crossed. "I think I'll run that by Bob Silverstone first. I'm sure you won't mind."

"Excellent idea. Interrupt our CFO to explain that I don't understand that reducing our investment advisory fees by ten basis points would result in a 0.1 percent increase in net investment income which, applied to our four billion dollars of invested assets, would create a bottom-line increase in net income before tax of four million dollars."

Art's crossed arms stiffen.

Kat snickers and Cindy smiles.

"And then you can tell him about the project I'm giving you. Do you know how much higher New Horizon's average investment yield is than ours?" He pauses, but Art doesn't respond. "It's three hundred basis points." He pushes his calculator across the table. "Want to do the math? It amounts to a hundred twenty million dollars a year more in investment income. And I want to know how they're doing it." Art looks pissed. Tyler doesn't care. "Now what do you think your priority is? Or do you need Bob to explain that to you, too?"

Art glares at him, and Tyler can see his diaphragm expanding and contracting as he breathes deeply. Finally, Art uncrosses his arms, rests his hands on the table, and smiles.

"I don't need Bob to put me in my place. You did fine."

Tyler relaxes and glances out the window. Nice and sunny. No hint of the tropical storm he's seen on the news working its way up the Eastern Coastline.

He turns to Kat. "What are you working on?"

"My team—along with Cindy's—is analyzing an oil derivative investment opportunity."

"Ed's baby?"

They both nod.

"Thoughts?"

Cindy speaks first. "I don't like it."

"Me, neither," Kat says. "It smells fishy."

"That makes three of us," Tyler says. "Kill that project. Help Art with analyzing New Horizon. I want to know their secret."

• • • • •

Two hours later, Greg waltzes into Tyler's office and plops down in a guest chair with an open bag of chips in his hand.

"You're seriously eating Fritos right before lunch?" Tyler asks.

Greg shrugs and munches on a chip. His lanky body sprawls across the chair.

"Where to?" Tyler asks. "Sally's?"

Greg shakes his head. "No, siree. No subs today. Today is a big day. We're going to Bo Brooks for steamed crabs to properly celebrate your promotion."

Tyler raises his eyebrows. "You think we can get back in an hour?"

"What do I care? I'm with a VP." Greg wads his empty bag and tosses it into the garbage can next to Tyler's desk.

Fifteen minutes later, they're seated in Baltimore's oldest crab house, placing their order. Their table is near a window overlooking the harbor. Several boats dot their view, and the salty scent of the water is palpable here, away from the hubbub of the nearby downtown.

"A dozen of the big boys." Greg speaks loudly to be heard above the noise of all the voices chitchatting at other tables, servers bouncing from group to group, shells snapping, and the occasional clanging of pots banging together back in the kitchen.

The server—her name tag says Missy—stops writing on her order pad and looks at him. "The extra larges are a hundred two dollars per dozen." She purses her lips. "Maybe mediums? They're sixty dollars."

Tyler agrees with her. "Yeah, that sounds—"

"*Extra. Large.*" Greg makes a wide gesture with his hands as he emphasizes each word. "This is a celebration. We're in the presence of a newly appointed vice president here."

Two older men in business suits at the table next to them pause their conversation to watch this occasion. Tyler looks at them and shrugs his shoulders.

As Missy walks away, Greg holds up his water glass. "A toast to Tyler Rush, the newest—and the youngest—VP at Mid-Atlantic Financial Services."

Tyler clinks his water glass against Greg's and asks quietly, "Did you know Cindy reports to me?"

"Makes sense. I knew she worked for Ed." Greg pauses. "Did you get some serious coin?"

"They're quadrupling my salary."

Missy returns and covers the table with a roll of thick, brown paper. She sets a bib and wooden mallet in front of each of them.

"What're you going to do with all that dough?"

"Help Anna."

Greg holds his glass up a second time. "To Anna." After they clink glasses, he asks the question Tyler knew was coming but wanted to avoid. "Now that you're a big shot, will you get into the poker game?"

Tyler looks away. "I doubt it." The more he has learned about the game, the less he wants to discuss it, even with Greg.

"How does someone get to join, anyway?"

"There's a core group. I think they can approve others."

Greg pulls his foot up onto the chair and wraps his arms around his knee. "I'm going to rent that old Kenny Roger's movie, *The Gambler*, this weekend. I'll be ready if you need me."

Tyler shakes his head, laughing.

A horn sounds in the distance and pulls their attention through the window next to them. On a piece of land jutting into the harbor farther east, a container ship is being loaded, and they watch as a crane operator carefully maneuvers a crate from the loading dock onto the vessel.

"Beautiful day out there," Tyler says. "Too bad it won't last."

"Tropical Storm Donald is putting the kibosh on my weekend plans. Jenny and I are supposed to go *down the ocean*."

Tyler understands the local expression that refers to a visit to the beach on Maryland's Eastern Shore. He nods and says, "Supposed to be a glancing blow. Maybe a front will come through and push it off to sea."

The mention of the beach tugs at something inside him. He can almost hear the crash of the waves, feel the grit of sand between his toes. Anna's giggles come to mind—the way she used to chase seagulls, her tiny feet kicking up water as she ran along the Ocean City shore. He pushes the memory aside, the ache too bitter to dwell on.

Missy is back, this time with a plate of steaming, extra-large crabs. The frothy smell of the ocean engulfs Greg and Tyler, laced with the peppery notes from a liberal dose of Old Bay seasoning. She sets the overflowing plate on the table between them.

Tyler grabs a crab but quickly drops it as hot juice squirts from the shell and burns his fingers. He rubs his hand on the paper bib around his neck that protects his shirt and tie then reaches for the crab again, this time avoiding the crevices and joints. After executing a successful transfer, he looks over at Greg.

"Do you know about tells? In poker?"

Greg is busy striking a crab claw with his wooden mallet and ignores the question. He splinters the shell and sucks the meat out before leaning forward and speaking softly.

"I hacked into Baltimore's power grid last night."

Tyler freezes, a piece of crab dangling from his fork. "You've been working on that for what … at least a year?"

"Two. I can't believe I made it in. I caused a brownout in Towson, but only for five seconds, to make sure I was really in."

Tyler lifts the crab, breaks the shell in half, and picks out the delicate meat smothered with spices. "Now what?"

"That's it. Mission accomplished. I'll have to think of the next challenge. Let me know if you have any ideas."

Tyler takes a sip of water.

"How about we work on a project together?" Greg says.

Tyler smirks. "I'm not a hacker."

"You could be." Greg points a claw at him. "Seriously, you're the best programmer I've ever met." He drops the claw and curls his fingers. "Join me on the dark side. Slum a little."

Tyler sucks the end of his index finger, now throbbing from lemon juice and spices stinging an unseen cut—posthumous payback from the crab. He glances at his watch, waves Missy over, and asks for their bill. She already has it ready and lays it on the table between them.

Greg looks at Tyler and points at the tab.

"What're you looking at me for?" Tyler asks. "You invited me. Plus, you insisted we buy the hundred-dollar crabs."

"But *you* got the promotion."

Tyler laughs and reaches for his wallet.

CHAPTER 15

The normally gentle waters of the Inner Harbor are agitated, slapping against the boardwalk, with spray flying up and over the empty walkway. The boats, usually overflowing with locals and tourists gallivanting around the harbor on a mid-August Friday evening, now sit empty, rocking in their moorings.

Far above the water, Tyler stands on the edge of the Mid-Atlantic's fortieth-floor terrace, observing the approaching tropical storm. He grips the railing, enjoying the thick, sweet air blowing in from the sea.

He's exhausted after his first week as vice president of investments and can't fathom reading another email or studying one more spreadsheet. Twenty minutes left to kill before he meets Mike in his office and heads up to the game.

Thunder rolls in from the east—a slow, steady rumble. He follows the dark clouds with his eyes as the air grows heavy and tense.

He had planned to attend Anna's final summer league game tonight, but it was canceled because of the approaching storm. So, when Mike invited him to the game, he eagerly accepted, thrilled to receive another invitation so soon.

At 5:59 p.m., he strolls into Mike's office, and together they climb the stairs to the forty-first floor. Tonight, there are no ladies and no signs of happy hour. But there is tasty food—baked redfish, seared scallops, shrimp cocktail, and a plate of gigantic chocolate chip cookies. The plan is to grab a quick bite then play. Tyler figures he can always sit out a few hands and enjoy more of the food later.

He spots Paul Thompson at the buffet table and finds it a little easier to approach him this time.

Paul nods at Tyler, locking eyes with him for a few seconds. "Son, I'd like to help."

Tyler waves a hand. "Thanks, but I don't need it." Mike's tell has given him a secret weapon.

Paul opens his mouth again then closes it. He turns away and sets his dish on a high-top table. Tyler watches, wondering if the offer was genuine.

Ten minutes later, Tyler finishes eating and heads to the poker room, ready to play. As one chair after another is claimed, he hesitates, waiting for Mike to sit first. Finally, Mike and Paul approach from the buffet, quietly conferring. Just before reaching the table, they separate—Paul takes the nearest seat while Mike continues to the far side. Tyler slides into an open chair directly across from Mike, positioned between Preston and Paul. He's achieved his first objective—a clear view of Mike's face.

Lance is already stationed at one end of the table, stacking chips into piles of various denominations. Barry Knowles, the actor Tyler remembers from the first game, is sitting next to Mike, animatedly discussing plans for a new game show he's hoping to host. Hedge Fund Evan is on Mike's other side.

"Chester, do I have the job or what?" Barry says, his deep voice carrying across the room to a man Tyler doesn't recognize. The man is still chewing a last bite of food as he approaches and takes the far seat at one end of the oval table.

"Give it a rest tonight … please," the man says to Barry.

A few halfhearted chuckles ripple around the table. Tyler gathers Chester is a television producer and is developing the show Barry is so excited about.

The building sways slightly as a burst of wind howls its way through the downtown skyscrapers. Rain follows—a soft pitter-patter at first— but it quickly intensifies into a pounding assault from the storm's outer bands. Tyler listens to it attacking the roof and the northeastern side of the building.

Preston nods at the empty chair next to Lance. "Who's missing?"

"Tony had to turn back to New York," Mike says. "The gusts were too strong for his chopper."

"That reminds me," Preston says. "A senate colleague of mine, Anthony Vincent from New Jersey, wants to play." He looks first at Mike then leans forward to catch Paul's eyes. "Any objection?"

Mike furrows his eyebrows. "You're a council member now. You can approve it."

"Still getting used to that."

"Mr. Knowles, chips?" Lance asks.

"Twenty thousand, please."

Lance slides Barry two chip racks filled neatly with white, red, and black chips, and a separate stack of ten of the thousand-dollar green variety.

Mike asks for fifty thousand dollars in chips, Evan and Chester each request twenty-five thousand, and Paul asks for fifteen thousand. Tyler had planned to get five thousand in chips like the week before, but he doesn't want to appear intimidated.

"Fifteen thousand please, Lance." His voice cracks on the word *thousand*, and he curses to himself under his breath. He feels Paul's eyes on him but doesn't return the look. He turns instead to Mike and receives a small nod of encouragement. No way he'll bet the entire fifteen, but it does feel good not to be a kid at the adults' table.

Lance finishes distributing chips, sits in the dealer's chair, and the game begins. Tyler is quick to fold most hands and content to watch the other players, one in particular. He studies how Mike holds his chips and places them in the pot with every bet. He sees that Mike's expression vanishes after making a large raise, and he notices Mike's higher voice inflection when he is on a draw. Tyler sees it all, and waits, folding hand after hand.

An hour into the game, he has seen enough to be comfortable that Mike's tell is real. He's observed Mike's slight eye twitch three times, and all involved big bets. The first was against Paul, who folded. The remaining two were against Evan and Chester, who called. In both cases, Mike showed dominant cards.

Twice Mike made large raises without Tyler observing any squint. In each case, Mike's opponent called and beat his hand.

Eye twitch equals stay away, Tyler repeats in his mind. No eye twitch, safe to play.

As Lance deals again, Tyler leans forward, his forearms resting on the cushiony bumper rail bordering the table. He lifts the edges of his cards off the green felt and peeks at them. King of spades and king of clubs. A tremendous starting hand. Now … how can he play it to extract the maximum amount of chips from the rest of the players?

He releases the cards so they lie flat on the table, leans on his elbows again, and tries to look bored. Nothing interesting with *those* cards, that's for sure. Beneath the facade, his heart pounds. He's aware of the sweat tickling the skin behind his knees.

Paul is first to act. "Rags again. I fold." He flicks his hole cards with his index finger and sends them careening to the center of the table.

Lance looks at Tyler. "The action's on you."

"I'll bet a hundred." One seventy-five is already in the pot from the antes, so the black chip he adds is a relatively small opening bet. He wants to seem interested but not overeager.

"What was his bet?" Barry's voice carries across the table. "I couldn't hear." The rain is pouring now, pounding against the roof above them.

"One hundred dollars," Paul answers for him. That's fine with Tyler because the fewer words he speaks, the less likely he is to accidentally say or do something that might tip the others off that he has the potential for a monster hand.

"Get some new hearing aids," Mike says, fake-shouting in Barry's ear and generating laughter from the others, even from Barry.

Preston and Barry both call. Mike peels up the edges of his hole cards, glances at them, and returns them to the felt.

"I raise five hundred." He places six black chips in the pot—one to match Tyler's initial bet and the other five for his raise.

"I was gonna call, but it's getting too rich for these borderline cards." Chester adds his hole cards to the muck in the center of the table.

"I call." Tyler builds a stack of red and white chips totaling five hundred dollars. He wants to appear uncertain about his decision and unwilling to part with his black chips.

Preston and Barry fold.

"Me and you, heads-up," Mike says.

Tyler is concerned about the possibility of an ace appearing on the flop. That would make the hand tricky to play because it's likely Mike has an ace in his hand since he made a large raise before the flop.

The flop cooperates for Tyler's hand, however. Jack of diamonds, seven of spades, and four of hearts.

Community Cards: J♦, 7♠, 4♥

Tyler's Hole Cards: K♠, K♣

Mike's Hole Cards: ?, ?

It's a good flop for Tyler. The cards are all different suits, and the numbers are spread out, making the chances slim that Mike has a straight or flush draw. Tyler wants to extract more money from Mike before showing his strength and ending the hand.

"Check," he says. He's ready to reraise if Mike raises.

Mike looks down at his chips. "No free cards around here. You want to stay in, you've got to pay." He forms two stacks of black chips side by side, each ten chips high, and pushes them into the pot. "Two thousand."

Tyler smiles. He no longer needs to be coy. Mike has fallen for his check-raise trap, and it's time to end the hand and collect his profit of almost three thousand dollars, huge by his standards.

"Raise," he says. He knows he must put enough in to make it mathematically correct for Mike to fold. "Five thousand."

Tyler now has half his stake committed to the pot, just over seven and a half thousand dollars.

"You fell for it there, Mikey." Barry shakes his head in mock disapproval. "Always so headstrong. Tsk-tsk."

"Check-raise, eh?" Mike looks at Tyler, down at his cards, then back at Tyler. He reaches for his drink and takes a slow sip.

Fold! Fold! Fold! Tyler struggles to hide the emotional turmoil within him. *Why is Mike taking so long? He should have folded by now.*

Mike appears oblivious to Tyler's internal alarms sounding at full blast.

Finally, Mike speaks, "I call." So simple a statement, yet so perplexing to Tyler. Over fifteen thousand dollars is now in the pot—way beyond Tyler's comfort zone—and with two community cards still to go.

Evan freezes after two steps into his stroll to the dining area, pivots, and returns to his chair.

"Here comes the turn card." Lance presents the fourth community card with a flourish. Seven of diamonds.

Community Cards: J♦, 7♠, 4♥, 7♦

Tyler's Hole Cards: K♠, K♣

Mike's Hole Cards: ?, ?

So far so good. There are hands that can beat him, but Tyler doesn't see Mike having them. The stakes and Mike's call on the previous card spook him, though, and he checks instead of betting.

He holds his breath. Mike checks behind him.

"Last but not least, the river card." Lance deals the fifth community card, the queen of diamonds.

Community Cards: J♦, 7♠, 4♥, 7♦, Q♦

Tyler's Hole Cards: K♠, K♣

Mike's Hole Cards: ?, ?

Tyler still thinks he has the best hand with his pair of pocket kings, but the three diamonds on the board scare him. Mike may have been hoping to hit a flush with a diamond on that last card. With that concern in mind, he checks again.

Mike does not.

"Fifty thousand dollars." Mike's voice is steady. His face freezes, and he stares straight ahead. Tyler searches for any hint of movement in his right eye—a squint, a flex, something. He sees nothing, no tell that would indicate Mike has a powerful hand.

He must be bluffing, trying to represent a flush with a big bet to scare me out of the pot.

Tyler trusts the tell, but one slip could cost him his life's savings, plus hamper his ability to free Anna.

Noise from the other players' kibitzing bombards him, but it fades into the background. He is wrestling with himself, with what he knows he has to do. He feels like a child again, on the end of the diving board at the Thompson's pool, too scared to jump. He remembers telling himself it would be okay, that it was the right thing to do, but still he stood there, glued to the end of the board. Finally, he turned off his brain and activated his body. And he does so now.

"I call." He feels his mouth form the words and hears what sounds like someone else speaking them. But it's his voice.

"You got it," Mike concedes before he even sees Tyler's cards. He flips over a pair of eights, giving him two pair, eights and sevens. Not good enough to beat Tyler's kings and sevens. "Good call. I thought I could get you to fold with a big bet."

It was a smart bet. Tyler most likely would have folded if he hadn't figured out Mike's tell. He shows Mike his pair of kings.

For a second, the enormity of the moment hits him, and he reaches out with both hands to rake in the mountain of chips. He tries to look casual, but he can't hide his overwhelming excitement that they're all his now.

Paul lays his hand on Tyler's shoulder and says, "Congratulations, son." Surprisingly, it doesn't bother him.

Mike points at Tyler. "Allow me to retrieve some cash so I can make good on my last bet." He had declared his fifty-thousand-dollar raise but hadn't yet added anything to the pot. "I have enough chips, but it would wipe me out." Picking up his briefcase from the floor beside him,

Mike sets it on the bumper rail, removes five stacks of hundred-dollar bills, and tosses them toward Tyler.

Tyler watches the stacks of bound bills tumble across the table, bouncing off each other in their slow-motion journey to reach his outstretched hands. The leathery surface of the bills feels wonderful against his fingertips, and he smiles the kind of smile that would leave wrinkles and a sore jaw if he held it too long.

Almost sixty thousand dollars in profit from one hand. Combined with the money he's already saved, and his elevated salary, he can do more than just hire lawyers to file motions and argue in court. He can hire top-notch attorneys who pull strings behind the scenes and get results quickly.

"How do you plan to spend that pile of cash?" Barry's question rises above the buzz of the other excited voices, all talking at once about the enormous pot.

"Hire good lawyers to help my sister."

Paul leans forward and whispers, "Anna?"

"She's thirteen now. I'm trying to free her from our aunt."

"My attorneys have an office here in Baltimore," Paul says. "I can make an introduction."

"I've got my own." That's a lie … but not for long.

A tingling chill sweeps across Tyler's body. It's all coming together, and he's done it himself. He pops out of his chair and parades to the buffet table. He isn't hungry, but he needs to release the energy from his internal fireworks going off.

"Sitting out this hand?" Lance asks. He pauses while holding the deck of cards, ready to deal the next round.

What is a monumental, life-changing moment to Tyler is just an interesting Friday night occurrence to these other players—nothing significant enough to disrupt the flow of the game.

"I'm going to grab some food." Tyler speaks loudly enough to be heard over the drumming of the rain.

It occurs to Tyler that he might like to call it a night. He's already up an unfathomable amount and has enough to rescue Anna. But he scoffs at his doubting conscience. He's doing fine … better than fine. Besides, his car is parked at his apartment building two blocks away. He has an umbrella, but it would be of little use against the swirling winds and torrential rain.

A bomb of deafening thunder explodes outside in the unseen sky. Standing at the buffet table, picking at a scallop, Tyler is thankful this floor doesn't have windows. It feels safer, like a bunker.

As he walks back to the action, a moment of vertigo hits him as the tilt of the floor changes. Tropical Storm Donald has given up its attempt to break through the northeast side of the building and is now trying an attack directly from the north. He pushes away the uneasy feeling, unwilling to let anything ruin what is a perfect night.

•   •   •   •   •

With more chips at his disposal, Tyler is playing lots of hands now. Without meaning to, he has become the player driving the action, the table captain. He's winning a lot of small pots as others fold when he shows strength with a meaningful bet. These little pots are adding up, too, and he's up another five thousand dollars in the hour since his life changed for the better.

His cards haven't even been that great. It's just that as the faces and stakes have become more comfortable to him, he's back in a dorm room and naturally taking command of the game, a step ahead of everyone else. The stormy weather is his friend, he's decided, its steady applause pelting the roof as his pile of chips expands.

"Ante up, everyone." Lance yawns as he speaks, making his words unintelligible. Everyone knows what he means, though, and each player tosses a white chip in the pot.

Lance's fatigue is contagious. Tyler erupts into a big, body-stretching yawn as the excitement of the night recedes, and he experiences the natural ebb toward low tide that eventually arrives. Casually, he glances at his hole cards, not even bothering to shield them with his left hand.

A quick swallow stifles the rest of his yawn. Adrenaline shoots through his tired body as he sees two aces, the best possible hole cards.

Mike starts the betting with a hundred dollars. Evan and Chester both call. Paul folds.

Tyler raises five hundred, in line with his recent, more aggressive betting pattern. No one will take his raise as an indicator he holds such strong hole cards. Mike and Chester both call after Evan folds in between them. Just like that, the pot stands at over two thousand dollars.

Lance deals the three community cards that make up the flop.

Community Cards: A♣, K♦, 9♣

Tyler's Hole Cards: A♠, A♥

Mike's Hole Cards: ?, ?

Chester's Hole Cards: ?, ?

Quite a nice flop for Tyler. He now has three aces, the best possible hand at the moment, the nuts, as it's called. He wants to pump his fist in the air and cheer. Instead, he forces himself to frown as he watches Mike. Staring too long at the flop or showing any positive emotion might give the other players a hint of how strong his hand is.

"A thousand." Mike tosses a green chip onto the existing pile in the center of the table. It is a decent-size bet based on the current size of the pot.

"Call," Chester says.

Tyler knows his hand is the best right then, but the two clubs on the flop concern him. It's likely either Mike or Chester has two more clubs as their hole cards and are hoping for a fifth club on the turn or the river to make a flush, which would beat his three aces.

He decides to make a big bet, show his strength, and hopefully end the hand and win a nice pot. That approach is certainly safer than limping along, praying a club doesn't show up in the next two cards.

Just as Tyler prepares to announce his raise, a roar from outside freezes him in place. Heads turn to the north, the players' expressions ranging from Mike's curiosity to Preston's outright fear. The deep rumble in the sky grows louder, like a freight train barreling toward them. Wind pounds against the building with increasing force, as if an unseen hand were pressing harder and harder. Rain lashes the roof and walls, striking with the relentless snap of a whip.

Then it passes.

Every head turns to the south to follow the sound of destruction as the twister works its way out of downtown Baltimore and heads toward Anne Arundel County.

The normal tropical rain and wind are almost calming now.

Barry rises to his feet. "I need a drink."

During the break that ensues, several players, including Tyler, walk down the stairs to Mike's office to survey the damage through his windows then decide to venture out onto the terrace. The building provides a measure of shelter from the blustery winds, but even so, Tyler's face is blasted with large bullets of rain as soon as he steps through the door.

He opens his mouth to yell at the others and gets a mouthful of water. After four steps forward, an errant gust pushes him sideways. He suddenly feels extremely vulnerable, forty stories up in the stormy night sky.

Retreating into Mike's office, he watches the storm through the windows. It's difficult to determine exactly what happened, but debris is strewn around the downtown streets, and panels are missing from the sides of two nearby buildings. He calls Anna to check on her, but his call goes to voicemail.

Paul comes down the stairs and walks over to Tyler. He nods toward the patio, where Mike, Evan, and Chester are clutching the railing at the far end of the terrace and peering over the edge. "Those fellows are certifiably insane," Paul says.

Tyler laughs and adds, "We dodged a bullet."

Ten minutes later, they're all back upstairs at the poker table, ready to resume the game.

Lance glances at each face around the table to make sure he has everyone's attention. "The pot stands at four thousand seventy-five dollars," he announces. "The current bet is one thousand dollars, and the action is on Tyler."

Tyler is ready, having had enough time to mentally rehearse how he will say it with just the right amount of confidence. "I'll raise five thousand."

The last of the chatter around the table ceases. Mike examines him, a look of curiosity on his face. Tyler thinks he's wondering if it's a bluff, with Tyler trying to cash in on his recent rush of wins.

"I call," Mike says, shocking Tyler. The odds simply aren't there to justify a five-thousand-dollar call with a flush draw … unless he's decided Tyler is bluffing.

Chester folds, leaving just the two of them in the hand.

No club. No club. No club. Tyler repeats the mantra in his head.

Lance pulls the top card off the deck, moves it toward the playing surface, and turns it over. It is black. It is a … *oh no* … a club! Mike must have made his flush. *Time for me to fold, cut my losses.*

Wait a minute. It's the *king* of clubs.

Community Cards: A♣, K♦, 9♣, K♣

Tyler's Hole Cards: A♠, A♥

Mike's Hole Cards: ?, ?

Now Tyler hopes Mike has, indeed, made his flush, because Tyler has the full house that will beat it.

The action is on Mike. He acts quickly. "I'll bet sixty thousand."

Whoa! That's a big bet, four times the size of the pot. Tyler watches Mike's face and sees it has melted into the expressionless mask familiar in these situations. There's no evidence of the tell, but in this case, Tyler wouldn't expect it. Mike must know his flush—if he has it—is not a sure thing … not with two kings on the board.

Mike might be suspicious that he has a full house, Tyler realizes. This bet must be a test, a fishing expedition, to see what he has. A funny thought occurs to him—what is simply bait for Mike to test the waters is a life-altering treasure to him.

He blots the stakes from his mind and plays his full house. "I call."

"Alllrriigghhtty thheenn," Barry's voice booms in full showmanship mode, as if auditioning for his job as the game show host. "We have ourselves a hand."

Paul leans over and says, "Careful, son."

Tyler watches breathlessly as Lance deals the last community card. It's a meaningless three of spades.

Community Cards: A♣, K♦, 9♣, K♣, 3♠

Tyler's Hole Cards: A♠, A♥

Mike's Hole Cards: ?, ?

Tyler is unsure what Mike will do, an unusual position for him to be in at a poker game. He's disoriented, the moment surreal.

Mike licks his lips, reaches for chips, then pauses. He speaks slowly and distinctly.

"One million dollars."

Tyler chokes. *Talk about no-limit!*

"Oh, shit." Paul says.

"Come on, Mike. What the hell is that?" Preston throws up an arm. "Bullying the kid like that." He stands and stomps off to the bar behind them.

"There are no training wheels in this game," Barry's voice calls out in a mocking tone. "You know that, Senator."

Mike grins briefly before retreating into his hollow you-won't-get-a-read-on-me pose. Tyler notes it. He's watching every hint of movement that Mike makes.

"Mike has a right to bet whatever he wants." Paul's voice is calm and measured. "However, there is a problem in this case because of the rule that all debts must be paid in full within six months. It is not conceivable to expect Mr. Rush to repay a million dollars in that time frame … should he call the bet and lose the hand."

Paul's words and some of the banter across the table between Evan and Chester wind their way into Tyler's ears, but they're only vaguely decoded by his brain. His focus is squarely on Mike.

Tyler's CEO strokes his chin for a full minute. Then he speaks. "I will keep my bet as stated. One million dollars. However, I will suggest

Tyler can call the bet with his commitment to infiltrate our competing financial services company, New Horizon, and deliver to me the investment algorithm they used to achieve the returns I see on their annual statement."

Tyler's eyes dart frantically from face to face. "I don't understand."

"To clarify the bet"—Barry has everyone's attention—"Mike is betting a million dollars in cash. Tyler can call by agreeing to obtain the requested information in lieu of handing over a million dollars … should he lose the hand."

Barry's summary seems to satisfy everyone.

It scares the hell out of Tyler. He turns to Paul. "He wants me to steal corporate secrets?" he whispers. "How can he bet that?"

"I was afraid of this," Paul says. "In our brand of no-limit, *anything* can be bet. Anything at all. Didn't Mike explain that?"

Tyler begins shaking. "I thought he meant any amount of money."

He's testing me again, trying to scare me … and it's working. Tyler has seen no sign of Mike's tell. *I know I've got him beat. But am I willing to gamble my future? Anna's future?*

Mike's earlier words echo in his mind—"Trust your gut. Don't overthink your destiny."

The room quiets, and the weight of all eyes is on Tyler. The only sounds are the wind and the rain, growing louder in the players' silence.

A million dollars could do wonders for Anna, help him finally make amends for his big mistake years ago. He knows he has the better hand. *I just have to jump off the diving board one more time. Take the plunge.*

"I call," Tyler says, flipping his cards over without waiting for Mike, and revealing the pair of aces in the hole and his monster hand. Full house, aces full of kings.

"Ha!" Mike shouts. "Ha! Ha! Ha!" Leaping to his feet, he hunches forward over the table, his face beaming, his loud war cry echoing off the walls and drowning out the rain.

He turns over his hole cards—a pair of kings.

Community Cards: A♣, K♦, 9♣, K♣, 3♠

Tyler's Hole Cards: A♠, A♥

Mike's Hole Cards: K♠, K♥

Mike has not made a flush. He's got four of a kind—the strongest possible hand, the nuts—as nothing Tyler could have would beat him.

This time, Tyler has not dodged a bullet. Instead, it has hit him smack in the jaw. His face burns with shame at the humiliation of being duped ... along with the realization that his life has just changed drastically again, but not for the better this time.

Mike winks at him—a big, exaggerated wink—and his next words thunder across the table. "Come on, Tyler. How stupid do you think I am?"

Tyler has been set up. He feels used and abused, a pawn in a game he doesn't understand.

He stands and stumbles backward, one, then two steps. Nausea sweeps over him. He leans to his left and vomits. Bright lights dance in his vision, and he is suddenly dizzy, very dizzy. He tries to turn and take a step toward the door, but his right foot does not respond. His legs give out, and he falls down on all fours, aware of nothing for a minute.

Then someone helps him up, hands him a cool bottle of water, and assists him toward the exit.

It's Paul.

Several minutes later, Tyler is sitting in Paul's black Escalade in the building's underground parking garage. The cool leather seat presses against his back, but it offers little comfort. He is breathing properly again, his chest no longer tight, though a lingering numbness dulls his senses. The faint whisper of the car's ventilation system and the distant rumble of the storm outside fill the silence.

He pulls out his phone, seeking the comfort of something familiar. The smooth screen is cold against his fingertips, and the display lights up, casting a faint glow in the dim interior.

Tyler sees Anna's text from nine minutes ago, and his heart drops. His hand trembles, and the phone slips from his grasp, clattering onto the floor mat.

Paul grabs it and reads the text aloud.

Help! I'm scared!

CHAPTER 16

Twenty minutes earlier, Anna opens her bedroom window a couple inches, hoping for relief from the stuffy air. The room has grown hot since the power went out when the storm was at its peak. She thought she heard a tornado pass nearby, but it was hard to tell. Now, cooler air drifts through the window, and though the rain still falls, it's no longer driving sideways. The musty scent of damp earth and asphalt wafts in.

Footsteps echo down the hall—heavy and deliberate. Marco.

Anna glances at the doorknob, shining her small laser flashlight on it to double-check that it's locked. Dealing with him is not high on her priority list at the moment. She sat with him and Aunt Virginia during the storm, but he made her uncomfortable by sitting so close to her on the couch that his big, hairy leg brushed against hers. And he was being overly polite—not normal for him.

Auntie noticed it, too. She told Anna to stop flirting with him.

As if! Anna thinks, remembering her aunt's words.

Anna finally excused herself to use the bathroom and afterward retreated to her bedroom. She thought she was in the clear.

Instead, Marco is here, fidgeting with the knob. Her muscles tense.

He knocks. "Open the door." His voice is low but forceful.

Anna steps away from the window, pulse quickening. "Not a good time. Maybe later."

"Open the door, Anna!" His voice rises as he rattles the knob harder.

She races across the room and presses her back against the door, bracing it with her shoulders. Her feet wedge against the opposite wall in the narrow nook of her tiny entryway. The flimsy lock won't hold—she knows that.

The door cracks open an inch, Marco's thick fingers curling around the edge. Panic surges through her. With a burst of adrenaline, she slams her weight against the door. The edge bites into his fingers and a sickening crunch echoes through the space.

Marco howls in pain. "You little—"

His shout rattles the walls, but Anna doesn't budge. She digs her heels into the wall, her whole body trembling with the effort of keeping the door shut. Marco finally wrenches his hand free, and the door slams shut again. His footsteps thunder down the hallway, his curses fading as he storms away.

Anna's knees buckle, and she slumps to the floor, drawing in short, shallow breaths. For a moment, she remains frozen, listening to the faint sounds of the storm outside and the pounding of her own heart. With effort, she pushes herself up, grabs her desk chair, and wedges it between the doorknob and the opposite wall.

Reaching for her phone, she realizes her back pocket is empty. A quick glance around shows it lying on the worn carpet a few feet away. She sinks against the bed and texts Tyler.

Help! I'm scared!

Her hand hovers over the phone as she debates calling 911. The silence is unbearable as she waits for a response from Tyler. Maybe Marco won't come back, she hopes. She considers sneaking out of the apartment and knows, this time, she won't come back. Then a door slams, and relief briefly washes over her.

Maybe he left?

Tiptoeing toward the door, she listens carefully, her stomach tightening as heavy, fast footsteps echo down the hall again, destroying her fleeting hope.

Just as she presses "9" on her phone, a loud crash shatters the silence. The door splinters as the head of a sledgehammer smashes through it. Anna gasps as the chair falls apart and the door collapses off its hinges. She drops her phone then snatches it back up with shaking hands and accidentally presses "2" instead of "1."

Marco steps through the wreckage, his face twisted in rage, holding the hammer in one hand, his other hand bloody and mangled.

Anna's instincts kick in. She scrambles across the bed, her heartbeat thundering in her ears. Marco throws the hammer at her, and she dodges just in time, the metal head thudding into the wall behind her.

He crosses the room and lunges toward her, his powerful hand clamping the back of her neck. He lifts her off the ground like a rag doll and flings her across the room. The small of her back smacks against the corner of the nightstand and her head crashes against the wall. A searing pain jolts up her neck and all the way down to her pinkie toes. The personal items on her nightstand scatter in all directions.

Dazed, Anna struggles to keep her eyes open, her vision swimming. Dizziness creeps forward through her skull, and she blinks to stay awake.

Marco approaches again, towering over her. Anna's hand frantically searches the floor, and her fingers close around something small and metal—her scissors.

Marco raises his fist and leans closer. His eyes are glassy and maniacal.

Summoning the last of her strength, she thrusts her arm forward.

Marco's scream fills the room as he stumbles back, covering his eye. Blood trickles from between his fingers. Heart racing, Anna scrambles to her feet and darts for the door.

Aunt Virginia stands frozen in the hallway, eyes wide with shock. Anna doesn't stop. She pushes past her and bursts out into the stormy night. The rain pelts her face, and the wind whips through her hair as she sprints down the darkened sidewalk, slipping on the wet pavement then regaining her footing.

She zigzags farther down the flooded sidewalk, strewn with leaves and sticks, stumbles over a large branch, and crashes to the ground. Pain shoots through her as she lands hard on the curb, her breath knocked out. She looks up to see a shadow behind the window of a nearby building. A pair of eyes peeks through the blinds then quickly disappears.

Blood trickles from the back of Anna's head, staining the pavement. The wail of sirens grows louder, and her vision blurs, her consciousness beginning to slip away.

The last thing she sees before everything fades to black is the headlights of a large SUV pulling up to the curb.

CHAPTER 17

Anna eyes the young man sitting across the red oak table. He seems well-educated and eager to help, but he's still growing into his suit and tie. It might not be his first case since law school, but she's sure the number could be counted on just one of his delicate, pale hands.

She glances over at Tyler. *Where are the good lawyers? The expensive ones?* He is staring back at her, his expression unreadable, as if he's waiting for her to speak.

She reaches up and touches the rough bandage wrapped tightly around her head. *So embarrassing.* It will take time, she knows, for her skin to heal and for the lingering dizziness from her concussion to subside.

It's her legs that worry her most. She lifts them, one at a time, off the footrests of the wheelchair to make sure they still obey her. They do, mostly, but the doctors aren't sure when—if—the numbness will fade completely. With the trauma to her spine still too fresh, they can't predict her recovery timeline.

A clicking pen pulls her attention back. The young lawyer scribbles something on a yellow notepad as he talks to Tyler, mentioning interim protective orders and emergency hearings. She knows she's not in trouble—the police at the hospital assured her it was self-defense. They told her Marco had been arraigned in his hospital room, and as soon as the doctors finish reconstructing his face, he'll be transferred to jail.

The cool air from the vent above hums gently, making Anna sleepy. Being anywhere but the hospital—even in this bland conference room with its faint scent of pine cleaner—is a relief after the sterile smell of antiseptic that still clings to her senses. She snuggles into the soft blanket they draped over her in the wheelchair, allowing her eyes to close for just a moment.

A sharp knock startles her awake. The door swings open, and four people stride in, their perfectly tailored suits gleaming under the harsh overhead lights. The woman in front walks with purpose, her curly hair bouncing slightly as she moves. Two younger women and a man follow her closely, all with their chins held high.

The young lawyer looks up. "I'm sorry, I'm with clients here."

"Not anymore," the woman says briskly. "We're their attorneys now." She glances at Anna and Tyler. "Unless you decline our representation."

The young lawyer frowns. "I was appointed by the court."

Without acknowledging him, the woman says to Anna and Tyler, "Paul Thompson retained us. At his expense."

Tyler looks confused. "Paul Thompson? Who are you?"

"Four of McCovey and Wright's finest," she says, gesturing to herself and the others. "I'm Darla Wright."

Tyler hesitates then starts to shake his head no, but Anna cuts him off.

"Yes!" She glares at her brother. "We do want you to be our lawyers."

The court-appointed lawyer snaps his briefcase shut, stands, and leaves without another word. The tension leaves the room with him.

Darla Wright's expression softens as she turns to them. "Good. Let's get started." She gestures to her associates, who set up laptops and begin taking notes.

Tyler leans in and sighs. "I understand this will take weeks to resolve."

Anna looks at him and groans. *Why does everything have to take soooo long?*

Darla raises a finger. "I spoke to Stanley on the way in." She pauses. "That's Judge Stanley Watson, who's presiding over this case. He wants to get it wrapped up this afternoon."

Anna's heart leaps. *Finally, something's moving quickly.* Just as Anna feels a spark of excitement, Tyler looks down and says, "I have a prior restraining order."

A cell phone rings. One of Darla's associates reaches into her pocket and silences it then leaves the room.

"The events of last Friday will take care of that," Darla says. "Waiving it will be a formality. The custody hearing will take a couple hours—and you and Anna will both need to testify—but Stanley already has the written ruling." Darla nods at the woman sitting next to her. "Marsha here filed a proposed order he will no doubt use. He likes to get these child protection cases resolved quickly. You'll be together tonight."

Tears sting Anna's eyes, and they feel wonderful. Tyler steps beside her wheelchair and wraps his arms gently around her in a soft hug. The warmth of his cheek against hers brings a glimmer of hope for the first time in days. She can feel the tears on his face, too.

Darla leaves the room, and the two remaining associates spend the next hour preparing Anna and Tyler for their hearing.

At 1:55 p.m., Tyler, flanked by his McCovey and Wright attorneys, wheels Anna into the family court. She thinks the room is imposing, its polished stone floors reflecting the bright overhead lights. Each step they take reverberates through the stillness, the sound amplified by the tall wood-paneled walls.

Tyler rolls her to the end of the glossy wood table where Darla sits. She leans over and says, "Hard to believe this used to be a post office, right?"

The judge enters—Honorable Stanley Watson, a small man with sharp features and a thin wisp of hair combed over his bald spot. Despite his diminutive frame, he wears a black robe that lends him an air of authority, and the courtroom rises then sits as the proceeding begins.

"I've read your brief and the motion you filed for custody," Judge Watson says, his voice stern as he addresses Darla. But before she can respond, Aunt Virginia's lawyer stands up.

"Your Honor, I filed a response to dismiss—"

The judge cuts him off with a sigh. "Didn't they teach you not to interrupt in law school?"

The lawyer stammers, then says, "Well, Your Honor, my client has followed the court's guardianship rules for ten years—"

The judge waves his hand and snaps, "You submitted a written response, and I can read."

Anna hears the tapping of fingers on keys from the court reporter as he catches up, and then it's quiet for a few moments.

The lawyer tries again. "Your Honor, Marco Burtone is no longer in the household. There is no risk to Anna's safety. Surely, returning her to my client's care is now the best—"

Judge Watson slams his gavel down. "There is no way on God's green Earth I'm sending this child back to that woman."

Virginia's face reddens, but she keeps her gaze fixed on the table in front of her, as if she didn't hear the scolding.

Anna is called to testify. The bailiff, a burly man with a white beard that reminds her of Santa Claus, gently wheels her to the stand.

Darla approaches with steady confidence. "Anna, can you describe what life was like with Virginia Rush and Marco Burtone?"

Anna's palms are slick with sweat as she grips the arms of her wheelchair. The microphone is too far away. She shifts, trying to reach it, but the wheels don't budge. The bailiff steps in, adjusting the chair and the mic.

Anna takes a deep breath. "I was always afraid. I never knew when Marco would lose his temper or when Auntie would be in one of her moods."

"Why were you afraid?"

The vinyl arms of her wheelchair are slimy against her sweaty palms. *Gross!* She wipes her hands on her pants.

"Anna, can you tell me what happened?" Darla asks.

Anna's bottom lip quivers. She doesn't want to talk about it, doesn't want to relive the mistreatment and anxiety of the past decade. She bites her lip hard, and then she talks.

Twice, Virginia's lawyer stands to object. Twice, Judge Watson overrules him. He starts to stand for a third time, but a cautionary glance from the judge sends him back into his chair.

The bailiff brings a small box of tissues to Anna.

She dabs her eyes while she describes the time she was locked in a closet as a punishment for playing with her food. "It was supposed to be for five minutes." She glances at the judge. "After a while, I banged on the door. But no one came to get me."

"How old were you?" Darla asks.

"Six years old."

Darla appears shocked, as if she didn't already know what Anna's answer would be.

"I'm sure … because it was my birthday dinner," Anna adds.

Darla looks at Virginia, shaking her head. "How did you get out?"

"I got tired and cold. I felt around in the dark and found a shelf with towels. I draped them over myself and tried to sleep, but there wasn't enough room to lie down." She pauses and takes in a broken breath. "Finally, Auntie came and got me. I don't know what time … somewhere between night and morning. She smelled like gin. I know that now. At the time, she just smelled like Auntie."

The courtroom is silent as Anna fights to keep her composure.

Darla nods and steps closer to her. "What happened last Friday?"

Anna stares straight ahead, not making eye contact with anyone, her voice almost detached as she recounts the events that brought her here.

Darla listens quietly, occasionally nodding, but when Anna describes Marco's attack, her face tightens with emotion.

"And whom do you want to live with?" Darla asks.

"My brother, Tyler," she says firmly.

Judge Watson leans toward the court reporter. "Let the record show the witness identified Tyler Rush."

Tyler's testimony follows. He speaks clearly and with purpose, defending his actions over the past several years. The judge interrupts to lift Tyler's restraining order then listens as Tyler explains his living situation.

Darla concludes her questioning, and Virginia's attorney begins a weak cross-examination.

After several minutes, Judge Watson speaks up. "Excuse me, Counselor. Let me interrupt here. I'm inclined to grant temporary custody to Tyler Rush at this time."

Anna wants to leap out of her wheelchair. It is *finally, finally, finally* happening! Tyler reaches for a tissue. He looks happier than she's ever seen him. Even the judge looks pleased, she thinks, and in her experience, judges never look happy.

Judge Watson turns to Tyler. "You'll need to arrange for a home study. I'll need to assess all the relevant issues—your place of residence, health, safety, schooling, anything that might impact Anna's well-being—before I grant permanent custody in a subsequent hearing."

Tyler's smile vanishes. "I'm not sure that will work," he says. "I'm moving to New York City soon. Can I do the home study there?"

Anna's stomach drops. *New York City?* The words echo in her head but make no sense. *He's leaving?* The room seems to tilt, and her world suddenly feels unstable again.

The judge shakes his head no. "You'll need to stay in Baltimore County until this gets resolved. You certainly can't move out of state with a temporary custodial order. You'll have to wait a few months before you move."

The clerk stops shuffling papers and watches as what now looks like a tragedy unfolds. Tyler's face is pale, his mouth hanging open. Then he says, "I can't wait. I have to go now."

Judge Watson looks confused. "Son, what's the rush? Is it a money problem?"

"No!" Anna shouts from her spot next to Darla, her body quivering. "He just got a promotion. He's never mentioned New York." She looks directly at Tyler, pleading. "What's happening?"

Everyone waits for an answer from her brother that does not come. He is speechless.

"All right," the judge says, his voice heavy. "I'm going to set a continuance for three weeks before ruling. I suggest you reexamine your priorities during the next twenty-one days, young man. Until then, Anna Rush will be placed in foster care. Court is adjourned."

Judge Watson bangs his gavel, everyone rises, and he marches out.

Anna's heart drops. Tears flood down her face, "No!" she screams. "Tyler! *Why? Why? Why?*"

It's the worst feeling she has ever experienced … to be abandoned by the one person in the world she trusts. Tyler just sits there, silent, with that stupid look on his face.

Anna's vision clouds over and her head throbs. Her injured brain cannot process what is being thrown at it. She feels herself being pushed out of the courtroom.

It's such a lonely feeling, she thinks, being deserted by your own brother.

CHAPTER 18

Tyler drags his feet as he approaches Mike's office, hands buried deep in his pockets, his fingers curled into fists. Every step is a fight to keep himself from unraveling. He woke up this morning drained, his mind stuck on the events of the courtroom catastrophe. No matter how many times he glanced at the clock during the wee hours, one thought burned through his brain—*I failed her*. Anna's teary face haunts him—tears he caused. He can't help but feel like his life, everything he's worked for, is slipping through his fingers.

His phone buzzes in his pocket, startling him. He stops mid-step and pulls it out. Greg's name lights up the screen. Tyler stares at it, his thumb hovering over the green icon. He should answer this time, explain why he skipped their Saturday run, let Greg know why he wasn't at work yesterday. *But what would I even say?*

Not now, he decides, silencing the call and shoving the phone back into his pocket. The guilt settles like a stone in his chest as he reaches Mike's open door and pokes his head in.

"Well, look who it is! How's it going, kid?" Mike asks, rising from his desk and motioning to the table at the far end of his office near the terrace exit. "Let's chat."

Every word is like salt on an open wound. Each syllable digs deeper, reminding Tyler of the trap he's walked into. His chest tightens as he approaches Mike's table, his heart pounding in his ears. He thought this game would be his ticket ahead, a way to help Anna. But it's clear now—it's not just his life he's derailed. His sister is paying the price, too.

A panoramic view of downtown unfolds through the windows in front of him, the scars from the recent storm visible everywhere. The debris has mostly been cleaned up, but the damage remains. Boarded windows, jagged tree stumps, broken masts of boats lying in their slips—it's like the city itself is wounded.

Tyler drops into a chair, the burden of his failure pressing down on him. He doesn't feel sorry for anyone outside. His own life is in ruins. He called and texted Anna repeatedly after the hearing, but she didn't respond. No matter how many times he replays it, there's no escaping it. He's let her down, plain and simple. Of course she feels betrayed. She should.

Mike sits down next to him, too close. Tyler drags his chair back a foot, widening the gap between them.

"How's it going, buster?" Mike asks. His voice is like a needle poking at a raw nerve. "Recovered from last Friday's fun?" He laughs and playfully slaps Tyler on the back.

Tyler shrugs Mike's hand away and doesn't respond, staring down at the polished table instead. His jaw twitches, the muscle jumping under his skin. He had expected an explanation, maybe even an apology. But this—this jovial nonsense, this callousness—it grates on him. Mike is the reason Tyler's life has crumbled, yet here he is, treating it like a joke.

Is all this just a game to him?

Mike's grin fades slightly. "Oh, come on. Get over yourself," he says, sounding disappointed. "You gave it your best shot, but hey, you got played by the best." He leans back, his hands behind his head, exuding the confidence of a man who knows he's untouchable. "Don't worry. You'll bounce back. It'll be good for you in the long run. And you should be honored I even selected you for this assignment." He lets the words settle before his tone sharpens. "I don't waste my time on people who can't handle the pressure."

The truth in Mike's words—that Tyler had tried to play him and failed—irritates him even more. Heat rises up his neck. Mike's casual indifference is maddening.

"You won. I lost. I get it," Tyler says through clenched teeth. "But *you* don't get it. It's my sister. If I lose her ..." His voice falters. He can't finish the thought and his hands shake. *If I lose her, I lose everything.*

Mike snorts, rolling his eyes. "That sounds like a smokescreen."

Tyler shakes his head and quickly summarizes the events since Friday night—the hearing, the continuance, the looming loss of Anna. His voice rises in desperation as he adds, "If we could put the bet on hold for a few months, I know I can get custody of her. I just need time."

Mike strolls over to the window, glancing out at the harbor. "It wasn't supposed to be this sunny today," he says, slipping on his sunglasses.

Tyler's stomach churns. His world is crumbling, and Mike doesn't care—won't care. Talking to him is like talking to a brick wall. *How did everything go so wrong so fast?*

Mike turns back, his voice controlled. "You're in a difficult situation. And I see why you're upset." For a moment, Tyler is hopeful. *Maybe he understands. Maybe he'll give me a chance to fix this.*

"Your request is not unreasonable," Mike says, slowly stepping back toward the table and settling in a chair, but then his eyes harden. "However, I can't allow it. You need to learn how to face the consequences of your actions, young man."

"If I leave now, I'll lose Anna!" Tyler's voice rises, cracking under the strain of his fear. His throat closes as he fights back the tears threatening to spill over. The image of Anna in her wheelchair—her face pale, eyes filled with hurt—flashes before him. *How did I let this happen?*

Mike leans in, his words cutting through the tension. "I don't want to be the bad guy here, but honestly, maybe that's for the best. Being alone might be just what you need to focus. And you'll need all the focus you can muster to fulfill your bet."

Tyler flinches. The coldness of Mike's words stuns him, leaving a bitter taste in his mouth. For a long moment, he just sits there, his hands clenched, his body tense. He wants to scream, to tell Mike exactly what he thinks, but no words come. The sting behind his eyes intensifies. *Not here. Not now.*

Finally, Tyler rises and turns toward the door. He wants to leave with his head held high. Just as his hand touches the doorknob, he stops. He turns, sucking in a sharp breath, his chin tilted up defiantly.

"What if I can't get hired?" His lips curl into a smirk. "What if I can't *find* the investment algorithm?"

Mike stands and his response booms across the room. "You do not even want to go there."

Tyler meets his eyes, his voice low. "Maybe I do."

Mike shakes his head, stepping closer, any amusement fading from his face. His voice drops to a growl, each word deliberate. "This game has rules, Tyler. Break them, and it won't just be your sister you lose." He pauses, his eyes narrowing. "One way or another, everyone pays."

Mike leans against the desk, his tone measured now, his expression fully serious. "Get me the algorithm, and you'll come out of this just fine." He lets the words hang in the air, watching Tyler closely, almost as if giving him time to absorb the significance of the situation. Then, softening his tone, he adds with a smile, "After all, I've got big plans for you."

"You're full of shit." Tyler turns and starts walking through the door.

Mike's laughter rings out behind him. "This is just a formality, but are you ready? You're fired!"

Tyler stops in his tracks, his back stiff. He slowly raises his hand and extends his middle finger toward Mike without looking back. He holds it high as he walks the rest of the way out the door.

Mike's hyena-like howl of laughter follows him into the hallway, so loud and forceful it feels like it makes the whole building shake.

Tyler's skyrocketing career had lasted for only the briefest moment. Now, as he steps into the elevator, the walls seem to close in, mirroring the collapse of his once-promising future.

CHAPTER 19

Three days later, Tyler strolls to the north side of the pool by the 9/11 Memorial in Lower Manhattan. Paul had said he'd meet him here.

Tyler checks his watch. Not quite noon yet. He scans the weekend traffic working its way up West Street. A few minutes and a hundred vehicles later, he spots the black Escalade easing to the curb in front of a line of cabs.

His phone vibrates softly in his pocket, but he doesn't bother pulling it out. He knows who it'll be. Greg's been trying to reach him since Saturday, leaving texts Tyler hasn't answered and voicemails he's avoided listening to. He needs to tell Greg something but is afraid to bring his best friend into the mess he's created.

Tyler shakes off the thought and waves as Paul steps out of the Escalade, wearing a straw hat—smart, given the heat. Tyler is hopeful because Paul heard about the judge's decision and said he would talk to Mike. Maybe he's worked something out, Tyler thinks. Maybe he's convinced Mike to drop his demand that Tyler infiltrate New Horizon.

"Over here!" Tyler waves an arm, feeling a rush of adrenaline. He was surprised when Paul suggested the New York meeting place, saying he didn't mind the long drive up from Baltimore. For Tyler, it was no sweat, a half-hour subway ride from his Harlem motel.

Paul approaches, looking calm. Tyler can't help but notice the contrast between Paul's relaxed demeanor and his own anxious energy. The midday sun bakes the air, and the scent of car exhaust and city grime lingers in the background.

"Thanks for sending Darla to help us," Tyler says. "She's a solid attorney."

Paul nods, his lips tight. "I asked her to talk to her contacts up here. See if they can work out a deal to get Anna with you."

"Is that possible?"

"Worth a shot," Paul replies, although he sounds uncertain. His expression becomes more serious. "I talked to Mike," he says, shaking his head. "He won't budge on the bet."

Tyler's stomach sinks, the brief spark of hope snuffed out.

They walk closer to the memorial pool, the sound of falling water growing louder.

"Have you been here before?" Paul asks, his voice softer now.

"No, first time. It's impressive," Tyler says, taking in the sight.

Water cascades from all sides of the giant, square fountain that surrounds what had once been One World Trade Center. Its sheer size overwhelms him. As the water spills into the dark granite basin, it never fills, continually draining into a large, square void at the center of the pool. The emptiness is palpable—like a wound that will never close, leaving a vast void where Tower One once stood.

"Gives me chills every time," Paul says, leaning closer to Tyler. The sound of the rushing water offers them a thin veil of privacy. "So, what's next for you?"

"I applied for an analyst position at New Horizon," Tyler says, drawing in a lungful of humid air. "If I get an interview and land the job, I'll poke around. Try to find the investing algorithm."

"And if not?" Paul asks, his gaze steady.

Tyler swallows hard. "Then I'll go back to Baltimore, find another job. Mike will have to deal with it."

Paul places a hand on his shoulder, his tone grave. "That's not good enough, my friend." His grip tightens slightly. "This game is no joke. The bet is very real. And the consequences of not fulfilling it are beyond severe."

Tyler jerks his shoulder away, his breath quickening. "This game is a bunch of crap. I don't need a lecture, Paul."

"This game is bigger than you and me, son," Paul says, frowning. "Much bigger. Bigger than Preston. Bigger than Mike. Bigger even than the president of the United States."

Tyler freezes, Paul's words hanging heavy in the air. The splashing of the water fills the sudden silence. He glances at the memorial pool, the water cascading endlessly, its soft rush contrasting with his inner anxiety. He inhales deeply, the chlorine stinging his nose.

A child runs in front of them, his hand running along the bronze panels that outline the fountain, his sneakers clapping against the speckled granite tiles. Then it's quiet again.

Paul finally breaks the stillness. "The secretary of agriculture is going to resign next Tuesday."

A chill runs down Tyler's spine, despite the heat of the sun. Paul's tone has a gravity to it that gives him goosebumps—too real to dismiss. He furrows his brow. "How do you know that?"

"Because it's already been decided. And it's not because of a 'family matter,' like they'll say. It's because he lost to a seed company executive who plays a better hand of poker—and who wants fewer regulations."

Tyler watches Paul, his mind racing. As head of the FDA, he could easily know about something like this. *Maybe he's just trying to scare me. No way it's because of the game.*

"That's not bigger than the president," Tyler says, sure he's right.

Paul exhales slowly, his expression intensifying. "There's a referendum in Britain in two months—right before Halloween. A vote on rejoining the EU."

Tyler scoffs. "That's no secret. It's all over the news. The polls say it won't pass. The people don't want it, the prime minister doesn't want it, and the EU is sick of the whole mess."

Paul's eyes turn steely. "And yet, it *is* going to pass. It's also been decided."

"By whom?" Tyler asks, his skepticism creeping in.

"By people who understand its importance in maintaining the economic strength and security of the world's democratic nations."

Paul's voice drops to a near whisper. "To answer your question more directly … by the game."

Tyler snorts. "You've been drinking Mike's Kool-Aid. Do you realize how ridiculous this game sounds when you put it that way?"

Paul stares at the horizon for a long moment. His voice is colder when he finally speaks. "How ridiculous does seventy thousand American lives sound to you?"

Tyler raises his eyebrows, openly questioning Paul.

"I've seen the game in action, Tyler. I've seen it save lives—more than you can imagine."

Tyler smirks, the disbelief written across his face. "That's hard to believe."

Paul steps closer to the memorial pool, pointing to the bronze panels surrounding it. "The names of the 9/11 victims are etched here. Look at them. Read them."

Tyler follows him and squints at the inscriptions. *Charles Parker.* He runs his finger along the rough edges of the etchings. *Denise Lopez. Marvin Turner.*

"These people died for our country," Paul says. "I imagine the water flowing down in front of us is their blood … a reminder that their deaths mean something, that they caused our country to finally awaken and take action against terrorism." His voice becomes gravelly. "They didn't sign up for that, of course. None of them did. But they became symbols—reminders of what's at stake."

Marc Bailey. Ricky Tran. Elizabeth Morgan. Tyler keeps reading the names silently. The spray of mist from the fountain cools his skin, but it does nothing to lift the heaviness settling over him.

Paul's next words slice through the sound of the water. "If not for the game, blood would be gushing into this pool from so many victims that it would overflow onto the streets of the city." Tyler looks down, shifting his stance. The enormity of what Paul is saying sinks in, pressing down on him.

"If it weren't for the game, Osama bin Laden would *not* have been caught. The documents recovered from his compound detailed intricate plans for an upcoming Super Bowl attack. His warm-up was 9/11. The Super Bowl was to be his twisted masterpiece … with the entire world watching."

Tyler wants to scoff, to laugh off the absurdity of it all—but the certainty in Paul's eyes pins him in place. It's as if the world around him stills, and for the first time, he's starting to understand just how deep this game runs.

"You're giving a poker game credit for catching bin Laden?"

Paul meets his stare. "I was there when it happened. Pakistani President Zardari proposed a game with Preston. They played for bin Laden's exact location."

"What was Zardari's price?"

"If Preston lost, he'd have to give a billion dollars' worth of state-of-the-art US weapons to Pakistan."

"A billion dollars?" Tyler's eyes widen. "Preston couldn't bet that."

Paul nods grimly. "As chair of the Armed Services Committee, he could've found a way."

"The president was okay with this?"

Paul seems surprised at the question. "Obama? Hell, he never knew. He thought the CIA tracked bin Laden down."

Tyler's knees weaken, and he steadies himself against one of the bronze panels, silently apologizing to the name his hand covers. The image of Preston and Zardari playing for those stakes flashes through his mind … no doubt using the gold coins in that game. The ramifications of their contest swirl in his thoughts, along with the online article he and Greg read. It all seems so far-fetched.

"I know it sounds unbelievable, but this game … it's real, Tyler. Mike asked me to talk to you because he likes you. He's worried about you, in his way." Paul sighs. "But the debt is real. Your six-month deadline is real, too."

Tyler shakes his head, the disbelief gnawing at him. "Me stealing New Horizon's algorithm will not save the country. All it'll do is fatten Mike's wallet."

"I agree," Paul says quietly, his voice barely audible over the water.

Tyler looks up, surprised. "You do?"

"It's a complete abuse of his power and a blatant disrespect to the spirit of the game."

Tyler feels a surge of hope.

"But he made the bet, and you called it, my friend. And you lost. Whether or not it's fair, that's the reality." Paul pauses. "This isn't just about money."

"It's all about money," Tyler fires back.

"You're not listening, son! Your safety is at stake."

The words hang in the air, and the icy clutch of fear settles in Tyler's chest. "My safety? What, my life means nothing?"

Paul hesitates, his face softening. "Not compared to seventy thousand others."

Tyler's insides twist, a knot forming in his stomach. His world seems even more out of control than before. "What if I go to the police? Or the FBI? Isn't this whole game illegal?"

Paul laughs, the sound sharp against the memorial's serene backdrop. "Son, with this group, there's no such thing as illegal."

CHAPTER 20

Tyler trudges along East 129th Street, his mind a tangled web of doubts and anxiety. His stomach was so tight when he woke up that he couldn't eat his breakfast, leaving his fork clean beside the untouched eggs and toast. The confidence he once leaned on has crumbled. A couple of weeks ago, he was tossing around hundred-dollar chips without a second thought, like boy wonder. Now, he's just a guy in a suit—an unemployed, inexperienced analyst with dwindling savings, a crushing debt, and a sister trapped in a mess of his own making.

Being boy wonder was so much more fun.

He checks his watch. Nine thirty-five a.m. Only two minutes since he last looked. His interview isn't until ten thirty, yet he feels like the clock is breathing down his neck. He quickens his pace.

A car rolls by, its tire splashing through a puddle. A spray of dirty water hits his pant leg and soaks one of his shoes. *Perfect.*

With a sigh, he pulls out his phone and scrolls through his contacts until he finds Greg's. After a moment of hesitation, he presses the call button. It rings three times before going to voicemail.

"Hey, Greg, it's me," Tyler says. "I know I've been hard to reach lately." He pauses, searching for the right words and finding none. The silence stretches before he forces himself to finish. "Call me back when you get this."

He hangs up and slips the phone back into his pocket, his heart heavy. The message won't satisfy Greg, but what else could he say? He can't tell the truth—not about any of it.

Plodding down the street, Tyler rehearses the answers he's prepared for the questions he's sure to be asked in his interview. *How did you rise to VP so quickly? Why leave Mid-Atlantic? Why New Horizon?*

This job has to work out. His conversation with Paul made that abundantly clear. But even if he gets the job, the real challenge will be much more difficult—extracting New Horizon's secret algorithm.

Tyler steps onto the street to avoid half a dozen orange plastic cones scattered on the sidewalk and runs a finger under his collar, mopping up a thin layer of sweat. He turns onto Lexington Avenue, which erupts with the energy of the city. High-performance engines zoom south like bees buzzing toward their hive. Vehicles are parked up and down both sides of the road and form a protective cocoon around the Mercedes, Range Rovers, and BMWs streaming south toward the financial district, their occupants insulated from the "regular folks," Tyler thinks, who inhabit these northern reaches of Manhattan.

A wave of the real New York washes over him with its perfume of myriad, multi-national ingredients, created by twenty-five thousand bodies being packed like sardines into each square mile.

Shouts ring out from a schoolyard across the street where a group of teenage girls and boys are playing soccer. His thoughts drift to Anna. She's never played soccer that he knows of, but he's sure she'd be good at it. He watches the kids in the schoolyard, their shouts floating through the air as they kick a ball around. A brief smile touches his lips then vanishes. The field and the kids are safely tucked behind a tall chain-link fence, protecting them from the harsh realities of the outside world.

There's no fence protecting Anna. Never has been.

Tyler squeezes his hands together, his heart thudding like a drum as a headache simmers at the base of his skull. *Please, no migraine, not today of all days.*

He glances at his watch and forces himself to move on. Cement sidewalks and asphalt streets stretch out in front of him toward the horizon. He strides past one- and two-story structures, each connected to the next like one long building with many faces. He passes a nail salon, a mobile phone store, and a bagel shop. Here the windows are free of handprints, and their paint trim is bright and neat.

As he walks, Tyler replays the court hearing in his mind for the hundredth time. The more he thinks about it, the more helpless he feels.

Just ahead, a man is sleeping, curled up on the sidewalk, a bunched-up camouflage jacket wedged under his head. A dog with fluffy, brown fur lies next to him, leashed to a grate covering a basement window. The dog guards his friend, its head perking up to inspect Tyler as he walks by.

Tyler's phone vibrates—snapping him back to the present.

"You alive, bud?" Greg asks.

"Yeah. Sorry I disappeared for a while. I moved to New York."

"Lots of rumors flying around about you, big boy."

"I bet."

"Word around here is that you got fired," Greg says. "Is that true?"

"I … I can't discuss it. I'm sorry."

Greg pauses, his voice quieter when he speaks again. "Is it related to the game? Doesn't make sense that you just got promoted and now you're fired."

Tyler clenches the phone tighter. "I'll explain it one day, Greg, but I can't right now."

"One of my favorite rumors is that you and Mike Hayward had a fling that went sour."

Tyler chuckles, though it's forced. "Disturbing. But funny."

Greg laughs. "Another rumor says you're a secret agent stealing classified information from other companies."

"I'm actually on my way to an interview," Tyler replies, his voice strained. *The interview*, he reminds himself. "Nothing clandestine on this end, I'm sorry to say."

"Stupid conspiracy nuts. Seriously, though, don't be a stranger. I'm worried about you."

"Everything's fine," Tyler says quickly, his stomach knotting. *Now I'm lying to my best friend.*

Greg lets out a soft laugh. "I'll tell Mike you said hello."

Tyler pockets his phone and arrives at the subway entrance. He trots down the steps, removing himself from the bustling world above into the midmorning lull of an uptown subway station. As he enters the dark labyrinth below, he does feel like a secret agent … a rogue agent, the weight of deception heavy on his shoulders.

He stands on the platform, waiting, alone. Voices arrive from behind and echo past him into the vast tunnels beyond. A digital sign informs him a train will arrive in two minutes, another serpent slithering through the underground twists and turns with many stops remaining before it returns to its lair. Tyler is keenly aware he is far away from the comforting waters of the Inner Harbor.

The whooshing noise arrives first. The creature is approaching. Its presence grows louder and sounds like a vacuum lock being unsealed. Wind blows against Tyler's face, agitating the still air, and a loud, rhythmic clack, clack, clack erupts as the belly of the beast skids across the tracks of the station in front of him. Finally, he hears the screeching cry of protest as its brakes press hard against the metal rails. The silvery metal cylinder comes to a stop and succumbs to its duty to deliver him to the financial hub of the world—Wall Street.

•   •   •   •   •

The man across the table—Stewart—radiates arrogance. Early forties, carefully groomed hair, and delicate mannerisms that indicate he's not the type of man who would last long on a farm. An Ivy Leaguer, Tyler bets.

"My degree is in business administration," Tyler says, trying to steady his voice. "Finance, with a dual major in computer science. Three-point-nine GPA."

"I see that on your resume." Stewart yawns and doesn't try to hide it or apologize for his disinterest. "Let's be honest, though—University of Baltimore. Not exactly Harvard or Yale, is it?"

Tyler adjusts his posture, keeping his voice even despite the simmering frustration, and forces a smile. "I worked my way through school. No one handed me a hundred-grand-a-year education on a silver platter."

Stewart holds up his hands. "No need to be defensive. It's just that most of our associates come from—how shall I say it?—more *established* schools."

Tyler reaches for his water glass. "Maybe that gives me a unique perspective. I might bring fresh ideas to the table." He smiles to lighten the mood.

Stewart's expression doesn't change. "You're clearly overqualified for a senior analyst role, considering you were a VP in your last job." He checks Tyler's resume. "But you've only got, what, two weeks of actual investment experience?"

"Which is why this is the perfect mid-level position for me."

Stewart glances at his watch and stands. "I appreciate your time. We'll be in touch."

Before Tyler can respond, there's a knock at the door. A woman steps in—much younger than Stewart, with auburn hair that bounces as she moves. She wears a comfortable smile, and her emerald eyes glisten.

Tyler returns her smile, an unexpected spark of attraction stirring within him, though it does little to calm the anxiety twisting in his gut.

"Tyler Rush?" Her voice is melodic, and he detects a slight Baltimore accent.

He nods as a tingle shoots down his spine. For a moment, he feels free. Then he remembers why he's here and nausea rises in his stomach.

"Jill Young," she says, extending her hand.

"Are you from Bal'more?" Tyler asks.

She steps closer to the table. "I moved to New York when I was twelve."

Stewart clears his throat. "We're wrapping up. Did you need something?"

"I'm joining this interview," Jill says. "Let's continue."

Tyler is momentarily thrown by the shift in tone. Relief washes over him, but unease lingers. He hadn't expected anyone to take his side. As

Jill takes Stewart's seat, crossing her toned legs and flashing a smile, he forces himself to refocus, unsure whether to trust the sudden change in the atmosphere. His eyes are drawn to her polished confidence, though his nerves keep him on edge.

Stewart coughs, breaking their connection. "We covered Tyler's education—University of Baltimore—and his lack of relevant experience for the opening."

"Tell me, Mr. Rush," Jill begins, ignoring Stewart, her tone casual yet probing, "are you a Mike Hayward disciple?"

"Oh, no. If that's what you're looking for …" The words spill out too quickly, and he hesitates, trying to craft a response neutral enough to allow him to gravitate toward the answer she might want. He can't afford to be wrong and lose this opportunity.

"Quite the opposite," she says, flashing a smile.

A sense of ease momentarily settles in. He exhales and glances out the window. The upper floors of One World Trade Center are visible a half mile away, towering a hundred stories above the unseen 9/11 memorial pools.

Jill scans his resume. "College grad to executive to fired. In barely a year?"

Tyler describes his rise at Mid-Atlantic, highlighting his accomplishments and clashes with the VP of investments. He also touches on his research into New Horizon's investment returns. The one thing he omits is any mention of the game and, above all, the bet—the very thing that has turned his life upside down.

"The CFO didn't like me," he says with a shrug, finishing with a blatant lie. "He set me up."

Jill raises an eyebrow, but her expression softens as she listens. Stewart, on the other hand, checks his watch. "I've got another interview lined up," he says.

"It can wait," Jill responds firmly. She turns back to Tyler. "Why New Horizon?"

"I want to be part of the best," Tyler says, shifting in his seat. "Your risk-to-reward metrics are off the charts." He's grateful Jill has entered the picture, but a sense of unease creeps over him, as if she knows more than she lets on, as if she can see through the untruths he is weaving into his responses. His skin is clammy, and his soul feels dirty.

Stewart points at Jill. "She created our investment algorithm, you know. Before she became CFO."

Jill looks down. "It's been a team effort."

She doesn't strike Tyler as the type to dislocate her shoulder patting herself on the back. "Still plenty of work to do to improve it," she adds.

Tyler finds it hard to believe she's old enough to have accomplished so much. Admiration swells in him, but it's quickly smothered by thoughts of his deception. He's here under false pretenses, a fraud in the presence of someone who has truly earned her place. The growing sense of being an impostor chips away at his confidence. Every smile, every nod, feels like a lie.

Outside the window, a small plane buzzes by on its way up the Hudson River. Jill watches it for a moment. "September 11th wasn't the first time a plane crashed into a skyscraper," she says. "In 1946, an army plane hit this building. Fifty-eighth floor." She stands and beckons Tyler to follow. "Come on. I'll show you where it happened."

Stewart's face is pinched. "I have interviews lined up all day. I suggest we leave tours for candidates who will return for a second interview."

"Go ahead with your interviews. I'll take care of Mr. Rush." She stands and holds the door open for Tyler. She winks as he walks past. "I didn't start out in investments, either."

He follows a step behind her as they tour the fifty-seventh floor and move to the fifty-eighth. A musky, almost spicy scent lingers in the air as they walk. She explains that the company is only a dozen years old— which Tyler knew—and that it occupies just two of the building's seventy-one floors, which he didn't know. He takes it all in.

They pass offices and small conference rooms that line the floor's perimeter. Cubicles fill the central space, where the buzz of conversation mingles with the droning of printers and copiers. The desks are more utilitarian than what Tyler expected in a Wall Street office. A gray carpet covers the floors, except for the break room, where black-and-white checkered linoleum tiles break the monotony.

Halfway around the building, Jill stops and gestures to an office. "When I'm not in meetings, I'm here."

Her office is smaller than the one he inherited from Ed, with a desk and a round pedestal table just big enough for four people. What it lacks in size, it makes up for with a stunning view of Manhattan's southern tip, a conglomeration of architecture from multiple eras stuffed into a sliver of land wedged between the merging of the Hudson and East Rivers. The edge of Battery Park is visible, bordering the water where a ferry has just departed, loaded with tourists on their way to the Statue of Liberty.

"We're practically joined at the hip with the New York Stock Exchange." She points almost straight down at a building a block away on the other side of the street. Two barricades close off a driveway that leads beneath the building, and Tyler counts three, four, five military-type personnel with very real weapons at various spots spanning the corner of Wall and Broad Streets. "Being physically close to the trading floor used to matter. A lot. It allowed us to get our trades in a fraction of a second faster than firms farther away. The difference is almost imperceptible, but it was the secret that put New Horizon on the map. All before my time."

"It's a long way down," Tyler says. He turns away from the window, and his eyes track her as she moves to the desk and sits behind her computer.

She looks up at him. "There was a big exposé on *60 Minutes* before I started working here. An investigation followed, and adjustments were made to the trading software used by the exchange. I remember hearing whispers that the company would shut down. After we lost our advantage, we became just another financial services firm."

The framed documents on the far wall catch Tyler's eye. He sets his briefcase down on the edge of her desk and wanders closer so he can read them.

"Until you invented the investing algorithm," he says quietly.

"I started the project when I was getting my MBA. With a partner."

His heart lurches, and he turns back toward her. His gaze drops to her hand, searching for a ring. He doesn't see one.

She picks up a tissue and dabs her eyes, her expression softening. "Excuse me," she says, turning away to blow her nose.

"Are you okay?"

She raises a finger. "Just need a minute."

He scans her sleek silhouette and admires the way her dress clings to her body, embarrassed by his thoughts. He turns his attention back to the wall, afraid she can see the images in his mind, and he is close enough now that he can read the documents. One is a diploma from Princeton awarding a bachelor's degree in computer science, with highest honors, to Jillian H. Young.

Computer science. That's interesting.

The other framed document confers the degree of Master of Business Administration from Harvard University, also to Jillian H. Young.

Didn't start out in investments, either, eh? Ha!

"Jillian H. Young." He enjoys the sound of her name on his tongue.

She wipes her eyes and moves around her desk to join him. "Jillian," she says and stares at her printed name, but her eyes quickly move someplace far away. "It's been a long time since I've been called Jillian."

He walks back to her desk to retrieve his briefcase and notices a picture of a black Labrador retriever and a French bulldog curled up together, sleeping.

"I love dogs," he says.

She rushes over to him and picks up the picture. "I'm working on a project with the Humane Society. Adapting the algorithm to help match strays with families." Her voice is full again. The tears are gone.

"Maybe I could help." His stomach tightens, and his gaze falters. He shifts his weight from one foot to the other, the warmth of her smile making the lie between them even bigger.

Glancing next to the photo, he notices a gold medal. He picks it up. "You won the World Finals of the ICPC?"

"At Princeton. We had a talented team." She eyes him closely. "You're familiar with the International Collegiate Programming Contest?"

"We didn't have a team, but I worked through the challenges on my own."

She smiles at him. He smiles back.

After a few seconds, she breaks their stare and glances at her watch. "Follow me. I'll show you where the plane crashed." She reaches behind her desk, grabs a ring of keys, then marches to the door.

After a quick walk to the opposite corner of the floor, she fiddles with her key ring, finds a fob that she presses against a security pad mounted on the wall, opens a thick metal door, and peeks into a large room.

She holds the door open. "Boardroom's empty. Come on."

She crosses to the far wall of the unlit room and, with her finger, outlines the 20 x 10-foot hole in the steel and limestone that was created two generations earlier by the accident. The crash site is now hidden behind layers of paint and drywall, but Tyler tries to imagine what that experience had been like, both for those on the plane and those in the building.

He steps closer to her in the dark, silent room. There's an undeniable pull between them, but just as it stirs, guilt surfaces, sharp and unrelenting in the stillness.

"Jill!" A man's voice breaks the silence, and Jill straightens immediately. "We've got a situation. Stock volumes are surging for companies specializing in gene-edited crops."

She frowns. "New regulations are about to be enacted that will make it difficult to bring those products to the market. The secretary of agriculture has been working on it for two years."

"He resigned a half hour ago. Family matter of some sort. The market seems to think those regulations will be shelved."

"I'm on it," she says.

Five minutes later, Jill and Tyler are at the reception area near the elevators on the fifty-seventh floor. He hands his visitor badge to a burly security guard.

He's still thinking about the secretary of agriculture's resignation. *How did Paul know? Is it really because of the game?*

"We'll be in touch," she says, her demeanor back to businesslike.

Tyler steps into the elevator, his pulse racing as Jill's parting words linger in his mind. It hits him with full force—how little control he has over his own future.

CHAPTER 21

Tyler strolls along Calvert Street in Baltimore on his way to the courthouse. The mid-seventies temperature is refreshing, courtesy of the first cool front of early fall. He's just had lunch with Greg and dodged most of his friend's questions—again.

Greg's not stupid. He knows something's wrong, and Tyler can see the frustration behind his usual jokes. *Maybe I should just tell him. It's not like it can get any worse.* But every time he thinks about laying it all out, he stops himself. How do you tell your best friend you've been lying to him—and risk dragging him into something dangerous?

Still, the weight of carrying this alone is crushing him. Greg's the one person who might actually be able to help. *And if I don't come clean soon, I may lose his trust completely.*

Tyler shoves his hands in his pockets, turning his focus to the upcoming hearing. What will he say when he finally sees Anna after three weeks? Will she even speak to him?

She's maintained complete silence since the last meeting. He wishes she would call, scream at him, lash out in some way. He'd rather face her anger than endure the icy wall between them. Anything would be better than the hell of being completely shut out.

Despite his fractured relationship with Anna, Tyler is optimistic about the upcoming hearing. His lead attorney, Darla Wright, has contacted an old friend, who is also a Manhattan judge, and he has agreed to oversee a home study in New York. He's promised to call Judge Watson to discuss transferring the case to his jurisdiction.

There's still the whole algorithm issue to deal with, of course, but at least he and Anna would be together. Without Virginia and Marco ... for the first time since Anna was out of diapers.

Tyler arrives at the circuit court building, bounds up the stairs two at a time, and steps into the Greek Revival behemoth. Earlier in the week, Marco was charged with eleven counts of aggravated assault of a minor in one of the nearby buildings. Tyler is scheduled to return later in September to meet with the district attorney's office and provide his statement. The thought of Marco sitting in a jail cell brings a fleeting sense of satisfaction. Surely, no one will bother to scrape up the money to bail him out.

The pleasure of thinking about Marco's troubles is fleeting, though, and Tyler returns to obsessing about his own upcoming hearing and his hope for a positive outcome from it. He walks down a marble hallway, and just outside Attorney Conference Room B, he meets Marsha and Benjamin from McCovey and Wright. He wishes Anna were with them.

Benjamin shuts the conference room door and they all sit. Marsha frowns at Tyler. "Darla's friend, the New York judge, called yesterday. Says he is no longer willing to consider the case."

Tyler slumps in his chair, crushed by yet another disappointment. Too many of these recently.

"He said to tell you that you need to fulfill your obligations and that you would know what that means." She raises her eyebrows in question.

Tyler bites the inside of his cheek and nods. He knows exactly what it means—that Mike's reach extends even further than he'd imagined. He's an octopus hiding within a human shell, his arms stretching from his Baltimore office into world events, through history, and now, the legal system. His tentacles are suffocating Tyler's every attempt to regain footing.

"Darla talked to Judge Watson this morning and really pushed him to loosen the requirement that you stay in Baltimore County. He said he might consider it if you would agree to stay in the state of Maryland."

She places her hands flat on the table between them. "Is that a possibility?"

He sighs. She doesn't get it. No one gets it … because it doesn't make any damn sense.

"I have to be in New York. No way around it."

Benjamin shrugs. "Perhaps if you explain why, and for how long, that might carry some weight with the judge. Right now, it's a total red flag. He thinks you're hiding something, and it irks his ego that you aren't jumping at the gift he believes he's offering you."

After ten more minutes of useless back and forth, Tyler trudges behind his hired help into the courtroom, the same one he was in three weeks ago. He's ready to get it over with. This time, three tables sit in front of the viewing benches, all facing the judge.

Virginia and her lawyer are at the far table. Anna and a court-appointed legal guardian are in the center. Darla is at the nearest table, and Tyler veers toward her, tightening the knot of his tie and wiggling it back and forth to make sure it's centered. It presses flush against his Adam's apple and makes it difficult for him to swallow comfortably, but that feels strangely good to him, as if he's receiving a small dose of penance for his stupidity in creating this mess.

The air conditioning is off, probably because of the cooler weather outside, but the room is on the warm side of pleasant and adds to the queasiness in his belly.

Anna looks up as he approaches the waist-high wooden rail separating the public gallery from the court participants, and he meets her eyes for a fraction of a second. Her expression sears into him—her anger, her hurt, her confusion. He spots the aluminum walker next to her chair, the metal dull under the courtroom lights. She sits hunched, her movements stiff, and Tyler notices the dark circles under her eyes. She seems like an old, beaten soul trapped in a young, teenage body.

The Honorable Stanley Watson strolls in, just like before. Everyone stands, just like before. But unlike before, no one in the room is hopeful of a favorable outcome.

What a waste of time and money, Tyler thinks. He figures five hundred an hour for the associates and a thousand for Darla. Assuming they can submit three hours to prepare for and attend this pointless hearing, there go seventy-five crisp, hundred-dollar bills down the drain. At least the bills are Paul's.

The legal guardian begins by providing an up-to-date verbal report. Anna is being cared for in a fine manner, but her grades have slipped. She's also been suspended from school for attacking another child.

"Miss Rush, is that true?" the judge asks gently.

Tears stream down Anna's face. "Yes, sir." She reaches for a tissue and blows her nose.

"Why did you do that?"

"The girl called me a homeless cripple. Everyone laughed at me." She sniffles. "It made me so mad. Later, when she was sitting at her desk, I hit her in the head with my lunchbox." She stifles a sob. "I know it was wrong."

The judge looks up at the loud sound of hard-soled shoes marching down the empty viewing aisle toward the rail.

"Excuse me. We're in session here." His voice is loud and full, much bigger than Tyler thought possible, given his petite frame. "Closed session, I might add."

"I'm sorry, Your Honor. My name is Paul Thompson. I'm a friend of the Rush family."

Judge Watson's tone softens. "I know your name very well. Please have a seat." He motions with an open palm toward the front row of the viewing area. "For the record, Mr. Paul Thompson, head of the United States Food and Drug Administration, is in the courtroom today."

Darla waves discreetly at Paul. Tyler nods in his direction, confused. Anna scowls.

"Mr. Rush," the judge begins, "I understand there's no change in your situation. You are in New York for reasons you aren't willing to share, and you will not commit to living in the Baltimore area to take temporary custody of Anna. Is that correct?"

Tyler fidgets in his seat and considers his response. He holds up his finger. "I do expect to return to Baltimore in about six months. At that point, I will commit to staying here for as long as needed. I'll do anything for Anna. I just need to get through the next six months." His voice is strained, and he knows he's on the edge of breaking down completely. He glances at Anna and finds her looking right back at him, her expression no longer as hateful. She seems confused but does not turn away.

"Are you in some kind of trouble?" the judge asks as he removes his glasses, his eyes locked on Tyler. "I suggest you talk with your attorneys. They are here to help you, you know."

Tyler looks down at the table and begins to count the grains of wood on the surface. There's nothing more he can say. No way can he reveal the truth to his lawyers.

The judge shakes his head, dons his glasses, and consults some papers in front of him.

"Does Virginia Rush or her attorney have anything to add?" He waits less than a second and then continues. "We'll move on then." He focuses on Anna, a social smile plastered on his face. "Miss Rush, I'll schedule a hearing in six months to revisit this decision, but until then, I'm afraid you'll need to remain in the custody of—"

"Excuse me, Your Honor?" Paul stands just behind the rail, a plastic water bottle in his hand.

The judge looks perturbed.

"I have something …" Paul's voice is husky. He takes a sip of water, sets the bottle down against the rail, and clears his throat. "I would like to provide care for Anna Rush for the next six months."

Murmurs and whispers erupt from everyone present, except the judge, who studies Paul from high on the bench.

Paul takes another sip from the bottle and stands fully upright. "I work down in Silver Spring most days, sometimes in DC." His voice is stronger now. "But my wife stays home. She can accommodate Anna's schedule. And we'll open our home for Tyler to visit as often as he can."

Tyler is shocked. *Is it possible something good is happening?*

"Mr. Thompson, please provide some background about yourself … just for the court record."

Paul speaks for several minutes. He describes his earlier experience as a parent, cut short by the tragic loss of his son, and he discusses the prayerful consideration he and his wife have put into this decision. He explains they had been approved by the state once for foster care, years before.

The judge looks relieved by the unexpected turn of events, and the four horizontal tracks lining his forehead relax and smooth out. He turns to Anna.

"I assume you are excited about this arrangement?"

She shakes her head back and forth. "No. I want to go with Tyler. Even though I currently hate him right now."

"Your Honor?" Anna's legal guardian rises to her feet. "In my professional opinion, she should be given to the care of Paul and Melinda Thompson until the next hearing."

Anna shoots her a dirty look and sinks down into her chair, her arms crossed tightly across her chest.

The judge makes his ruling by agreeing with her guardian then ends the hearing.

Tyler shakes hands with his lawyers and hustles over to Anna's table. She turns away but then quickly jerks back, a gigantic smile spreading across her face. She reaches up and accepts his embrace.

Tyler feels as if he's been hugged throughout his body, inside and out. He leans over and whispers in her ear. "Go with Paul. Trust me. I will visit, and we really will be back together soon."

She pulls him tighter, wrapping her arms around his neck, saying nothing. He feels her moist tears against his skin and hopes they are tears of relief. As he breathes in, the familiar scent of her floral shampoo fills his senses, grounding him in the moment, reminding him of a time before everything fell apart.

Several minutes later, Paul and Tyler stand alone in the courthouse foyer, waiting for Anna and her legal representative to retrieve her suitcase. Paul motions to a bench against the wall, and he and Tyler sit down.

"When I first saw you a couple months ago, I was angry," Paul says. "How dare you barge into my life again after I had worked so hard to forget what happened? I could barely eat. Sleep was out of the question. All the emotions came flooding back. But even worse than the reminder of Melinda and I losing our beautiful and only child was the realization of what had happened to you and Anna. That had not been my intention."

Tears well up in Tyler's eyes.

"Providing care for Anna will allow me to feel human again. Melinda and I will experience the joy of being parents once more, even if it's with a teenager." He laughs, and so does Tyler. "Thank you for letting me help you."

Tyler nods and thinks about that. It feels good, Paul helping him.

·   ·   ·   ·   ·

Tyler sits on a wooden bench in Baltimore Penn Station, just north of downtown, waiting for his train to Manhattan. His phone rings, displaying a 212 area code—New York City.

"This is Jill Young … with Stewart Beechum." Her voice is silky and confident.

"Good afternoon," Tyler says, trying to sound as self-assured as she does. This is it, do or die. Is it going to be a second interview, or will he be turned down and forced to come at this thing from a different angle … from a direction he can't seriously consider until he becomes more desperate?

"I'll get to the point," she says.

A garbled announcement blasts through the station announcing the four o'clock train to Pittsburgh is about to depart. He pushes the phone tight against his ear.

"On paper, you don't match up well against the competition," she says matter-of-factly.

The serenity he's been feeling since the court hearing evaporates.

"But I believe—Stewart and I believe—that you could bring a unique perspective."

"Agreed," Tyler says, feeling a bit lighter as he straightens a little.

The bench rattles as a large man in overalls settles next to him, pulling a phone from his satchel.

"There is one issue, though." It's Stewart's voice now. "You lied about having a disagreement with the CFO at Mid-Atlantic."

How do they know that?

Tyler stands and strolls away from the bench.

"You actually had a run-in with Mike himself, didn't you?"

"That's a fair statement." Tyler chooses his next words carefully. "Please understand, though, I'm not able to discuss the situation beyond that simple acknowledgment."

Jill speaks again. "I figured a confidentiality agreement was in play."

"Doesn't change the fact that he lied to us," Stewart says in the background.

"It does for me," Jill says. "I'm very aware of how mercurial Mike Hayward can be."

How does she know that? Tyler wonders. He leans against a stone pillar in the vast terminal as she continues talking. "While I do understand the fib, I want to be clear that this is a strike. And you only get one. Untruths are not tolerated from new analysts—or anyone else, for that matter—at New Horizon Financial Services."

Did she say, "new analyst"?

CHAPTER 22

"Jill Young?" the woman's voice comes through the phone, hesitant but direct.

Jill tightens her grip on the phone. She recognizes the voice immediately.

"I'm Olivia Stanard. I spoke to you briefly at my father's funeral."

"It was a beautiful service," Jill says.

She's still having a hard time accepting he's gone. The experts concluded suicide. She doesn't buy it. Following his death, rumors surfaced about inappropriate relationships with coeds, as if that would explain his puzzling action. Hopefully, Olivia has been insulated from that nonsense.

"I understand he worked quite closely with you." Olivia's voice chokes up. "I'm sorry. This is difficult for me."

I understand, Jill thinks. *More than you could possibly know.*

"My dad's bank records … they're shocking. I had no idea he was involved in something like this."

Jill tenses and leans forward in her office chair. She knows now exactly where the conversation is heading.

"I found large monthly deposits from Jill Young Associates."

"Consulting work. I paid him a monthly retainer."

"Eighty thousand a month?"

"He did valuable work." Jill waits for the inevitable follow-up.

"The last check was processed on August 4th," Olivia says. "But I can't find a contract or any documentation about this arrangement. There's nothing. What kind of consulting work was this?"

Jill glances out the window, not wanting to answer the question and not wanting to lie. She notices that leaves are beginning to fall from the trees. Soon, the city will be transformed into a cornucopia of beautiful fall colors. She and the professor both loved this time of year. Dear Francis, she thinks, he didn't care about the money—it was always secondary to the mission. Their ever-evolving algorithm had funded initiatives around the world, a testament to his altruistic heart and their mutual belief in using technology for good.

She takes a deep breath. "It was highly specialized and confidential work. There was no formal contract because of the nature of the engagement."

Olivia hesitates. "So ... no documentation at all? It's like his relationship with you doesn't exist."

"I'm sorry. That's how it had to be." Jill's voice softens. "Your father was a great man. I'll miss him."

"That's not enough. I need something for the estate. Anything."

"A 1099 will be sent to his estate early next year for tax purposes," Jill says. Tears sting as they run down her cheeks. "I'm sorry, Olivia. That's all I can provide."

She sets the phone down, leans over, and buries her face in her hands.

Eight years earlier, a simple handshake had cemented their partnership. Together, Francis and she would create the world's first truly intelligent algorithm—to be used for good. Each for their own reasons. New Horizon was their first commercial client. Money from the exclusive licensing deal helped them fund pro bono partnerships with a dozen non-profits across the globe.

It also made them rich.

One day, she'll present a check to Olivia and her siblings—a big one. But she can't risk it yet. If she lets them in now, what had always been a gentleman's agreement between her and Francis would likely turn into a court battle. A public one. For now, their advances and breakthroughs still need to be kept secret from the broader world that will eventually benefit from them. In the wrong hands, their technology could be exceedingly dangerous.

She does need to let someone else in—someone who can help brainstorm with her, shape ideas, and accelerate the project. Progress has slowed since the professor's death, and she's realized this path is not an easy one to traverse alone. Her choice will require caution, though, as letting someone in involves risk on many levels.

She has twenty minutes of free time before her next meeting, and she ventures down to the fifty-seventh floor. Simply going for a stroll around the office helps her stay connected and often pays unexpected dividends. A stray comment from an employee in another department might be the link she needs to connect the dots on a seemingly unrelated project. Exercise of any sort also helps clear her head, and she needs to do that after her call with Olivia.

Meandering down the hall, she nods and says hellos to a few New Horizon employees. In one of the small conference rooms, she sees Stewart and his team holed up in what looks like an intense discussion. Tyler is standing in front of them and pointing at a wall-mounted monitor. She knocks on the window and opens the door.

Stewart stands up to greet her, a broad smile on his face. "Looking for the fourth quarter projections?" he asks.

Her attention focuses squarely on the monitor. "Gradient-boosted, machine-learning models? Decision-tree ensembles? I'm impressed."

"The new guy wants to be a quant," Stewart says, "but we already have an investment algorithm."

She studies the new guy, Tyler. He really is quite intriguing. The instant attraction she'd felt at their first interview scared her, though, leaving her uncharacteristically unsteady. So she's kept him at arm's length since he joined New Horizon. And yet, she keeps looking at his face, recognizing a depth to him that beckons further exploration.

He looks at her. "We can improve the process we follow to select stock recommendations for clients in our *Beyond the Horizon* prospectus."

Stewart dismisses the notion with a wave of his hand and scoffs, "Waste of time."

Tyler doesn't back down. His voice, calm but confident, cuts through Stewart's condescension. "We can apply machine-learning statistical techniques to all publicly available data for the sector we're analyzing. You know, identify the past data attributes of companies that are now successful. Create a predictive model we can use to filter out most of the companies."

The faint whir of electronics and the buzz of fluorescent bulbs fill the room. The soft flicker from the overhead lights highlights the sleek, minimalist conference table. Despite the sterile office environment, there's an undercurrent of tension in the air—Stewart's dismissive tone, Tyler's determination, and Jill's quiet attention.

Her hunch about him had been right.

Stewart sneers. "You won't get a robot to do Rachel's and Wei's jobs." He glances at the other two analysts with him.

Tyler persists. "We can use computing power to narrow the field. Use the quant techniques first then spend our time digging into the qualitative aspects of those companies that are most promising."

"Agreed," Jill says, continuing to watch him while ignoring Stewart. "Good work."

His enthusiasm to discover new paths reminds her of a younger version of Francis—a version she finds herself attracted to, but in a new and different way. She watches him with a mix of admiration and something else she doesn't want to name just yet. It unnerves her—how easily her thoughts drift from professional to personal. Tyler is someone she'll have to handle with care, not just for the company but for herself. He's also a bit on the young side, she thinks, and she feels her face warm.

Good heavens. What am I thinking?

There is also that company policy prohibiting relationships between employees. She's never been tempted to violate it before, but she knows some others have ignored it. And she knows how to be discreet.

Too soon, she cautions herself. *Patience.*

•   •   •   •   •

Back at her desk, Jill pulls up the website for the University of Baltimore's donation page and begins typing.

Amount: "Eighty thousand dollars." *Designation:* "Create Team for International Collegiate Programming Contest." *Donor Name:* "Anonymous." *In Memory of:* "Dr. Francis Stanard."

He'd like that, she thinks.

Tyler probably would, too. Her face warms again.

CHAPTER 23

"Wei, check this out," Tyler says, peering over his cubicle wall. He pushes aside a paper pumpkin dangling from a fishing line attached to a ceiling tile.

The young man on the other side of the divider holds up a finger and points to the phone he is holding to his ear.

Tyler runs a few more data queries, and five minutes later, Wei appears beside him.

"What is it?"

Tyler looks up. "I've been investigating the pharmaceutical industry."

"Right. You have pharmas, I've got insurance techs, Rachel has retirement facilities. What's up?"

"I created a beta version of a predictive model and used it to filter my list of companies to the eighteen best candidates. I'll investigate those one by one and select my best pick for the publication. But I saved a ton of time."

"Let me try it with the insurance techs," Wei says. "I've been grinding through them all week."

Tyler doesn't respond, too absorbed in his own work. "I started playing around with adapting the model to predict stock gains based on social media posts."

"Send it to me," Wei says.

Tyler points at his screen. "I found this company, Lexon Pharmaceuticals. They're way too small to be listed in *Beyond the Horizon*, but they look incredibly interesting."

Wei focuses on Tyler's monitor.

"They went public a year ago," Tyler says, "after running out of venture capital seed money. They needed funds to finish testing their big, new drug to halt kidney failure." He shuffles through his notes. "It's called Tabladol. I ran analytics on social media posts and found a lot of chatter. Success stories."

"Has the drug been approved?"

"They're expecting a decision in the next few weeks." Tyler hears the creak of Rachel's chair as she returns from lunch. He speaks louder to her over his other cubicle wall. "Can you come over?"

"Hold on," she calls. "I'm in a bit of trouble."

"What's wrong?"

"The UK's referendum to rejoin the EU passed. I nearly lost my lunch when I heard the news."

Tyler is silent, stunned.

"That's a surprise," Wei says.

Rachel walks over from her cubicle and joins them. "I was supposed to write an opinion paper on investment opportunities should Britain's citizens vote to rejoin the EU, but the polls said it wouldn't happen, and I never got around to it."

It wasn't supposed to happen, Tyler thinks. Yet it did. Just as Paul said it would.

"Come look at this," Wei says. "Then we'll both help you write that paper."

Tyler shakes away the intrusive thoughts of Paul's prediction swirling through his brain and shows his two coworkers some of the posts he's found about the kidney drug. They read them together.

Patricia in Des Moines stated:

"My kidney function was steadily declining. Down to 19 percent when I started taking Tabladol. My numbers immediately stopped dropping, and after a couple of weeks, increased. Right now, they're

functioning at 23 percent. My doctors say it's impossible for this to be happening, but it is!"

Rachel smirks. "People used to think it rained because they danced."

"Look at these stats," Tyler says. "I found 851 references, with a favorable to unfavorable ratio of 22:1. Ever seen a ratio like that?"

Wei slaps his back. "Barely two months in, and you might've found a whale."

Tyler wonders, has he really found a whale? He's heard a couple stories of previous analysts who had identified stock opportunities that resulted in gigantic windfalls for the company. They sounded like myths to Tyler, and the two analysts referenced in the tales are long gone. One founded and currently manages a hedge fund in Switzerland. The other is a senior VP at Goldman Sachs.

After an hour of intense research, Tyler and his coworkers crowd around Stewart's desk.

"There's another Tabladol reference," Rachel says, pointing at his monitor. "It's up to eighteen hundred reposts. It was at four hundred when I found it fifteen minutes ago."

"I think you're onto something," Stewart says.

"Tyler found it."

Stewart glances up at him then back at his screen. "What do you know about the company?"

Wei nods. He has further researched this angle of the project. "They're basically a one drug company. Founded three years ago by a PhD student at Columbia University, Ronnie Wang. He was experimenting with various drug cocktails to slow the progress of viruses that attack the kidneys. He dropped out of school and went to Silicon Valley. Lexon Pharmaceuticals was born."

Stewart rolls back quickly in his chair. Rachel has to dart to the side to avoid a collision.

"Something doesn't seem right," he says, looking away and staring out the window. Tyler follows his gaze and absentmindedly counts the rooftops of other buildings as he waits.

"Why is the company publicly traded?" Stewart finally asks. "Doesn't make sense since it's so small."

"The first year was a failure," Wei says. "The initial drug didn't work. Ronnie wasn't able to raise more venture capital, so he took the company public as a penny stock. There were enough speculative investors in the market to make the offering successful, and he was able to develop Tabladol. It appears the efficacy of this drug far surpasses the goals he'd set with the original one."

Stewart returns his attention to his screen and pulls up a site with live market quotes. "The stock is at $2.85. It's been slowly but steadily increasing over the past three weeks." He glances at the ceiling for a moment then looks back at them. "Let's take this to Jill. *Now.*"

They parade down the hall and climb the stairs leading up to the fifty-eighth floor. They duck under netting that resembles a giant spider web and stretches across the hallway, connecting two cubes. Halloween witches, ghouls, and goblins are perched on walls and tables, with others attached to strings dangling from the ceiling.

The decorations remind Tyler of Anna. *Will she be trick-or-treating on Saturday? Is she too old?* He wonders if she even feels like a kid anymore after everything she's been through. Another pang of guilt tugs at him for being so far away.

The crew of four marches into Jill's office, heads held high. She's on the phone and nods toward the four chairs surrounding her circular table.

"I need to go," she tells her caller. "An urgent issue has arisen." She hangs up and pushes her chair over to the table. The others scrunch together to make room.

"Who wants to fill me in?" Her voice is pleasant. She appears undisturbed by their sudden interruption.

Stewart straightens his spine and clears his throat. He's been a good listener, and he now regurgitates the information almost verbatim as Jill takes notes. He must have been a good test taker in school, Tyler thinks. Stewart never divulges that Tyler discovered the opportunity or acknowledges the work of Wei and Rachel. He just preens his feathers, and the others sit silent.

Jill taps her pen on the notepad lying on the wood veneer table surface. She reaches for the conference phone at the center of the table and dials a three-digit extension.

"Mateo," she says, "you're on speaker with my investment team. We've got a live one here. I need your trading group to pounce."

"What've you got?"

"Start accumulating Lexon Pharmaceuticals. The ticker is LXON. Really go after it … like you're a hoarder. Use all the channels you've got because it will pop once word gets out."

"What's the stop price?"

She studies her notes. "It's almost $3 a share now. Stop buying when it hits $15."

After she hangs up, Tyler speaks for the first time. "Don't you need to double-check or get additional validation?"

She smiles. "We identified an opportunity. We performed quick due diligence. Now we act. That's the way it works here."

·   ·   ·   ·   ·

The rest of the afternoon, Tyler, Rachel, and Wei track market activity for Lexon. The volume of shares being traded spikes, and the price rises, slowly at first then rapidly as other traders notice the unusual activity and jump on the bandwagon.

When the stock market opens the next morning, the three of them gather at Tyler's cubicle and watch his monitor as a hastily arranged press conference takes place. Lexon's CEO is responding to rumors by announcing the drug tests have been wildly successful and production is moving forward.

The price of Lexon's stock skyrockets after the announcement.

That afternoon, Stewart gathers his team in his office. He is unusually effusive, and he waves his arms emphatically as he speaks.

"We just engineered the biggest one-day gain in the history of New Horizon!"

Tyler leans against the wall next to the window. Maybe this score will get him on the investment team, he hopes … get him within sniffing distance of the investment algorithm.

"How much?" he asks.

Stewart glances at him then turns back to Rachel and Wei seated in the two guest chairs. "We accumulated almost two million shares—about ten percent of the company—before the price hit $15."

"Wow!" Wei says, grinning.

"We started selling shares when it got to $25, and we were completely out at $40 a share. The net profit is *forty-nine … million … dollars*! Holy crap. I can't believe it!"

Stewart looks completely off kilter now. It's funny what money can do to people, Tyler thinks. Stewart gives each of them an exuberant but awkward high five and announces, "Take the rest of the day off. Start your weekend early."

•   •   •   •   •

An hour later, Tyler pushes through the turnstile at his subway station and climbs the stairs to exit. As he steps onto 57th Street, the greasy scent of hot dogs from a nearby cart hits him, overpowering the crisp autumn air. His stomach growls, but he strides past without a glance—his apartment is only five minutes away.

He pulls out his phone as he strolls along, enjoying the tingling warmth of the midafternoon sun in the crisp autumn chill. While walking and flipping through his email, he stumbles over a fake Gucci bag, one of about twenty haphazardly displayed on the sidewalk.

"Watch it!" the street vendor yells.

Tyler does not react. The guy is simply hustling, trying to make a buck just like everyone else. Tyler knows he has the added pressure of living like a minuteman—always on edge, ready to pack up and split at a moment's notice if the cops appear.

When Tyler reaches 6th Avenue, he notices an email from Jill Young with the subject, *Celebration*. It's addressed to Rachel, Wei, and himself, with Stewart carbon-copied. He opens it.

Great job helping Stewart on the Lexon deal. Sorry to hear you won't be at happy hour to celebrate. If you change your mind, it's at The Dead Rabbit. Four p.m. till? We win with teamwork!

Tyler is only a block from his apartment, but he pivots and returns to the station, thinking about Lexon and then about Stewart. *What a jerk.* But then he reconsiders. Stewart's just another guy hustling, trying to get ahead—no different than the street vendor. It doesn't make him any less annoying, though.

Tyler redirects his focus to finding the best train to The Dead Rabbit Grocery and Grog. He has heard of the trendy bar on Water Street, but he's never been there.

At four-thirty, he reaches the bar and ascends two flights of stairs. One more flight to go, but the noise of the celebration already spills down the stairwell. Dozens of voices blend with the pulsing beat of a pop-inspired Celtic tune. A shout, a squeal, a burst of laughter—the sounds of hard-working people letting loose and celebrating a major win.

He reaches the third floor and joins in, the infectious energy washing over him. Music reverberates from the rafters spaced along the ceiling, bounces off the faux-wood tiled floor, and echoes back at him from the walnut panels lining the walls. The abundance of dark wood throughout the room creates a warm and comfortable atmosphere.

Tyler slides up to the bar and admires the glasses glistening in neat stacks against the mirror on the back wall. He orders a club soda with lime and turns to survey the room. Framed pictures on the walls provide a glimpse into the proprietors' previous existences in Belfast. Small pods of New Horizon employees around the room are chatting, eating, and drinking.

Tyler walks over and spends a few minutes talking with his coworker Rachel and her friends, all speaking loudly to be heard over the hubbub of music and competing voices. One woman—is her name

Denise?—seems more interested in what he has to say than the others, but he's having trouble following the conversation.

He glances repeatedly at a table where Jill is sitting, cornered by four men. He's tried more than once to reconnect with her since they first met to see if the spark he felt during the interview was mutual. And to get closer to the algorithm. All he has to show for his efforts so far is banal chitchat with her about running and one halfhearted commitment to go for a jog together … one of these days.

A man rises from Jill's table and strolls to the bar. Saying a quick goodbye to Denise, Tyler makes a beeline for the vacated chair.

Jill sees him approaching and waves. "Over here."

Tyler sits on the open chair between Stewart and one of the traders. Mateo and Jill are across the table, and platters of partially consumed nachos, wings, and cheese fries fill the surface of the beer-stained wood that separates them.

"What a day, my brother!" Stewart says to him, obviously sloshed. His breath is so thick, Tyler can taste the bourbon in the air just sitting next to him.

Stewart points at Tyler and exclaims to the others at the table, "This right here is a fine American."

Tyler ignores him and starts a conversation with the trader on his other side.

After a few minutes, Mateo departs, and Stewart slides around the table, claiming he has private information for Jill. Tyler grabs a handful of fries and continues to chat with the trader about the Lexon trades. It's the talk of Manhattan.

Across the table, Stewart whispers in Jill's ear and flings an arm around her shoulder.

"Jello shots!" a male voice shouts from the pack of people in front of the bar.

Tyler glances at the commotion then back at Jill. She takes advantage of the shouting to gently remove Stewart's arm and points toward the excitement.

"Go on, Stewart. Do a shot for me."

That's all the encouragement he needs.

The trader Tyler has been talking to decides he should join in as well, and he follows Stewart to the bar crowd.

Tyler smiles across the table at Jill. She stands, rounds the table, grabs his arm, and tugs it. "Let's go somewhere quiet," she says.

Making their way down a flight of stairs, they find a table tucked away on the mostly empty second floor. He orders drinks from the bartender—a glass of Chardonnay for her and another club soda for him.

They start off talking about food. She loves Italian, and he loves everything. Then they discuss hobbies. She is, indeed, an avid runner, just like him. And to Tyler's delight, they agree to meet the following morning for a run.

Soon, they're exploring each other's hopes and dreams. She has her sights set high, wants to make a positive difference in the world.

They talk enough for Tyler to determine that, yes, the electricity he'd felt was legit. It's surging through him again. He feels a calm connectedness with her, a natural comfort he's not felt with anyone else in the past decade, other than Anna. It both comforts and unsettles him as he remembers his mission.

Jill nods at his beverage. "My turn to get drinks. Gin and tonic?"

He lifts his glass. "Club soda. Without the gin but with a lime."

"Not a bad idea." Leaving her empty glass on the table, she makes her way to the bar.

"This is my last," she says after returning with fresh drinks. "You set a good example."

For a moment, he completely forgets the reason he's in New York and the task he faces. A flood of happiness sweeps through him. He has an urge to share something with her, a secret he has never said out loud, an embarrassment he's never talked about.

"My dad was an alcoholic."

Even hearing himself say the words brings instant relief from a burden he didn't realize carried so much weight.

She nods but glances down and picks at the napkin holding her silverware together.

"Sorry," he says. "Didn't mean to get too deep."

Jill wipes her eyes with her sleeve, which confuses him. *Is she that upset about my dad?* He looks at her face, and she meets his stare.

"That makes me think of my father. Something I try to avoid." She pauses. "He's a *work*aholic. And an ass. He divorced my mom when he grew tired of her. Evicted her … his words, when I was in seventh grade."

She slides her wine an inch to the left. "Mom worshipped him. Even after she couldn't stand him."

"My dad wrecked my family, too," Tyler says quietly.

"She died almost ten years ago." Jill glances over at the television mounted above the bar before continuing. "He crushed her spirit. Cancer finally killed her, but she was already dead." She shakes her head and makes a fist. "Won't ever happen to me."

A shiver runs through Tyler, and a dull ache settles in his chest as he looks away, searching for anything to distract him from the shared pain. His eyes land on the TV, which is showing a replay of the Jets game from the previous Sunday.

"Ever see your dad?" he asks.

She frowns. "He reconnected with me a few years ago. Gave me a present. More than that, a family heirloom." She peers into her glass. "I tried to forgive him."

She swirls her wine and watches it flow round and round in the crystal. Finally calmer again, she looks at him. "You said your dad '*was* an alcoholic.'"

Tyler nods. "He's dead. Killed my mom, too."

She pulls a tissue from her coat pocket and dabs her eyes.

"And my brother and several others." He glances down at the table. "We were on a church outing. Dad was driving, and he'd been drinking. Not unusual." Tyler nudges his drink forward and places his hands flat on the polished wood. "But that day, there was freezing rain. We went off the road and crashed into a flooded creek."

Jill reaches across the table and lays her palms over his hands. "You don't have to talk about it."

He takes a deep breath and looks at her. "I was thirteen. My little sister, Anna, and I are the only ones who escaped. She was a toddler."

Jill nods, and he sees compassion in the depths of her emerald eyes.

"The two of us were trapped in the back of the van as it sat nose down in the overflowing water. Somehow, I found a metal jack and managed to bust a hole in the back window. We barely got out in time."

She reaches farther up his wrists and squeezes them.

"The worst part was my mom's wailing from the front seat as she banged against the passenger door, trying to force it open. Of all the screams in the van, it's her voice I still hear, even after all these years. It reverberates in my mind, gives me chills every time."

Jill rounds the table and sits beside him. Her hand lingers on his back, steadying him.

"The water was ice cold and rose fast. The van became quiet. No more yells. No more screams. Nothing. Just Anna's wide eyes pleading with me to do *something*."

Tears run down his cheeks, and he lets them drip on the table.

"The whole thing was my fault."

Jill places both hands on his shoulders and turns him to face her. "You were thirteen. It was not your fault."

Tyler thinks about that. Nice of her to say. He wishes it were true.

"Do you know who Paul Thompson is?" he asks.

"*The* Paul Thompson?"

Tyler nods. "His son, William, was my best friend. He was with us in the van along with a few other kids from church."

She pulls him closer, her breath warm against his skin, providing comfort.

"I told Paul the truth afterward—that I knew my dad was drunk before we left the church. I didn't want to embarrass my mom by saying anything in the parking lot." He exhales loudly, his head lowering. "That's a mistake I'll never live down." His lower lip trembles. "Paul turned on us. He was supposed to be our guardian but refused once he found out. Who could blame him?"

Pulling away from Jill, Tyler takes a sip of his club soda. "Lawsuits from the families of the other kids drained my parents' estate." He brushes his fingers over the grains of salt scattered on the table then blows them into the air. The sight makes him think of their nest egg, how it had once seemed so solid but dissolved slowly under legal fees and settlements, like a sandcastle in a rising tide.

"It wasn't your fault," she says again.

He looks at her. Could she be right? *How amazing to be sitting with this woman who understands me so quickly,* he thinks, *who accepts me so completely.*

Who holds the secret code I will have to steal.

He flinches and drops his glass, which tumbles and spills water across the table. Jill grabs a pile of napkins and helps him clean up the mess.

He glances up again at the TV. The game is still on, a welcome distraction from the painful memories.

"Are you a football fan?" he asks.

"I like football." She nods toward the TV. "I love the Jets."

"Well, don't get too into this one." He leans forward and whispers, "They lose at the last second."

"I know. I saw it." She smiles. "Don't worry. It's just a game."

Just a game, he thinks wistfully. *Wouldn't that be nice? If all this were just a game.*

· · · · ·

Tyler climbs ten feet up Umpire Rock in Central Park to his favorite nook. The rock's firm surface is cold against his bare hands and the crisp dawn air bites at his skin. He watches his breath puff out in small clouds as he scans the horizon for Jill. It's less than a fifteen-minute stroll from his apartment and an oasis from the endless sea of concrete and glass, man-made wonders that comprise Midtown Manhattan.

Silence reigns this time of day, and the fall colors abound this time of year. A gust of wind makes its way through the trees, sending a curtain of leaves into flight. In just shorts and a long-sleeved running shirt, he shivers for a minute but then settles comfortably into the chair-shaped rock.

He hugs himself for warmth and watches for Jill through the fall leaves slowly dancing their way to the ground, a glorious display of cinnamon red, deep yellow, and sweet-potato orange.

He spots her as she passes across the playground. Yelling her name, he scrambles down the rock formation to meet her at the base. She looks cute—and very fit—in her black running tights and form-fitting jacket.

An awkward pause passes between them, their conversation waiting to begin until a crack appears in the thin layer of ice that has naturally formed after such an intimate exchange the previous evening.

Is she still feeling the connection? He knows he is. *Is this just a run … or our first official date?*

She takes off down the path, giggling as she leaves him standing still. He runs after her, determined to keep up.

Damn, she's fast.

He catches her after a hundred yards, his feet turning over at a roadrunner-like clip. She turns her head and looks back at him. "Pace too slow?"

Speak or breathe?

"It's fine," he lies and tries to suck in a breath.

"I'm taking it easy for a few weeks," she says. "Resting up before I start training for Boston."

"The marathon?" he asks.

"I qualified for it already."

"Congrat"—*breathe in*—"ulations."

Jill is laughing now, not a hint of strain in her voice. "You should learn to tell the truth," she says and slows considerably.

He is starting to catch his breath. "The only way I'd qualify is to get a fake ID that says I'm an eighty-six-year-old woman."

She punches his arm playfully. "Time and twenty-five grand can make that happen."

The soft pounding of feet on asphalt is audible from around the curve ahead. Two men and a woman emerge from the bend and pass by.

"What else do you do for fun?" she asks.

How to answer such a simple question? Worry about my sister. Worry about my future. Worry about whether I'll be able to steal the proprietary investment algorithm you worked so hard to develop and provide it to the ruthless CEO of your biggest competitor.

"Read. Work. Play cards on my phone. Poker mostly."

She glances at him. "I play in hold 'em tournaments several times a year."

He's surprised. He'd hardly figure her for a poker player.

"Usually charity events." She smiles. "I bet you're a good player."

"I used to think so."

They veer to the right onto a path that leads them into the heart of the preserve. Tall trees line both sides of the trail, their branches high above the ground and reaching across the path, as if to embrace them and form a canopy above, bursting with the vibrant hues of fall. The leaves underfoot, dead and brown, crunch beneath their steps, sending musty flecks into the air. One tree is already bare, beating its fellow hardwoods in the race to discard their flesh, a race that will soon leave twenty thousand wooden skeletons to face the harsh winter that will descend on the park.

What a beautiful setting. What a beautiful morning. Tyler's ever-present anxiety lessens its hold for a moment.

"I like you," he says.

She looks at him with a curious expression but then focuses on the path ahead. "I was afraid of that," she says and quickens her pace.

They run a few more minutes in silence and reach the end of their run back at Umpire Rock, both lathered in sweat. He leans forward to give her a light embrace, but she surprises him with a quick kiss on his lips.

Definitely our first date.

CHAPTER 24

Three weeks later, Tyler darts into Jill's empty office. She is currently in a meeting scheduled to last another hour, and her office door is wide open. The company's shared-calendar policy works in his favor, as does Jill's personal open-door policy.

He strides to the far side of her desk and reaches for the familiar protruding hook. But the key ring isn't there. His heart pounds as he stares at the empty spot, the hook taunting him.

The image of Jill pulling the keys from behind her desk during his interview flashes through his mind. He's double-checked their location twice since then—they're always here. But not today.

His breath quickens as his eyes sweep her desktop, searching. Footsteps echo outside. He freezes, then jerks his head up to see Stewart standing a few feet inside the doorway.

"Where's Jill?" Stewart asks.

Tyler's mouth goes dry. His eyes dart to the empty hook then back to his boss.

"In a meeting," he says, forcing a smile. "She printed some articles for me to review about the use of statistics in investing."

Stewart scowls, his skeptical gaze boring into Tyler. "I'm not aware of that."

"She asked me to fill you in," Tyler says, willing his voice to stay steady. "Said she knows you're busy and didn't want to bother you."

"Right. I am terribly busy. Don't have time for goose chases," Stewart says as he turns and leaves the office.

Tyler exhales, the tension releasing, but only for a moment. His mind races, and he scans Jill's desk again. No keys. He opens her desk drawers, one by one, his fingers trembling. The third drawer reveals the key ring.

A three-block walk, fifty dollars, and twenty-five minutes is all Tyler needs to possess a copy of her security fob. His hands are clammy when he slips into her office again and returns the keys to her drawer.

His stomach clenches. *What will I tell her if Stewart asks about my lie?*

The excitement of the theft and the fear of being caught temporarily trump the guilt that he knows will set in later.

He spends the rest of the afternoon and evening in his cube, bouncing from project to project, unable to focus. His nerves are still jittery, his thoughts scattered, until exhaustion finally drags him down. He falls asleep in his chair, his body positioned to appear as if he is engrossed in the stock chart displayed on his monitor.

"I'm all done." The night janitor's voice cuts through the fog of Tyler's half-sleep and wakes him. "I'll leave the walkway lighting on."

"Thanks, Carl." Tyler waves without turning around. "Adios."

It's all clear now, Tyler thinks, yet he doesn't move for a good ten minutes, wrestling with himself, hoping an alternative course of action will materialize from the turmoil of his thoughts.

He enjoys and appreciates Jill. They are kindred souls in many ways, and no one seems to know about their relationship. Conversation is easy and comfortable, whether they're dining at a restaurant or unwinding on her balcony after a long day at the office, soaking up the early evening bustle of the city below them.

They spend hours talking about investments and corporate finance, places they want to travel, people they want to help. Several times, she hints that the investment algorithm is a beginning to something much bigger. He can read the excitement in her demeanor, but when he tries to pry with a targeted question, she demurs and tells him the time is not right. Soon, she says.

She has no problem asking him detailed questions, though, and often inquires about his progress on enhancing the predictive model he developed to use for the analysts' picks. She wants to know how he's going about it and specifics regarding his approach to the programming code. He's happy to tell her.

But each time he does, the knot in his stomach grows tighter. It has become a familiar companion these days, twisting deeper as he is drawn further into Jill's orbit. Just when he becomes fully engrossed in this new world, a stray thought brings the realization crashing back into his consciousness that he eventually must double-cross her.

He finally heaves himself out of the chair and tiptoes up one flight of stairs, unsure if Carl has finished this floor as well. The northeast corner is dark, so he must have departed. Tyler passes the boardroom and stops in front of the executive records room. He presses his ill-gotten possession against the electronic reader. The red light turns green, and the lock disengages. He is in.

With the aid of a pen-size flashlight, he completes a quick inventory of the space. Twenty-two file cabinets are crammed into the twelve-by-eight-foot room, with one table—the size you would play cards on, he thinks—positioned in the center. He devises a plan to make the most efficient use of the six hours he has available. Most likely, no one will be in the office before five the next morning, but he wants to be out by four to provide himself a cushion.

Starting with the nearest metal cabinet, he opens the top drawer and flips through the manila folders. They're all neatly labeled. He quickly eliminates most of them from consideration. Whenever he finds one with potential, he slides it out and scans through the first two or three documents.

It takes half an hour to finish reviewing the first cabinet. He finds the minutes from the Investment Advisory Team meetings and many logs of stock transactions. But nothing useful.

Maybe you all could shred things once in a while. Sure would help a thief like me.

He is a third of the way through the second cabinet when the lights in the hallway illuminate. He slams shut the drawer he's working on, cringing when it clangs into place, and searches for a place to hide. Two of the file cabinets are pulled away from the wall. He climbs over and drops behind them. Warm air from a vent blows against his legs.

The door opens. He hears the click of a switch being pressed, and bright light fills the room. His breathing sounds so loud. Too loud.

"I'm sure it's good." It's Jill's voice. "We can present the enhancements to the board as planned."

"I don't understand how the algorithm works like you do," a second voice says. A man's voice. Maybe the COO's. "But I do know we'll need to run extensive due diligence tests."

"Agreed," Jill says. "I know they're concerned about the anomaly we found. We must demonstrate conclusively what I already know— that it's fixed."

Tyler hears a scraping sound then a light clicking noise. He lines his eye up with the crack between the two cabinets and peers through. It *is* the COO, James Nelson. He's on his knees under the table. A panel sits on the floor beside him. Tyler watches as he opens the top of a floor safe and removes a gray metal case. He stands and sets it on the table.

Jill presses her thumb on one corner of it for several seconds and then opens it. James watches her as she places a file into the metal case.

"Do you think it's really necessary to store a physical copy of the code?" he asks.

She smiles and nods yes. "We have state-of-the-art backup, but technology is only great until it's not. If anything were to happen to the secure server, all my work would be gone. This hard copy would be the only way to recreate the algorithm."

"Got it." James is back on his knees, replacing the case and securing the safe.

After they vacate the room, Tyler climbs over the cabinets and stares at the floor panel housing the safe that holds what he desperately needs. He'll need to research floor safes and come back another time to try to get in. There's no point in sticking around now, so he carefully makes his way to the stairs and quietly leaves the building.

CHAPTER 25

Tyler stares out his office window at the particularly gray morning, feeling dull. Commuters bundled in London Fog overcoats scurry from the frigid air outside to the warmth of their offices. He glances at his desk and sighs at the long list of companies he's assigned to research. *Such a waste of time.* The model he developed is working fine. He, Rachel, and Wei regularly sift through the results and identify companies to recommend to Stewart. But Tyler knows he needs to find another Lexon—something that will help propel him forward, get him noticed to a point where he can get closer to Jill's investment algorithm.

Any pretense he harbored about being a genius stock picker has long since been replaced with the realization he had just been lucky. Lottery winner lucky. He has reviewed hundreds of companies since his earlier success, futilely searching for a needle in the stock market haystack that likely isn't even there.

While he's busy trying to accomplish the impossible, the New Horizon investment algorithm continues to chug along, steadily producing above-average returns through the ups, downs, and curves of the market. He needs to get inside the engine, to understand how it works. So far, though, he can only observe from the fringe.

His phone dings. The high-pitched tone indicates it's a text from Jill.

Hey – r u there?

Oh, good, he thinks, a break from the monotony. He types a response.

Yes.

I hope she's not about to cancel our dinner plans. His phone dings again.

Come to the boardroom.

The message seems ominous, and his eyes widen. *Uh-oh.*

Donning his sport coat, he makes his way to the room he hasn't visited since the tour during his initial interview. His brain churns out a list of plausible explanations for the questions he might face.

Why did you try to access the secure investing drive eighteen times over the past three weeks? Why do you have a copy of Jill's security fob? Why are there videos of you sneaking around late at night? Why, why, why?

Getting fired would be the equivalent of a death sentence but without the benefit of an appeal. There would be no way to string out the process to give him time to clear things up.

And he would lose Jill forever, which seems inevitable anyway.

He tries to ignore those thoughts, but the realization of what he's doing pops into his head at the worst times—*like right now*—and renders him useless until he can reengage in the moment. After spending a Saturday with Jill two weeks ago, he woke the next morning with sore abdominal muscles because they'd been so tightly clenched while he was with her.

The boardroom door is closed. He knocks twice then slowly opens it.

The CEO is standing at the opposite end of the board table, using a laser pointer to show the movement of a line along a graph on a large screen. It looks like New Horizon's rising stock price over the past year.

The man turns his head then his entire body toward the door. "I'm Sebastian Shultz. Thank you for joining us."

Tyler feels a prickling sensation at the back of his neck.

"This is our esteemed board of directors." Mr. Shultz sweeps the air with an open palm, framing a distinguished-looking panel of eight seasoned executives—five women and three men—sitting around the table. Jill sits slightly apart from the others, next to the spot where the plane crash created the hole over seventy years ago. Tyler wishes it were still there so he could escape through it if needed.

Everyone looks serious, and he counts four frowns. Jill's eyes are moist and reddish.

"Sit down, please," Mr. Shultz says.

Tyler moves to the nearest available chair, which is at the head of the long table, directly opposite the CEO.

"We have a serious matter to discuss." Mr. Shultz has a deep voice with a slight rattle.

The room is focused on Tyler, the owl eyes peering into his soul, attempting to read the treacherous thoughts he is trying so hard to hide.

"One of our core values at New Horizon is honesty."

Oh, boy.

"It has come to our attention that this important tenet has recently been violated."

Here it comes.

Tyler wants to confess so badly, he can feel everything about to come out like a rain cloud so full of moisture, it has no choice but to burst. He wants to explain his impossible situation, that he genuinely cares about New Horizon—particularly its CFO—and that he will quit immediately, go home, and beg for Mike Hayward's mercy.

He starts to open his mouth, but Mr. Shultz waves him off.

"Let me finish, please. It has come to our attention that Mr. Stewart Beechum was not truthful in his report to the board regarding the Lexon Pharmaceuticals transaction."

Tyler sinks into his chair, chilled and shaking. His fight-or-flight adrenaline response dissipates as quickly as it arrived, but he's a quivering mess.

"I know," Mr. Shultz says in response to Tyler's visible reaction. "We are all deeply disturbed by his actions."

Tyler is quite thrilled with Stewart's actions. He nods, still looking somber, but inside, he is alive again. His sphere of awareness expands, and he scans the room. He notices the branches of holly adorning the windows and the wreaths on the walls.

The fragrance of freshly cut pine reminds him of Christmases at his childhood home, before the tragedy. He can hear his mother's laughter and Anna's squeals of delight when a pile of dough and an angel cookie cutter were plopped down on the tray of her high chair. The result was a collection of the ugliest—and most beautiful—cookie angels ever to visit Earth. He would give anything to be back there, when life seemed so simple and secure.

He sees Jill wipe her eyes with the back of her hand, quickly and unobtrusively.

Why is she so emotional? She's not a big Stewart fan.

Mr. Shultz walks around the table and stops in front of Tyler.

"However, we were greatly pleased to learn that the key person responsible for this tremendous success did exhibit another of our core values—humility—to a level that is difficult to believe." He pauses, a faint smile tugging at his lips. "Mr. Rush, it has been made clear to us that *you* are the reason we achieved a one-day profit that dwarfs any other day in our history, that *you* are the reason we harpooned the whale of all whales, and that *you* are the reason our stock price increased twenty percent and has held that gain."

Applause breaks out, and Shultz reaches for Tyler's hand.

At the other end of the table, a tall, solid man with a full head of bushy gray hair stands. Two more people stand. Then everyone is standing. And still clapping. Ten faces beaming with delight that the value of their stock options is soaring into the stratosphere. It will be a very Merry Christmas for each of the board members in the room.

Next Christmas won't be, Tyler thinks, not if he succeeds in his mission. He forces a smile but can't look a single one of them in the eye.

"Stewart Beechum's employment has been terminated, effective today." Mr. Shultz waves to Jill, inviting her forward. As she rises, an oval locket on a silver chain falls out from her blouse. She tucks it back under and addresses the room.

"Tyler, you've been promoted to the position of Manager of Investing, reporting to me. This is effective immediately. I'll meet with you later to discuss salary, benefits, and the team that reports to you."

His smile widens as Jill wipes her eyes again and smiles back. Only then does he realize he had misread her tears—they weren't of sorrow but joy.

I work for someone. I do well. They get fired. I take their job. Seems to be a pattern here. Are you sure you want this black widow reporting to you?

"You deserve it," Mr. Shultz says, misinterpreting his reaction.

Jill continues, "You'll also be on the Investment Advisory Team, along with me, Mateo Garcia, James Nelson, and Mr. Shultz. We provide a report to the board each quarter on our investment strategy and its execution."

Finally! The holy grail.

He knows what the Investment Advisory Team is. From his sleuthing, he probably knows more about it than she does, and she chairs it. He's not been able to get within sniffing distance of the algorithm, but that will surely change now.

He glances away, not able to face Jill. She's giving him a life preserver, and he's going to drown her with it so he can save himself.

He stands, as that seems to be the thing to do when speaking in this room.

"I'm truly honored by the recognition," he says, but he still can't look anyone in the eye.

"There's one more thing," Mr. Shultz says after returning to his chair. "Our Chair of the Board, Barron Kensington, would like to address you."

The fit, older man—the one who had started the standing ovation—pushes himself from his leather throne and walks over to Tyler, thrusting out his hand.

"On behalf of New Horizon's Board of Directors, I congratulate you." He keeps pumping Tyler's hand, encasing it with both of his. "In recognition of your contribution to this historic achievement, you are hereby awarded a finder's bonus of five percent of the profit generated from the Lexon Pharmaceuticals deal."

Tyler's mind spins. He's having trouble with the calculation that would normally occur automatically.

Kensington hands him an envelope, and a wide smile lights up his face. "Enclosed is a check for 2.5 million dollars."

Tyler takes it and falls into his seat, dizzy.

One by one, each person shakes his hand as they file into the adjoining executive break room. Jill invites him to join them for coffee and pastries, but he excuses himself and leaves. Holding a check with so many zeros makes him uneasy. He'll go straight to his bank. Mobile deposit doesn't seem like a good idea in this case.

On the elevator, somewhere around the thirtieth floor, a solution to his impossible dilemma occurs to him—he sees a way out of this mess. The original bet was for a million dollars. Mike changed it because he had no chance of scraping together that kind of money within six months.

Well, now he has it.

Hell, I'd pay the whole two and a half to end this nightmare and get on with my life. I'll need to work out how to be with Anna in Baltimore and Jill in New York, but that will be like solving a children's puzzle after the terrible jigsaw I've been struggling with.

The stress that's been building steadily over the past five months—really, over the last ten years—disappears all at once, and his vision blurs. He can't read the floor indicator as it decreases toward ground level. If he closes one eye and really focuses, his splotchy vision dissipates enough for him to make out the numbers … eight, seven.

An ache starts in the back of his head and grows like the nuclear cloud from an atomic bomb. *I don't need this right now.*

At the bank, Tyler isn't able to enjoy the fuss made over him. When he presents his check to the teller, she calls the manager. The manager calls the large account specialist. The large account specialist calls the branch vice president.

There is talk of growth opportunities, investments, protection of the principal, blah, blah, blah. His head is still exploding.

"Are you okay?"

He isn't sure who asks the question.

"Do you have any Advil? I'm getting a migraine. A bad one."

Someone hands him a bottle of water and two pills, which he quickly swallows, grateful the nausea hasn't set in yet. Closing his eyes, he searches for relief from the outer bands of the pain, but he fears the storm that will soon rage in his head.

A limo whisks him away and drops him at his apartment doorstep. On the way, he manages to send a misspelled text to Jill, letting her know he has a massive headache and will call her later.

By three, the hurricane has finally left his head. He's a little groggy as his body works to repair the damage to his brain, and he knows he'll feel a little off until he has a good night's sleep. By four, he's well enough to text Jill that he'll still meet her for their seven o'clock reservation that evening at Joseph's, their favorite Italian restaurant in Lower Manhattan.

Venturing from his third-floor flat, Tyler's full of something that has been absent from his life for a while—real, genuine hope. The sun has fought its way through the thick, marshmallow clouds, bringing a cheer to the chilly air. The world is brighter, more vibrant than it was only a few days earlier.

Christmas tunes blare from speakers mounted above the open doors of a souvenir shop, inviting tourists to pop in and purchase memories of the city. He stops for a minute to listen.

A block farther down 56th Street, the ringing of a Salvation Army bell welcomes him outside his favorite coffee shop. He fishes a twenty from his wallet and drops it into the bucket.

"God bless you," the uniformed woman says.

With a nod, Tyler enters Café Francoeur. Though hungry, he's not ready for food just yet, so he settles for a hot chocolate and takes a seat on a stool at the long counter, facing the road. The steaming, sugary drink courses through his body, a beautiful feeling.

Snowflakes begin to fall, slowly decorating the landscape. With an hour to spare before he needs to start his trip back to the financial district, he considers getting Jill a present—something personal but not too extravagant. Maybe perfume. Or better yet, a pair of earrings. There's a jewelry store nearby. Silver earrings to match her locket … with inlaid emeralds to match her eyes. Yes, he'll get her something nice, the kind of present a millionaire would give to his lady friend.

He laughs at himself.

Finally dragging himself from the cozy cafe, he finds that it's snowing heavily. Bare tree branches reach out to catch the falling flakes as if looking for something to cover their nakedness. The fluffy, white powder contrasts nicely with the deep-brown bark. Tyler shivers as the sun begins its early winter descent, bringing darkness and real cold.

As he walks to the jewelry store, he thumbs a message to Mike.

I'll be in town in two weeks. Can you meet on 12/24? I've got a Christmas present for you … something personal and quite extravagant.

CHAPTER 26

At three p.m. on Christmas Eve, Anna flings open the front door to Baltimore Penn Station, runs up to Tyler, and jumps into his arms. He lets go of the suitcase he's wheeling—but not the briefcase in his other hand—and catches her with one arm before stumbling backward.

"Guess what part I got in the Christmas program?" she asks, eyes sparkling with excitement.

He sets her down and retrieves his bag, nodding an apology to several other arriving passengers who are forced to veer around them.

"A donkey?" he teases.

"Shut up." She punches him playfully on the arm. "I'm going to be Mary."

"That's terrific. Fair to say you like your church?"

She nods. "The special service starts at six o'clock, and our program is right afterward. And then refreshments!"

"Sounds perfect." And it does. "What's the name of your church again? Our Lady of Perpetual Hope?"

She rolls her eyes. "I've told you that like a hundred times, dopey."

Tyler chuckles. He's looking forward to the service, and not just to watch her perform. Almost every Sunday morning for the first thirteen years of his life, he sat in the fourth pew from the altar at St. Paul's in Baltimore, less than a mile from his family's waterfront condo. He was always freshly scrubbed, wearing pants that were a little too tight and a white shirt with a pressed collar that made his neck itch.

After his family was killed, Tyler was angry at God and gave up on religion. Plus, Virginia and Marco would've ridiculed him—even more than usual—if he suggested they go to church. As Anna talks, though, a tug in his heart brings back memories of being in Christmas programs of his own, when the world still felt right.

They exit the station, and he spots the black Escalade parked by the curb. The temperature is pleasant for late December, probably in the low fifties, and Paul waves at them from the open window of the driver's door. The liftgate pops open, and Tyler deposits his larger bag in the back of the SUV then gets in the front seat. He swings his arm to create momentum to hoist the briefcase while Anna slides in back.

"There are going to be like five hundred people there. I'm so nervous." Anna pushes hard on the back of Tyler's headrest. "And excited!"

"You've been practicing a ton," Paul says from the driver's seat. "You'll do a great job." He pulls the vehicle into the circular drive that exits the station.

"Such a waste of money," Paul mutters, looking at the Male/Female statue that stands fifty feet tall in the middle of the roundabout. He shakes his head. "They could've planted a tree. Instead, in their infinite wisdom, they decide to spend almost a million dollars to erect two giant, aluminum cutouts of a man and woman intersected together, and call it art."

Tyler glances at his sister. She's grinning. Paul had expressed the same sentiment—in almost the same exact words—when they'd picked Tyler up for his Thanksgiving visit. The statue does clash with the classic architecture of the train station, but Tyler still kind of likes it.

Twenty minutes later, they arrive at the Thompsons' two-story, gray, wood-frame home in suburban Ellicott City. Their yard, like quite a few they've passed entering the neighborhood, is decorated with twinkling net lights draped over the bushes and more bulbs strung across the roofline.

"Can we drive around and look at Christmas lights tonight after the service?" Anna smiles and tilts her head in the cute way that usually results in her getting what she's after. "Please, please, please."

"Let's check with Melinda. She's been working hard to prepare a nice dinner." Paul peeks at Anna in the rearview mirror and sees her face has melted into a mock frown. "But if not right after church then certainly after we eat."

"Can we take Daisy, too?"

"Sure. She may not be a puppy anymore, but she still likes to get out."

A large wreath with a big red bow welcomes them at the front door. So does Melinda, a handsome woman in her early fifties, dressed in an apron adorned with reindeer pulling a sleigh. Daisy appears and pushes her way through Melinda's legs, her tail wagging so hard that her entire body jiggles.

"Hi, Mom." Anna hugs Melinda then leans over and rubs Daisy's face.

Mom? Tyler is startled but smiles.

"Come on, Tyler. You have to see my room. It's totally more awesome than last time you were here." She scampers down the hallway with Daisy ambling after her.

"I've been summoned," Tyler says. He sets his bags down in the foyer and follows the parade.

Later that afternoon, while Anna is getting dressed to be Mary and Melinda is cooking, Tyler joins Paul in the study and closes the door. He sits on the sofa, leans back, and smiles.

"Anna tells me she's co-captain of the eighth-grade basketball team."

Paul swivels in his chair to face him. "She's come a long way, even since Thanksgiving." His pleasant demeanor then dissolves into concern. "But she's having nightmares."

Tyler leans forward, frowning.

"I wasn't too worried at first," Paul says. "She's been through a lot."

"What are they about?"

"Being chased, mostly."

"Is she worried about Marco?" Tyler asks.

"Probably," Paul says. "He pleaded guilty. Five years. He'll probably serve two, which is a gift considering what he did."

Tyler stomps his foot. "Two years? That's crap!"

"He does have an additional punishment. According to his lawyer, the patch over his left eye will be permanent."

"Does Anna know he'll be gone for a while?"

"I told her last week." Paul looks down. "But the nightmares haven't stopped."

"Maybe she needs to see a professional."

Paul shifts in his chair. "There's something else."

"What is it?"

"She thinks someone's watching her."

Tyler falls back in the chair, crushed by an overwhelming weight on his chest. The door to the study shifts slightly. "Anna," Tyler calls. "Is that you?"

The door opens, and she slides into the room, tossing her phone up and catching it.

"I've told you before not to eavesdrop," he says.

"I was coming to tell you it's time to go. I don't want to be late."

The two men rise. As they leave the room, Anna turns to Tyler. "Did you bring a picture of Jill for my corkboard?"

He retrieves a photo from the inside pocket of his jacket, a nice picture of him and Jill in front of the Statue of Liberty, imitating Lady Liberty's pose. Jill had humored him by agreeing to be a tour guide for a day and show him the sights that everyone new to the city wants to see.

Paul glances at the picture, frowning.

Anna holds the photo in her hands and studies it. "She is so pretty. And you make a great couple." She looks up at him. "When can I meet her?"

"How about your birthday weekend? That's less than two months away."

"Yay!" she says and skips away, down the hall to her room. "I'll meet you at the car," she yells back.

Paul shakes his head and speaks softly.

"What are you thinking, son, pursuing her? Are you insane?"

•   •   •   •   •

Late that night, Tyler wonders what he's doing riding the elevator to the forty-first floor of the Mid-Atlantic building. Children everywhere are sleeping, he thinks, while Santa is busy traversing the world, squeezing down through chimneys when there is one, and improvising when there isn't. *And here I am, clutching my briefcase and going up, not down, a tall, metal shaft.*

The Escalade he borrowed—without explaining exactly why—is parked in the underground garage. Other than asking how things are going, Paul has not regularly pestered Tyler about the bet. Their conversations have generally centered on Anna.

Tyler walks down the long hall and enters "ground zero" for the first time since he stumbled out of it over four months earlier. He transfers the oversized briefcase to his left hand to relieve the cramp forming in his right.

"You have the information?" Mike asks him. He's sitting in the same chair he was in when the big bet unfolded. It appears to Tyler he's even wearing the same suit and tie.

Nice. The jerk has flair.

Tyler marches across the ebony floor in his jeans and gray hoodie, the light tapping of his Nikes echoing in the empty space. He passes the first poker table and approaches the second, where Mike is seated.

Several highball glasses dot the green felt, each filled to varying levels with a mixture of half-melted ice and leftover booze. An empty beer bottle rests in a drink holder. No cards or chips are visible. It's quiet. Surreal.

Tyler feels a twinge in his lower back as he leans forward to place the briefcase on the table. His outstretched arms support the heavy load while he faces the handle toward his adversary.

A loud click breaks the silence as Mike unfastens the clasps and pulls open the lid. He peers at the contents, glances at Tyler with wide eyes, then looks down again.

Neat stacks of hundred-dollar bills fill the case. Ten thousand of them.

"How did you get a million dollars?" he asks. Obviously, Mike has seen large piles of cash before.

"I'm pretty resourceful."

Mike grimaces then glares at him. "You told someone about the bet. That's how you got the money."

Tyler sits but leaves an empty chair between them. "I'm not stupid. Foolish at times but not stupid."

"I was expecting to see the investing algorithm. I wasn't sure why the briefcase was so large, but I thought with your *resourcefulness*, you might have brought a load of documentation."

"The original bet was a million dollars." Tyler pauses but Mike does not react. "The alternate agreement was made because no one believed I could deliver the money. But I did. So we're even."

Mike abruptly stands and paces, first away from the table then back.

"I appreciate your ability to achieve the improbable. I really do. But I don't want a million dollars." His eyes narrow, and his lips curl apart, revealing snarling teeth. He's furious. "I want the algorithm. And that was the bet. *That's* what you owe me."

"This is an equal value. Everyone agreed. Take it. Better than ending up with nothing."

Mike shakes his head no. "You're wrong on that one, Tyler. The algorithm is much more valuable than you realize, much more powerful than almost anyone understands. You need to focus on getting it. And stop playing silly games."

He walks over and sits down beside Tyler. "Let me tell you a story, young man, and I recommend you listen closely."

Tyler inches his chair back.

"Once upon a time, a man was cheating on his wife with a mistress, a well-known actress. He lost a bet that required him to end the affair. Several months went by, and he was still seeing her. He was warned to stop and reminded that he had six months to comply with the results of the bet."

Mike's phone erupts, ringing and vibrating on the card table. He silences it.

"Six months passed, and it appeared the man had finally ended the affair. Only he hadn't. Pictures surfaced a month later. What do you think happened to this man?"

Tyler shrugs, trying to look uninterested, but inside, he churns with curiosity. *What did happen to this man who ignored the rules?* He leans forward.

"He was shot in the head." Mike lets the words penetrate Tyler's defenses, his face contorting into a sneer. "Do you understand how serious this game is? Do you understand you do not renege on your bets?"

Maybe the story is made up, Tyler thinks. "Who is this mystery man?"

Mike shakes his head and laughs. "John F. Kennedy. Heard of *him*?"

Tyler falls back in his chair as though a bullet has hit him. He thinks about Mike's words. He thinks about bin Laden. He thinks about the internet letter again. This time, he also thinks about the fate of its author, Brett Sommerfield.

Gas leak. Right.

"Go, Tyler. Fulfill your agreement. The elevator will be waiting for you. I hope it's a smooth ride."

Mike stands and saunters toward the far wall, leaving the briefcase untouched. He disappears through the door that leads down to his office.

Tyler picks up the case full of money and goes out the other door.

•　　•　　•　　•　　•

Mike wanders down the stairs to his office and pours himself a small glass of aged Scotch. He scans the vista of his sleeping metropolis. The pattern of lights before him is as breathtaking as the Milky Way, and the darkness of the night hides the less desirable aspects of his universe.

He makes a toast to his empire and lets a sip of the expensive nectar glide down his throat.

Meandering over to his desk, he notices the flag on his monitor. An email awaits his attention on the secure server. It's from Dr. Chakra.

Mr. Hayward,

I am pleased to advise that our network now exceeds ten million computers. We expect to achieve your target of fifteen million within the next two to three months.

While progress remains slow on developing the code, I have good news to report. Dr. Morris from Sydney and Dr. Gupta from Mumbai have joined our team. They are brilliant neuroscientists and are most excited about our project. Both were carefully recruited and are secure.

Mike nods, satisfied that his lead scientist knows how to hire the right talent. He continues reading.

I would be remiss if I did not report that I have learned the destination of Dr. Conti. After leaving our team, he did, indeed, move to Râmnicu Vâlcea. He was hired by the Popa clan. We have since lost two assistants to them as well.

I will keep you informed of future progress.

With deepest respect,

Deepak

Not good news, Mike knows. The Popa clan is the largest in the Romanian mafia. Anton Popa is a shrewd businessperson who has created a fortune by leveraging his country's history of mathematical and programming talent to build a lucrative cybercrime syndicate, specializing in ransomware.

Could he have gotten wind that the Einstein Code is an achievable endeavor? Why else would he hire a neuroscientist?

Mike tenses. He wants to take immediate action to propel his project forward, but there's no one to yell at, no one to cajole, no one to inspire on this very early Christmas morning.

Anton isn't sitting still—that much is clear. Anton's resources are also vastly greater than Mike's and will allow the Romanian to quickly make up the ground that separates them. And being first is all that matters, all that is needed to take control of the world's flow of information. Future attempts will be strangled, deprived of the data oxygen needed to feed a new breed of intelligent computers.

Have my hopes really boiled down to the exploits of a twenty-three-year-old analyst? Tyler needs to deliver. Or else it will come down to my last option.

That thought creates a twinge of guilt, but Mike quickly pushes it away.

CHAPTER 27

"How's the new girl working out?" Jill asks, sitting behind her desk with the office door uncharacteristically closed.

Tyler glances at her. She's been acting strange ever since Nicole joined his team after New Year's.

"She's doing well," he says.

"You do remember she graduated from Yale?" Jill flashes a smile. "For a minute there, I thought you might say something nice about an Ivy Leaguer."

Tyler shrugs and moves to the window. The waters of the New York Harbor glimmer in the mid-January sunlight. A beautiful view, but it does nothing to improve his mood.

He's returned to the executive records room four times, but the steel lock of the Hamilton floor safe has proven impenetrable. His fingers are within inches of the code, and yet it remains untouchable. Frustrating isn't even the word.

"What's wrong?" Jill asks.

He keeps staring at the harbor.

"You've been preoccupied lately," she says.

Yes, I have. Anna's nightmares haven't stopped. Her paranoia is getting worse. She's convinced someone is following her, watching her at basketball practice, trying to hack her social media accounts.

Jill steps closer, lowering her voice. "It's not just the algorithm or Anna, is it? You've been distant, and I can feel it—you're hiding something."

Tyler swallows hard. "It's just been a lot, Jill. Everything with Anna, work … it's overwhelming."

"Look at me," Jill says firmly.

He glances in her direction then quickly drops his stare to her desk. It's too difficult to look her in the eye. He's lost ten pounds, and he can't sleep more than a few hours before waking up in a panic. His entire world has shrunk to one thing—figuring out how to steal what she has dedicated her life to creating.

His ear twitches—another sign of his stress along with constant guilt.

"I know what you're up to." Her voice cuts through his thoughts.

He freezes, looking straight down at his shoes. His heart pounds, and the pressure of her eyes is like a laser on his head. This is it—the moment he's dreaded.

"You're seeing her, aren't you?"

He's caught so off guard that he laughs. "Nicole?"

Jill's voice sharpens. "You think it's funny?"

Now he can look her in the eye. "There are only two women in my life—you and Anna. That's the truth." He inhales slowly, steadying himself. "I'm worried about Anna."

She watches him silently. "There's more to it," she presses.

"I'm fine," he replies, too loudly.

"It's okay to talk to me. You can tell me anything. You should tell me." She stands and walks toward him. "I can't help if you don't."

Should I tell her? The whole truth?

"I'd like to work on the algorithm," he says instead, unable to confess the truth.

"That's what's bothering you?" She looks annoyed.

"I've been on the Investment Advisory Team for a month, and it's all concepts, guidelines, and reviewing trades. I haven't contributed anything," he says, clasping his hands together.

She sighs. "It's not a choice. Our Enterprise Risk Management Plan requires that anyone—even the CEO—be an employee for at least six months before seeing any algorithm details."

"But I thought it was your algorithm?"

She places her hands on his shoulders and rests her forehead against his. His anxiety dissipates instantly at her touch. "It is, but there are still licensing agreements in place with terms I must honor."

He smiles. "You can show me at your condo. When we're breaking those other company rules."

"I can't break this one," she says.

"I know I could help improve the algorithm."

"And I can't wait to show it to you. All of it."

He pulls back, raising an eyebrow.

"Certain sections are off-limits to everyone except a select few," she says. "And by a select few, I mean you're looking at her." She squeezes his arm. "I need someone to collaborate with, and you will be that person. Soon."

Tyler's frustration bubbles up. She wants to show him the algorithm, and he desperately needs to see it. "Forget that stupid six-month policy," he says, hearing the desperation in his voice.

She takes his hands and massages his palms with her thumbs. "It's out of your control. Be patient. Give it time."

The one thing I don't have. Her touch, normally soothing, is now a reminder of everything he's hiding. His heart races, not from her gentle contact but from the stress born of his lies.

"Besides," she says playfully, "that six-month policy is there for a reason—I have to make sure you're not a spy."

Her unintentional jab hits him hard, the word "spy" echoing in his head. He pulls away and turns toward the window, catching his reflection in the glass. At first, it's just a distorted image—his nose more prominent, his hair uncharacteristically wavy, almost curly—but then it solidifies into something darker, more familiar. The shadows under his eyes, the furrow in his brow, they all remind him of someone he's read about—Benedict Arnold, the infamous traitor who sold out his allies for personal gain.

In this moment, Tyler feels the full weight of his duplicity in every aspect of his life. The deceit with Jill burns the deepest—pretending to be the loving boyfriend while secretly plotting against her life's work. Then there are the half-truths he's told Anna, meant to protect her but also to shield himself, the lies that misrepresent him in the office, and the secrets he's kept from Greg.

He's not just betraying one person—he's betraying everyone around him. His colleagues, his family, the woman he loves. Every choice he makes feeds the traitor growing inside of him, a traitor staring back at him now, reflected in the glass.

Tyler looks away, sickened, unable to face the stranger he has become.

Jill misreads his reaction. "You can't wait six weeks?" There's an edge in her voice. "Give me a break. Go mope somewhere else." She walks back to her chair, clearly annoyed. "You act like it's life or death."

·　　·　　·　　·　　·

Back in his office, Tyler flips between financial news stations on the flat screen, stewing over the dead-end he's hit. Nicole interrupts his thoughts, her face fresh and full of enthusiasm.

Lucky for her she still has hope and ambition. How long will it take for her to become institutionalized ... for her ideals to be drained like lifeblood from a wounded animal?

He gives it two years on the outside.

"I'm ready for another project," she says.

Of course you are. How about you create an investment algorithm for me? The sarcastic thought lingers for a second before sparking an idea. There's more than one way to get what he needs. He is suddenly energized.

"I've got something in mind. Please get Wei and Rachel."

He prints a list of trades generated by the investment algorithm over the past three years. At least he has access to that. Tyler realizes he can reverse-engineer the process. By adapting the predictive model he's developed, he can replicate the trades made by the algorithm. He'll need a copycat version convincing enough to deceive Mike, even if only for a few weeks. That will buy him the time he needs to satisfy Jill's six-month rule, after which he can access and deliver the genuine algorithm.

When his team assembles in his office, he begins. "Our predictive model is working well, but I want to take it up a notch. I want it to make specific stock recommendations for *Beyond the Horizon*, not just narrow the field. That would completely remove the manual work we still do."

"Amen," Wei says.

Tyler continues, "We'll reprogram our model using the additional data we've been collecting manually and also feed it the final stocks we've selected."

Wei frowns. "A lot of that data is subjective information we gather through research, not numbers we can input directly."

Nicole has been thinking quietly and now addresses the group. "We'll create a system to convert that information into data. I can lead that part."

Rachel nods. "Props to Nicky."

"There's one more angle," Tyler says, pushing a stack of papers toward them. "These are the trades that Jill's investment algorithm has made over the past few years, including dates purchased and dates sold. We're not trying to recreate it." He pauses, searching for the right words since that's exactly what he's trying to do. "But incorporating this data will only help the model perform better."

They all nod.

"This is your top priority. I'd like to have a new model by the end of the month."

Rachel looks skeptical. "Two weeks isn't much time."

"If it drags out, Jill will lose patience," Tyler says. "We'll have a fifteen-minute huddle at the end of each day to check progress."

As his team leaves to unknowingly assist him in betraying Jill, excitement gives way to crushing guilt. Struggling to breathe, he walks out, completes two laps around the office floor, then returns to his desk. He dials Jill's extension.

She answers with silence.

"I haven't been myself," he says. "Please forgive me."

After a pause, she responds, "Not my strong suit, but I'm working on it."

"Dinner?" He isn't the least bit hungry.

Another pause, longer this time. "I'll meet you at Joseph's," she says. "Six o'clock."

At five-twenty, Tyler is on the crowded elevator descending to the ground floor, planning to stroll along the streets to clear his head before meeting Jill. He merges with the stream of workers emerging from a dozen of the human cages, all funneling toward the freedom of the front exit.

Two large men push their way through the crowd, moving against the flow. Tyler notices their crew cuts and the way their muscles bulge against their sleeves. The flow of departing employees naturally parts around them, as if around a large rock in a river.

The men separate just enough to let Tyler walk between them. Suddenly, they close in, hooking an arm under each of his shoulders, lifting him off the ground. His stomach lurches violently as his feet flail uselessly in the air. The weight of his own body pulls him down, sending a sharp, burning ache through his shoulders, as if the muscles are being slowly torn apart under the strain.

No one in the sea of people around him seems to notice. Their faces blur together as he's hauled backward, feet dangling, past the main elevator banks and into the service area. He thrashes back and forth, trying to free himself, but their grips tighten, biting into his skin and keeping him pinned between them. His heart pounds harder, the reality of the situation sinking in.

Glancing over his shoulder, Tyler watches as the taller man pulls out a key card and swipes it in front of the freight elevator. The beep of the lock feels like a death knell, and his chest tightens. A dragon tattoo peeks above the man's shirt collar, a twisted reminder of the danger he's in. The door slides open with a mechanical thud, and the sharp scent of oil and metal fills the air as the two thugs toss him hard against the back wall.

Fear flares into anger. Tyler's sick of being manhandled like this. "Where are we going?" he demands.

The thugs ignore him as the elevator begins to rise.

"I said, where are we going?" His voice breaks, desperate.

The shorter thug responds by forming a tight, three-fingered fist and slamming it into Tyler's gut. The blow knocks the wind out of him, and he doubles over, gasping for air.

They arrive at the top floor, and he is shoved onto an empty observation deck. His mind tells him not to worry, that they're just here to scare him—no doubt Mike's doing. But his legs shake anyway.

The pair hustles him over a safety railing and onto a narrow rooftop ledge with nothing between him and the street below except seven hundred feet of air. The dragon-tattooed man pins Tyler's arms behind him while the shorter man pushes hard against his neck, forcing his torso to hang over the edge.

His entire body is trembling, rebelling against this unnatural posture. His head spins as he watches folks file out the front doors of 40 Wall Street. Each speck seventy-one floors below is unaware they are in danger of being hit by a two-hundred-pound asteroid.

"Say, who's that leaving the building now?" the shorter man says, pressing a pair of binoculars into Tyler's face. "Ain't she a sweet girl?"

He sees Jill below, getting into a car. The man in the chauffeur hat looks up and waves.

"Almost as sweet as your sister," the dragon-tattooed man whispers in his ear.

Tyler twists violently, his muscles burning as he struggles to free himself, his heart hammering against his ribcage.

"Careful," the dragon-tattooed man says, mocking him. "Stumpy has a history of dropping squirmers."

A cold sweat breaks out across Tyler's skin as he glances down at the tiny objects so far below. Panic overwhelms him.

"Shut up, Drag," the shorter man growls.

The hold on his shoulders tightens, and for a moment, Tyler thinks they might pull him back to safety. Then, without warning, Stumpy's grip on his shoulders disappears.

"Whoopsie," Drag says with a sickening smile as he lets go of Tyler's hands. "My fault this time."

Tyler's stomach lurches as time slows and his arms flail in the empty space. They aren't saving him. They're letting him fall.

Suspended in the air with nothing beneath him, he senses the yawning void below. *This is what it feels like to die.* His head tips forward, stomach plummeting as though he's back on the high dive at the pool—except this time, there's no water waiting below. Just a deadly fall.

When gravity is on the verge of claiming him, tension yanks at his ankles. Stumpy has grabbed them. Tyler's torso follows a violent arc, crashing into the gritty facade of the building. The jagged stone grinds against his face, tearing through his cheek, and a hot flash of pain shoots through his skull.

His body is dragged up and back over the ledge, upside down, his face scraping along the rough edge. Finally, he comes to rest, balanced precariously on the top of the building.

Tyler lies there, trying to comprehend what just occurred, trying to take stock of the damage, trying to prepare for what will happen to him next.

He hears a door close behind him, followed by the sound of his own heavy breathing and the occasional muted horn from the traffic far below. Pushing himself away from the edge, he lifts his head to glance behind him. No one's there. His arms give out, and he collapses, grimacing as his battered face smacks against the cold asphalt rooftop.

He rolls onto his side and sits up. Scrambling to retrieve his phone from his back pocket, he's relieved to find it's still there. The screen is rippled with cracks, but it's functional. He calls Anna.

"Ty! What's up?" she answers, cheerful.

"Anna …" His voice cracks, barely containing the flood of relief. "You're okay?"

"Of course I'm okay. I'm with friends right now. I'll call you later."
She hangs up before he can say anything else.

Thank God.

He pushes himself away from the building's edge and against the
safety rail, clutching the phone. His fingers hover over Jill's number,
and he dials. Straight to voicemail. He tries again with the same result.

Gritting his teeth against the pain radiating from his ribs, he forces
himself to stand and climb over the railing. His legs are shaky, and every
movement sends sharp stabs through his face and body. He stumbles
to the wall and slumps down against it.

There's one more call he needs to make.

"Sup, bud," Greg says.

"Help me. Please." It's the first time he's said those words in a
decade.

"Are you okay?"

Tyler leans to his side and spits. A wad of blood-clotted saliva hits
the dark surface beside him. He wipes his mouth with his sleeve.

"Are you ready for a project to really test your skills?" Tyler asks.

"I'm in the middle of getting my PhD in neuroscience … from
Harvard."

"You're doing what?"

"I've almost gained access to the graduate records. Already
purchased a nice frame to house my diploma—genuine seal on it and
all—and once I'm done, I'll delete myself from the university's records.
No trace."

Tyler chuckles then flinches as pain spider-webs across his busted
face and through his chest.

"Put that on hold. I need you to help me on a project, one that'll
determine whether I'm alive a month from now."

Greg's voice drops, laced with concern. "What kind of trouble are
you in?"

Tyler hesitates, the words catching in his throat. *How much do I tell
him right now?* "I'll fill you in, but we need to meet in person. Call in
sick tomorrow. I'll do the same, and we can meet halfway … in Philly."

They hang up, and he tries Jill again, but there's still no answer. Making his way into the building, Tyler steps into an empty hallway. He limps over to the freight elevator and touches the security pad with his fob, but the light stays red. Figures—it must require a separate clearance.

Searching in the dim glow of the hallway, he discovers the entrance to the stairway and stumbles his way down fourteen flights, exiting on the familiar fifty-seventh floor. Since it's late and most employees have already left, he's able to duck into the men's room without being seen.

Tyler cleans up with soap and water. His nose has stopped bleeding, and he's relieved to determine it isn't broken. The flesh around both eyes is raw and will soon turn black and purple, but he detects no chipped teeth—just some scrapes on his hands and a few sore ribs. All in all, he's fared pretty well—physically.

Mentally, he's a mess. His head swims with the dizzying realization that he's barely escaped death—and now he's even deeper into this nightmare.

He leaves the restroom and makes sure no one is watching before slipping into the elevator. Two men and a woman are already inside, and their conversation halts abruptly when they see him. He shrinks into a corner, pretending to check his phone. All the while, he's hoping Jill is okay, and he's thinking about the lies he'll have to tell her.

·　　·　　·　　·　　·

Tyler arrives at the restaurant fifteen minutes late and hurries past the curious glances of patrons and servers. He finds Jill at their usual table, seated near the crackling fireplace in the rear room. The heat from the flames feels like sandpaper against his raw skin.

She looks up as he approaches, her expression shifting from annoyance to alarm.

"Are you okay?" she asks, jumping up to guide him into a chair. Tyler flinches as the chair's slats dig into his sore back.

"I'm fine. Just … sorry I'm late." He tries to smile at her, but his swollen lower lip stings.

She kisses him on the side of the head, returns to her seat, and lowers her voice to an urgent whisper. "I'm taking you to the hospital. Or the police station."

He glances at the couple sitting one table over staring at him, and they quickly look away.

"I got mugged by the river. They took my watch and cash." He shows her his bare wrist. In truth, he ditched his watch a block before reaching the restaurant, tossing it to a panhandler along with the eighty-five dollars in his wallet.

A server approaches, tray balanced on his hip. "Now that we're all here—oh, my … are you all right?"

"I'll have a Joker-Cola," Tyler says, hoping the caffeine and sugar will help with the dizziness. "Wait, make it a Republic." He chuckles then sucks in a quick breath as a sharp pain shoots through his chest.

The server raises an eyebrow and glances at Jill. "Ma'am?"

"We need to leave," she says firmly, clearly shaken by his appearance.

"I'm fine, really. Just tired." He forces a smile, but even he can feel the hollowness of it. His eyes dart around the room, scanning the faces of strangers, wondering if one of them is watching, waiting. His hands shake as he reaches for the glass of water, and he's thankful Jill doesn't seem to notice.

Now he feels even worse. He's the one who caused all of this—the constant tension, the deception, the predicament he's dragged them into. All because of that idiotic bet.

He looks at the server. "She'll have a glass of Chardonnay."

The server makes a note and scoots away.

"Did you call the cops?" Jill whispers.

"Not yet," he replies, shifting uncomfortably. He looks around, hoping to change the subject. "I'm thinking of getting Anna a signed Caitlin Clark jersey for her birthday."

"Ty, is there something else going on?" Jill presses, shaking her head. "Something else bothering you?"

He hesitates. *I can't tell her. Not yet.* "You mean, besides getting mugged?" he says sarcastically and chuckles. He picks up the breadbasket and hands it to her, trying to appear nonchalant.

She pauses then sighs and shifts the conversation. "Well, that's quite a gift for her. She'll be ... fourteen, right?"

"Yeah. I'm going to get it from a reputable dealer—you've got to watch out for fakes." Tyler winces as he stretches, his battered body protesting. "We'll give it to her when we visit in a few weeks."

He reaches into his pocket and pulls out an envelope, setting it on the table between them. "Luckily, this was in my back pocket. Didn't get stolen."

She points with her knife. "What is it?"

"An early Valentine's Day present."

She opens the envelope and pulls out two tickets. Her eyes light up as she reads them. "*Hamilton* on Broadway?" She covers her mouth, clearly delighted. "My favorite show!"

"I should have gotten tickets for *Beauty and the Beast* instead," he jokes, pointing at his bruised face.

She rolls her eyes, but she's smiling.

CHAPTER 28

The speedometer hovers above eighty, the Porsche 911 purring as if asking Jill for more.

"I thought you'd be a speed limit driver," Tyler says, glancing over at her as they cruise along I-95 through light Thursday evening traffic into South Jersey. They're on their way to Baltimore to celebrate Anna's birthday weekend.

Jill turns her head and smiles. "You thought wrong."

She presses the accelerator, pinning Tyler against the plush leather seat. The speedometer jumps to a hundred before Jill relaxes her foot, letting the car coast back to her cruising speed in the low eighties.

Tyler adjusts his seat and takes a deep breath, the oily scent of new leather filling his senses. He turns to her, grinning. "You're full of surprises."

They pull into Paul Thompson's driveway just after ten. The driveway splits into a semicircle with a small offshoot where Jill parks the Porsche. Paul emerges from the front door as they unload their suitcases and Anna's presents.

Daisy bounds past Paul, intent on being the first to greet them. Tyler crouches down as she rises on her hind legs and presses her front paws into his stomach, panting excitedly in the cold February night. He rubs behind her ears, and her tail whirls in a happy blur before she plants several wet licks on his face.

"Welcome back," Paul says, stepping forward to shake Tyler's hand over Daisy's head.

Tyler turns to introduce Jill, but Paul beats him to it.

"You must be Jill Young," Paul says with a warm smile, extending his hand and winking.

To Tyler's surprise, Jill skips the handshake and leans in for a hug. Normally, she's more formal with new acquaintances. Then again, Paul's easygoing nature is instantly disarming.

"Clearly, you're way out of his league," Paul says.

Jill laughs then squats to greet Daisy. "I love dogs."

"The ladies are asleep," he says. "I didn't tell Anna you were arriving tonight or she never would've gone to bed. It's only a half day of school tomorrow, but she'll need her rest for the game tomorrow night."

Tyler nods and grabs their bags. "Same room as usual?"

Paul gestures toward the house. "You got it."

Tyler shivers as the cold bites through his jacket. "Let's get inside. We'll be quiet."

They carry their luggage down the hall, but Jill stops at a framed picture of a young boy in a suit and tie.

"Is that …?" she asks softly.

He nods, memories of his old friend flooding back. She wraps her arms around his waist, and they stand still for a quiet moment, reflecting.

•　　•　　•　　•　　•

The next morning, Anna insists Jill drive her to school in the Porsche. After they leave, Melinda excuses herself to get ready for the day, and Tyler follows Paul into his study.

"Are you getting close to fulfilling your bet?" Paul asks, settling into the armchair.

Tyler sighs, sinking onto the couch. "I'll find out later today. If not, I'm working on a backup plan."

Paul frowns. "Don't fool around with this, son. Please."

Tyler feels the burden of everything he's been holding back. His voice wavers as he speaks. "Mike had a couple thugs send me a message a few weeks ago. They threatened me. And Jill and Anna." He cradles his head in his hands. "I can't eat. I barely sleep. I call the two of them every five minutes to make sure they're okay."

Paul pulls out a handkerchief, his eyes moist.

"Can't you do something?" Tyler asks.

The older man stands and paces. "Anna's with me, the safest place she can be. I'm giving you advice, the best I can. I even talked to Mike again, asked him to change the bet, let you off the hook. But he still won't budge."

Tyler is deflated. "So that's it, I guess."

Paul wipes his eyes with the handkerchief, his voice hoarse. "I can't undo what you did, my friend. There's no magic wand that will fix this. You need to get the algorithm. And soon."

"I'm giving it everything I've got." Tyler curls his hands into fists then lets them drop to his sides. "This whole thing is bullshit."

Paul studies him for a long moment. "The bet is bullshit, I agree. But the game? The game is not."

"How can you say that?" Tyler snaps. "After all this?"

Paul hesitates. "Look, I know it's not perfect, not always clean. But that peace treaty between India and Pakistan—do you think diplomacy did that?" He shakes his head. "It was the game. A bet. Influential people pulled the strings and got the key figures in the room, brokering peace where decades of conflict failed. That's the kind of power this game wields."

Tyler's disbelief deepens, and he sets his jaw. "You're telling me people gamble on world peace now?"

Paul's face hardens. "You don't get it. They gamble on everything. That's how the world works at this level. And yes, when you mix those kinds of stakes with the risk-takers who find this game irresistible, both terrible and great things happen. But it's the people, Tyler, not the game itself. And the net result of this game has been an enormous benefit to the world."

Tyler's frustration boils over. "Mike told me about JFK. How the hell can you justify that?"

"Get off your high horse, son!" Paul turns away from Tyler and kicks the air. "Shoot," he says and turns back, "you've hit a nerve with me is all." He sits down again. "You've heard of the Bay of Pigs? The US's failed invasion of Cuba back in the early sixties?"

"Of course."

"You know why it failed? Why it really failed?"

Tyler shakes his head no.

"Castro knew it was coming. The KGB tipped him off, and they found out through mobsters in New York. Those mobsters had their claws in a certain blonde-haired beauty with access to sensitive information—the same woman Kennedy was seeing."

Paul leans closer, his voice low and firm. "Don't you get it, Tyler? Kennedy played Russian roulette with the future of our country. He lost a bet, agreeing to end the affair, but he didn't."

Tyler can't bring himself to care about the history lesson. "Whatever," he mutters. "I'd shut this game down if it were up to me."

Paul sighs. "It's not up to you. And let's be honest—you wouldn't feel this way if you'd won that last bet."

Tyler flinches. "But I didn't. And now, I've got to fulfill it."

"I'm afraid so."

A lump forms in Tyler's throat. "Or else I die."

Paul's silence says all it needs to.

· · · · ·

Later that morning, Tyler pulls Jill's Porsche to the curb on Charles Street outside the Mid-Atlantic building. Greg hops in and folds his winter coat over his lap.

"You look better than when I saw you in Philly last month, big boy," Greg says, surveying the vehicle's interior. "Nice wheels. Doing okay up there in the Big Apple, huh?"

"Jill's wheels, not mine," Tyler says, his tone flat.

Greg rubs his hands together in front of the heater vent. "Freezing out there. I'm ordering soup for lunch." He angles the vent upward and increases the fan to max speed. His curls bounce in the warm stream of air. Tyler examines how he's wedged himself into the seat with one leg pulled up, his hands wrapped around his knee, his foot resting on the seat. He never does things quite like everyone else.

"Hey, nut job," Tyler says. "Don't leave marks on the leather."

Greg returns his shoe to the floor and sits straighter. As they inch through downtown traffic, he glances at Tyler and clears his throat. "I don't have good news."

Tyler's heart sinks. He suspected as much. If Greg had found a way in, he would have called sooner. Still, hearing it stings. He'd hoped, even just a little, for a miracle.

"Don't sweat it," he says, focusing on the road.

"New Horizon's network is tighter than anything I've seen," Greg explains. "Layer after layer of security. It's like Disney World—you think you're about to reach the front of the line, then you turn a corner and find there's another line."

"There has to be a way in." Tyler wishes he had taken his friend's advice and developed his own hacking skills. Now, he feels helpless.

Greg shrugs. "There might be, but I haven't found it yet."

Tyler grips the wheel, frustrated. He slams the brakes as a pedestrian darts in front of them. "Sorry."

Greg chuckles. "No sweat. Some fresh underwear, and I'll be good to go."

Tyler tries to smile, but his mind is elsewhere. "So, what's the next move?"

Greg hesitates. "We're running out of moves. The only option left is using your credentials to get into the system. But that's risky as hell. Once I use your log-in, you'll be on the radar. There will be a trail, and if the tech nerds spot it, it'll lead straight to you."

Tyler pulls over near the restaurant and parks. He stares out the windshield, weighing his options. If his team can finish the predictive model in time, he might be able to pass off a proxy of the real algorithm and avoid all this. But, as his mind sifts through possibilities, fear feeds his brain, and his survival instinct kicks in. He'd tossed out his societal norms and morals somewhere back on Charles Street.

I need to play every card I have as hard as I can.

He turns to Greg. "Go for it."

Greg hesitates then says, "You sure about this? I mean, you said in Philly you had no choice, but are you ready for the fallout? Because there will be fallout."

Tyler exhales. "I know. I'm ready."

Greg leans back, his usual humor gone. "You'd better be. Once I pull the trigger, there's no going back."

Tyler nods. "I need the answer by next Sunday. Or it won't matter."

Greg folds his arms, studying Tyler. "You know, you're the last guy I'd expect to get dragged into this kind of a mess." He pauses, his expression hardening. "I just hope you're not in over your head."

Tyler clenches his fists in his lap. "So do I."

•   •   •   •   •

The clock reads 11:59 p.m. Tyler stands in the crowded reception area of the Mid-Atlantic building, naked, holding the algorithm folder in front of him. People are staring, their faces blurred and featureless. Should he board the elevator and deliver the folder or go back to his office for his clothes?

The elevator doors open, revealing a dimly lit interior. A heavy silence presses against him as he steps inside, and the walls of the elevator begin closing in. He tries to scream, but no sound comes out.

Suddenly, Jill is standing at the far end of the elevator, her back turned to him. He reaches out, but the folder feels like a weight he can't drop. His arms tremble with the effort of holding it.

"Jill," he tries to say, but the words die in his throat. She turns her head, her face just barely visible through the dim light, and then she steps backward into the shadows, fading away.

A hollow laughter echoes through the elevator shaft. Mike's laughter. It reverberates, growing louder and louder until Tyler feels like his head is going to split open. The walls press closer, the air thinning. His lungs cry out for breath, but his chest tightens, refusing to expand.

"It's not faaiiiirrrr!" he screams, but once again, nothing comes out. Only silence.

Tyler jolts awake, drenched in sweat, the sheets twisted around him. He glances at the clock and groans. It's 1:13 a.m., and he's wide awake. Jill is sound asleep next to him, her breath soft and steady. But no matter how close she is, she seems unreachable. He rolls out of bed in the dark, tiptoes to the bathroom, and splashes cold water on his face. On his return, he stubs his toe on his suitcase. Muttering a curse, he crawls back into bed and tosses and turns for hours. When he finally drifts back to sleep around five, his dreams are haunted by a ticking clock.

He opens his eyes at eight-fifteen with sunlight filtering through the blinds. He never sleeps this late. Jill is in the shower, and he closes his eyes and listens to the relaxing sound of the falling water. He imagines himself near a light waterfall along a lazy, woodsy trail, far away from poker games and algorithms.

Steam escapes from under the bathroom door and floats into the bedroom, mingling with the faint scent of sizzling bacon. His stomach growls, but he lies still for several minutes more in his peaceful reverie. When he hears the water stop, he stretches his arms way up in the air, yawns, and forces himself to get up.

He pulls on his sweats and shirt from the night before, smiling as he remembers Anna's eleven points and tough defense in her team's victory. While retrieving his phone from the dresser, his hand brushes against Jill's silver locket. He picks it up, the chain dangling beneath his hand, and admires the intricate detail of the lion crest embossed on the front. He runs his thumb across the rough surface, and then, without thinking, he starts to crack it open.

The bathroom door creaks, and Tyler snaps the locket shut, chastising himself for absentmindedly almost invading Jill's privacy. She emerges from the bathroom wrapped in a bath towel, beads of water dripping from her hair onto the plush carpet.

"It's beautiful, isn't it?" she asks.

"Exquisite," he says, smiling. "Like you."

She blushes. He loves that about her.

She studies the surface of the locket. "That's our family crest. It was a gift from my dad—he hoped it would bring us together." She shrugs. "It didn't."

Tyler places the locket back on the dresser and looks back just in time to see Jill drop the towel and wrap her arms around him.

·   ·   ·   ·   ·

By the time he makes it to the kitchen, the others have finished breakfast, but the dishes are still on the table. Tyler balances four wrapped presents as he enters the room.

"Jill said you didn't sleep well," Melinda remarks.

Yawning, he says, "I finally crashed this morning. A cup of coffee and I'll be fine."

He sets the boxes on the floor and reaches for the pot sitting in the middle of the breakfast table. As he pours a cup, he glances around at the others and raises an eyebrow. "I know there's something special today, but I can't remember what …"

Anna rolls her eyes. "Oh, Tyler. I outgrew that when I was, like, ten."

Outgrew it. What else will she outgrow—maybe trusting me? She'd hate me if she knew the truth.

He sighs. "Happy birthday, sis."

She smiles and gently pushes him away. "Hurry up with the presents. Jill and I are going shopping in her Porsche."

Tyler watches as Anna's excitement permeates the room, her laughter filling the air. A smile flickers across his face, but it doesn't reach his eyes. He glances through the bay window at the courtyard patio where, even in the dead of winter, the world seems calm. Too calm.

If they only knew the storm brewing inside me.

CHAPTER 29

Tyler sits in the small conference room adjacent to his office, his arms crossed as he leans back in the chair and looks at his team.

"Show me what you've got," he says.

February 14th—the six-month deadline to deliver the algorithm—is only two days away. He hasn't been able to get the real one, and if the version his team created isn't convincing enough to fool Mike, his life is over.

Other than that, it's a pretty chill day.

Rachel taps at her keyboard, and an Excel report appears on the wall-mounted monitor. Tyler's eyes skim quickly over the numbers, and his jaw tenses.

"The new-and-improved model," she says, beaming alongside Wei and Nicole. "We tested it using the trades you gave us that were generated from the investment algorithm last year."

Nicole points to a chart displayed on the left side of the screen.

"We were able to accurately predict seventy percent of the buy-and-sell transactions made by our investment team," she explains, looking at Tyler expectantly. It's an impressive accomplishment, and they clearly know it.

"Terrific," Tyler says, manufacturing a smile. He does his best to inject enthusiasm into his voice, though his mind spins with doubt. *Will this be good enough?*

"We can improve it further," Wei adds. "It'll never be 100 percent accurate, but this is a solid start."

Tyler nods, his arms still crossed. "What return would this model have generated if we had used it last year in place of the investment algorithm?"

"That's the problem we're still working on," Wei says. "New Horizon produced a nineteen percent return, excluding the Lexon windfall and a few other big wins. Even though this new model correctly predicts over two-thirds of the transactions, it misses the key successes the algorithm achieved."

"So it would have generated …?"

Wei grimaces. "Only a seven percent return."

Tyler forces himself to smile again. "Nice job," he says, keeping his voice steady. "Please send me a detailed report this afternoon."

His team relaxes, sharing quiet grins with each other. They have no idea what's really at stake.

The funny thing is, he really does like their work. The model is a definite improvement over the previous version and will certainly make their jobs more efficient in the long run—if he survives long enough to care.

He dismisses his team and tries to focus on other projects, but his mind keeps reverting to the looming deadline.

At 5:30 p.m., Jill pokes her head into his office. "Happy hour at The Dead Rabbit? Mateo's team is going."

"I need to finish up a project," Tyler says, stretching his stiff shoulders. "How about a run tomorrow morning?"

She smiles, but the usual warmth in her eyes is missing. "Seven?"

He nods.

"Bundle up," she says and turns to leave. "You don't want to be exposed in this weather."

He glances out the window, knowing ice is already creeping across the streets below. A shiver crawls up his spine.

Tyler spends the rest of the evening buried in his office reviewing the report provided by his team and repackaging the information into the form of an investment algorithm Mike can deploy. The result is a ten-page document—as official looking as he can make it—that explains the market data that needs to be fed into the model, the specific formulas that need to be programmed for the algorithm to work, and the guidelines for applying the output to drive automated buy-and-sell decisions.

By the time he finishes, it's nearly midnight. He stifles a yawn and backs up the file, using a combination of Hedera Hashgraph for secure validation and a decentralized storage network, ensuring it will be securely fragmented and encrypted across dozens of nodes. Afterward, he calls a car service to take him home. As the car cruises through the city, his mind is preoccupied with anxious thoughts.

How long will this deception hold up? How long until Mike realizes he's been given a counterfeit?

"It might look like the real thing," he says to himself, "but it's missing the secret sauce."

The next morning, Tyler receives a text from Greg as he's lacing his running shoes.

Spent all week on this. Tricks and traps galore trying to access the secure server. No luck but will keep trying.

Tyler drags himself through a half-hearted run with Jill. The biting cold stings his skin, and neither of them says much. She seems annoyed with him—likely for bailing on happy hour the night before.

He spends the rest of Saturday morning and the early afternoon doing much and accomplishing little. At three p.m., he calls Greg.

"Still nothing?"

"Sorry, man," Greg says. "You should be proud to work for such a secure company."

"Right," Tyler says, his frustration simmering beneath the surface.

"Will you be okay?"

"I've gotta go," Tyler says abruptly then hangs up.

A wave of emotion surges through him. *How did I get into this nightmare?* He's asked himself that question countless times, but today, the answer finally surfaces—greed. Plain and simple. He's tried dressing it up a million ways, but that's the truth.

Admitting it, for once, is oddly liberating.

After a hot shower, Tyler puts on fresh clothes and heads out into the cold. His steps are heavy as he walks down 6th Avenue then turns onto 53rd Street. The Museum of Modern Art looms on his left, but he barely glances at it. His mind is fixated on the task at hand.

He blows into his cupped hands to warm them as he approaches the library. Once inside, he settles in front of a computer far from the main traffic. Logging into a fake email account, he retrieves a secure access link for the file stored on the storage network. The link is encrypted, granting Mike temporary access to the report without compromising security. He pastes it into an email addressed to WinkInc@darkmail.net —Mike's alias, *such a wiseass*. His finger hovers over the send button.

Tyler considers pausing to embed a virus, turning the link into a Trojan horse. He chuckles, imagining the havoc he could wreak on Mike. It would almost be worth ruining his own life to see Mike's smug confidence shattered. But then he thinks about Anna and Jill.

He is just about to hit send when he's interrupted by a loud buzzing from his pocket.

A heavyset, gray-haired woman two cubicles down leans back and glares, pressing a finger to her lips.

Tyler smiles at her as he pulls out his phone. Her afternoon is about to get even more exciting because there's no way he's ignoring this call. "Hi, Greg."

The woman's mouth drops open, seemingly caught between shock and indignation at his blatant disregard for the sacred library silence.

"I got in!" Greg says, his excitement crackling through the phone.

Tyler's heart leaps. "Tell me you're not joking!"

He glances at the woman down the aisle. "Go outside!" she barks.

"Call you right back," he says to Greg. Then he hangs up, deletes the draft email, and practically sprints out of the library, adrenaline surging through his veins. It doesn't feel so cold in the wintery air now. He stops at the top of the granite steps and calls Greg.

"How'd you do it?"

"Not sure. I followed the same steps I've been through a hundred times, but it worked this time. It's like someone left the front door open and the porch light on. Security lapses do happen—sometimes you just have to get lucky."

Over the past several months, Tyler's learned how strict New Horizon is about protecting confidential information. Still, he doesn't dwell on it. He simply accepts the gift.

"When I get back to my place," he says, "I'll call you so you can walk me through the steps needed to access it."

Back at his apartment, he settles on the couch, ready to dig into the task ahead. His fingers are unsteady as he opens his laptop. With Greg's guidance, he carefully navigates into the secure server, and after ten stressful minutes, he's in, staring at the coveted code.

Tyler leaps from the couch, pumping his fist in the air, hardly able to believe it. He screams with joy—he's finally safe. But just as quickly, the thought of Jill drags him back down, the crushing weight of his betrayal extinguishing his enthusiasm.

He pushes the guilt from his mind and focuses on the code. The small table in front of him holds his computer, several notepads, and a large pepperoni pizza. Hours tick by as he digs deeper into the algorithm, taking notes and sketching diagrams on a pad of paper.

At eight o'clock, Jill calls. He looks at the phone for a second then lets it go to voice mail. Grabbing a slice of the room-temperature pizza, he sighs then forges ahead.

As the night wears on, Tyler's optimism grows. Document after document yields answers to the many questions listed on his legal pad, and he checks them off one by one, forming a comprehensive picture of how the algorithm operates. He picks up his pen and draws a schematic then grabs his laptop to type notes illustrating the steps needed to replicate it. Although he finds sections of code that surpass even his exceptional programming skills—and one that is completely Greek to him—he's relieved to discover plain-English explanations in summary reports and board presentations that clarify how the code works and the results it achieves.

At midnight, he is sure this last-ditch effort will succeed, even though he hasn't completed all his entries yet. He texts Mike and asks to meet the next day. Sending a secure access link to the actual algorithm and his report makes him uneasy. Even with encryption, the stakes are too high. Instead, he plans to catch the seven a.m. train to Baltimore, exchanging his Valentine's Day date with Jill for a train ticket to visit Mike. Not exactly an even trade.

At three a.m., Tyler types the last sentence, snaps his laptop shut, and collapses on the couch, exhausted. Less than two hours later, his phone alarm blares, jolting him awake. Groggy and disoriented, he double-checks that the report and the code are secure in his online storage. With fresh clothes and a heavy heart, he ventures into the early dawn.

He takes the subway to Grand Central then boards the Baltimore-bound train. Settling into his seat, he stares at his phone, wishing his text to Jill would write itself. His eyelids droop as he reclines and rests his head against the soft cushion.

Tyler is out cold until another passenger walking down the aisle bumps into his leg. His watch says it's almost ten. They'll arrive in thirty minutes. He searches for his phone, finds it wedged between the seat cushions, and types a message.

Sorry for not calling you back last night. Have to go to Baltimore today. Emergency. Everything's fine, but I'll miss the matinee. I'll find tickets for another weekend. Let's still have dinner tonight. So sorry. Happy V-Day.

Love You! Ty

He feels a pang of guilt as he hits send. She'd been so excited about their Valentine's Day date. He opens an internet browser and searches to exchange their seats. Valentine's Day may be screwed up, but at least he'll be alive to take her to the show another time.

He takes a cab from Penn Station to the Mid-Atlantic office and pays the driver in cash. No need to leave a trail. Not that it matters, he supposes, but it seems like something someone in his situation should do.

Tyler enters Mid-Atlantic through the main doors. When he doesn't scan himself through the turnstile, the security guard speaks without looking up from behind his desk.

"Forget your badge?"

"I'm not an employee." Tyler approaches the man. "I'm here to see Mike Hayward."

The guard looks up now, squinting. "You're here to see Mr. Hayward?"

Tyler is wearing jeans and a sweatshirt.

"You realize it's Sunday?" the guard asks.

Tyler winks. "And Valentine's Day."

Might as well have some fun with a rotten situation. Maybe I'll start a rumor or two.

"I'll call up there, but I wouldn't hold my breath," the guard says and presses three numbers, holding the phone to his ear. "Mr. Hayward? This is Bill in security. There's a gentleman here to see you." He glances at Tyler and listens. "I'll send him right up."

He produces a visitor badge and hands it to Tyler. "Second set of elevators, floor forty."

Once Tyler is inside the elevator, the doors creep shut, caging him and shutting out the light of day. He feels the pressure of being an unwitting double agent, trapped by circumstances in a place where there is only darkness, no matter which way he turns, no matter which path he follows.

A short time later, the doors open, delivering him into the hands of his tormentor, who is waiting eagerly in the reception area of the fortieth floor. Tyler hands Mike a sheet of paper with the login credentials needed to access the report and code securely stored on the Hedera Hashgraph network. He turns to get back on the elevator, but Mike waves him forward.

"We're going to vet this together," he says, beckoning Tyler to follow him. They march in silence down the shadowy hall to his office.

For the next half hour, Tyler watches as Mike goes through the report, his face betraying nothing. Tyler's not worried, at least not about Mike. The information is legit, but he's thinking about how he'll face Jill and the elaborate fabrication he'll need to construct to explain his disappearing act.

After five minutes of chastising himself once again for the choices he made that led to this moment, Tyler looks over and examines Mike's monitor. He's on page five of eighteen. Tyler pulls out his phone, scrolling through random articles, tired of berating himself.

"Ha! So that's how they do it." Mike is on page six now. "It looks so simple when I see it all laid out like this, at least conceptually. I'll need my computer techs to confirm the code works."

Another twenty minutes pass before Mike closes the file and swivels in his chair to face Tyler. "It's impressive. More than I expected." His lips form a sly smile. "I'll test it fully, but I think we both know what you've given me is gold."

"It's the real deal," Tyler says flatly.

Mike scrutinizes him. "You can understand my skepticism, receiving it on the absolute last day of your six-month window. I thought you might try to pass off a phony out of desperation."

Tyler crosses his arms tightly across his chest. "I don't think you're that stupid."

"Of course not." Mike hesitates. "I always knew you were special."

Mike has that look on his face—the intense stare with a hint of a smile, the expression that makes Tyler feel like Mike really cares about him, as if he were the only person who matters.

"You did an excellent job, Tyler. It's more fantastic than you understand. You did the impossible."

As Mike praises him, Tyler can't help but feel hollow. The more Mike admires his work, the more disgusted he is with himself. "I'm leaving now," he says.

Mike displays the full Hayward smile. "You should be proud of yourself."

Tyler feels completely ashamed. "Are we done?" he asks.

Mike stands and strolls around the desk. "Why such a rush? Let's go celebrate with a champagne brunch at the Raven's Club." He places an arm around Tyler's shoulders. "We can talk about the timing for you to come back to Mid-Atlantic ... and to rejoin the game. You can have your pick of jobs." He smiles. "How about CFO?"

"You've got an opening for a CFO?"

"I'll fire Bob. You deserve it."

Tyler brushes Mike's arm from his shoulder. "Screw you. I've had enough of your favors." He stands and stomps out of the office.

On the train back to New York, he receives a text from Jill.

Not feeling well. Let's postpone dinner.

He deflates into his seat. If she's really sick, it's because of him.

CHAPTER 30

The quick rap on Jill's open door, followed by three footsteps, tells her exactly who has entered her office. She remains glued to her monitor, her body tensing as it has each time Tyler has visited recently. Her fingers hover above the keyboard, pretending to scroll through the day's breaking news.

"Jill?" Tyler's voice carries a note of hope, but she doesn't look up right away.

After a few moments, she lifts her eyes, feigning surprise. "I'm really busy, Tyler. What do you need?"

"I've got seats for Hamilton this Sunday, second row." He holds out a pair of tickets, a hopeful smile tugging at his lips. "Thought we could have our Valentine's Day celebration, a fortnight delayed."

She wants to say yes. The warmth he's offering is so tempting, but the words that come out of her mouth are colder than she expects. "I wish I could, Tyler, really … but I've got a major project due Monday. I just … I can't. Another time, maybe."

She turns her back to him and shuffles through a stack of papers as if nothing in the world could pull her away from her task.

He stands there a moment longer, his presence lingering in the air before he finally leaves. The warmth he offered disappears with him, leaving behind a cold emptiness she can't seem to shake.

Once she's sure Tyler has left, she pivots back to her monitor and pulls up the protected section of the algorithm. The familiar intensity returns as she examines the lines of code. She ponders the Einstein subroutine, the piece of the algorithm she's been trying to crack for over a year. If she could just enhance its ability to connect seemingly unrelated points of data, she could finally push through the plateau she's hit, make the breakthrough that will lead to success, not just for New Horizon but also for her work with the World Food Programme.

And then what? she wonders. Stop the extinction of endangered animals? Fast-forward space exploration? Eradicate viruses before they become pandemics?

Calm down, sister.

Her mind often whirls with excitement when she thinks about fulfilling the professor's dreams. She can't escape the unwavering belief that she's on the brink of something transformative—an achievement that could affect the world on a global scale.

If only she could call Francis, her mentor. Since his death, she's been working solo on this most secretive section of the code, and the need for collaboration has never been so vital. She's never felt so alone, so in need of a partner.

There is someone who could help her, of course ... someone with the right combination of technical knowledge and creative problem-solving. Someone she trusts. Or did, until recently.

For the third time, Jill rereads the same line of code, trying to concentrate, but the gnawing sense of guilt inside her won't let go. She sighs, acknowledging the truth she's been avoiding. Stewing in resentment only provides temporary comfort. There's no denying the need to confront the situation head-on.

Her therapist's voice echoes in her head, instructing her to observe her thoughts with curiosity, to watch them as if they belong to someone else. She rewinds the events of the past month like a movie reel.

Tyler was acting distant, not looking her in the eye, tensing when they touched. It wasn't another woman—he'd been telling the truth about that. Three weeks ago, she found the real reason for his odd behavior—he was trying to access the algorithm. That's a fact. She has the security warnings to prove it. Yes, others have stumbled into the protected zone before but never fifty-one times in four days.

She wonders, though, if her immediate conclusion was wrong. Could it be that Tyler wasn't trying to steal the algorithm but was just too eager? Was his persistence—his scrappy determination, the very trait she admired—what drove him to dig deeper, what made him unable to wait out the six-month rule? After all, patience wasn't one of his strong points.

She's amazed at how people—so-called experts—like to slice others into situational parts, as though those pieces can be easily reassembled into a cohesive person. They applaud entrepreneurs for being rule-breakers when their investments turn into fortunes but are shocked when the same entrepreneurs end up in hot water for taking things too far.

"Bless his heart, if only he'd known when to stop," they say. "Why risk it all when you've already won so much?" They never understand.

It hits Jill then—her own hypocrisy. Tyler wants the model his team is building to succeed. He wants to help her further develop the algorithm. He asked again and again, and finally, when denied, he tried to help himself.

Nothing bad has happened. None of her suspicions materialized.

And I really miss him.

Her next appointment with her counselor is two weeks away. She imagines explaining how she's once again driven away someone she cared about, all because things were getting too serious.

At least she hasn't forwarded the security warnings to anyone.

Jill considers Tyler's burdens—the shame he carries about his father, the rejection he experienced from Paul, his desperation to protect Anna. A surge of clarity overtakes her guilt, propelling her to act. After a moment of hesitation, she logs off the secure server and types a message to him.

Sorry for earlier. I'd love to go to the show.

Five seconds later, a smiley emoji pops up on her screen. She smiles, too.

•　　•　　•　　•　　•

"Good morning, Deepak speaking."

His sleepy voice reminds Mike that Bangladesh is a world away.

"How's the plan unfolding? Is the testing going well?" Mike asks then leans back in his chair, enjoying the warmth of the late afternoon sun streaming through one of his many office windows. These are his favorite moments, when a strategy is coming to fruition, allowing him to fully employ his tactical brilliance. These are the times he truly feels alive.

"Good so far. The algorithm appears to be functioning properly, but we need more time to thoroughly vet it."

Mike shakes his head. Those eggheads will test forever if he lets them. They'd let Anton Popa stroll right past him.

"I'll give you two more days then start disseminating it to the drones. How long will that take?"

"Mr. Hayward, please allow us more time to work with this code. It's very sophisticated. None of us has encountered anything quite like it." A clap of thunder follows Deepak's words and reverberates through the phone.

That seemingly meaningless rumble eight thousand miles away might be a sign to load up on a stock, Mike thinks. Once the almost infinite volume of data and information flowing throughout the world can be properly harnessed—instead of uselessly washing away like loose gold in a poorly constructed sluice box—it could trigger a series of events that would tell him to buy Republic or Joker-Cola. Or perhaps it's a clue a recession is on the horizon. Who knows what it might foretell? No one knows, not now.

But soon, I will.

Mike lifts his tumbler and takes a long sip, savoring the thought of one day sitting back and watching his adopted technology utilize data and information in ways that were heretofore unimaginable. With the algorithm integrated into his army of computers, he'll create an electronic cocktail powerful enough to shock the financial elite— especially New Horizon.

Before long, he will be deftly moving in and out of stocks, currencies, and markets with the precision of a surgeon while the rest of the investing universe is checking the weather report.

"Mr. Hayward?" Deepak asks tentatively.

The interruption annoys him. "The code's fine," he snaps, setting his glass down hard on his desk. "I'm going to do a test run to make sure—a limited, focused deployment. Kick the tires, so to speak. In the meantime, have your team move forward with getting the program distributed to our network of computers. No more delays." He grips his fingers tightly around the phone. "For the second time, how long will it take?"

"Eighteen million computers. Two to three weeks."

"Good. Move forward. Anything else?"

"No, sir." A slight pause. "It's just that I still think we should—"

Mike hangs up before Deepak can finish. Scientists are such nervous Nellies.

Excitement floods through him as he imagines unleashing his new weapon on the world. Patience, he cautions himself. First a test drive then the open roads.

He can't help thinking about his future. Financial rewards will be just the beginning. Global leaders will bow to the power of his knowledge. He'll shift the world stage like a modern-day Nostradamus, wielding insights as precise and unstoppable as prophecy.

He takes another sip, a longer one this time. The glass trembles slightly in his hand, its cool surface pressing into his palm as the amber liquid burns its way down his throat. The warmth of the whiskey courses through his chest, just as his power will soon spread across the globe. Here he is, at the outset of a grand journey, the birth of a new era. The dull buzz of the office lights, the familiar creak of his chair, all fade into insignificance beneath the power of his vision. History will mark it as a bifurcation of time. The period of BC ended with the arrival of Christ. The period of AD is about to end with the introduction of his cyber god.

Soon, the Hayward era will begin.

Mike drains the tumbler slowly, letting the satisfaction linger as a smile creeps across his face.

CHAPTER 31

Jill and Tyler spring to their feet, along with the other thousand people in the Richard Rodgers Theatre, delivering a standing ovation. What a performance, Tyler thinks. It was worth every penny of the two five-hundred-dollar tickets. He looks back around at the vast crowd behind him and above in the balcony section, all roaring with applause.

But what makes the moment most special for him is that he and Jill are enjoying a splendid Sunday together. The recent tension that had formed an icy divide between them has finally melted.

As he pulls his suit coat back on, he sneaks a glance at Jill, who gently wraps her vibrant pashmina shawl around her bare shoulders. She looks stunning tonight in a clingy, black dress that shows off her toned arms, and she's wearing the silver-and-emerald earrings he gave her—a good sign. He's relieved their relationship feels normal again.

His arm around her, he breathes in the light, spicy flavor of her perfume as they work their way up the aisle to exit the theater. He's been deprived of that scent for weeks now, at least from such a close vantage point.

Stepping out of the theater, they are greeted by the soft thrum of the city at dusk. The warm breeze kisses their faces, carrying the mixed smells of street food and blooming flowers from the nearby park. February is about to turn into March, and they're blessed with their first taste of spring. The sun has been shining all day in a cloudless blue sky, and even as it sets, the air remains pleasant.

As they stroll down West 46th Street with plenty of time before their dinner reservation at La Masseria, Tyler feels better than he has in months. His stomach isn't constantly in knots, and for once, he can look at Jill without the gut-wrenching anxiety that has haunted him. For now, at least, the cloud of his betrayal seems to have cleared.

Since his Valentine's rendezvous with Mike, nothing has happened. No big announcements from Mid-Atlantic. No questions from New Horizon's security team. Maybe the algorithm isn't that big a deal after all, he thinks. Maybe no one will know. Maybe he can be free to pursue his future without repercussion.

What's the statute of limitations, though, on betraying the woman you love?

Jill points toward an open-topped, double-decker bus passing by. Four children wave from the top level, and Tyler waves back. He notices the theater marquee across the street.

"We should go see *Wicked* sometime," he says.

She nods, her smile genuine. "And how about we take Anna to *The Lion King*? Maybe when she comes up for spring break?"

He hopes Anna will fall in love with the city as much as he has with one of its residents. After the spring semester ends and the legal issues are resolved, he wants her to join him. He's been in contact with social services in New York, and they've agreed to help him complete a home study report that will satisfy Judge Watson.

They continue walking until they turn into the electrified neon glitz of Times Square. It's like they've purposefully entered a human traffic jam. Tourists from all parts of the world mill about amid the flashing lights of digital screens and advertisements. The energy is palpable.

Tyler squeezes Jill's hand tighter, secure in their relationship as they pick their way through the crowd. He feels so close to her and vows not to let anything change that connection.

·   ·   ·   ·   ·

Three days later, Tyler is summoned by Tara Mays, President Sebastian Shultz's personal administrative assistant. He hurries to her office, excited to be invited to the inner sanctum.

"To the war room," she says, pointing to a door across from her desk.

Tyler moves quickly, a twinge of pride rising in him as he enters the large, high-tech room for the first time. The war room is an impressive space, with several distinct sections that include round tables for discussions, individual workstations, and a classroom-style setup at the far end with large monitors covering the wall.

Mateo is at a nearby table and waves at Tyler. "Find a new whale for us to hunt?"

Tyler laughs. "I wish."

He scans the room, spotting the COO, James Nelson, glued to his phone at another table. Then he sees Jill across the room, pacing in front of the monitors, her face taut with worry. Financial market trades scroll down the screens—the middle one shows real-time activity in the major commodities, with gold highlighted.

Jill stops in front of President Shultz, who's sitting at one of the desks, mutters something to him, then moves on.

Tyler walks over to Mateo, a sense of unease settling within him as he feels the stress in the air.

"Gold market's heating up," Mateo says.

Tyler glances again at the screen. The demand for gold is spiking, and buy orders are accumulating, waiting for the supply of sells to catch up. As a result, the price is increasing, a natural response, Tyler knows, to the demand and supply imbalance that has been created.

Jill passes in front of the center monitor again, waving her arms. Tyler's never seen her like this. He walks toward her and President Shultz.

"I thought we addressed that problem ... that we fixed the glitch," Shultz says to Jill, his voice sharp. "At least, that's what I told the board in December." He leans back in his chair and crosses his legs.

Jill turns to answer but hesitates when she notices Tyler.

"Should he be here?" she asks Mr. Shultz, her tone clipped.

Her words sting Tyler. *Why would she say that? Is she embarrassed her baby isn't behaving properly?*

Mr. Shultz frowns but responds smoothly. "This is an emergency meeting of the Investment Advisory Team. And Tyler *is* a member of the team … albeit the most junior member."

Jill glances at Tyler then faces the screens. "We've accumulated just over 10,000 shares of GLD … 1.3 million dollars' worth," she explains, pointing to the statistics displayed on one of the side monitors. "The alarm triggered at 7,600 shares, but I don't think there's a problem. I think it's working."

Mr. Shultz rises and moves to her side to get a closer look. "GLD is a reputable exchange-traded fund, right?"

She nods. "Yes, it's an ETF, but it's supposed to move in lockstep with the price of gold itself."

"Is it?"

She glances at the main screen. Tyler can see that buy orders are continuing to outnumber sells, causing the price of gold to rise.

"Gold is up almost four percent on the day," she says, pointing. "GLD is up over five percent."

She grabs the mouse on the shelf in front of her, slides the cursor onto the lower left-hand display, and taps once. A blank graph appears. She types "GLD" on the keyboard then drags it onto the graph. She does the same procedure with "gold." The result provides a comparison of the trading activity for the gold commodity and its ETF proxy.

"To answer your question, they're moving in the same direction. Both are up substantially … but not in lockstep."

"That's odd," Mr. Shultz says, a puzzled look on his face. "The ETF seems to be leading the way. It's increasing first then gold follows. That seems backward to me."

Jill's face tightens. "You're exactly right. Usually, a big change in the value of the commodity—in this case, gold—would cause the ETF to have to catch up since it's really just a proxy for the real asset. Here, the situation is reversed."

"Who's buying the ETF?" Mr. Shultz asks. "Pull it up on the big screen."

Jill moves in front of the large monitor and swipes her finger across the screen three times to replace the commodities with a list of exchange-traded funds. She finds GLD and selects it. The screen now shows only individual trades for GLD.

"Mateo! James!" Mr. Shultz calls loudly so they can both hear him over the hum of the computers stored in the glass cases beneath the screens. "Over here!"

The entire group congregates in front of the desks to stare at the display in front of them and watch New Horizon's accumulation of GLD increase.

"We're up to 11,000 shares now," James says. "It looks like Rosie is picking up the pace of our trades."

"Rosie?" Tyler whispers to Mateo.

"From *The Jetsons*, the old cartoon TV show. Rosie the robotic maid."

Too funny. For a second, Tyler can enjoy the humor.

The transactions are appearing on the screen at a faster pace now, and the lot sizes are increasing.

"We need to override her and slow this down," Mr. Shultz says.

"Not yet," Jill replies. She places her hands on her hips and watches the activity as if she's daring the algorithm—her algorithm—not to function properly. "Look, there appears to be another buyer as aggressive as us."

They can all see that, interspersed among the seemingly random flow of transactions, there are two buy orders for large blocks of shares. One is coming from them. But they're wondering about the other one.

As Tyler silently watches the transactions flashing across the screen, foreboding stirs in his gut. Someone else is buying too, matching New Horizon's every move.

The thought crosses his mind like a cold shadow—*could it be Mike?*

"We passed 15,000 shares, and the price is up eight percent," James says.

There's a knock at the door of the war room, but no one notices as they continue watching the shares roll in. There's another knock, louder this time. Again, it is ignored. Finally, the door opens, and Tara Mays pokes her head in.

"Mr. Shultz?"

His head swivels. "What is it?"

"Chief Finley from the Securities and Exchange Commission is waiting for you in your office."

"Not now, Tara."

"He's come all the way from DC, sir, at your request."

"Please, Tara. Reschedule."

"Very well."

Tara is clearly annoyed, but no one other than Tyler sees it. They all remain mesmerized by what's unfolding on the screens in front of them.

"Twenty thousand shares. Up nine percent," James says, now their unofficial play-by-play announcer.

Rosie drops in another trade—the largest so far—for 1,000 shares. Their mysterious investment partner quickly matches it.

"Who *is* this other buyer?" Mr. Shultz asks and glances from face to face.

Though Tyler could voice his guess, he simply furrows his brows and shrugs, feigning as much bewilderment as everyone else.

Mr. Shultz's eyes settle on Mateo. "Chase that down."

Tyler knows Mateo has a tough task ahead. Obtaining non-public information about stock transactions in real time is no easy feat. Maybe the relationships he has cultivated with select employees at the stock exchange will now pay him dividends.

Mateo nods and jogs over to the table where he was sitting earlier, locates a pen and a pad of paper, and starts working his cell phone.

"Look! There." Jill points at two new buy transactions. "An order from us for 1,500 shares ... and .03 seconds later, an order from someone else for the exact same number of shares."

"They're copycatting us," Mr. Shultz says, "or using the same investment algorithm." He looks at Jill. "Have you received any alerts?"

She hesitates and tosses a stink-eyed glance in Tyler's direction. "Nothing unusual," she says.

Tyler looks down at his shoes. Yes, his laces are neatly tied. A wave of fear engulfs him and washes away the serenity he has enjoyed with her the past few days.

Mr. Shultz turns to James. "Quick! Find out if we've had an enterprise breach. This has to be more than a coincidence."

James marches out of the room to obey Mr. Shultz's order, who now returns his attention to Jill. "Remind me how the fail-safe works."

Without hesitation, she rattles off the answer as if she were reading it from a textbook. "When the incremental price increase of the shares being offered for sale exceeds three standard deviations of the average daily fluctuation, Rosie should—I mean, she will—stop buying."

Tyler receives the next directive from President Shultz. "Figure out what that number is. Fast!"

As the tension escalates, so do the trades. They have now accumulated over 20,000 shares, and the price of GLD is up fourteen percent. Their total investment is staring them in the face from the screen above them … three million dollars … and it's still climbing rapidly.

Tyler scurries to the computer on the desk behind the president and works through the calculations. He returns in less than two minutes to Mr. Shultz and Jill, who are still gawking up at the big screen. New Horizon now owns 40,000 shares of GLD with a total investment of six million dollars.

"Five dollars and seventy-five cents," Tyler says.

Mr. Shultz glances at him and frowns.

Tyler continues. "Ninety-nine point seven percent of the time, the daily price change of GLD is less than $5.75, which is the third standard deviation. That's when Rosie will stop buying, according to Jill's explanation."

Their eyes return to the monitor where another transaction appears. It's from Rosie again, and it's a doozy … 4,000 shares. It settles at two dollars higher than the previous buy order, far from the $5.75 cutoff point Tyler calculated.

Mr. Shultz is shaking his head back and forth. "I don't care what the formula says. We need to stop," he says.

The door to the room opens. It's Tara again. "Mr. Shultz?"

"I told you to reschedule," he snaps.

He has a reputation for being a patient leader, but today is extraordinary.

Tara flinches but stands her ground. "I did reschedule," she says, pointing directly at him, her voice brimming with urgency. "You just received a call from a White House staffer inquiring about your knowledge of the mayhem in the gold market. They are demanding an immediate response."

The room falls silent as her words sink in. Mr. Shultz's frown deepens. He runs both hands through his already disheveled hair, the mounting stress visible in the set of his shoulders.

"Someone pull up CNBC on one of these damn screens," he demands.

Jill swiftly activates the cable news network on another monitor. The dry, monotone voice of a news analyst fills the room.

"… resulting in the largest increase in the price of gold since the COVID-19 crisis and on pace to be the largest, single-day gain in history …"

Tyler's heart pounds as he considers the implications. The second buyer has to be Mike—it's the only explanation. Tyler wills himself to stay composed but feels like he's about to explode. Is this the moment he's dreaded, the moment his betrayal will come crashing down? He never imagined the entire world would be watching when it happened.

The TV continues to blare. "The unprecedented increase is creating a ripple effect throughout the precious metals market. Silver is up twelve percent …"

Mr. Shultz pulls his focus back to Tara. His tone has calmed, though the strain in his voice is unmistakable. "Please buy me twenty minutes, Tara. Then I'll take the call."

Tara nods and leaves the room.

Mr. Shultz turns his attention back to the market update.

"… and the lack of any discernible cause for this meteoric rise in gold prices is creating fear and causing panicked investors to flee equities. As a result, stock markets worldwide are plummeting."

The team remains frozen, staring at the screen in shock. Jill doesn't say a word, appearing too confused to even begin processing the chaos. It finally dawns on Tyler that his actions have started a global economic meltdown. He can practically feel the tremors spreading through the financial world, and suddenly, he can't breathe.

"… the dollar is up three percent, and Bitcoin is surging fourteen percent as investors scramble to find shelter amid the uncertainty. Global leaders are in emergency talks, searching for an explanation, and working to develop a coordinated response to address the crisis."

Suddenly, a loud alarm pierces the room. The main screen flashes red, and a warning message pops up in bold letters: "Liquid Reserve Threshold Exceeded."

Everyone in the room instinctively turns toward the screen. New Horizon's accumulation of GLD has skyrocketed to a staggering 120,000 shares. The price has surged by forty-six percent—an unheard-of figure for a commodity-based exchange-traded fund. The twenty-million-dollar reserve threshold has been breached.

Mr. Shultz thrashes his hand toward the monitor. "No more delays—shut this thing down now!"

Before anyone can react, Tyler speaks up. "No need."

Mr. Shultz spins toward him, his face turning crimson, ready to unleash his fury. "What do you mean, 'no need'?" he barks.

Tyler holds up his hands, speaking quickly. "The price on the last trade went up $5.80. That's beyond the third standard deviation. Rosie should be done."

All eyes return to the screen, and sure enough, the buy orders from New Horizon have ceased. Rosie has stopped trading.

Mr. Shultz loosens his tie and unfastens the top button of his shirt. He runs a hand through his matted, salt-and-pepper mane, and his face sags with relief. He is spent but sports a weary smile.

"It looks like the fix worked after all," he says.

This is the second time Mr. Shultz has referenced a fix of some sort.

"The fix?" Tyler asks.

Jill shoots a cautionary glance at Mr. Shultz, but he waves her off. "It's fine," he says. "Last summer, Rosie created a panic one morning when she went on a shopping spree for corn futures. An unusual, off-cycle uptick in demand got her started, but then she didn't stop. She kept buying more and more but not like today. There wasn't another big buyer. It was just us."

Tyler pieces it together. "So she fed off her own momentum?"

Mr. Shultz moves over closer to him. "Exactly. Rosie artificially inflated demand with her early large trades then mistakenly interpreted her own purchases as a sign that the corn futures market was heating up, when it was really just a temporary early morning spike. Instead of reading the market, she was creating it, then she was unable to control her desire for more, more, more."

Unusual activity in the corn futures market. That sounds vaguely familiar, Tyler thinks.

James returns from his assignment, positioning himself next to Mr. Shultz, eyeing the monitor. "We finally stopped buying GLD?" he asks.

Mr. Shultz nods. "Rosie shut herself down, but the other player is still going strong." He raises his eyebrows. "Find anything?"

"Everything appears secure on our network, but I've got a couple others doing a deeper dive."

"What happened," Tyler asks, "with those corn futures?"

"Mateo noticed the unusual volume of purchases and sounded the alarm," Mr. Shultz says. "We shut her down after investing eight million dollars. It took us two weeks to unload the excess shares, and we ended up with a five-hundred-thousand-dollar loss. That got the board's attention."

Tyler's stomach drops. *Whose attention will today get?* As he tries to steady himself, Jill calls everyone's focus back to the screen.

"Look!" She points at the chart. "GLD is up fifty-two percent, and the other buyer hasn't slowed down. Their last purchase was eight thousand shares. Either they know something no one else does, or we're watching a train wreck about to happen."

Nervous energy fills the war room. Jill is clearly enjoying the action, thriving in the market chaos. They all watch the monitor as buy orders continue to mount.

Tyler turns to Mr. Shultz. "You were able to find the problem with the algorithm and correct it?"

James nods, interjecting. "Jill did. She found the issue after last summer's incident and worked out a solution. We tested the fix exhaustively before deploying it last month. Even then, we kept Rosie on training wheels for two weeks."

Mr. Shultz pulls a handkerchief from his pocket and wipes the sweat from his brow. "None of us expected a scenario like today. Thank goodness the safeguards held. If we'd had to manually shut her down, we'd be in a predicament trying to figure out when to sell."

"Speaking of which … look!" James exclaims, pointing back to the screen. "Rosie's starting to unload our shares."

GLD has soared fifty-five percent, and while New Horizon is shedding its position, the other buyer is eagerly gobbling up the shares, netting New Horizon a handsome profit with each transaction.

"It looks like they didn't get the fix for *their* algorithm," Mr. Shultz says with a chuckle, relaxing now that their risk is turning into reward with each passing second. "Mateo," he calls across the room, "any update on the mysterious buyer?"

Mateo covers the mouthpiece of his phone and yells back, "Not sure. Lots of speculation it's Mid-Atlantic, but I've also heard Sachs mentioned twice. It doesn't sound characteristic of either."

Why hasn't Mike stopped buying? Fear settles deeper in Tyler's bones. He can't stand still and hurries to fetch a round of cold spring water from a small kitchen tucked in the corner. He returns, four bottles in hand, to find the price of GLD still increasing, even with Rosie dumping their shares. It finally peaks at a ninety percent increase and then declines.

New Horizon's shares are soon fully liquidated, and trading activity slows noticeably. The other buyer finally stops, the other algorithm apparently now shut down.

With no more buyers to maintain the inflated price of GLD, its value starts to collapse like a house of cards. Tyler smiles nervously and takes a slow sip of water, his grip tightening around the bottle.

The shifting market dynamics catch Rosie's attention, prompting her to short-sell shares—shares they don't actually own—in the hopes the price will continue to drop, allowing them to buy back later at a lower cost.

That investment concept had confused Tyler at first, but one of his finance professors explained it to him as being like an online retailer selling a product they don't actually have in inventory yet. First, they make the sale. Then, after the fact, they acquire the product and deliver it to the consumer.

With the artificial downward pressure from short-selling, the price of GLD plummets even faster.

"Should we let this continue?" Mr. Shultz asks, clearly rattled and not ready for another roller-coaster ride. "We can stop trading now and walk away with our profits."

Jill doesn't hesitate. "We must keep going. A moment like this doesn't come along often, and we need to exploit it."

The other buyer—now apparently without their algorithm—is left on their own to chart a course on when and how to sell, like a family lost in the wilderness with a busted GPS. Their human reactions are no match for Rosie's cold, calculating precision.

The emotionless algorithm calmly processes the market action, riding the price fluctuations like a world-class surfer. GLD craters—down ten percent at one point—rebounds to plus twenty percent then drops again. Everything is happening at a fast-forward pace, and the transactions have become a blur on the screen.

The odds are tilted so unfairly, Tyler realizes, like a speed chess match between a grandmaster and a novice—it's not really a contest at all.

Finally, Rosie stops. The other player is done, down for the count. New Horizon's profits are locked in, and the carnage is over.

As the numbers settle on the screen, a figure appears—staggering in its size. Eighty million dollars. The preliminary net profit.

Mr. Shultz slumps onto a desk, burying his face in his hands. Mateo howls with victory, pumping his fists, while Jill laughs, a proud mama, her smile wide with triumph.

Tyler stands apart, emotions swirling inside him. He didn't ruin New Horizon—quite the opposite. But the victory is fleeting. An icy shiver runs down his spine as the weight of what he's set in motion presses down on him. He may have accidentally helped the company make a fortune, but he's triggered something far more dangerous.

As the others celebrate, he takes a deep breath, trying to shake the anxiety gnawing at him. His mind races through the potential fallout—the global consequences, the lives that might be affected. Guilt tightens around his chest, but beneath it, a dark satisfaction emerges as he thinks about Mike Hayward. The feeling grows, slicing cleanly through his guilt. Tyler knows he's lit a fuse on something Mike can't control, and the thought brings a twisted sense of triumph.

CHAPTER 32

The next day is a celebration. More like a zoo, really, Tyler thinks.

Everyone at New Horizon is buzzing, talking about Wild Wednesday. Rumors explode and spread like wildfire, each one more outrageous than the last, only to be discarded as soon as a new, more tantalizing one emerges.

The board of directors includes Tyler on a Zoom meeting to extol the virtues of the Investment Advisory Team. He is nervous the entire time, waiting for someone to ask exactly how another entity got their hands on such a similar algorithm.

At 1:30 p.m., Mr. Shultz strolls through the halls, beaming with goodwill, handing each employee a surprise spot bonus of ten thousand dollars. All he's missing is a Santa suit.

The unexpected bonus sends the office into overdrive—cheers, laughter, and high-fives echo through the two New Horizon floors. It's electric, but Tyler is disconnected from the energy. The money feels tainted. He donates his bonus to a local food bank without hesitation. Ten grand is a pittance next to the 2.5 million already in his account. And to him, it's blood money—his conscience isn't entirely dead. *Maybe there's hope for me yet.*

As the day winds down and the office slowly empties, Tyler sits at his desk, lost in thought, processing the events of the past couple of days. He stops by Jill's office before leaving and glances at her empty desk. A frown creases his forehead. She'd been on the Zoom earlier but hadn't shown up to the office to celebrate, nor replied to multiple texts he'd sent. She's probably wiped out. *Or is she avoiding me?*

The next morning, Tyler allows himself a few extra minutes in bed, his body heavy with fatigue from the excitement of the week. He stretches, yawning, thankful it's Friday. Despite everything, he feels lighter than he has in months—exhausted but content.

His thoughts drift to Jill. He checks his phone, but she still hasn't responded. Her phone's probably blown up since the events of Wednesday, he thinks. It still hurts, though, that she hasn't reached out. Eager to see her and celebrate the victory, he pushes himself out of bed and walks to his kitchenette. After pouring a bowl of cereal, he absentmindedly turns on the television. The background noise of the news barely registers until a familiar phrase grabs his attention.

"… and in financial news, multiple sources have identified Mid-Atlantic Financial Services as the key player in the Spring Break Gold Rush two days ago."

Tyler freezes, spoon in midair, and turns up the volume.

"An automated investment mechanism malfunctioned, causing a massive disruption in the gold markets. Analysts estimate that losses for Mid-Atlantic will be in the hundreds of millions of dollars."

The cereal bowl slips from his hand and milk splashes onto the counter. He wonders whether anyone other than Mike knows what really happened. *Could Jill have figured it out?*

"Pre-market trading has pummeled Mid-Atlantic's share price to under a dollar, prompting market officials to suspend further trading, pending an investigation."

Tyler stares at the screen, his pulse racing. This makes sense, he thinks. It was inevitable, but he hadn't fully considered the fallout. Mid-Atlantic's collapse is more real than he'd imagined. People like Greg, Michelle, and Lance will be jobless.

"CEO Mike Hayward has been unavailable for comment," the reporter says.

Tyler turns off the television to get ready for work. His mind is swirling, the reality of what he's done settling into his soul. He stumbles into the bathroom to splash cold water on his face, hoping to dispel the dread steeping in his belly.

Maybe I'll start my own company. Rent a floor in a Baltimore high-rise. Hire Greg, Michelle, and the others. I have the Lexon seed money. It could work, could be a fresh start. But the thought feels hollow, a thin veneer over the damage he knows he's caused. There's no erasing what he did.

As he strolls along 57th Street, heading to catch the train, the cool spring breeze cuts through him, betraying the warmth of the sun. His phone buzzes in his pocket. It's a text from Mike Hayward—his first contact since Tyler delivered the algorithm.

Nice try, cheater. I'm filing a protest with the council.

Fear slams into Tyler. *The council.* He's not sure who comprises the game's governing body, but surely Mike has assembled a cadre of disciples. Not exactly a jury of Tyler's peers, he is certain. His former mentor is playing chess, and once again, he's a move ahead.

What were the terms of the bet, the exact wording?

His memory is hazy, shrouded in the fog of that night's chaos. Desperation claws at him as he stops in his tracks and texts Paul.

Need your help. I'll arrive on the train at nine tonight.

He turns onto 6th Avenue, the wind picking up and gusting from the north. It carries the scent of early spring blooms, rich and floral, but to Tyler, it only smells like allergies.

Halfway to the subway, two large men appear on the sidewalk ahead. Both are huge, with shaved heads and suits a size too small. The white guy on the left glances at Tyler and says something to his friend, who snickers.

Tyler tenses, glancing at nearby rooftops, then ducks into a donut shop and gets in line. Looking over his shoulder, he sees the two men walk past without so much as a glance in his direction, continuing their conversation.

He exhales, leaving the store without ordering. His stomach is too knotted for food, and his nerves definitely don't need any caffeine.

The subway ride to Lower Manhattan gives him time to think and plan. *I'll go to Baltimore tonight, talk to Paul. He'll know how to handle Mike's latest threat.*

By the time he arrives at the office, things have calmed down. The fever pitch from yesterday has dissipated, replaced by a quiet purr of productivity. Tyler sits at his desk, sorting through papers that have gathered over the past few weeks. They all end up in the shredder.

He sends a message to his team to meet in his office. They need to focus on further developing the predictive model. It didn't fully replicate Rosie's trades, but it showed promise in sifting through the financial data to highlight key opportunities for *Beyond the Horizon*. Tyler is determined to make it a success—to make amends for his betrayal, even if it's only a small step toward redemption.

Rachel, Wei, and Nicole enter his office. Rachel and Nicole sit while Wei stands behind a chair, leaning against it.

"Did you hear about the merger?" Wei's voice is almost giddy.

Tyler shakes his head. "Merger?"

"It's all over the news," Rachel says, standing up. "Where's the remote?"

Tyler flips on the television. Mike Hayward's face fills the screen, standing behind a wall of microphones. He's on the patio outside his boardroom, squinting into the morning sun.

"Our board of directors met late into the night and again this morning," Mike's voice squawks through the speakers. "They have approved an acquisition offer from New Horizon Financial Services Company, effective immediately. The terms are confidential."

Tyler is stunned. Electricity courses through him. *This is real. Mike's empire has crumbled.* And people like Greg, Lance, and Michelle—people he thought he doomed—will be okay.

Mike is still speaking, though Tyler barely hears him as his mind is reeling. Everything has happened so fast, he thinks, it hardly seems possible. But he realizes that if the share price had crashed to zero and clients had jumped ship, there would have been nothing left to acquire.

Mike's legacy would have simply vanished—just like Tyler's chance for a normal life after that fateful elevator ride.

He hears Mike's voice again. "I want to assure our clients that you will continue to be well cared for. Account representatives will be reaching out today to discuss your investments."

Tyler's team looks to him, unsure of how to react. "I'll find out more about this," he says. "In the meantime, please prepare a summary of the model's status. I want to present it to the board this month. Actually, I want you three to present it. You've done the heavy lifting."

Rachel, Wei, and Nicole exchange proud smiles as they leave.

Tyler heads to find Jill, excited to congratulate her on the merger. He now knows why she was unreachable yesterday—she had to have been deeply involved. But there's a knot of unease in his stomach. *She's been hiding this from me.*

His hypocrisy makes him laugh. *After everything I've hidden from her?*

Still, a sliver of doubt tugs at him. Trust works two ways, he decides. It's time he comes clean so they can start fresh.

He finds her at her desk, wearing a weary but determined expression.

"Hey, honey," he says, stepping closer. "You've been hard to track down. Congrats on the monumental win."

"I've been busy," she replies without looking up. "Serious issues came up."

"I know. I saw Hayward's press conference. This is huge."

"You don't know the half of it," she says, looking up at him, eyes red and swollen. "Close the door."

Poor thing. This merger has completely exhausted her. He shuts the door then steps toward her, ready to offer comfort. He moves to embrace her, but she shoves him away—hard.

"Get away from me," she hisses.

Her words are venomous. The force of her push sends him stumbling back, shock ricocheting through him. Panic flares in his chest as he braces for the storm.

"You've been working for Mike Hayward this whole time," she snarls. "You didn't think I'd figure it out? How stupid do you think I am?"

Tyler is speechless, his mind spinning.

"You used me, Tyler. You even got me close to your sister." Her voice cracks, her rage teetering on the edge of collapse. "You're a hell of an actor. A *hell* of an actor." She pushes him again, and her fury sends him back two more steps, bumping against the wall. "But a terrible thief. You took the fool's gold, you moron."

He holds his hands up, surrendering. "Please, let me explain."

"This isn't the first time a man has treated me poorly, Tyler." She backs up to her desk and collapses onto her chair.

"I can explain—"

"Get. Out."

"Jill, I love you. Please—"

"GO!" Her voice shatters the air. Tyler is certain the entire office can hear, but he doesn't care. All he sees is the devastation in her eyes.

"Just one chance—"

"And you're fired," she whispers, her voice wavering.

Tears stream down her face as he turns to leave. He swallows his own tears until he's alone in the elevator. The doors slide shut, and his devastation reflects at him from the polished walls.

·   ·   ·   ·   ·

Once outside, Tyler plods his way down Wall Street, passing the imposing facade of the New York Stock Exchange. He barely notices it, lost in his thoughts.

What shaped people's lives in centuries past, before stocks and private jets, before millionaires and billionaires?

Was it really that different? People have always been driven by the same desires—territories to conquer, riches to accumulate, symbols of power to flaunt.

Greed is a beast that's difficult to tame.

At least for me.

But in the end, what has it all gotten him? A bloated bank balance and a world of pain. Nothing he truly cares about is intact anymore.

As he wanders aimlessly, he ignores the familiar turn toward the subway. The gray clouds overhead blot out the remaining sunlight, casting the city in a gloomy pall that matches his mood. The sky is heavy with the promise of rain, but he doesn't care.

I've done the impossible. Mike said so himself. And yet, my life is in shambles.

He kicks a crumpled newspaper, its headlines faded and smeared, and lumbers forward with no destination in mind, just a dull ache in his chest.

·　　·　　·　　·　　·

After going home to change into jeans and a windbreaker, Tyler nestles into his favorite spot atop Umpire Rock in Central Park. The uneven surface of the large boulder is familiar, comforting in a way the rest of his life no longer is. He wedges himself into the natural curve in the stone, watching a few tourists and young families milling about below.

The world is moving on, unaware of the turmoil roiling inside him.

He dials Paul's number, hoping for some sense of direction.

"Tyler," Paul's warm, fatherly voice answers. "I've been watching the news."

He presses his feet against the rock, grounding himself. "Jill found out," he says flatly.

"Oh," Paul replies, his tone softening with understanding.

"She thinks I've been working for Mike the entire time. I tried to explain, but she was too upset to listen."

A teenage boy clambers up the rock nearby, his sneakers scraping against the surface, and Tyler turns away, shielding the phone with his hand.

"Maybe when she calms down, you'll be able to tell her the full story," Paul offers after a moment. "I think she'll understand once she knows the truth."

Tyler moves carefully across the uneven rock, the jagged edges sharp beneath his shoes. He wishes he shared Paul's optimism.

"I don't think I'll get that chance. She fired me, Paul. Kicked me out of her life." He pauses, swallowing hard before continuing. "I won't be on the train tonight. Instead, I'll rent a car, pack my things, and drive down tomorrow. If it's okay, I'll stay with you for a few days."

There's a long silence on the other end of the line, and Tyler waits, the enormity of his next steps sinking in.

"You're welcome here, son. For as long as you need," Paul finally replies, his words offering a small lifeline. "But I've got business to take care of tomorrow—something important. Sunday works, though. Join us for brunch at the harbor before you come to the house. Eleven o'clock at the Rusty Scupper."

Tyler nods, though Paul can't see it. "Okay. Sunday then."

They exchange goodbyes, and as the call ends, Tyler lowers the phone from his ear and stares out at the park below. The wind picks up, tugging at the loose strands of his hair, and the gray clouds overhead seem to press down even harder.

He closes his eyes for a moment, feeling the roughness of the rock beneath him, and wonders how he'll begin to rebuild. The path forward is unclear, but he knows this—he's not done fighting for the life he wants.

CHAPTER 33

After a fretful night's sleep and a light breakfast, Tyler fills a suitcase and two boxes with the belongings he wants to keep and packs them into his rented SUV. He stops by the bank to close his account and is on the road by midmorning.

Since he isn't meeting Paul until Sunday, and with nothing else to do, he decides to take a long detour on his trek to Baltimore by spending the night in Ocean City on Maryland's Eastern Shore. Not a bad place to escape and recuperate from the events of the past week.

He pulls into the oceanfront hotel parking lot with a good four hours of daylight remaining. The hotel looks different than he remembers it from his trips there as a child. It's still nice and luxurious but not quite the majestic castle it had seemed when he was twelve. It held a magical electricity to it then, in the van full of his excited family and close friends, itching to exit the vehicle and start their vacation.

After turning off the SUV, Tyler stares at the hotel. So much has slipped away in just twenty-four hours—Jill, New York, his job. He feels numb, like his pain is being held back by an emotional dam. Hopefully, it won't burst through all at once but just trickle out in doses small enough for him to handle.

He checks in at the front desk, drops his bag off in the room, and heads straight to the beach. On the open sand, his windbreaker flaps in the strong wind. The briny, fishy, and slightly sulfurous smells of marine life that normally please him today smell putrid.

Tyler knew from the beginning Jill was the one. He'd never felt an instant attraction quite like that before. Maybe he should have told her everything months ago. Asked for her help. *Would things have turned out differently?* He thinks about that.

Mike's threat pops into his mind, and his brain starts to spin again. *What if the jerk wins the protest? What if the council sides with him?* His chest tightens, and the committee in his head manufactures thoughts so scary, he freezes in fear. It's not just the fear of losing the protest— it's everything. The lies, the betrayal, the constant pressure that has been his companion for months. Each new "what if" lands like a heavy stone on his chest, making it harder to breathe.

Anxiety builds, swirling through his head, body, and even his soul. It tightens like a vice, squeezing his chest until every breath is a battle. His hands tremble as he clenches them into fists, his nails biting into his palms. Tension pounds in his head, the familiar drumbeat of an oncoming migraine. His vision blurs, nausea curling in his gut, and he sways on the sand as though the ground itself is shifting beneath his feet.

The weight of everything is pressing down, urging him to give up, to roll over and let the chaos win—just like he's done before by refusing to ask for help. He senses he's hit rock bottom. It would be so easy to surrender, to let the pieces of his life scatter and disappear. Maybe then the pressure would stop, and the relentless fight would end.

But a stubborn resolve stirs within him. Giving up would be the easy path, but it would also mean losing himself completely. He can't change the past, or control Mike and the council. But he can control this moment—and his next choices. He still has the power to decide who he wants to be.

He tries to focus on the horizon, on the waves rolling in rhythmically, but the panic returns in full force. His pulse hammers in his ears, drowning out the sound of the ocean. Each attempt to calm himself proves futile, like trying to dam a river with his bare hands. The stress has been building for so long, he's lost sight of what life felt like without it. How long has it been since he could think clearly, breathe easily? He doesn't even know anymore. Tyler feels trapped, like his body is betraying him, locking him inside his fear. It's as if he's been carrying this burden for years, letting it shape his decisions and define his existence. How long has he been running from this moment?

His heart races faster, his breath coming in short, shallow bursts. The strain inside him mounts, threatening to break him apart. He's on the edge of the worst migraine of his life, and he knows it. But this time, something's different. This time, everything seems to be closing in, like there's no way out. He's always found a way to keep going, to hold it together, but now … now, he feels himself unraveling.

He presses his hands to his temples, as though he can physically hold the pressure in check. But the storm inside him is too strong, and he can't control it anymore. The panic keeps swelling, twisting around him in a relentless spiral. His mind whirls with worst-case scenarios. *What if I lose everything?* His pulse quickens and his breaths become shorter. Every heartbeat slams against his chest.

And then, through the fog of panic, a new thought pushes through. *What if I stop fighting? What if I stop caring about things I can't control?*

Bring it on, he screams to himself silently. A gust of wind, cold and bracing, slices through the haze clouding his mind. *I don't care anymore.*

The thought shocks him. He's spent so long trying to keep all the pieces of his life together that he never considered this—what if he just lets go? *What if the council sides with Mike? What if everything falls apart? What if it doesn't matter?*

The realization hits him like a wave. Maybe it's okay. Maybe it's all beyond his control, anyway. Letting go doesn't mean giving up. Maybe it's just about seeing things for what they are and figuring out the next right step. Slowly, carefully, he takes a deep breath, and his shoulders relax, even if just by a fraction.

The migraine that had threatened him begins to fade. His heart stops pounding. He straightens, breathing deeply as his body lets go of its tension, the tightness in his chest easing as if a knot has finally come undone. His head feels light, his muscles no longer coiled in panic.

His mind clears. Completely.

He looks out at the horizon again, this time really seeing it. The waves lap gently at the shore, a steady rhythm that matches the calm now inside him. The wind, which had once felt like a battering force, now settles into a light breeze. He breathes in the salty air, the cool wind brushing his skin.

There will be no migraine. He is no longer afraid of Mike. The council will say what they say, regardless of Mike's protest. Tyler's mind is quiet. Silent. He listens to the waves, letting them wash over him.

For the first time in years, he is truly free. He dances along the water's edge and splashes in the little tide pools formed by the receding waves. The sand, the water, and his newfound freedom rejuvenate his soul.

Tears spring to his eyes, a wave of relief washing over him.

He fills his lungs with frothy air. Anna is safe and doing well. Being with Paul and Melinda has done wonders for her. Mike and his thugs can threaten him all they want, but harming her is not part of the bet. His conversations with Paul have made it painfully clear there are rules being followed in this game.

For now, there is nothing more Tyler can do. About any of it.

What an odd time to feel free. He will return to Baltimore with his fortune, deal with the repercussions of his previous actions, and enjoy Anna's life, even if his own is completely derailed.

His feet sink into the cool, wet sand. Looking behind him, he observes the trail of footprints he's created. He spots a gap in the trail, the result of an overachieving wave that erased a small portion of his legacy. He remembers the delight Anna displayed so many years ago on this very beach, giggling and laughing at the marks she left as she frolicked along the shore, her diaper-clad, little body covered in sand.

She's more a young woman than a girl these days, he knows, but her giggling and laughter have returned recently. He could listen to that sound for hours.

Standing there, waves washing over his feet, he forgives himself—for the mistakes, the missed chances to ask for help, and the choices that spiraled out of control.

For everything.

•   •   •   •   •

The next morning, Tyler continues his trip to Baltimore to meet Paul for brunch. An accident south of Glen Burnie delays him, and he arrives ten minutes late. He parks in the lot next to the restaurant and hurries toward the Inner Harbor eatery. The red letters on the side of the building announce its name—Rusty Scupper. A dozen boats rock gently in slips along a dock.

He passes through the double-door entrance to the restaurant. Light jazz fills the air, and he sees two thin, bearded, older guys—they look like brothers—who are set up in a back corner, one playing a keyboard, the other strumming a guitar.

There is no sign of Paul, Melinda, or Anna.

Tyler ventures back outside and scans the parking lot more closely. No black Escalade. He meanders to the harbor side of the three-story structure, content to relax for a few minutes. He stands and looks at the water and the downtown buildings beyond.

"Tyler!" a voice booms from a nearby dock. "Over here."

Paul is standing behind the center console of a thirty-seven-foot, Grady-White Canyon 386. He has one hand on the controls, and the other is waving at Tyler.

Tyler knew Paul kept a boat at the Harbor East Marina, past downtown on the far side of the harbor, but he's never seen it. The Grady-White's seaport-blue hull doesn't appear to have a scratch on it, and the humming of its triple 350 horsepower Yamaha engines hints at the power it has.

Tyler boards the vessel and offers his hand, but Paul ignores it and gives him a fatherly hug.

"Quite a week you've had," Paul says.

"Melinda and Anna aren't here?" Tyler asks.

"We'll pick them up on the other side of the harbor."

Paul revs the engines as Tyler takes a seat. He steers the boat along the shoreline and away from the city.

Tyler wobbles up to the bow, his steps uneven on the bobbing vessel. He sucks in the clean ocean breeze, free from the pollen of flowers, the exhaust of cars, and the smells of a bustling city. The cool wind stings his cheeks and tickles the bare skin of his arms. Goosebumps form along his legs.

He can't get enough of it. He's watched with envy other families enjoying the harbor on many sunny weekends but always from a distance as he jogged along the Waterfront Promenade on his way to Fort McHenry.

"You can't seem to hang on to a job, my friend," Paul calls from behind the controls.

Tyler steps back carefully and rejoins him, grinning. "True enough."

"Melinda and I talked about this," Paul says in a serious, fatherly tone. "We'd like to give you a loan. Take the pressure off for a few months so you can focus on Anna and your future without being strapped for cash."

Tyler bursts into laughter.

Paul appears annoyed, even hurt. "We just want to help," he says.

"I do need your help, but I'm okay financially. That's the only area in which I am okay."

Water laps against the side of their slow-moving vessel.

"There's no shame in accepting assistance, you know."

"A lesson I have learned." Tyler smiles. "The only concern I have right now from a financial perspective is that you might take a turn too quickly and send me flying into the very wet water of the harbor."

Paul tilts his head, questioning.

"I've got a cashier's check in my pocket that needs to stay dry … a 2.5-million-dollar check, to be exact."

Startled, Paul inadvertently pulls on the throttle and sends the boat lurching forward. Tyler falls backward in his seat, his feet flailing in the air.

"What have you gotten yourself into that I *don't* know about?" Paul asks as he slows the boat down.

Tyler straightens up and recounts all the events surrounding the Lexon Pharmaceuticals deal.

They troll past the invisible line separating the waters of the Inner Harbor from those of the Patapsco River, with Paul skillfully navigating between the boats of anglers anchored in their favorite spots. A water taxi passes them and speeds off in the other direction. Two young children wave from it, and Tyler returns their greeting.

"Why didn't you tell me?" Paul asks.

"I was ready to use it—all of it if I had to—to buy my way out of the bet. But Mike didn't care about the money."

Paul smirks. "I bet he would now."

Tyler chuckles then stands and steps out from behind the protection of the console. The light breeze once again fans his face. He squints and surveys the greenish-blue waters ahead.

"I guess it wasn't too difficult for you to figure out I fulfilled my obligation. That I gave him the algorithm."

"Wednesday kind of made that clear to me." Paul takes one hand off the wheel and waves over toward the horizon. "And, to some extent, to the rest of the population across all seven continents."

Tyler laughs then sighs. "Unfortunately, Jill is one of those people."

They're quiet for a moment, listening to the rippling wind as it breaks across the outline of the Grady-White. Tyler steps to the port side, leans over the edge, and runs his hand through the swells, enjoying the silky water as it climbs his arm, then dribbles back into the sea.

Paul clears his throat and says, "You've been chasing control for a long time, son. But sometimes the things we can't control are the ones that set us free."

Tyler looks up at him, considering his words. The fear that has ruled his life for years lingers in his chest, but he allows himself to imagine fully letting go. The peace he felt on the beach radiates through him. He smiles and nods.

Paul glances ahead. "There's Fells Point."

"Are we picking the ladies up there?" Tyler asks.

"No," Paul says, "they're back a ways. They needed a few minutes, and I thought a little ride would be nice, give us a chance to catch up." He turns the boat in a slow arc. They ride in silence, viewing the conglomeration of bars and restaurants unfolding before them.

"Mike says he's protesting to the council," Tyler finally says. "He's claiming I cheated and didn't fulfill my obligation."

Paul glances at him.

"The algorithm I gave him wasn't the newest version," Tyler says. "I didn't know it at the time. Not until last Wednesday."

"Is it the version that produced the returns on New Horizon's Annual Statement?"

Tyler stands and grasps the top of the console. "Had to be. They just unleashed the new version in January."

"That's how the council remembers the bet."

"You're on the council?"

The hotels are approaching, the big name, expensive kinds with many floors—Four Seasons and Marriott, both to starboard—tall, glass structures towering over each other, competing to provide their guests with the best views of the harbor.

"We had an emergency meeting yesterday," Paul says.

Suddenly woozy, Tyler sits down on the side of the boat. His life depends on what his older friend's next words will be.

He listens to the engines' purr in the silence that follows as they propel the boat slowly forward. A trio of figures mills about on an empty dock in front of the hotels, too far away for him to make out details.

Paul finally speaks, calm as ever. "Mike made his case, but the custodian of the game, along with most of us, ruled in your favor."

He holds Tyler's gaze for a moment before smiling. "You're free, my friend. The albatross has flown away."

Tyler goes numb, relieved, but also confused. "The custodian?" he asks and stretches his legs. "I thought Mike was in charge."

Paul shakes his head no. "It's a good thing for you he's not."

Tyler leans over the side of the boat again and lets his fingers dance along the top of the water. He thinks about what could have happened and feels relief one more time.

A huge boat zips by, and he looks up to see the large waves of its wake coming at him.

"Hold on!" Paul yells, gripping the wheel tightly as his eyes widen.

The Grady-White rides up to the crest of a wave before plunging into a dip, and a wave of salty water splashes onto Tyler's face. He swallows a mouthful and starts coughing uncontrollably.

"Are you okay?" Paul asks.

Tyler nods, now laughing, and he runs a hand through his damp hair. He is refreshed from this unexpected baptism, but he checks his pocket to ensure the check is still dry.

Standing, he scans the view in front of them and glances past the three people waiting on the dock. He stops and does a double take, his heart stuttering in his chest. It's Melinda and Anna.

And Jill.

· · · · ·

Tyler looks at Paul, bewildered.

"You'll have to ask Anna about that." Paul grunts and shakes his head. "She accosted me yesterday as I was eating breakfast, demanding that I take her to the Four Seasons, the one just ahead." He nods toward the glass tower rising behind the ladies. "She told me Jill would be coming into town to handle issues related to the merger and that they were going to have lunch together."

"But how—"

"Melinda and I are going to drop the three of you off for brunch and give you a chance to sort everything out."

"I can't talk about the game."

Paul chuckles. "I think you can in this instance. I wouldn't do anything foolish like write a book about it, but talking about it with your sister and your girlfriend is okay."

Tyler frowns. "Jill hates me."

"She loves you." Paul pushes forward on the throttle, slowing the boat. "That's why she was so upset when she thought you were secretly working with Mike."

They pull alongside the dock. Tyler helps Melinda step aboard, then Anna, and finally Jill, who accepts his hand and climbs on.

"Thought we lost you there for a second," Jill says, "when that other boat sped by you."

"Yeah, dopey," Anna says and pushes against his chest. "Be careful."

Tyler laughs.

Paul nudges the boat away from shore and glides across the gentle waves. Foamy bits of spray are dancing along the crests. The Rusty Scupper is directly ahead across the harbor. Many boats are out now with their passengers enjoying the warmth of the noon sun on their shoulders as they float along the protected waters of the Inner Harbor.

·   ·   ·   ·   ·

Brunch is both pleasant and awkward.

Anna insisted that Paul and Melinda join them, and she leads the conversation as Tyler thinks about how best to bring up his questions without disturbing the calm of their relaxed meal on a pressed white tablecloth. He decides instead to listen to Anna as she talks about the one hundred she just earned on an algebra test.

He smiles, so happy that she continues to thrive in her new environment.

Jill remains quiet. She glances at Tyler several times, as if about to speak, but holds back.

Melinda and Paul help fill the conversational voids by telling Anna about the stores located in the shopping gallery across the harbor. Anna declares it will be their next stop.

After the meal, the five exit the restaurant. Tyler looks at Paul. "You all take the boat. Jill, would you walk around with me? We can meet them at the shops."

She simply nods, her eyebrows raised in an expression he can't decipher.

"Better hurry," Anna says. "Might not be anything left in the stores once I start shopping."

She runs to the boat and hops on. Melinda and Paul laugh and follow her.

Tyler and Jill stroll along the promenade. He is still uncomfortable, unsure of what to say. Nodding toward the city, he asks, "Has it changed much since you were a kid?"

Jill slows her pace and looks from the tall downtown buildings back to the horizon of the harbor water then turns to Tyler. "It's changed. I've changed. I still come down here about once a year. I'm on a board that meets annually." She glances at the water. "Family trust, of sorts."

"I was shocked to see you on the dock," Tyler says.

"Twenty-four hours ago," she says, "I would've bet anything that I'd be anywhere in the world except standing on a dock in front of my hotel, waiting to get picked up for brunch with you."

They turn right onto the main boardwalk leading to the restaurants and shops. Tyler moves a little closer to her.

"You might want to be careful betting *anything*. I got into some trouble with that."

Jill raises her eyebrows at him.

He shifts uncomfortably under her stare, the cool breeze from the harbor doing little to calm his nerves. After rehearsing what to say ever since he saw her waiting on the dock, the words now feel jumbled and inadequate.

He remembers the wind on the beach, how it felt to finally release the weight of his fear. That same freedom pushes him forward now, giving him the courage to face her with honesty.

"Jill, I've made some big mistakes," he blurts out, breaking the silence. "I'd really like to explain."

He watches her closely as she glances silently at the horizon then to the pavers beneath her feet. She reaches for her necklace and massages the dangling silver locket, apparently deep in thought. He can't tell if she's holding back words of her own or deciding whether he deserves to speak at all.

For a moment, he braces himself for rejection. Then she nods. "I'm listening."

They continue to move slowly along the promenade, the bustling sounds of the harbor blending with the rhythmic slap of water against the boardwalk. Tyler swallows hard and begins.

"From the start, I was in over my head. Mike roped me into this incredible poker game, and I thought I could handle it, but I was wrong. I let the stakes spiral out of control, and I lost a bet that forced me to get your algorithm … to steal your algorithm."

He stops, the gravity of his confession settling heavily in the space between them. Jill's expression remains unreadable, her lips pressed into a thin line. Tyler's pulse quickens. *What's she thinking? Does she hate me? Forgive me?* He can't tell, and the uncertainty gnaws at his resolve.

"I didn't think about who I'd hurt. You, Anna …" He hesitates, his voice breaking. "I've been selfish and reckless. I've lied to you, and I used you, Jill. For that, I am so, so sorry."

He risks a glance at her, unsure if his words are enough—or too late. The tension in her posture softens, but she says nothing, her gaze shifting back to the water. So he continues. "When I stole the algorithm, I thought it was the only way to protect Anna. But I know now that I was just making excuses. I betrayed your trust because I wasn't strong enough to face the consequences any other way."

They pause near a bench overlooking the water. Jill leans against the railing, her arms folded. "Anna told me what happened. She's the reason I'm here." A few steps later, she adds, "She told me a lot, but hearing it from you …" Her voice trails off.

Sweet Anna. For so long, I thought she needed me to protect her, but maybe she's been stronger than I ever gave her credit for. Strong enough to bring me and Jill together here, to help me see what I needed to fix.

Tyler steps closer. "I want to make things right. I know I can't undo what I've done, but I'm here, Jill. Whatever it takes to earn your trust again, I'll do it."

She takes a hesitant breath, falling silent for a moment before speaking again. "I hated you for what you did, Tyler. For the lies, the way you made me feel like I didn't matter. But I couldn't shake the thought that there was more to it. Maybe that's why I'm here now. Deep down, I wanted to believe what we had was worth saving, that the Tyler I knew wasn't entirely gone." She pauses then offers a tentative smile. "Forgiveness has never been easy for me—it's been a tough road, learning to forgive. But I'm here, trying."

The depth of her emotion leaves him shaken. For a moment, he's silent, letting her words settle like ripples spreading across still water, a testament to how far they've both come. They walk for a few moments, stopping by the pier to watch a sailboat leaving its berth, its sails catching the light breeze.

He turns to her. "How did Anna know about the bet?"

"She said she heard Paul and Melinda whispering about it, worrying about you."

"Quite the eavesdropper, isn't she?"

Jill nods. "She sent me a text Friday night." Making eye contact with him, she adds, "Her timing was spot-on. I was still feeling sorry for myself … but also a little for you."

Tyler smiles faintly. "And apparently, she's a good saleswoman, too."

Jill looks at him with big, sad eyes. "In her text, she said she almost lost her big brother. And that she doesn't want to lose her big sister, too." Her voice falters. "I cried when I read that."

He feels tears forming himself. Holding his breath, he reaches for her hand. She accepts the offer, and they walk along together.

This feels good. This feels right.

"She also said she knows what it's like … being betrayed by you."

That doesn't feel so good. Not so right.

Jill's warm hand in his does not completely erase the unease between them. They walk in silence again, each lost in their own thoughts. Finally, she breaks the quiet. "I'm not saying this fixes everything, Ty. We still have a lot to work through." She glances at him. "But I'm here. And that's a start. And in the end, who doesn't have secrets?"

Tyler nods, satisfied. She's seen the worst of him, all his character warts exposed. Yet here she is, holding his hand.

He glances up at the skyscrapers of the city beyond the harbor buildings. The Mid-Atlantic building looms dead ahead, a quarter mile away. She follows his eyes then stops suddenly and turns to face him, her expression more serious now.

"There's something else," she says, her voice steady but cautious.

Tyler meets her eyes, unsure of what's coming next.

"I've got a meeting at Mid-Atlantic tomorrow," she says, "with Mike and his lawyers."

"Paul mentioned you're here to deal with merger-related issues."

"It's more than that. I'm actually moving to Baltimore."

He stops and his jaw drops.

"Mid-Atlantic will remain intact as a subsidiary of New Horizon," she says. "And I'm going to be the new president of the subsidiary."

Tyler wraps his arms around her waist and twirls her in a circle, forgetting they're still breaking the ice from their temporary separation. He steps back, his hands resting on her hips, staring into her eyes.

"Does that mean …"

She finishes his sentence, "That we'll all be here—you, me, Anna, and the Thompsons."

They continue along the boardwalk. Two children dart in front of them, engrossed in a game of tag and playfully taunting each other, oblivious to the crowd of people around them.

Tyler pauses mid-step, just long enough to avoid running into the kids. "At least you can give them the correct investing algorithm," he says and chuckles.

"Ty," she says, her voice soft but resolute, "it's so much more than an investing tool. It's a way to reshape the future. Which you'll fully see when you help me improve it."

He whips his head around to look her in the eye, his mouth slightly open. *Did I hear that right?*

In response to his questioning look, she holds up a finger as they thread their way through the growing thicket of people out in full force to enjoy the first taste of spring.

"I need someone I can trust, someone who's on my level to help me accelerate progress on the algorithm. It can do so much good in the world." She pauses, her eyes shifting momentarily before locking back on his. "I know this might be a lot to process, especially now, but I want you to take the CFO role at Mid-Atlantic."

Tyler blinks, caught off guard. He opens his mouth to respond but hesitates. "You're serious?"

"I am," she says, folding her arms. "Look, this doesn't erase what's happened between us. But I know you, Ty. You're good at this. And right now, Mid-Atlantic needs someone who can steer things back on course." She takes a breath. "We need each other. In more ways than one."

Tyler considers this. There's a lot that still needs to be said, a lot they need to work through, but maybe this is how they start.

"I turned that job down," he says, "less than a month ago."

Jill's eyes widen. "What?"

"Mike offered me the job after I gave him the algorithm." He snickers. "That guy has no clue." It's funny how things come full circle, he thinks. The same job he didn't want because it would have dragged him deeper into deception is now an opportunity to start fresh—with Jill. After a pause, he continues, "It's more appealing this time, though."

"Is that a yes?"

He chuckles. "Only if you agree there's no chance for a promotion anytime soon. That doesn't seem to work out well for anyone."

"Deal." She gives him a little sideways push. "Your first assignment is to attend the meeting with me tomorrow morning." She does not wait for acknowledgment. "Meet in the Four Seasons lobby. Eight thirty, sharp. We'll walk over together."

He nods, and they continue walking to the gallery, where they find the other three at a sporting goods store. Melinda and Paul sip coffee while Anna rummages through a sale rack. Her face lights up, and she rushes over to Jill holding a Baltimore Ravens jersey.

"What do you think?" Anna asks.

"Don't spoil her," Tyler says as Jill pulls a credit card from her purse.

Paul chuckles. "Looks like you're a little too late there, son."

"Can Jill stay at our house tonight?" Anna asks.

"Sorry, sweetie," Jill says gently, running a hand through Anna's hair, "but I've got a mountain of work to get through." She turns to Tyler, a small smile playing on her lips. "Perhaps I could come over for dinner tomorrow?"

Tyler nods, feeling a quiet understanding pass between them.

CHAPTER 34

A team of expensive suits huddles outside the door to the boardroom, the Armanis filled with enormous bellies and fat wallets. Even bigger egos appear to lurk above their collars.

Jill marches down the hall toward them with purpose. Tyler fast-steps alongside her, trying to keep up, as do New Horizon's general counsel and a second attorney who specializes in mergers and acquisitions. Mike's assistant, Lance, lags behind and breaks into a jog to overtake them.

"Ms. Young." Lance catches up as Jill slows to a walk on the final approach. "This is Jeremy Stone." He motions toward a large man waiting near the door. "He's lead attorney for Mid-Atlantic."

"Pleased to meet you," Stone says, his deep voice rumbling from behind a bushy black beard. As they shake hands, he adds, "Mr. Hayward requests the courtesy of a private conversation before we attorneys come in and muck things up." He finishes with a throaty chuckle.

"I advise against it," Jill's general counsel says out loud, then whispers, "There's a reason you pay me big dollars."

Jill looks past the gaggle of advice-givers, and Tyler follows her gaze into the boardroom. Mike Hayward sits alone at one end of the rosewood table, watching them. He locks eyes with Jill. Then with Tyler. Then back to Jill.

Everyone waits.

Finally, Jill breaks the silence. "It's okay," she says to her attorney. "Give me a few minutes." Without taking her eyes off Mike, she adds, "Tyler, you're coming with me."

They enter the boardroom. The door closes behind them, cutting off the loud voices and general office din from the hallway. The soundproof glass encasing the room creates a cocoon of silence.

Mike reaches under the table and flips a switch. The see-through windows instantly turn opaque, and the overhead lighting increases in intensity, transforming the fishbowl into a private meeting space.

Jill approaches the head of the table and Tyler follows. Mike leans back, his elbows resting on the chair's plush armrests, his right leg crossed over his left. He studies Jill with vacant eyes.

She stops five feet away, and Tyler stops next to her. Together, they look down at the fallen giant. Mike seems to wake up, and his eyes focus, Jill in his crosshairs.

"Hello, Jillian."

Tyler glances over at her, confused.

"Don't call me that," she says.

Mike smiles, his eyes twinkling. "Well done, young lady. The apple doesn't fall far from the tree, they say."

"Don't you dare try to equalize us," she hisses. "You use people, destroy them, and toss them away like they're nothing more than yesterday's trash."

Tyler's mind spins, trying to make sense of what's unfolding before him.

Grew up in Baltimore … moved away with her mom … financial leader. Could it be?

"Our actions are very much the same. I know that displeases you," Mike says, clearly enjoying himself. "Embrace your Hayward heritage. Don't run from it. You've proven yourself the superior puppet master. You used my own pawn against me."

Tyler remembers Greg's words after he finally accessed the secure server. "It's like someone left the front door open and the porch light on." He hadn't given it much thought at the time. He'd just been grateful to get the algorithm.

"I'm nothing like you." Jill's voice is a fierce whisper slicing through the still air.

Did she set me up? Tyler is still staring at her, a quizzical expression on his face.

She ignores him and looks straight ahead at Mike, but her cheeks flush red.

Tyler remembers what she said when she fired him. "You took the fool's gold." She'd given it to him to steal. *He* was the fool.

"You *are* my daughter." Mike is laughing as he speaks with the annoying, condescending cackle Tyler has learned to despise. "You can't deny that."

Tyler is humiliated and angry. Twice he has tried to outwit a Hayward—once out of greed and once out of fear—and both times, it's backfired. He is zero for two.

"I *was* your daughter," Jill says, her voice rising. "You took care of that when you drove Mom and me away. You killed her."

The hurt in her voice evaporates Tyler's anger. She thought he was a spy, that he was using her and would stab her in the back. Instead, she turned the tables—and saved him in the process.

He moves closer to her and places a hand on her shoulder.

"You can get mad," Mike says with a smug smile. "But you can't escape the fact you're my offspring."

She steps closer to Mike, pointing her finger down at him. "For every ten parts Mom, I'm only one part you!" she yells.

Tyler clears his throat. "Only one?"

She glances at him then adds softly, "Maybe two."

They both grin, and the tension in the room falls away like a sail without wind.

Even Mike appears amused.

Jill pulls a chair away from the table and turns it so she faces her father. She sits, and Tyler follows suit.

Mike nods in Tyler's direction. "What's this loser doing here?"

"This loser is my new CFO. He'll be the one signing your pension check, so you better be nice to him." She rests a hand on Tyler's knee.

"I've already got a CFO."

Jill's fingers tense on his kneecap.

Mike laughs. "You don't think I'm going to walk out of here and hand over the keys, do you?"

"You approved the merger," Jill says. "It clearly states that the New Horizon executive team will take control."

"No, darling." He waves a finger. "My *board* approved that cowardly cop-out of a deal. I didn't vote for it."

"Either way, it's binding."

"So you say. But I've got a pit bull out there who'll say otherwise. We'll tangle this up for years in the courts." Mike stretches his arms. "Unless you want to pay me thirty mil to walk away quietly."

"Oh, Dad, you're such a pain in the ass."

Tyler coughs. Mike glances his way but quickly focuses back on Jill. "Can you get rid of him so we can really talk?"

"Mr. Hayward," Jill says, her tone firm, "as an executive of New Horizon Financial Services Company, there is no way I can satisfy your extortion request."

"Let's drop the charade." Mike flashes his signature smile. "We both know you and I should be working together." He stands and steps forward. "I wasn't the greatest father, I'll admit. But I'm not responsible for your mother's death. You need to move past that and do what you are meant to do."

"That's exactly what I am doing."

"No! You're putzing around—with the most significant invention in human history." He stretches his palms out, beckoning, as his deep voice rises. "Join me, and the Hayward empire can begin. Our reign will know no boundaries—not on this Earth."

She pushes her chair back. "You're delusional."

"Fine." He shrugs. "We'll bring the lawyers in and let them get to work."

"You'll lose."

"Eventually." He sneers. "But that's irrelevant. This will buy me time."

Tyler is mesmerized as he watches these two giants volley salvos at each other. He realizes he's holding his breath and forces himself to exhale slowly then breathe in fresh oxygen.

"You made a mistake by giving me the algorithm," Mike says. "You think ruining my company is the end—game over for me. But what you fail to comprehend is that you've given me the seed I'm after. Yes, it's a flawed version. Yes, it'll take time to perfect. But I have a team of scientists eager to fertilize and nurture it into the magnificent flower it will become."

"I'll get there first," Jill says, crossing her arms tightly over her chest. "You're wasting your resources."

"Your bluff isn't fooling me, sweetie. You may be ahead now, but I know, for a fact, that your partners have had trouble staying alive."

She gasps and her eyes fill with tears. "You son of a bitch!"

He steps forward and closes the gap between them.

"Come work with me, Jillian. You turned me down five years ago. Don't make that mistake again. We are destined to do great things together. We can do so much more than toss gold back and forth."

"Not a chance."

"Then we're back to lawyers and legal delays."

"I guess we are."

Mike turns quickly, angrily, and strolls to the window.

"You think you're saving this city, don't you? Think you're saving the world, keeping me from seeing the Einstein Code. But you're wrong, sunshine. You're obstructing the wrong fella."

The Einstein Code? Tyler thinks about the algorithm and the parts of it he doesn't understand. *Could it be real?* He's read that it's a pipe dream, the kind of goal fringe lunatics waste their time on. *But if it's real ...* His heart thumps as he considers the ramifications.

"You're the one bluffing now," Jill says.

"Am I?" Mike snorts. "Heard of Anton Popa? Think he'll be a good steward of this technology?"

"I'll get there first," Jill says, her hands forming into tight fists. "And when I do, I'll make the code open source, allow everyone access."

Tyler understands the brilliance of her solution. If everyone has the code and can use it to interpret data and information in the same new and powerful ways, the would-be power mongers will have no advantage, no edge to exploit. And yet, all the positive benefits will still manifest.

Mike turns toward them and leans over the board table, bracing himself with his arms. "Nice try, but we both know New Horizon will never allow you to do that."

Jill assumes a similar position on the other side of the East Indian rosewood. "I don't need their permission. It's my algorithm. New Horizon leases it from me."

Tyler would never admit it publicly, but he sees many similarities between the two titans.

"Smart girl." Mike strolls around the head of the table. "But it's all academic. You don't have the resources to get to the finish line. The Popa clan does, and then they'll shut the rest of us down."

Jill glares at Mike then marches to the terrace door. She opens it, and a blast of cool air blows into the room. Stepping outside, she walks over to the far end of the grass and places her hands on the metal railing, scanning the metropolis below.

Seconds become minutes. Tyler stays seated, pulls out his phone to check his email, then glances again at Jill, who is still staring out across the harbor. An idea suddenly pops into his head.

While Mike sits back down at the head of the table and scratches his chin, Tyler continues to think through his idea.

Several minutes later, the terrace door clicks shut. Tyler looks up to see Jill studying him with bloodshot eyes. She walks over to Mike.

"I cannot allow the Romanian mob to perfect this technology," she says. "It would erase everything I've dedicated my life to achieve. Destroy the ideals for which Francis gave his life." She clenches her hands. "It would obliterate global advances in human rights and democracy."

Mike nods and smiles. "I do know I'm not your first choice." He stands and offers a hand. "Partners then?"

Jill opens her mouth to speak, but before she does, Tyler steps forward, his eyes locking on Mike. "I have a better way to settle this," he says, his voice firm and deliberate.

Mike raises an eyebrow, clearly intrigued. Jill turns to look at him as well.

Tyler speaks with unflinching resolve. "You and I will play poker," he says to Mike. "If you win, you'll exit with your thirty million. And you'll get Rosie … with all the code. If I win, you walk away with nothing and hand over your scientists."

Jill's eyes widen in surprise, then she quickly regains composure. "Tyler—"

He raises a hand. "It's the only way. We end this now."

She is momentarily stunned. He can see the conflict written across her face. She looks at him, brows furrowing as if trying to read the motives behind his offer. Her chest rises and falls with a deep breath, and Tyler senses the silent calculations taking place. She shifts her attention to Mike then back to him, and he wonders if she's questioning whether to trust him with so much on the line.

"Why would you suggest that?" Her voice softens, as if considering whether he's serious.

The enormity of the stakes presses down on him. Engaging in a contest like this would be exhausting and extract a grueling mental toll. But like the game itself, this bet would be much bigger than him. A bad call could shatter Jill's dreams, jeopardize her vision of having a transformative positive impact across the globe, even disrupt the world order.

He lifts his chin and meets her eyes. "It's my chance to set things right, to make amends for everything," he says. Then he smiles and adds, "Besides, it's in my new job description."

Jill tilts her head.

"Other duties as assigned," he adds with a grin.

Mike laughs, loud and deep. "Oh, this is good. Very good." He sits and leans back in his chair, fingers drumming on the table as an unreadable expression crosses his face. The silence stretches, the room charged with an almost tangible energy. Finally, he stands and claps his hands once. "I agree."

Tyler turns to Jill. She hesitates, her eyes narrowing as she appears to process the magnitude of what's unfolding. He knows it's a life-changing gamble, one that could alter everything she's fought for. Her gaze shifts from Tyler to Mike then back to Tyler again, searching his face. The weight of the decision hangs heavy in the air.

After a long moment, Jill exhales slowly and gives a small nod of agreement.

"See, honey," Mike says, grinning. "You are my daughter, after all."

She walks toward the door but stops just before exiting, turning back to Tyler. "Don't screw it up this time," she says with a wink before disappearing through it.

Mike grins as Tyler stands alone with him in the now-quiet room. "Don't screw it up," Mike echoes with a sarcastic laugh.

• • • • •

Tyler stops by Greg's office before leaving the building.

Greg jumps up from his chair as Tyler enters then peeks nervously down the hall before quickly closing the door behind him and returning to his seat. His leg bounces under the desk, and his fingers tap a restless rhythm on the edge of the table.

"Relax," Tyler says, amused. "I've never seen you so jumpy."

"I heard the new president is here finalizing details to shut this place down." Greg gestures toward the office buildings outside his window. "I've already sent my resume to a recruiter, hoping she'll find me something local."

"Your job's safe," Tyler says calmly.

"Yeah, right," Greg says, fingers tapping faster now.

"They wouldn't hire a new CFO if they were planning to fire everyone and consolidate the business in New York," Tyler says with a grin.

Greg squints. "Who'd they get?"

Tyler smirks, leaning casually against the desk.

Greg tilts his head. "You're not serious."

Tyler's face stretches into a wide smile.

"You?" Greg's voice is incredulous as he shakes his head. "You are serious."

Tyler nods toward Camden Yards. "Soon, we'll be going to O's games again. Except this time, better seats. On me."

Greg slaps the desk and laughs, his leg finally still. "You picked one hell of a path to a promotion, my friend."

Tyler chuckles. "You have no idea." He walks out the door then pauses and pokes his head back in. "I hear there's an opening for the VP of IT. I may have already put in a good word for you with the president."

Greg beams. "You're a lunatic, my man, but thanks."

Tyler waves and steps out, a surge of confidence buzzing through him.

CHAPTER 35

Tyler stands beside Jill, gazing at the White House as they wait for Anna, Melinda, and Paul to return.

"That's where the big decisions are made," he says. "Where the deals that really matter get done."

"At least the ones not decided at a poker table," Jill says, her voice edged with wariness.

He laughs nervously, the sound of it lingering between them. Tonight is the night. The showdown between him and Mike is scheduled to begin at the Willard Hotel, a half mile away. Paul had suggested the neutral site, the same location where the very first game was played over a century and a half ago.

Tyler glances down Pennsylvania Avenue. The road is closed to vehicles, but it's packed with people. The third Saturday in March always attracts tourists in droves for spring break, but today, with the sun warming the air to a perfect seventy-four degrees, even the locals have come out to enjoy the day.

"The cherry blossoms are starting to bud," Jill says, pointing at trees poking out from behind the grand residence, the first hints of pink scattered among the branches. "Full bloom will be here soon. So beautiful," she adds, sighing.

Tyler smiles, though anticipation builds within him. He stands a little taller, reminding himself that he's the one who proposed this game.

"You know, Jill, for the first time in a while, I'm sure I'm doing the right thing—facing Mike head on. Even if I'm nervous as hell."

Jill looks at him, her forehead creased, but there's warmth in her eyes. "You *are* doing the right thing, Tyler. This isn't just about the game or the algorithm. You're taking control of your life again. And you're not alone in this. We're all behind you."

Her words calm him, easing the tension that's been winding tight inside. "Thanks. I'm so glad you're here."

She squeezes his hand. "I wouldn't be anywhere else."

For a moment, he lets himself relax. The warmth of the March sun mirrors the budding hope in his chest, but then the nagging thought that's been bothering him for the past couple weeks pushes to the surface. He needs to know.

"When did you find out I was looking for the algorithm?" he asks quietly.

Jill crosses her arms, bracing herself before she speaks. "A few days before Valentine's Day, I received an automated alert about failed attempts to access our system. I didn't know for sure it was you until I got the security logs the next Saturday morning." She pauses, looking at him carefully. "I remember it because it was right before I left my condo to meet you for our run."

"I thought I might have been detected," Tyler admits. "I actually expected to be escorted out of the building." His cheeks flush dark crimson. "Instead …"

"I was so mad," she says. "It was all I could think about while we ran—how you'd come from Mid-Atlantic and were so eager to see the algorithm. I just knew you must be working for Mike." She places a hand on his shoulder, softening her tone. "Thank God I was wrong."

Tyler rubs his jaw, a wave of regret settling deep within him.

"As soon as I got home," Jill says, "I moved Rosie out and put the old version of the algorithm in there. Turned off the firewall. That's how you got in."

Tyler chews his lip.

Jill adds, "After a couple weeks passed and nothing happened, I felt guilty for having suspected you. Until Wild Wednesday."

He shakes his head. "I can't believe what this game pushed me to do." He pauses. "Okay, more like what I made myself do."

Jill leans against him, resting her forehead on his shoulder. For a moment, the seriousness of everything melts away in the closeness between them. "It's easy to lose perspective when things get so intense," she says. "It's all been so surreal."

Tyler wraps his arms around her, drawing strength from the warmth of her presence. "If it were up to me," he says, "the game would be disbanded. Shut down for good."

She pulls back slightly, giving him a funny look. He continues before she can respond. "Paul insists it's good for the country, necessary even, but I'm not buying it."

She studies him for a long moment, her face thoughtful. Finally, she speaks. "I was shocked when you suggested this final bet."

His eyes widen, taken aback. "I had to do something. It felt like the only way forward." He pauses, his voice softening. "Plus, I created this mess."

"It'll be a disaster if Mike gets the algorithm," Jill says. "He'll exploit it for his own gain, and that won't do anything to make the world a better place." She frowns. "I can't even imagine how big his ego would get."

Tyler runs a hand over the back of his neck, glancing away. "But if the Romanian mob gets it? That's a whole different level of danger."

She nods, her expression grim. "That's why I agreed to it, Tyler. We can't risk the algorithm falling into their hands." She pauses, her eyes searching his. "I can't risk my invention being used to destroy the world, even if it means taking a chance on Mike."

They stand quietly for a moment, listening to the buzz of the throngs of people soaking in the spring air.

"And if you win," she says, "his team could really speed up our progress. He's right about the Popa clan—we must beat them. This is our shot."

He breathes deeply. "I won't lie. Mike's good, and he knows how to get under my skin." He meets her gaze. "But that's why I challenged him. I've run long enough."

Jill's eyes soften. "You're stronger than you give yourself credit for. But I get it—he's confident, cocky really. He thrives on people doubting themselves."

Tyler exhales, a smile tugging at his lips. "I know I can beat him. I just … I don't want to screw this up."

She steps closer, wrapping her arms around him. "You won't. I'll help you press his buttons, too. You've got this, Tyler."

She holds him for a moment longer before releasing him, just as Paul, Melinda, and Anna return. Paul is munching on an ice cream sandwich, half of it already gone. Anna has a smudge of chocolate on her lips.

"His mission is to keep the street vendors in business," Melinda says with a smile, nodding toward Paul.

Everyone laughs, the anxious anticipation breaking for a moment.

Anna skips to the metal fence, peering through the bars at the White House. She turns to Tyler, her eyes wide with excitement.

"My field trip is next Thursday," she announces. "We're taking a walking tour to see the cherry blossoms."

He wraps an arm around her shoulders. "Sounds perfect," he says.

The five of them meander toward 15th Street. Anna walks alongside Tyler while the others stroll behind.

"Our hearing is coming up in two weeks," Tyler says quietly to her. "Paul's lawyer says Virginia will officially be out of the picture."

Anna whistles softly. "I haven't seen her in forever."

He nods, pulling her close. "I know. We've waited a long time, but we're almost there. We can finally be together again."

She looks up at him. "Uh-huh."

Jill appears beside them, and together they walk along the sidewalk that borders the Treasury Department, its imposing stone columns towering over them.

"Look familiar?" Paul calls out, holding up a ten-dollar bill. He points to the Treasury building's profile inked on the back of the bill.

"Cool!" Anna runs over and snatches the bill from his hand, tucking it into her pocket before hurrying back to Tyler and Jill.

"There's another option," Tyler says to Anna, his tone serious now. "Paul and Melinda would love to continue being your parents. Officially."

Her face breaks into a huge grin, which is the answer he needs.

"I'm also looking at that house for sale down the street from the Thompsons," he adds. "I might make an offer."

"Oh, Tyler!" Anna exclaims, throwing her arms around him, halting their parade down the sidewalk. A lump rises in his throat as he hugs her tightly, overwhelmed by how far they've come.

He glances over at Jill, a playful smile forming on his lips. "It'll be a bit of a commute to the office, though. Maybe we can carpool."

·　　·　　·　　·　　·

At the Thomas Jefferson Suite of the Willard Hotel, Anna bounces through the entry hall, her footsteps echoing in the grand space. "This place is bigger than my house!" she yells out.

She's right. The three-thousand-square-foot beauty is the crown jewel of the hotel. They had to wait until four o'clock to check in, giving the staff time to prepare the room for the reason they are here, the event that has kept Tyler awake almost every night this past week—the game.

"It's March 20th," Paul says, sprawled in a plush wingback chair in the foyer. "Know why that's significant?"

Tyler sits across from him in a matching chair and shakes his head no.

"Abraham Lincoln and Jefferson Davis began their contest on this very date … in 1861." Paul points to a large portrait of a Victorian woman set in a gilded frame hanging on the wall. "It's more luxurious now, but this is where it all began. And now you're here, a different battle, but just as important."

Tyler feels as if the hands of Zeus himself are pressing on his chest. He stretches his arms in front of him to ease the tension, but the sense of responsibility weighs heavier than ever.

"And now it's my turn," he says. "Will I be Lincoln … or Davis?"

Paul leans forward and says, "That was a different time, my friend. This is now. You'll be Tyler Rush, which is all you need to be."

Paul's phone chirps, breaking the moment. He glances at the screen then drops the phone back into his pocket.

"What is it?" Tyler asks.

"Preston. He says he okayed a request from Senator Corbin to bring a new Texas staffer to the next game." He smiles. "Still thinks he needs our approval."

"Who's the staffer?"

"I don't know. Maxwell something."

Tyler rises and walks with Paul past the door to the primary bedroom. They enter the living room, where the green felt-covered table and five executive chairs with thick cushions and arched backs wait for them, like silent witnesses to what's about to happen.

The anxiety in the air is palpable as they make their way to the second bedroom where Anna sits on the king bed, legs crisscrossed, absorbed in a cooking competition show on TV. Paul leaves the room quietly.

Tyler unpacks his suitcase, hangs his shirts in the cavernous closet, and tries to make himself comfortable in this grand room that will serve as his home for the next few days. His mind is racing, thinking about the game, about what's at stake. He stands by the window, taking in the sweeping view of the city below.

Jill and Melinda enter the room, Jill dragging a suitcase that looks like it's ready to burst.

"I'm not sure we'll have room for all your stuff," Tyler says, earning a smirk from Jill.

"I packed light," she says.

Before Tyler can respond, Anna shoots them both an annoyed look. "Shhh! This is the best part."

They smile and lower their voices, giving her space to enjoy her show.

Fifteen minutes later, everyone gathers in the converted living room. Paul sits down in one of the executive chairs and motions Tyler over.

"Mike's here," Paul says. "He's getting settled in and will be out soon."

Jill and Anna stand in front of the floor-to-ceiling windows that line the far wall, admiring the panoramic vista of the city below that is bathed in the warm glow of the late afternoon sun. It's a calm moment, almost peaceful, but Tyler knows it won't last.

A door closes from outside the room, and footsteps echo across the foyer. Mike saunters in, decked out in a light-gray leisure suit, his chin cocked high in the air. He wears his signature smirk, the one that makes Tyler's stomach twist with unease.

Mike removes a pair of sunglasses from the pocket of his tailored shirt and slips them on. "About time for me to give the young man another poker lesson." He glances at Tyler, his sneer cutting through the room. "Hopefully, these'll help you from making a poor decision. You know, in case I accidentally wink."

Lance Hudson, the dealer for tonight's game, enters behind Mike and retrieves a cart parked by the wet bar. He transfers racks of gold coins onto the felt-covered table. Tyler selects a chair that allows him to face the tall windows, hoping the view of the outside world will give him a psychological edge as the hours stretch into days. Mike, on the other hand, will be staring at a wall.

Tyler pulls a coin from the closest rack and examines it, wondering whose hands have touched this very piece of gold. These unusual poker chips have quietly and anonymously shaped the course of history … and they will again today.

His hand trembles, and the coin slips from his fingers, bouncing off the rack before settling on the soft felt. Mike chuckles under his breath.

Melinda and Anna step forward. "Time for us to go," Melinda says, squeezing Tyler's shoulder. "Good luck."

Anna pouts, her eyes wide. "I want to stay."

"We've got a fine room down the hall," Melinda says. "And now it's time for us to sightsee. And shop." Anna perks up. "Besides, you and I need to be home by tomorrow night. You're not missing school on Monday."

Anna's frown returns.

Lance sets the last rack of coins on the table. It's one coin short.

"That's it, gentlemen. Nine hundred ninety-nine. I'll add the odd coin to the first pot, and the rest I'll split evenly."

"Someone lost a coin?" Tyler asks. "Or stole one?"

Paul glances up. "The missing coin is the custodial coin."

Tyler remembers the internet letter again.

It is embossed with a special mark, a chevron with thirteen stars. The person who possesses this coin is the custodian of the game.

Melinda and Anna leave the suite while Paul and Jill settle into chairs on opposite sides of the table. They will serve as witnesses, sitting between the two players.

Paul stands and leans on the cushioned bumper rail bordering the playing surface.

"To codify the rules and stakes for this contest, Mike and Tyler will play no-limit Texas hold 'em. Antes will begin at five coins each and increase by five coins every hour. When a player holds all the gold, they win that game. The first player to win three games wins the contest."

Tyler nods, excitement building inside him.

"If Mike wins," Paul continues, "Jill will pay him thirty million dollars and provide a complete printout of the code that powers the current version of her algorithm, including all her research notes. If Tyler wins, Mike will destroy his copy of the algorithm along with all its documentation and provide his team of scientists to Jill. Either way, he will step away from Mid-Atlantic without a fight."

Paul glances at Mike and Jill. "Agreed?"

"Yes," Jill says.

Mike nods. "Hundred percent."

Lance shuffles the deck and deals.

Tyler lifts his hole cards, but his fingers slip, flipping one card face up onto the table—a two of diamonds.

Mike snickers. "Well, well, off to a great start."

Tyler grits his teeth, his face flushing with embarrassment. He tosses his cards into the muck, folding before the first bet is even made.

"Relax," Jill says softly. "One bet at a time. One hand at a time."

He takes a breath and glances at her, appreciating her steady eyes and encouraging smile. A sense of confidence returns.

Lance deals the second hand.

Mike raises five coins immediately, that smug look never leaving his face as he surveys the table.

Tyler doesn't like how the game is beginning. *Mike is too comfortable, thinking he can run over me.* He decides he needs to shake things up. But how best to do that?

Mike leans forward, elbows on the padded rail. "C'mon. Let's go. Lots of hands ahead of us."

Tyler surveys the room, acting deliberately slow as he sizes up the situation. The sunlight streaming through the windows casts long shadows across the table, and in the reflection of the glass, Tyler sees a different man looking back at himself—older, sharper, more resolved. *I've been through too much to let him intimidate me now.*

Mike lifts his drink from the mahogany shelf that circles the table underneath the rail, taking a leisurely sip. Then, with his other hand, he raps his knuckles twice on the wood, impatient. "Do I need to call for the clock already?"

Tyler locks eyes with Mike. His heartbeat slows. Without even looking at his hole cards, he pushes a handful of coins into the pot.

"Raise," he says.

Mike frowns and his confidence wavers, just for a second. "Playing blind?" he asks. "What the hell are you doing? Look at your damn hole cards."

Tyler crosses his arms and leans back in his chair. "No need. I know you've got rags."

The gamble is measured, driven more by instinct than pure logic. He has no clue what Mike holds, but if he can create enough doubt—just enough confusion—it might tilt the balance. He watches Mike carefully, noting the subtle tension in the man's jaw.

Mike removes his sunglasses, chewing on one of the arms, clearly irritated. He picks up his cards and examines them closely, as if reconsidering.

After a long pause, he flicks the cards toward the dealer. "Fold."

Tyler pushes his cards to Lance without showing them and scoops the coins toward him. He keeps his expression neutral, but inside, he surges with confidence.

Mike snorts, apparently unimpressed. "Lucky guess," he mutters, but Tyler can tell it stung.

Tyler maintains his aggressive play, keeping Mike off balance. The intensity in the room mounts with each hand as Mike grows increasingly frustrated, calling when he should fold and folding when he should raise. The time ticks by, and by 9:15 p.m., Tyler finds himself in a strong position, flipping over a pair of queens to win a large hand with a full house. He beats Mike's three aces, forcing Mike to push the last of his coins into the pot.

Mike stands, sighing heavily. "Time for a break."

Tyler's heart pounds, but it's not from fear this time. It's from the adrenaline rush of victory. *One game down, two to go. At this rate, I might only witness a single sunrise before heading home victorious.*

He spends the next hour devouring a grilled chicken sandwich and a bowl of mixed fruit then heads down to the hotel gym. The treadmill whirs beneath him as he pushes himself through two miles, the steady rhythm of his steps clearing his head. Afterward, a hot shower feels like a brief sanctuary, the steam rising around him as he leans against the tiled wall.

Paul and Jill give him space, sensing his need to reenergize. By the time he returns to the table, he is centered and ready to begin game two.

At 10:18 p.m., Lance deals the first card of the second game. Tyler plays with focus and discipline, and by one a.m., his steady approach has paid off with him holding seven hundred coins to Mike's three hundred.

But Mike, always unpredictable, soon catches a hot streak. Tyler watches in frustration as he slowly regains his footing and executes what Tyler suspects are several well-timed bluffs. By five a.m., Mike has amassed eight hundred coins, dwarfing Tyler's stack by four to one. Tyler feels the pressure building again.

Lance deals the next hand. Both men check, and Lance reveals the flop.

Community Cards: 9♥, Q♠, 6♥

Tyler looks down at his hole cards—the ten and eight of hearts. He's got multiple draws to hit a flush, a straight, even a straight flush.

Community Cards: 9♥, Q♠, 6♥

Tyler's Hole Cards: 10♥, 8♥

He feels a rush of energy as he recognizes this is the moment to make a bold move.

"All in," he declares, pushing his remaining coins forward with resolve.

Mike tilts his head from side to side, pondering for a moment, before he slides his own stack into the center.

"Call."

With Tyler all in, no additional betting is possible, and both players turn over their hole cards.

Community Cards: 9♥, Q♠, 6♥

Tyler's Hole Cards: 10♥, 8♥

Mike's Hole Cards: Q♥, Q♦

Mike is ahead with three queens. But Tyler knows this hand is still anyone's game. Fourteen cards in the deck could give him the win, and he has two chances to hit one of them.

Lance deals the turn card—the two of clubs—a neutral card, no direct help to either of them, but an immense benefit to Mike's odds of winning the hand since Tyler has only one chance remaining to improve his hand. A knot tightens in his stomach as his odds of winning diminish sharply.

Lance grasps the river card delicately between his fingers, ready to reveal it. Tyler has a premonition, a gut feeling that's impossible to explain. It happens to him occasionally, at the card table and in life.

"Seven of clubs," he says.

Lance hesitates before flipping the final card, a slow reveal.

It's the seven of clubs, making a straight for Tyler to win the hand.

Community Cards: 9♥, Q♠, 6♥, 2♣, 7♣

Tyler's Hole Cards: 10♥, 8♥

Mike's Hole Cards: Q♥, Q♦

Mike's jaw tightens, and he stares intently at the card. His eyes dart from the seven to Tyler as if trying to comprehend how it could have happened. He picks up the card, examines it as though it might reveal some trick then drops it back on the table, shaking his head in disbelief.

Tyler feels compelled to explain it's dumb luck—or maybe something more cosmically significant—but certainly, it's not that he's cheating. Instead, he stays silent, relieved that he's still alive in this second game. He reaches for the mountain of coins in the center of the table that brings him much closer to being even.

But Mike isn't done. He stands abruptly, his chair scraping against the floor. "Hold on," he growls. "I'm calling for a redeal. Something's off. You all saw that, right?"

Paul glances at Jill and Tyler. He scratches his bald spot, clearly uncertain. "Son, is there something you need to tell us?"

Tyler raises his hands. "Nothing more than a hunch," he says in an even voice.

Jill steps forward, her calm demeanor diffusing the conflict. She walks over to the supply cart, selects a fresh deck, and hands it to Lance. "Use these for the next hand," she says, casting a measured glance at Mike. "Odd, yes. But nothing illegal. A new deck is the best we can do for you."

Mike grunts, stalks over to the bar, and pours himself a large tumbler of whiskey.

Lance opens the new deck and fans the cards across the table for all to see. Satisfied the set is complete, Paul nods. Lance shuffles seven times in careful, methodical precision, before dealing again.

Tyler now holds about four hundred coins, and Mike has six hundred. But the air has shifted. Mike's confidence wavers, and Tyler senses the doubt creeping in, fueled by whiskey and frustration. Tyler leans back, watching Mike closely as he sips his drink. The alcohol will only cloud his judgment further.

With renewed determination, Tyler increases his aggression. He raises bigger, more often, forcing Mike into a defensive position. Tyler's pile grows to five hundred, then seven hundred. The tide is turning.

An hour passes. Then two. The antes rise steadily, and every hand sends their fortunes swinging wider, but Tyler continues to build his lead. As dawn breaks, the room fills with the soft glow of the first rays of sunlight. The doorbell chimes, and Paul answers. Hotel staff arrive, quietly setting up a table behind them, laying out trays of fresh fruits, eggs, and bacon. Tyler fixes a plate, but his mind is still locked on the marathon second game.

Four hours later, the tension finally breaks. Tyler wins a monster hand and sweeps up the last of Mike's coins. He stretches, his body aching from the hours spent at the table, but the thrill of victory overrides the fatigue. He's feeling fine, up two games to none in the race to three.

Paul yawns, rubbing his eyes. "Thought that would never end."

Jill smiles, her expression one of pride. "Three-hour break. We'll restart at 2 p.m."

Mike strides to the bar, refills his glass, downs half in one go, and retreats to his room without another word.

Exhaustion settles over Tyler as the game pauses, and he fills a bowl with cantaloupe before heading to his room. He runs a hot bath and sinks into the water, letting the steam rise around him. Within minutes, he's asleep.

When he wakes, the water is lukewarm, and his muscles have stiffened. He pulls on a robe before collapsing onto the bed.

His alarm blares two hours later, pulling him from a deep sleep with a sharp, shrill sound. His head throbs, and he can already feel the dull ache that threatens to become a full-blown migraine.

Please, not now.

He pops two Advil, hoping they'll kick in soon, and stumbles into the parlor. Paul is seated in one of the blue chairs, sipping coffee. The rich, bitter scent fills the air, and Tyler is drawn to it like a lifeline.

"You okay?" Paul asks, concern lining his voice.

"Where's the coffee?" Tyler grunts, barely coherent.

Paul nods toward the buffet. Tyler trudges over and fills a mug then presses the warm porcelain against his forehead, the heat soothing the pain.

Mike strolls in, his hair still damp, the sharp scent of aftershave cutting through the air. "Afternoon, young man," he greets with a smirk. "You look like a sprinter who tried to run a marathon." He chuckles to himself. "But we're just getting started."

Jill enters moments later, dressed in tight black leggings and a loose turquoise blouse. Her emerald earrings catch the sunlight streaming through the ten-foot windows, and Tyler notices the familiar silver locket resting against her chest. She pats his back as she walks by then takes her seat.

Tyler's head pounds as game three begins. His thoughts are sluggish, clouded by exhaustion, and Mike takes notice. It takes everything Tyler has just to focus on calculating pot odds and fending off Mike's relentless aggression. He loses the first five hands, folding and folding again, as Mike pummels him with a series of raises, refusing to give him room to breathe. The pile of coins in front of Mike quickly grows while Tyler's stack dwindles.

Enough, Tyler decides, time to take a stand. He's done playing passive, done letting Mike dictate the pace. He'll make a move on the next hand—no matter what cards he's dealt, simply to disrupt Mike's rhythm.

Tyler peels back the edges of his hole cards and spots a pair of tens— a premium hand in a heads-up battle. Makes it easier to execute his plan than if he'd been dealt rags. He pushes a stack of twenty coins forward. "Raise."

Mike crinkles his nose. "You've been trudging through quicksand the past half hour, and suddenly you make a move. Looks a bit scripted, buster." His eyes harden as he studies Tyler.

Tyler rubs his forehead, his headache still gnawing at him. Mike casually stacks twenty coins then reconstructs the pile, as though stalling, savoring the moment. Finally, he pushes the stack forward, toppling the coins across the felt. "Call."

Lance deals the flop.

Community Cards: K♠, 10♥, 8♣

Tyler's Hole Cards: 10♦, 10♣

Tyler perks up, trying not to let his excitement show. His pair of tens has just turned into a set. He bets twenty coins again—a Goldilocks move, large enough to build the pot but small enough to keep Mike interested. He knows this is his chance to make up for all the chips he's lost.

Mike stands up and saunters to the refreshment bar, casually refilling his mug as if he has all the time in the world. Without even looking back at the table, he calls over his shoulder, "Raise. Twenty more."

Tyler's pulse quickens. *Mike hit something. He's in this hand for real. If I play this right, I can set myself up for a big win.* He fidgets for a moment in his chair then stands and grabs a bottle of water from the mini fridge. His mind spins, searching for the right move.

He suspects I'm bluffing. How do I confirm it? Tyler opens the water and takes a sip. *If I were bluffing, I might fold in this spot. I might also reraise to fire another shot and continue the charade. No way I would simply call.*

"Raise," Tyler says. "Thirty more."

The pot now holds more than a hundred and fifty coins.

Mike returns to the table, shaking his head, and rests his chin on his fist. He looks at the board, glances at his hole cards, then, without warning, flips them face up for everyone to see.

Community Cards: K♠, 10♥, 8♣

Tyler's Hole Cards: 10♦, 10♣

Mike's Hole Cards: K♥, 3♦

Tyler watches in disbelief. *What's he doing?* Tyler has hardly ever seen anyone show their cards in the middle of a live hand.

Mike spins the king of hearts in a circle on the table with his index finger. "Pair of kings," he announces with a smirk. "Powerful hand in a heads-up game. Especially if your opponent is running a bluff." He leans back, his grin growing wider.

Tyler stares at the reflective surface of Mike's dark glasses, trying to read the man behind them. *He knows something. But what?*

"The problem is," Mike continues, tapping the card, "I don't think you're bluffing anymore." He pauses and shakes his head. "No way I'm betting my pair of kings against three of a kind." He flicks the king across the table. It cartwheels and lands in front of Tyler, the king's mocking eyes staring up at him. "I fold."

Mike committed enough coins to the pot before folding to even their stacks. In a single hand, Tyler has made up for the prior thirty minutes of being henpecked. He should feel good, yet he's unsettled. That pot should have been much larger. *How did Mike know? How the hell did he read me so perfectly?*

Mike must have picked up on a tell, Tyler thinks. "Gutsy fold," he says, shrugging, trying to sound nonchalant, not wanting Mike to know he was right. "Foolish, maybe, but gutsy."

Mike pulls a cigar from his breast pocket, bites the end off with his teeth, and speaks through the tobacco clamped in his mouth. "You're pathetic."

Tyler feels the sting of the insult but lets it slide. "Timeout," he says, getting up from the table.

The afternoon sun blinds him as he steps onto the patio, his headache intensifying. He quickly retreats inside and rushes to the bathroom, splashing cold water onto his face. The icy shock helps but not enough. He presses a cool washcloth to his forehead, trying to steady his nerves.

Paul knocks on the open door. "Did you have it?" he asks.

"How did that jerk know I had a set?" Tyler says. "Did you notice a tell?"

Paul shakes his head. "Thought he was just outsmarting himself."

Tyler unfolds the washcloth and drapes it across his face, the cold pressing against his skin. He takes a few slow, deep breaths.

"Don't sweat it," Paul says gently. "You've got this. Come on now, shake it off."

When Tyler returns to the table, the last hand still nags at him. It feels like Mike can see right through him, so he calls for a new deck. He even borrows Paul's sunglasses, desperate to mask whatever tell gave him away earlier. But none of it helps. Mike picks him apart, hand by hand, methodically separating Tyler from his dwindling pile of coins.

As the sun sets, Mike wins game three.

"I'm catching up, young man," Mike taunts as he rises from the table. "See you in an hour." He strolls to the bar, pours half a glass of Scotch, and saunters off to his room, his confident grin following him out the door.

Tyler sits, defeated. Maybe I should take a shot, he thinks, eyeing the bottle Mike left behind. Seems to be working for him.

Instead, he forces himself to eat a sandwich then leaves the hotel for a much-needed thirty-minute walk in the cool evening air. The chill bites at his skin, but it clears his head. He focuses on his breathing, one breath at a time, one step at a time. Just like the game.

When he returns, Jill is seated at the table, toying with three of the gold coins. She looks up as he enters, offering him a smile. "Doing great," she says, but she looks concerned.

"Don't worry," Tyler says, leaning over to kiss her on the forehead. "I've got this."

"I still can't quite believe you suggested this," she says with a tired grin.

He inhales sharply. "I know. I wish there were an easier way. But we had no choice."

"It was the right move," Jill says, her voice quieter now. "It's just that my life's work is hanging by a thread—and you're holding it."

The gravity of her words settles heavily on Tyler's shoulders, but he forces himself to nod. He can't afford to let doubt creep in. He's got to put the last loss behind him and push forward. Just then, Mike and Paul reenter the room, and Lance prepares to deal the first hand of game four, with Tyler leading two games to one.

Tyler's mind clears, focusing sharply on the task at hand. The stakes are as high as ever, but this time, he doesn't let them distract him. He channels his attention to the cards—each hand, each bet. Slowly, methodically, he begins to regain control. With every pot he wins, his confidence rebuilds, one step closer to victory.

Mike watches, tight-lipped, as Tyler scoops another pot. "You must be up two hundred chips already."

Tyler doesn't respond, ignoring the mind games. He stacks his coins in silence, one neat pile at a time, while Lance shuffles the deck.

"I must say," Mike continues, "I'm impressed, young man. Mighty big stakes we're playing for."

Tyler remains silent.

"No shame in a fella getting a little nervous when so much is on the line," Mike says, shaking his head. "But not you. Calmly chipping away. So close to victory."

Sweat breaks out along Tyler's brow. He knows Mike is trying to get under his skin, but the reality of how close he is seeps in. *Just hold my lead, and I've got it. One more game and I'll redeem myself with Jill. Her life's work will be intact. Our future together will be bright. Just hold on.*

Lance deals the next hand, and Tyler peeks at his hole cards. Jack and six. Mediocre. He checks, then folds when Mike bets ten coins.

He folds again and again, stuck in a bad run of cards. Mike is pressing, raising aggressively, not letting Tyler limp into any hands. After an hour, their piles are even again.

How did I blow this lead? I had it in the bag—the whole contest.

In the next hand, Mike raises twenty coins. Tyler studies him closely, figuring he must be betting on a high hole card. He looks down at his own pair of sevens. Not bad. He raises another twenty. Mike calls without a second thought.

The flop reveals an ace, king, and three. Mike immediately pushes fifty coins into the pot. Tyler groans quietly. Not the flop he needed. Mike must have an ace or a king and has made a high pair.

Time to fold. Again.

"I'm not stupid," Tyler says, tossing down his pair of sevens face up as he folds.

"Good fold," Mike says with a smirk, flipping his cards over—five and six of hearts. Absolutely nothing. He bursts into a hearty laugh.

Tyler clenches his fists under the table, anger bubbling beneath the surface. *Bluffed out of another hand.*

The next several hours blur together in a haze of poor decisions and dwindling chips. By two a.m., Tyler is dangerously close to being wiped out. Then, as if the cards themselves sense his desperation, a streak of winning hands arrives, allowing him to battle back and fight to even the stacks once more. He leans into his chair, letting out a massive, body-stretching yawn. His vision blurs as he stares at the cards. The numbers and suits seem to swim before his tired eyes.

Lance deals another hand.

Tyler lifts his hole cards, staring at them for a moment until the image sharpens. Two black kings. A surge of excitement rises in his chest.

"Twenty," Tyler says.

"Call," Mike responds, nonchalant.

Lance deals the flop.

Community Cards: 9♠, 2♥, 4♣

Tyler's Hole Cards: K♣, K♠

No flush or straight draw on the board—his kings are rock solid. Tyler slides five stacks of coins forward.

"Fifty," he says.

"All in," Mike fires back without hesitation.

Tyler's heart skips a beat. *What the hell kind of bet is that? If Mike has the better hand—maybe aces or trips—he wouldn't risk scaring me away with such a bold move. This must be a bluff.*

But a bluff doesn't quite add up either, Tyler thinks. Mike has a slight coin lead, but if he loses, he's handing over almost everything. This is it—a make-or-break moment.

He taps his foot nervously against the floor, both wired and exhausted. He replays Mike's previous bets in his mind and watches his face for any sign of weakness. Finally, after careful consideration, he decides—Mike is bluffing. It's the only explanation.

Tyler pushes his remaining coins forward. "Call."

Mike flips over his hole cards.

Community Cards: 9♠, 2♥, 4♣

Tyler's Hole Cards: K♣, K♠

Mike's Hole Cards: 4♦, 4♥

Tyler leaps from his chair, his stomach dropping. He's about to lose game four unless he hits a miracle on the final two cards. "What a dumb bet," he says. "How could you risk wasting that hand by making me fold?"

Mike's grin doesn't waver. "What a stupid thing to say," he replies coolly.

Lance deals the final two cards—a harmless seven of diamonds and a three of hearts. Mike's trips hold, sealing the hand.

Tyler's world spins as Mike rakes in the mountain of gold he's just won. Each clatter of the coins hits like a personal failure, the strain of the loss sinking deep into Tyler's bones. Mike rises, ambles over to the bar, and pours his usual. "We're tied up. Two games to two. Next game's the only one that matters." He laughs and wanders off to his bedroom. "I love it," he shouts back before he shuts his door.

Tyler stands frozen at the table, staring at the spot where Mike had just sat. His heartbeat drums in his ears, each beat punctuated by the gnawing doubt crawling up his spine. He's the one who pushed for this contest, but now everything is unraveling.

There's a three-hour break until the final game will begin. Tyler sits quietly, thinking, as everyone else leaves the room. He finally stands and walks mechanically to the bar, grabs a tumbler, and clanks it against the cool marble counter. The sound rings hollow in the empty room. He splashes Scotch into the glass.

Before he can take a sip, the familiar warmth of Jill's hands caresses his shoulders, gently massaging the temptation away.

"Deep breath," she whispers behind him. "You don't drink."

Tyler hesitates, the cool glass of alcohol firm in his hand, but her words break through the fog clouding his mind. He dumps the liquor into the sink and sets the glass down.

Jill slips her hand under his elbow. "Come on. Follow me."

She leads him to the patio, her pace brisk. As they pass the door to the hallway, Paul appears and wraps Tyler in a strong, fatherly hug. "You can do this, son," he says. "But you need to believe."

Once outside, Jill releases his elbow and paces across the stone patio. A thick predawn fog blankets the skyline behind her. Tyler watches as she turns and comes back toward him. He's expecting the warmth of a hug or the comfort of a kind word. He opens his arms, waiting for it.

Instead, she stops, her eyes sharp in the moonlight. "Straighten up," she says. "You need to get over yourself."

Tyler bristles. "What's your problem? I'm doing this for you."

Jill doesn't flinch. Her hand moves to the locket dangling from her necklace, her fingers brushing over it. "Oh, this is about me? I'm the one who got greedy and fell for Mike's tricks? I'm the one who committed corporate theft? I'm the one who put the world in jeopardy?"

He winces at the truth in her words.

"You've got all the tools you need to win this match, Tyler," she continues. "You've always had them." She takes a step closer, her eyes boring into his. "But Paul's right—you're the one who needs to believe that."

She steps forward, kissing him gently on the cheek. "I'm sorry, but you needed to hear that." Without another word, she walks back inside, leaving him alone on the patio. He stares out at the fog covering the city, the crisp air biting at his skin.

I don't have to do this alone, he realizes, sensing a shift inside him. Jill, Paul, Anna—they're all here with me. I'm not alone.

He grips the stone railing, straightening his back.

This is my game. And I'm going to finish it.

CHAPTER 36

"Game five," Paul announces. "Winner takes all."

The room feels like it's holding its breath, the soft shuffle of cards the only sound in the tense silence. Everyone is watching, waiting. As Lance shuffles and deals, Tyler exhales slowly, his mind clear. *This is it. My game.*

Mike raises his glass, a slow grin spreading across his face. "Hope you're ready for your final lesson, kid."

Tyler meets his eyes, unfazed. "Let's play," he replies calmly.

Lance deals the first hand, and Mike raises immediately. Tyler checks his cards—seven and three, off-suit. He folds. The next hand, Mike raises again. Tyler looks down at a nine and deuce. Another fold.

Mike continues raising almost every hand, winning most of them. Each small victory chips away at Tyler's confidence. He starts to question every decision. Nothing feels right—he's sure Mike's cards are better.

After half an hour, Tyler is down a hundred coins. Mike's relentless aggression doesn't let up—raise, raise, raise. The pressure mounts with each pot Mike claims, like the game is slipping out of his control, taking his future with it.

He's bullying me. There's no way his cards are that good every time.

On the next hand, Mike once again raises ten coins before Tyler can even look at his own hole cards. When he does, he finds a queen and ten, both spades. It's the best hand he's seen so far. *Time to fight back.*

"Reraise," Tyler says. "Twenty more."

Mike's hand freezes midway to the pot. He cocks his head and raises an eyebrow, clearly surprised by Tyler's sudden shift. "Got a real hand, eh?"

Tyler crosses his arms, his face unreadable. Mike glances at his cards then his stack. "Raise you back another fifty," he says, moving a pile of gold coins forward.

Is he bluffing, or did I just pick the wrong time to push back?

Tyler pauses, considering Mike's recent string of impatient raises. *He's acting too fast, not thinking, hoping I'll fold.*

"Raise one hundred," Tyler finally says. *That'll teach him to slow down and respect my action.*

Mike hesitates, his eyes narrowing. He glances at Tyler's stack, measuring it against his own then looks back at his cards. "You leave me no choice," he says. "All in." He shoves all his coins into the pot, and they clatter together in a chaotic heap.

Tyler feels the panic rising but forces it down. *This is reckless. Mike should never commit all his chips here—something's off.* If Tyler calls Mike's crazy raise and loses, it's all over—Jill's dream, his ambition, maybe even their relationship. But if he folds, his stack will take a massive hit.

He thinks through the hand. Mike started with a small raise then increased it when Tyler showed strength. If Mike has a high pair—like aces or kings—his all-in bet makes a lot of sense. He would want to end the hand now, which he could do with an outsized raise. And even Mike isn't wild enough to make a bet like this with everything on the line unless he were holding a premium hand. It becomes obvious to him that Mike holds a high pair.

With that realization, Tyler groans and tosses his cards toward the deck. "Fold." He glances at Mike. "Aces? Or kings?"

Mike chuckles. "Either would be logical, I agree." He flips his cards over, revealing an unsuited seven and deuce—the worst possible starting hand in Texas hold 'em, a complete bluff.

Tyler becomes dizzy, feeling the self-doubt creeping in. *Why didn't I call? I would've been almost guaranteed a nine-to-one chip lead. The game would have essentially been over.*

He pauses and forces the negativity back. Paul catches his eye. "Take a moment, son," he says. "You're still in this."

He nods, thankful for the opportunity to step away and clear his head. In the bathroom, he splashes cold water onto his face, the shock bringing clarity. He studies his reflection in the mirror, seeing not a man on the ropes but someone still very much in the fight. "This isn't over," he whispers, his voice gaining a new steadiness. "Not by a long shot."

A comforting chill sweeps through him. After drying his face, he straightens his posture and strides back to the table, clapping his hands as he reenters the room. He's not just ready to play—he's ready to win. As he approaches the table, he notices Anna and Melinda entering from the foyer, causing him to stop in his tracks.

"Are you okay, dopey?" Anna asks.

The sight of Anna lifts Tyler's heart. He rushes to her, scoops her up, and twirls her until she giggles. For a moment, the significance of the game fades, replaced by the simple joy of family.

"Never been better," Tyler says, and he means it.

"She insisted we stay another night," Melinda says. "We're just stopping by to wish you luck, and then I'll drive her to school."

"Get breakfast before you go," Paul says. "There's plenty more over there than we can eat." The buffet table has been restocked with oatmeal, fruit salad, eggs, bacon, and pastries.

Mike returns and sits down, setting his phone on the wooden shelf under the bumper rail. "Break time's over. Let's play."

Jill steps forward, her fingers curled around something small and golden. She pauses, her eyes meeting Tyler's then Mike's before flipping a coin into the air. It spins in a slow, deliberate arc, catching the light as it turns end over end. When it lands softly on the green felt, they can see it is embossed with a chevron and scattered stars. Jill stands at the far end of the table, clasping the face of her locket, letting it fall to rest on her chest.

"I'm adding this to the prize," she says.

Tyler is baffled. He opens his mouth, but no words come out.

"Pick up that coin," Mike roars. "Now!"

Jill smiles. Mike jumps to his feet. "You will not risk losing that coin. It's been in the Hayward family for two centuries. Jonas's own hands secured it from Elijah James's son." He glares at her, clutching the bumper rail. "No Hayward will be weak enough to give up this power."

Tyler recalls Jill's words—"He reconnected with me a few years ago. Gave me a present. More than that, a family heirloom."

Jill shakes her finger at Mike. "I don't take orders from you. I make my own decisions."

Over by the buffet table, Anna drops her plate, and it shatters on the tile. The sound rings out, but all eyes remain locked on Jill and Mike.

"How dare you risk losing the custodial coin to that loser?" Mike says. "You know it must stay in the family."

Jill looks around at the people in the room, her eyes finally resting on Tyler. She turns back to Mike. "Exactly. This is my family. If you're so worried about your precious coin, win the game."

Mike slumps back into his seat, his head in his hands. The wizard has been exposed, Tyler thinks. The curtain has been removed from his fortieth-floor Oz. His puppets have turned on him.

Jill … I love you.

"I'm calling time," Mike sputters and shuffles off to his room.

Anna skips over and hugs Tyler while Melinda picks up the broken pieces of the plate. After they leave, Tyler moseys out to the balcony. The early morning sun is bright, burning off the fog. He stretches his arms and sucks in the refreshing spring air. Jill steps up beside him.

"You are certainly full of surprises," he says.

She laughs.

"If you're the custodian," he says, "you must have known about my bet the whole time."

She shakes her head. "No. Mike had thought giving me the coin would bring me closer to him, get me to join his team." She sighs. "It almost worked. He can be quite captivating."

"Then who is the custodian?"

"It's me, all right. I do my duty by showing up for the annual council meetings, and I've gotten to know good people like Paul and Preston, but I never wanted to play in the game. I could have returned the coin, but I'm glad I didn't, now more than ever." She wraps an arm around Tyler's waist. "I didn't know about your bet until I arrived at the emergency council meeting."

"Why didn't you tell me?"

"I still had a nagging doubt you might be playing me," she admits. "That part of me is gone now."

Tyler steps to the railing and lays his hands on the concrete, already warm from the morning sun. "Good people, you say? Paul tried to justify this game, tell me it's necessary. I can't understand how he can rationalize that this game is good for the world."

Jill comes beside him and kisses his cheek. "Oh, I think you can. Think about what we're doing right now."

He thinks about her words. She's right again.

"If I win, I'm shutting down the game," he says.

"I hope you do," she replies then turns and walks back inside.

Did she mean win or shut down the game?

He surveys the city, seeing signs of freedom everywhere. The Washington Monument rises high, reminding him of the strength needed to lead a fledgling nation. The buildings of the Smithsonian prepare to welcome streams of visitors, promoting the sharing of knowledge to all who hunger for it. The fountains and pools of the World War II Memorial stand proud, honoring the men and women who rose tall when the world needed them most.

A surge of purpose flows through him. Tyler is strong, he is hungry, and he will stand tall for all the people who need him.

He takes a deep breath and walks back inside to the game table. Mike is talking, loudly, on his phone. "What? You won't support me?"

he bellows into the receiver. "I'll remember that." He throws his phone onto the table and glares at Tyler. "Let's go, hotshot."

Tyler's mind is razor sharp, and his confidence is buoyed by the love of his family, new and old. A peaceful connection radiates through him while his former boss fumes, repeatedly glancing at the custodial coin still sitting by itself on the table.

Tyler is ready to face the one obstacle that stands in the way of his future.

Over the next hour, Tyler reduces Mike's lead, then pulls way ahead with the help of one good win from a pair of pocket aces that Mike calls.

Mike removes his sunglasses and rubs his watery eyes. Tyler sees the black bags drooping beneath them.

Three hands later, they each have a hundred coins in the pot after the flop. Lance flips over the turn card, a nine of clubs.

Community Cards: 10♣, J♠, 9♥, 9♣

"I bet seventy-five," Mike says.

Tyler assesses the situation. *Mike's tired. Maybe desperate.* "Raise. One fifty."

"All in," Mike snaps.

Tyler leans back and stretches his legs, his heart pounding. He has a powerful hand, but not the nuts. He would have liked a guaranteed winner before committing all his chips, but that rarely happens—at the table or in life. His pulse quickens and a drop of sweat slides down his temple as his fingers rest on a stack of coins. The weight of the decision bears down on him.

His instinct tells him he has Mike beat. This is his diving-board moment—the point of no return. Replaying the hand in his mind, he reviews every bet, every movement. He glances at Jill, at Paul, at the city glowing outside the window, drawing strength from them all.

This is it, Tyler thinks. I'm not folding this time.

He takes a slow breath, his heart still racing but his mind clear. Locking eyes with Mike, he speaks with steady resolve.

"Call," he says, sealing his fate.

Mike grins. "Ha! I wasn't bluffing this time." He flips over the nine and ten of spades, giving him a full house, nines over tens.

Tyler's voice remains calm. "I'd hoped you weren't." He flips over his cards and shows Mike a pair of jacks.

Community Cards: 10♣, J♠, 9♥, 9♣

Tyler's Hole Cards: J♥, J♣

Mike's Hole Cards: 9♠, 10♠

Tyler has the higher full house.

Lance waits a second then deals the river card. It's the four of diamonds. No change to their hands.

For a moment, the room is still. Then, as the realization sinks in, Mike slumps forward onto his elbows, staring at Tyler's hole cards as if he can't quite make his eyes focus on them. The silence breaks as Jill leaps out of her chair, her fist pumping the air.

"Yes!" she yells.

"Attaboy," Paul says, and his face breaks into a toothy smile. "Well done, son."

Tyler feels a wave of calm, a sense of finality. He stands, exhausted, stumbles to his room, and crashes onto the mattress.

•　　　•　　　•　　　•　　　•

Tyler stretches out on the bed, momentarily disoriented as he tries to remember where he is. The digits on the clock read 3:12, and the bright sunlight seeping through the corners of the heavy drapes tells him it's afternoon, not the middle of the night.

The events of the past two days flood back to him, and a surge of excitement jolts him fully awake. Glancing beside him, he sees Jill sound asleep, her face buried in a pillow. He says a prayer of gratitude for his freedom, for Jill having her algorithm, and for their future together.

Rising from the bed, he remembers he is still fully dressed. Jill mutters something in her sleep and rolls toward him. Quietly, he tiptoes to his suitcase, retrieves a small box, and returns to the bed.

Kneeling beside her, he removes a diamond ring from the box and gently slides it onto her ring finger.

She yawns and rolls onto her side, her eyes still closed.

Tyler exits the room and strolls into the main living area. Mike is there sitting in a chair, holding a mug, staring at the custodial coin that lies glistening on the green felt.

He looks up at Tyler. "Afternoon, young fella."

Tyler nods and gets himself a cup of coffee.

"What's next?" Mike asks.

"No more poker for me. That's for sure."

Mike yawns. "What about the game?"

"Shutting it down."

"Such a waste. All these years, I've labored to help my city. Never asked for anything in return. And now it's all been snatched away. Just like that." Mike sighs, rubs his eyes, and leans back in his chair.

"You're really going to walk away?" Tyler asks.

"I made the bet. I lost. I have no choice but to honor the game." He smiles at Tyler and adds, "At least my legacy is intact."

Tyler raises his eyebrows. "Your legacy?"

"You, Tyler," Mike says, his tone softer now. "You are my legacy. You've shown yourself to be exceptional. And I picked you. You've proven me right." There's a trace of pride in his voice, but Tyler knows there's something more—an acknowledgment of everything that's come between them.

Mike's attention shifts behind Tyler. "Along with my daughter, of course … the master of all minds."

Tyler turns around and sees Jill standing ten feet away, tears streaming down her face. She holds up a finger that now bears a stunning diamond surrounded by small emeralds, her eyes shining. She nods, speechless for a moment, before simply whispering, "Yes. Absolutely yes."

Tyler sets down his coffee, rushes to her, and pulls her into a joyful kiss.

Mike chuckles softly. "Just do me one favor," he grumbles, "don't start calling me Dad."

The tension of weeks and months releases all at once as Tyler and Jill break their embrace and laugh, with Mike joining in.

After a moment, Mike's expression turns more thoughtful. "You know," he says, sitting up straight, "none of this would have happened if those maintenance guys had done their job and deactivated the elevator during their break. A simple oversight, and here we are."

Tyler's breath catches. "Are you serious?"

"Fate is fickle," Mike says with a shrug then turns his attention to Jill. "What about you, young lady? What's next? Other than getting hitched to this loser."

Jill places her arm around Tyler's waist. "Perfect the algorithm and start a foundation ... one that helps people."

"And get rich in the process," Mike adds.

Jill smiles, tilting her head slightly. "Probably so. But the more I have, the more I can do. That's the point."

She lets the words hang in the air, her gaze steady and thoughtful. "What about you?" she asks.

"Not sure." There's sorrow in his voice. "It'll be difficult to get my bearings. Think I might buy a tractor, move to the country. Breathe fresh air during the day, watch the Milky Way at night."

"That'll last about a day," she scoffs.

Mike leans forward and picks up the custodial coin then looks at Jill. "You know he's going to shut down the game?"

She nods.

"What about the coin?" Mike asks.

"I'm going to melt it," Tyler says.

"No!" Mike and Jill say in unison.

Tyler jerks his head around to look at Jill.

"I mean ... please don't," she says. "Mike is wrong about a lot, but he's right about one thing. I am a Hayward. And I want to hang onto that coin. We'll put it in a safe. It'll never see the light of day again. But please don't destroy it."

Tyler nods. He understands.

"See," Mike says, "you are my daughter, after all." He holds the coin to the light and examines it, tears forming in the corners of his eyes. Then, with a flick of his wrist, he flips it across the table.

Tyler catches the coin, its weight heavy in his palm—not just the gold, but the burden of everything Mike had been to him—mentor, enemy, rival. For all his flaws, Mike had seen Tyler's potential—his strength—before he himself had.

"Nicely played, son," Mike says with quiet pride. "You earned it."

THE END

ACKNOWLEDGMENTS

Thank you, Mom, Bonnie Armstrong, for encouraging me, rooting for me, commiserating with me, providing enormous amounts of your time and energy to discuss strategy and provide edits, and ultimately, celebrating with me.

Thank you, Jill Keller, for pushing me to attend the weekend workshop that started this journey, for being my love and partner in life, for supporting me in this process, and for putting up with my periods of obsessive writing.

Thank you, Erin and Aidan Keller, for your love, support, and the joy you have brought to my life. I could not be prouder than to be your dad.

Thank you, Dad and Cissa (John and Cecilia Keller), Jack Armstrong, Kristina Vogler, and David Keller for your love and support all along the journey.

Thank you to my furry friends, Abby, Chloe, Izzy, and Tom, for your unconditional love and the warmth you bring to our days. A special thank you to Abby, who lay beside me for countless hours as my steadfast companion while I painstakingly edited the manuscript over and over.

Thank you, Ron Rozelle, for teaching me to write and for reviewing and improving the earliest version of the manuscript. You turned the "writing light" on for me and ignited a passion that continues to burn brightly. Thank you also for your friendship.

Thank you, Randall Klein, for helping so much so very early on to elevate and bring the plot and characters of *The Game* to a new level. You had a lasting impact on my writing and my journey.

Thank you, Renee Fountain, for assisting me in improving the beginning, the ending, and in between, and for taking a chance on me by introducing me to the marketplace.

Thank you, Joyce Mochrie, for your copy editing expertise in polishing the manuscript so nicely.

Thank you, Mary Ellen Bramwell, for your sharp editorial insights and dedication in shaping the manuscript into its final form.

Thank you to the other talented editors and writing instructors I worked with, including Debby Kearney, Eve Porinchak, Rob Carr, Sam Jordison, and Laurence King, for having a positive impact on my writing and the novel.

Thank you to Jericho Writers for the tips, inspiration, and resources you provided during my writing journey.

Thank you to The Manuscript Academy for creating the connection to my agent, which was a key turning point in this process.

Thank you to Reagan Rothe and the talented team at Black Rose Writing for making my dream a reality.

Thank you, Brent Sager, for encouraging me to be the best version of me.

Thank you to my early readers, including Bonnie Armstrong, Debby Kearney, Cecilia Keller, John Keller, Jack Armstrong, Aubrey Johnson, Evelyn Arquette, Aidan Keller, Chip Harding, Paul Ehlert, Rhonda Ehlert, Tom Paz, Liz Hecht, Mark Akerley, Mike Bayless, Erin Keller, Jill Keller, Min Choi, Kristina Vogler, David Keller, Jana Willey, Kelleen Arquette, and Hayden Mierl.

And a big, gigantic thank you to you, my reader, for investing time to take this adventure with me.

ABOUT THE AUTHOR

Brandon Keller has spent three decades as an actuary and insurance executive, currently serving as the President and CEO of Germania Insurance Companies in Brenham, Texas. His passion for storytelling ignited in 2017 when his wife encouraged him to attend a writing workshop. That spark turned into an obsession, and hundreds of thousands of keystrokes later, his debut novel was born.

When he's not crafting gripping thrillers, Brandon enjoys adventures with his family, playing chess with an intensity that rivals grandmasters (at least in his mind), running to clear his head, and unwinding with Netflix alongside his two dogs and two cats.

Join Brandon's Readers Club at brandonkellerbooks.com.

NOTE FROM
BRANDON KELLER

Word-of-mouth is crucial for any author to succeed. If you enjoyed *The Game*, please leave a review online—anywhere you are able. Even if it's just a sentence or two. It would make all the difference and would be very much appreciated.

Thanks!
Brandon Keller

We hope you enjoyed reading this title from:

www.blackrosewriting.com

Subscribe to our mailing list – *The Rosevine* – and receive **FREE** books, daily deals, and stay current with news about upcoming releases and our hottest authors.
Scan the QR code below to sign up.

Already a subscriber? Please accept a sincere thank you for being a fan of Black Rose Writing authors.

View other Black Rose Writing titles at
www.blackrosewriting.com/books and use promo code
PRINT to receive a **20% discount** when purchasing.

Made in the USA
Las Vegas, NV
04 August 2025

25788612R00187